brain fever

ALSO BY VALERIE SAYERS

Due East

How I Got Him Back

Who Do You Love

The Distance Between Us

DOUBLEDAY new york london toronto sydney auckland

brain fever

I I I I I I I I I

VALERIE SAYERS

PUBLISHED BY DOUBLEDAY
a division of Bantam Doubleday Dell Publishing Group, Inc.
1540 Broadway, New York, New York 10036

DOUBLEDAY and the portrayal of an anchor with a dolphin
are trademarks of Doubleday, a division of
Bantam Doubleday Dell Publishing Group, Inc.

Book design by Gretchen Achilles

Library of Congress Cataloging-in-Publication Data

Sayers, Valerie.
Brain fever / Valerie Sayers. — 1st ed.
p.   cm.
I. Title.
PS3569.A94B73   1996
813'.54—dc20   95-4807
                                                  CIP

ISBN 0-385-47366-4

For **Casey Fuetsch**

TO HAVE FAITH IS PRECISELY TO LOSE ONE'S MIND SO AS TO WIN GOD.

—SØREN KIERKEGAARD

one

DAY ONE **THE EASTER RISING**

I pulled in from the Holy Thursday services just before midnight. Mary Faith heard my car in the driveway and came over from next door wearing, I swear to God, a straw Easter bonnet with a mess of blood-red cherries bobbing on top. I could tell with one look that she got the hat cheap at a discount store, but it was good-looking, and it was good to see her loosened up enough to wear it even if I didn't have a clue why she came over to my house at midnight in an Easter bonnet.

"Well," she says, doodling the toe of her shoe into the rug, embarrassed. "How you like the hat?"

"I like it fine. I know what would improve it, though."

"What?" she says. "You think I should pull off the cherries?"

"No. I like the cherries, like em fine. They'd stand out even more, though, if you took off everything else and gave em a chance to just . . . glisten, up there."

She smiled big, and I folded her up in my arms. I am a tall man, but in her high heels (high heels!—Mary Faith doesn't *wear* high heels), she was breathing the same air I was. I could feel her beaming against my collarbone, and I let that smile warm me, and I rested in the moment. Smiles were a long time coming. When I first came home to Due East, Mary Faith never beamed one my way.

Of course, I was not in the best of shape in those days. I had come to my father's house to have a crackup, and though I was done with my crackup by the time I made her acquaintance, I was still unfit for human company. Every afternoon I forced myself to rise for an hour and walk out into daylight and one day I saw her—the little neighbor girl, nearly grown—chasing her own little boy across the green.

She was wearing one of those flowing flammable Indian skirts, pink enough to shame the Rajah himself, and when she ran after her son it tripped up her long legs. But she managed to look graceful all the while she was tripping, her ankle in its sandal twisting with a dizzy languor. I watched her catch herself and turned my attention to her little boy, flying by radar to a big live oak that dripped moss right onto the street. Mary Faith in her pink skirt had shaken me from my own dizzy languor. I joined the chase and snagged the little guy.

When I delivered him up to her, she thanked me over the little boy's hollers with grave gray eyes, and she never once smiled. And when they walked away I could see her shoulders slumped with the weight of him: she carried a burden, and maybe it should have depressed me further than I was already depressed, but the Thorazine came between me and any feelings whatsoever. I was inclined to run home and flush my medication down the toilet. I was inclined to see exactly what it was she stirred in me.

Now I saw. Now it just slayed me to see Mary Faith smile and I pulled back from her to watch her narrow mouth spreading over her sharp chin. She was still way too young for me, and I knew it, and she knew it, but we had worked our way past that, and if I was already unbuttoning her new dress without any of the guilt I felt when I first went after her, why, that just showed we were both healing up. From our combined troubles.

"Look at this," I said. The dress I peeled off her was fake white linen, unlined, with red buttons to match the cherries. The high heels were red too. Mercy. Mary Faith had gone all the way with what our Southern girls call an *outfit,* and if it weren't for the graceful curve of her white shoulder revealing itself as I liberated the white dress, I might not have recognized her. This was a young woman who, having missed her childhood, ordinarily dressed herself up in dungarees and flannel shirts and those flowing pink skirts.

I took care to fold the new dress and laid it out unwrinkled in the wing chair, then turned to see the goose bumps popping out on Mary Faith's long white arms and a squiggle twitching on her mouth. She was waiting for the verdict. In the spring night, the old house had gone cold, and Mary Faith stood before me without a slip. She wasn't wearing pantyhose, either: no, a garter belt and old-fashioned white lace stockings stopping high on pale taut thighs. My woman loved me. Mary Faith was brought up the only child of dour fundamentalist Baptists, and she was as modest as she was eager. She waited for me to take formal notice that she'd gone to this trouble to doll herself up. That she offered herself to me this way.

Trouble was, I had no desire to speak and tell her so. I wanted only to gaze on her in her red high heels. She had promised to marry me, after all this time, and I was going to adopt her son, and in the last few months I had felt for the first time in many years that home—this house, Due East, this world—held the promise of peace and not just the admission of failure.

"Mary Faith," I said finally, "you are a vision. You are Ingrid Bergman. No, wait. Too full a face on Bergman. You're Lauren Bacall. And that makes me Humphrey Bogart and whooee, let's have us a life. What got into you, dressing up so swell?"

She stepped out of one of the high heels and stood lopsided. I would have been slipping that silky bra strap right down that white shoulder if it hadn't been for the way she was chewing her lip, bubbly with the knowledge of some surprise she had for me but stoppered by the worry that the surprise wouldn't please me. How could she not please me? Here I was, a man who crawled back to Due East seven years ago, a middle-aged failed academic, failed musician, failed husband.

How could she not please me? When I first saw her chasing her son on the green I knew that I had no business chasing after her in turn, so I sat on my lusting hands and bided my time and wore my hairshirt and tried to join a monastery. But I couldn't find me a single monastery in the market for a recovering madman, and after a while it looked as if the prodigal son was staying on home territory. And it looked as if Mary Faith Rapple wasn't such a kid anymore. One day it did not seem so wrong to, if you will pardon the old-fashioned expression, court her. The truth was—and here's an old-fashioned concept as well—I wanted to lift some of the weight off those shoulders of hers. Sometimes her gray eyes would bear down, maybe focused and maybe not, in that combination of fatigue and concentration you see on someone who's been driving the car all night and knows it might slip off the side of the road any second. I wanted to drive the car for her. And if she wanted to sit in the backseat with white lace stockings and a garter belt, well, hey, I was open to discussion. How could she not please me?

"Well," Mary Faith said. "Well . . ."

"Well what, darlin? What's going on? We got us a party to go to?"

"No, not a party." Naturally, not a party. We did not go to parties. Her household and mine constituted a social orbit all our own. Now she stepped out of the other shoe and stood, it seemed to me, with her shoulders bowed, just a degree. It made me a little itchy on my palms.

"What then?" I said. "Spill the beans." I should have been unlatching that garter belt, not stopping to chat.

"Well," she said again, and I felt the itch spreading up my neck. "Well, I thought I could come along to church with you. For Easter."

"Come along?
    to church?
        with me?
            for Easter?"

If you are old enough to remember Maynard G. Krebs on the *Dobie Gillis* show, then you will know just how I cracked my voice to answer Mary Faith. What you will not know is why this caused me to lurch into such a sudden panic. Well, see here. All through those long years of my odyssey, cast out of Due East, an exile, I had held tight to my faith. I was not a good Catholic. Often I was tempted to take a whip to some of the Pharisees who pass for Church fathers nowadays, and doubtless those Church fathers were often tempted to take a whip to me, twitching as I was with sexual desire all the livelong day. Nonetheless, I had clung to that Church through all my troubles and Hers.

And Mary Faith was an atheist. And that had strangely pleased me: the daughter of dour fundamentalists, unwavering in her disbelief. After the long slow courtship that finally wore her down, I told her I needed to get married in a church, and she put up a fuss in her quiet way. She said that I, who'd been through all the torments of the Church (she didn't say sexual torments, but she didn't need to), should know better than to wish the Church to bless our marriage.

Well. I could be as stubborn in my way as she was in hers: wasn't I a man who had called every monastery on the eastern seaboard as I struggled up from madness? I wasn't about to leave the Church. But it slayed me, too, that Mary Faith tried to stand between me and the endless obligations of this Church of mine. It was the one point on which she was firm and immovable. Hadn't I been married in the Church before? she asked. The same Church that snapped its fingers and granted me an annulment and made that marriage go away?

Now she stood half naked before me and said that she wanted to come to church with me for Easter. The last impediment to our marriage, the last speed bump on our ride to the marriage license bureau, was disappearing. Mary Faith stood half naked and *smiling.* It was as if a different woman had come and taken her place.

I stared again at the goose bumps on Mary Faith's long arms and saw for the first time that the hair resting on those arms was dark and coarse. The sight was akin to the beginning of a hallucination: because, you see, her arms had always looked graceful and delicate, and I had certainly never before registered the presence of coarse dark hair.

I closed my eyes against this new vision, but she didn't seem to notice. She said: "I've been thinking. We might could get married in a church after all, Tim."

I opened my eyes and saw her tremulous and eager, her arms crossed over her breasts.

"If it's that important for you. And Jess has been going on about getting a white tuxedo. He'd need a church, he wants to wear a white tuxedo." Jesse is her son, that little wild child running across the green, now grown to be eleven years old. All these years she has been protecting him from church. "I thought if I went with you at Easter I could see how long the middle aisle is, anyway. See if any those old biddies blow a gasket when I come walking in."

It seemed to me that her chin sagged down, heavy with flesh, as she spoke. "How old are you, Mary Faith?" I knew perfectly well. It was a rhetorical trick question. I had to keep talking, because if I did not she would keep changing before my very eyes. One minute I was looking at peace and perfection, a long-legged flat-bellied girl wearing white lace stockings could have come out of a Frederick of Hollywood catalogue. The next minute her chin was going loose and her underarms were growing stubbly. Her perfect nose was too long and too sharp. Mary Faith wanted to get married in the Church she loathed, and I was losing it, and I was afraid.

"I'll be twenty-eight in July," she said.

"Sugar lamb," I said, and it cost me all my effort to speak, "you are still young enough to tell people an age you're coming to instead of one you long since passed. How long have you been an atheist?"

Maybe she heard how harsh the words *sugar lamb* formed in my mouth. She cast her eyes down and thought it over.

"Twenty years," she said when she was done with her calculations, meaning she had stopped believing in God when she was seven years old. And she meant it. And I believed her.

"I don't think," I said, "that you can run atheism through your pipes for twenty years and then just turn off the faucet." I could hear my own faucet running frigid. I could hear that metallic clicking in my voice which means panic.

She was scared too. In the dim lamplight she bowed her head lower and yet I thought, if I strained to see, that I could see hair between her eyebrows, down over her lip. Mercy! I had never seen hair on her face before, not in the brightest sunlight. My panic increased exponentially. It was hard for me to keep my feet on the floor. The hallucinations were beginning. I was in for another crackup, a big one.

Mary Faith said: "I didn't say I was turning off the faucet. I just said, maybe it wouldn't be so terrible if we got hitched in church."

Hitched. That word almost brought me back, that and the way she stared down at her white lace toes and moved her arms tighter to cradle her breasts. Almost. But now I imagined that I saw her nose hairs curling, clotted.

"We aren't getting hitched," I said, and found that as soon as I uttered the words my panic eased.

"Tim?" She looked up, her wide-set eyes darting the question back and forth.

"We aren't getting hitched," I said again, and the second time I said the words my breath came forth easily and my heart stopped its pounding and she stood before me as Mary Faith Rapple, twenty-seven years old, long-limbed and lovely and needy, and I didn't want to marry her. That was what this was all about. I wasn't having a crackup. I did not want to marry her. I didn't want anybody in the backseat. I was a middle-aged man finally free of my troubles, and I wanted to barrel off down the highway all by myself.

"Tim, what's the matter with you? You been saying it has to be in church for the last six months. If I testified in a court of law how you been crawling down my back the jury'd say *harassment,* plain and simple. And now I try to be—I come over dressed for—and you—"

"Look." I had to turn my back to her, because for a moment I had been held again in the sway of her white shoulders, a vision whose swoop has put me to sleep every night since I first saw her holding her son on the green. And when I leaned toward her shoulders, when I leaned in the direction of the comfort they promised, they turned knobby and a good six inches broader than I'd ever seen they were.

No. I had seen the truth, whole and sudden, the way the truth is always delivered. I had seen the truth and the only way to put an end to this marriage was whole and sudden too. All the panic I had felt a minute before had been transformed into calm and purpose. I knew exactly what I had to do.

"Mary Faith," I said, "the marriage is off."

"Tim—"

"I can't be responsible for a false conversion."

"I am not—"

"Let's not prolong this. Let's leave you some dignity." I pulled her white fake linen dress off the wing chair and shoved it into her arms. "When you leave my house, leave it with your clothes on."

"Tim," she said, "have you gone mad?"

Well, no wonder she thought it a possibility. That Christmas seven years ago when I came home for my crackup I took a whiz in the front row of Our Lady of Perpetual Help at the midnight mass. I made various claims to be the Christ child and Blaise Pascal and Bobby What's-his-name, the sympathetic one on *Dallas.* Mary Faith had seen me through the clozapine years, the lithium years, the Prozac years, the drug-free years. I have been diagnosed schizophrenic, and I have been diagnosed simple neurotic. One doc says I'm manic-depressive, bipolar. Sounds pretty geographic to me.

Well, he's the one crazy as a June bug. I'm not depressive at all anymore. I'm all manic. I'm unipolar. I yam what I yam. And what I was at that moment was a man who saw that he did not want to be married. Not a question of madness. Not a question of madness at all.

"Mary Faith," I said again. "The wedding is off."

The light wide-set eyes never wavered from my face the whole while she was stuffing her long arms into her fake linen dress, and I didn't like the patient fear that bore down on me. She was a charmer and I was the snake, and if I let her hold me with those eyes we would be back to my panic.

No. This snake was ready to slither off down the road, ready to pack up and leave Due East and this vision in white lace stockings. The least I could do was crawl off fast and leave her her own life to lead. Before Mary Faith had time to stuff her white lace foot into her red high heel, I turned my back on her without another word.

I climbed the stairs and went on up to bed, and knew that the world had been reconfigured.

My grandmother Rose McGillicudhy was famous for her excuses. She was a sweet vapid woman, but every now and again she'd go berserk and take it out, long distance, New York to Due East, on one of us. Then she would call back the next day, ashamed:

"Oh, sweetheart. I want you to know that wasn't me talking last night. I woke up this morning with my temples pounding and my nose throbbing. I've got some virus, maybe even a brain fever. That must be what made me say those terrible things to you."

But as I heard the front door slam shut, I was already drifting off to sleep with no care for Mary Faith's safe passage home, and I knew that there was no excuse for what I did. This was no brain fever.

I was nothing but a foot soldier in the marriage wars now, one of those legions of men in this vale of tears who beat a retreat when the altar starts looming close. Yes indeed. For the first time in my life I was guilt-free, an ordinary Joe, a slob marching through enemy territory, a punisher for no good reason of that innocent sex that lays itself down in the dust to be kicked again and again. No excuse for it.

I fell immediately into a deep sleep from which I thought I might never wake. Glory hallelujah.

woke with a full-blown case of the heebie-jeebies an hour after I cast Mary Faith out of my house. I found it hard to believe that what had transpired had transpired. I did not want to send her away. I did not want to take off anywhere, not in the shape I was in.

We mental patients are accustomed to that kind of temporary set-back, yet each one comes as a shock and a blow. We think we've beat back madness, but there it lurks in the shadows, wielding the cudgel of confusion. I picked up the phone to call Mary Faith, to beg her to forgive me, to ask for her comfort.

Across our yards I could hear an empty jangling into the night. A light shot on: her son Jesse rising to answer my call. My bedroom looks directly into his and I saw Mary Faith's tall imperious shape come stand in his doorway to hush him back to his bed. Still I held the phone in my hand, but it rang on, unanswered. She was not going to show me any mercy. How could I blame her?

I did not sleep the rest of the night, try as I might to summon a vision of her.

The next morning I dialed the Fly Away Travel Agency, where she's been working these past five years, every twenty minutes from the time they opened. But she would not take my calls.

"Sorry, Tim, she's in the little girls' room." Little girls' room! After lunch I rang every five minutes, and soon she was shamed into picking up her line.

"Tim, you'll get me fired."

I did not remind her that I had talked her into leaving her sad job anyway, to marry me. She'd already given notice. Instead I said: "Mary Faith, I don't blame you if you never forgive me. I can only plead temporary insanity."

She held her breath on the other end of the wire.

"I can only pray you'll forget it happened," I said. "Because I can't *believe* it happened."

Still the long silent suck of judgment from her end.

"I didn't think I'd ever lose it again," I said. "I can only hope it was better to have that one burst of craziness and get it over with before the wedding. You wouldn't want me to go nuts *then.*"

"Tim?"

"I'm sane as a Republican now, Mary Faith, sane as those amber waves of grain, sane as John Wayne. I swear."

"Oh Tim."

"I'm sane, and I want to marry you and take care of you. Come to supper with me, will you? Will you meet me at the Scuppernong, round about six?"

"I will," she said, her voice down to a whisper, and I heard in its low register that same patient fear I'd seen in her eyes bearing down the night before. But her *I will* soothed me, and when I hung up the phone I fell into a deep sleep of relief and missed the daylight hours. I didn't know then that this routine was to shape the days to come.

When I woke, it was going on seven already and her house next door was dark as a tomb. Jesse was sleeping over at somebody's, then, and like as not he'd get himself in some to-do around midnight and Mary Faith would have to tear out into the night to fetch him home. Where was she now, though? Waiting for me at the Scuppernong?

Don't you know I had wings on my feet dashing round there to catch her. I ran down River Street in time to see her slinking out of the café, hoping not to be noticed by the general public. Stood up on Friday night:

that is about the worst fate a woman in Due East can endure, I am told.

As if she'd read my mind in recent days, she was wearing that old pink Indian skirt she wore when I first caught sight of her. She might have been a teenager, her hair pulled back in a rubber band high atop her head. She caught sight of me chugging along toward her and drew her shoulders all the way up to defend herself.

"Don't," she said, in the voice of a woman who's been waiting alone in a restaurant for an hour. "Don't twist me around. Don't play those kooky mind games on me."

She said *kooky.* Did I hear her right?

"Mary Faith," I said, "I'm sick," and heard my grandmother Rose's voice issuing from my own mouth. "I slept all afternoon," I said. "And I think that whatever made me sleep all day accounts for that craziness last night."

"Tim," she said, "I think maybe you have to go back on the medication."

"Maybe," I said. "But the crazy part's gone today. Today I just feel . . . odd. Physically, I mean. I believe I've caught a virus."

She narrowed her eyes, but her shoulders had eased down to swooping. She was fretting, yes, but I was forgiven.

"Did you eat?" I said, and she shook her head no. "All right then. Let's get us something on our stomachs anyway."

She strolled with me back down the block toward the restaurant she'd just exited, tucking her arm in mine as if she believed again, for the moment, that I would take care of her. My soul swooped.

We only had a few doors to go: River Street is not but one long stretch, commercially speaking. On the river side of the street the squat stores back out onto a tabby-and-grass riverfront park. Lately the bars and the restaurants have blossomed with the tourist trade, and like as not you'll sip your beer next to a total stranger wearing good boat shoes and a proprietary air that says he knows what would *really* fix this little town up. But the Scuppernong has a porch that looks out onto the bay, and even the tourists from New Jersey can't take away the sweep of that water. Mary Faith and I have made a custom of sitting out there, I picturing the rickety docks I saw when I was a boy, back before all this neat-and-tidy progress, back before you could get a good meal in this town but when you could still get you a good story served up with your fish fry.

On this night, though, before we reached the Scuppernong we caught sight of a large crowd forming down at the marina end of River Street. You don't see large crowds forming in Due East that often, not unless somebody's throwing a shrimp boil or a beauty contest.

"What's that?" I said, and a dim recollection nagged. I grabbed for the date, the hour. The sleep had thrown me off: I didn't know day from night, up from down. Was I expected somewhere?

Mary Faith said, "Oh, it's probly the religious nuts. On Good Friday."

The day was Good Friday. And I *was* expected somewhere. I was expected in that throng knotting up on the marina end of the street. Does it strike you as strange that Mary Faith, atheist, knew the date, and I did not? Does this ring any role-reversal bells from the night before?

"Mary Faith," I said, fast, "let's not eat at the Scuppernong at all. Let's go . . . somewhere else. Let's go home and I'll get the car and drive you out to Lady's Island."

She stopped dead in the street. "What's wrong, Tim?"

A spring breeze lifted our clothes from our bodies. "I don't want to be at the Scuppernong," I said, "when Father Berkeley passes by."

"Why would Father Berkeley be passing by the Scuppernong?"

The jumble of bodies beyond us, down at the end of the street, began to move in our direction. I touched her elbow and steered her until our backs faced the crowd.

"Father Berkeley," I said, "has the cockamamie idea to walk the Stations of the Cross through the streets of Due East."

She began to giggle.

"And what are you laughing at?"

"You have to admit, you belong to an em*bar*rassing church."

"Admit it? Didn't I just introduce the notion? Used to be you could count on the Protestants to be out making damn fools of themselves."

She slipped her hand into mine. Now I was more than forgiven. I was being egged on.

"They're all atwitter," I said, "everybody in the parish. I guess they've already prayed the Condemnation to Death. That was supposed to be down at the welfare office."

"What are they praying for on River Street?"

"They better pray for mercy," I said. We were just passing the bookstore, where Father Berkeley had persuaded the owner to drape the windows in black crepe and fill them with titles on the murders of the Jesuit priests in El Salvador and the years of detention and torture in South Africa and the madness in Bosnia. Mary Faith's hand slipped out of my crooked elbow and she peered in.

"They're going past here for Christ's first fall," I said.

I watched her scanning the titles and for a moment I was transported back in time. I could have been watching my mother standing at this very window. In those days, it was a narrow storefront, a combination office supply-bookstore with the clear advantage given to the adding machines and legal pads. My mother used to stand on the sidewalk peering in, her hair tucked back in an old-fashioned French twist, her skirt a tad longer and fuller than the other women were wearing their skirts, her shoes girlish flats instead of the pumps the other ladies wore. My mother would lean right into the bookstore window, knowing full well that she'd only be frustrated if she walked inside and checked the short stacks tucked away behind the boxes of vellum stationery. And here's the strange part: what my mother would have wanted them to carry in this bookstore (besides Thomas Aquinas and St. Augustine, which even she was not naive enough to pray for) would have been books the likes of which now crammed the glass display shelves at Father Berkeley's behest. In those days they would have been books on the Hungarian underground or the bombing of Haiphong or the assassination of Martin Luther King, but they would have been the same books, really. My mother subscribed to *The Catholic Worker* and she lined her children up at the kitchen table to write appeals to our congressmen for civil rights and human rights and poverty rights and the right to be as right about the moral issues of the day as she always happened to be. We all wrote the letters, my sisters a little more dutifully than my brother and I. We were all crazy for her.

And now here stood Mary Faith, long brown hair gathered high above her long brown neck, wearing, besides the pink Indian skirt—you guessed it—a pair of flats. Here stood Mary Faith, peering in at the bookstore window.

"Maybe it's not so bad," she said, "that Father Berkeley has them out on the street. Maybe the welfare office and the bookstore window are better places to be than the inside of a church."

I snorted. "They're doing Veronica Wiping the Face of Christ at the Scuppernong. I'm not kidding." I wasn't. I was reflecting that before Mary Faith met me she hadn't had the time of day for current events, much less politics. She'd had her little boy and her father, who was dying on her, and she'd been scraping together a degree in math, course by sorry course, down at the local branch of the university. Now she peered in at bookstore windows with political titles, and approved, and looked like my mother.

"Anyway," I said, "I've done my years of creative liturgy and witness to social justice. I find it unseemly for the parishioners of Our Lady of Perpetual Help to parade through the streets of Due East like a tribe of loonies."

"Look who's talking."

"Cute," I said. This was a good sign, wasn't it, that she was ribbing me? That she was not tiptoeing around the subject of my leaving my senses the night before? Why, then, did the spring breeze pass chill through my body? "I wasn't born to carry the burden of evangelicism," I said. "I have always preferred to worship within four walls."

"Well, all right," she said. "But I'd rather see them marching past a bookstore than an abortion clinic." We had passed by the black-draped window by then, and the bank, and now in the twilight we crossed in front of the bridge. We hobbled along on foot toward home and my car and this plan of mine to drive somewhere for supper. But the spring breeze lifted my clothes, and as my skin rose in goose bumps, my agitation rose with it.

"Mary Faith," I said, "I wonder if that virus isn't making its way into my lower depths. I'm starting to feel queasy."

She stopped in the twilight street to face me and look me over. We stood on the cracking sidewalk. Behind us was one old Due East house, verandahed and white and graceful in its square strong lines. Before us was one of the new brick jobs, with garish puffs of floral femininity defacing all the windows. The smooth lines of Mary Faith's young chin, her long elegant neck, arched up toward me. How had her image been shattered so the night before? Now she was whole again. And yet, having said I was queasy, I felt it. I could barely look down on her for the dizziness.

"Tim," she said, "you're green. I believe you're right about that virus. Let's get you back home. I'll fix you some toast and soup."

"No," I said. "I don't think I could eat a thing. It's back to bed for me. Anyway, Jesse'll be calling soon. Needing you to come fetch him."

Her shoulders rose again. "Jesse can make it through the night at somebody's house. He's done it before."

I did not dispute this. There are some truths none of us is willing to face. I let her lead me down the street, and let her turn the key in my front door, and kissed her a long good-bye before it occurred to me, mid-kiss, that I might pass the virus on. Mid-kiss I believed that I'd misjudged my grandmother Rose all those years she hid behind a mask of sickness.

A virus is a terrible thing. It leaves you downright witless. That night it left me weak in the knees and the heart and the groin.

And yet . . . and yet as soon as I saw Mary Faith's house next door light up, I felt perfectly fine, strong even, hungry certainly. I fetched myself a large meal of cold pizza and warm beer. I sat at the piano, the grease still congealed on my fingers, and began to plunk around, softly, so's not to arouse Mary Faith's attention.

The fact is, the tune I played was just between me and Mary Faith's boy. Jesse and I were collaborating on an opera about his dog. Jesse wanted to call it *The Hound from Hell,* but the last time we spoke I told him it was on the way to being called *The Stepson from Hell.* He copied all his tunes from television jingles and scorned my efforts to educate him.

That last time he came by, I said: "Jesse, you know the way Art Tatum plays?"

He wiggled his hips, frenetic. I've played him enough Art Tatum.

"All right," I said. "You know how he plays Massenet? With that swing?" I played him a few bars and his eyes went dead. All right. It's a big complicated lesson. I played Art Tatumlike until I was feeling a little frenetic myself, and I lost Jesse in the playing. He did a goofy jitterbug with his poor mutt and he turned the TV back on. The TV, in the middle of our composition session. It's a terrible thing to have high hopes for a child. We took to words. He hadn't come by the house in a few days.

But I didn't mean to repeat my father's tantrums when he taught me the piano: not that old trap. I tinkered around with Jesse's TV tunes, stolen outright from the pounding headache ads, and tried to transform them into something with a little swing shebop shish swish swing. I wanted to demonstrate that we could be true collaborators, a father-son team after all. The deal was, we'd start the adoption papers as soon as the marriage license was signed.

I had the damper pedal on, fooling around, and over the single notes I thought I heard a car sliding by outside in the night. A slow slide. A sound so smooth I could have imagined it.

I had the sense that I was being watched.

Paranoia, that back-stabbing old friend. I shook it off. I was not going to have last night repeated.

But I found after a while that I could not press the keys. My fingers were jittery with the certainty that someone watched them.

Like an intruder in my own house, I put the lights out fast and went and stood sideways at the front window. I had to grab hold of the lace curtains hanging there and pin them back to get a good picture of the street. The curtains are the same panels my grandmother put up thirty years ago on one of her visits meant to bring civilization to the Rooney children down in darkest Due East. They stank of dust, like my mother and grandmother in their graves.

I sneezed and couldn't see the car I'd sensed outside before, but I knew sure as I knew trouble was circling that the car would circle back too. It did. It came back blacker than the night: a black Volvo sedan, one of the new models. Could have belonged to just about anybody on the Point, one of those well-heeled, well-autoed burghers, but not just anybody would have slid the car into a dead stop and turned the lights out. Not just anybody would have parked in the street, craning his neck up to see my girl next door, hoping to catch her in her nightie before a lighted window.

Did Mary Faith have a lover?

I shudder to tell you what happened next. I stripped down naked, standing by the window, watching that car skulking like some palmetto bug waiting for all the lights to go out. Why naked? you say. I can't tell you, exactly. Taking my clothes off was a spontaneous act. Maybe naked the odds were better I could restrain myself from springing out into the night to pull him from his car and throttle him on O'Connor Street.

Instead, there I was, fool cuckold, or maybe-cuckold—I had no proof yet—crouched down in the cool night air, waiting for the black machine to make a move. Familiar enough. I did my time watching Mary Faith's lovers come and go, though never before from this particular position. Back when her father was alive, back when I was sitting on my hands, she pretty near worked her way through the male population of Due East— married lovers, single lovers, smart enlisted boys on their way to Officer Candidate School, her professors at the Due East branch of the university —all these before she condescended to step out with me. But if she thought. If she was going to. If there was some.

Dust. Sneezes. My grandmother's curtains. I ran to get some of those sinus pills and when I came back he was still there. I was beginning to soften toward her. She couldn't know anything about his presence, else why would he still be spying on her? Or were they both lying in wait?

Sinus pills sneak up on you. There I was, squatting, holding vigil, waiting patient in the night, when that chemical clarity came over me. The car was a stark outline in the night. The sinus pill delivered sweet dizzy sleep all at once. I never conk out before midnight, never, but that night I surely did, my hands around the dusty lace, my nuts cold as sin, my clothes at my bare feet, my eyes on the dark road.

And when I woke, couldn't have been five minutes later, the car was gone.

Now I shudder all over again to tell you the first thought that occurred to me. I was still seeing with that dry-sinus clarity, and my first thought was, *That car wasn't real.* I was so chilled I had to go sit on the toilet. It was cold in the bathroom, and I drew a towel around my shoulders. Oh, I knew what I looked like: a little old man.

I took the towel off my shoulders and willed my shivers to quit. The car was real. I heard it. I saw it.

When you hallucinate, see—if you're old enough to remember Dobie Gillis, then you have probably tripped or at least smoked enough hash to get you some vision, and you don't need my explanation for this, but just the same I feel I should give you some context—when you hallucinate, you know what's happening. You know if it's not real. And if you go with it, if you go with the vision, you're cool. But if you freak out and say to yourself, *Mercy me! I am losing control!* then you are doomed to a short stay on a psycho ward.

I can deal with the hallucinations. I have had plenty of peyote and psyllocibin visions I cherish, a couple of acid trips I remember fondly. The breakdown visions were not great, though I am told I did a pretty good imitation of Bobby What's-his-name. The hallucinations I can deal with.

But there is a creepy time beforehand, when you're not sure. That shadow. The buzzing sound. The chill. Real? Or early stages?

And though I have never had a suicidal thought while actually hallucinating—not me, bub, I'm swimming to shore—when it appears that a vision is imminent it occurs to me to jump in my car and drive fast. I have stepped out into traffic unawares. I am told I have jumped out of trees. There are x-rays to prove it.

This time I only let my bowels run loose and shivered while I pondered the reality of that black car idling outside my lover's front door.

A rap on the door? Or only a branch knocking?
I went naked to spy again through my own front door.
Dark night. The wind sweeping. Pollen splintered through the quiet.
I closed the door, sane and cold.

DAY THREE **HOLY SATURDAY**

The next day was pure Due East spring, bright and dark by turns. The clouds were purple-tinged, puffy. I woke at noon, refreshed and abashed, hard pressed to believe that two nights in a row I had flirted with madness. Another setback. Another aberration. But wasn't my stripping down naked the kind of thing any man might do, facing evil and his own violent impulses? It's a terrible thing to doubt your sanity when you've been years earning it back.

Next door Mary Faith's car was gone—she'd be out at the Piggly Wiggly—but I made my way over there to rap on the kitchen door for Jesse. I could see him inside at the breakfast table wearing his sleeping clothes: an Arrested Development T-shirt and those boxer shorts printed with scenic vistas in neon colors. He looked up when he saw me knocking on the glass pane and then looked back down again into his cereal bowl without a change in his expression or a move toward the door. I can be patient. He is eleven years old.

"Jesse." He could hear me perfectly well through the glass but kept his mouth set mean and his head down. He has black curls that grown women find angelic, the bane of his existence in this era of skinheads and lost childhood. He was the first kid in Due East to try a bilevel haircut, but it didn't turn out, what with his curls. "I got that opening number polished up. Got an idea for a scat song."

He chewed harder. I can't be all that patient.

"Open up for the love of Mike." I happen to know he finds *for the love of Mike* quaint. He mutters these expressions after me.

I rattled the doorknob and discovered it was unlocked all along. I have warned Mary Faith about the times we live in, but since she lives in a permanent cloud of optimism and faith that technology will solve all our problems she has not paid me any mind regarding personal safety.

I went on in. He did not so much as look up, but he was muttering *for the love of Mike.*

"Jumping Jehosaphat."

"Jumping Jehosaphat."

"Oh, man," I said. Talking to him, I felt completely sane. I was completely sane. "You're still pissed."

"Watch your language," he said. The milk ran down his chin.

"At least I approach conversation as a two-way street. At least I do not mimic my elders under my breath and then reprimand them with my mouth full."

He chewed down his Cap'n Crunch as slowly as is humanly possible. Vengeance led me to plot how quickly this boy would be on a diet of low-fat granola once I signed those adoption papers.

"C'mon, Jess. Let's work a little today."

He gave me a look out of dark eyes and narrow cheeks. All right. I was willing to make myself a fool for this boy. That is, I *am* a fool for this boy, always have been, would admit this to anyone except this boy's mother, who might think . . . oh, who knows what. She sees, anyway.

I sang him his first completed number, Words mostly by Rapple, Music mostly by Rooney:

> *Got me a mutt by the name of Clover.*
> *Can't get him to sing or dance or roll over.*
> *He's known around here as a champeen loafer.*
> *If he ain't lying on the chair*
> *Then he's lying on the soafer.*

I admit I was corning it up some, doing a little Tony Bennett finger snapping.

Jesse said: "Oh, dip."

"It's not dip. It's phat. It's real phat, babe." Then I did a fool-for-you imaginary electric guitar thing.

"Phat," he said under his breath, but we were spared a scene. His mother's car pulled into the driveway and he jumped to give her a hand with the bags. He is surly sometimes, but he is crazy for his mother.

Mary Faith came in biting her lower lip and carrying the, you know, weight of the world on her shoulders. Clover, who is a big yellow lump of a mutt, roused himself to get under Mary Faith's feet, and Mary Faith gave him a good nudge with her knee. I resolved to forget the black sedan which, God knows, she had not summoned. The sight of her made me saner yet. Better than sane: I was washed over with empathy and love.

"Hey, hey," I said. "What's making you so blue?"

She put down her sack and saw me skulking in the corner of her kitchen. "Hey yourself," she said. "How you feeling? And I'm not blue. I'm trying to puzzle out some of that Linde theory."

"I'm feeling fine now," I said. "Just a virus."

"The Linde theory!" said Jess, ecstatic. "Where all the imaginary numbers go." He knew about inflation theory, about alternative universes, about fractal fluctuations. She talked to him about these things the way other mothers would talk about how you have to pick up your dirty socks. I wanted her out of the Fly Away Agency so she could start applying to doctoral programs, hole up somewhere where she could conjure any universe she liked. I told her I'd follow her anywhere. I said I'd scrub her kitchen floors in Cambridge if she could get MIT to overlook her early education.

She was beautiful, chewing her lip over her theory. Her brown hair was twisted up high on her head, tucked in this time with pins. "I do not believe in alternative universes," I said. "I believe in heaven on earth, which is what I have found me with you two right here in this very kitchen with frozen foods leaking through the bottom of the grocery bags."

They groaned together, but they looked right pleased, as they always do. It's been a long haul for her, what with her father laid up in bed a full year before he died of heart disease and her son near failing in school on account of grief and boredom and a bad attitude.

I pulled out a couple of packages of the leaking frozen food, meaning to help her unpack, and gave myself a start. There on the kitchen counter, tucked away behind the grocery bags, lay a stack of envelopes, stamped and ready to mail. The top envelope, written out in Mary Faith's round sloping scrawl, said *Senator Strom Thurmond.* I knew without asking what the envelopes below said. Mary Faith was writing to her congressmen and her state senator and her city councilman. Mary Faith was protesting injustice in the world. Why did this make me so uneasy?

One day soon after we began keeping company, I caught her rifling through my mail, the letters coming and the letters going: Amnesty International, Pax Christi, White Southern Males for Peace and Justice, Underemployed Intellectuals for the Right Thing, Fools for a World That Will Never Exist.

"What are you doing?" I said when I caught her at it. I felt she was rifling through my underwear drawer, looking to see if I hid condoms or magazines.

"Oh!" she said, not embarrassed in the least. "Just seeing who you write to."

"Don't do that," I said. "Mail is a private matter."

And I don't recall that she ever fingered my mail again, but look what she'd gone and done: she'd taken on herself that letter-writing habit my mother formed so early in me. Mary Faith wrote the fool letters now. For all I know, she had Jesse writing letters too.

"You hungry?" she said. I must have nodded. She got her groceries away and fixed us some puffy cheese things she popped in the microwave. *Technology is our friend,* she's always saying.

Jesse burned his tongue with the first bite. "Arrrrrrrrrrrrr." He over-turned his chair in protest.

"Serves you right," I said, "eating a microwave plastique lunch on top of that bowl of crap you call breakfast."

"Watch your language," Mary Faith and Jesse said, on the same breath. They did not crack a smile at the coincidence.

"Sit down, Jesse," she said, and he righted the chair.

"I will have you both eating macroecstatico diets once we are bliss-fully wed," I said, and they both beamed back that pleased and annoyed look. It is eerie to think back on those words. Ecstatico. That is just how I felt, the three of us wolfing down our too hot too cheesy too carcinogenic instimeals and bickering over my use of the word *crap.* In the bosom of my family. In the bosom of my woman who loves her microwave. Mary

Faith's father was a mechanic, and he taught her enough that she was able to build the only geodesic dome doghouse in Due East for Clover. She is threatening to build one for us, she ever gets to engineering school.

We ate on in silence, two great minds working on important theories and one puny mind working out a double-four tune, until I saw Mary Faith was not eating her cheese puffs. She had started chewing on a long finger instead.

"Now you really do look blue," I told her, "besides which you will injure yourself if you dig into your skin any deeper."

"I guess I am blue," she said then. Jesse looked up from his lap. "What's wrong?"

"Oh," she said. "Something I heard on the radio. About Bosnia." She watched me with the shadow of that look she uses when she needs a man-thing done, a twisting of the wrench or a heaving of the furniture. But the shadow of the look was nothing compared to the substance of it: her eyes were pale and full of demand and expectation. Here, Tim. You take care of this for me. "I'm worried," she said.

"Aren't we all," I said. "Worried."

"No, really, Tim. We have to do something."

"Maybe we could do marches," Jesse said. "Like the ones you used to go on. Maybe we could go on marches, huh, Tim, and stop the war?" The first civil words he had spoken to me all day, and they too had an expectant, demanding sound.

"What you know about Bosnia, Jesse?"

He shrugged. "They got a siege on."

"Don't tell him those things, Mary Faith. He shouldn't ought to bear that weight."

I thought her face flushed. "He sees it on the news," she said, and then, under her breath, "unlike the operas you expect him to write."

We stared at each other, and Jesse stared at us staring.

Finally she said: "We should be writing letters, anyway."

Now I felt my own face heating up. "Tell the truth, Mary Faith. You've already written your letters. They're sitting over there on the kitchen counter. And now you want me to write my letters. Letters from Due East, South Carolina, that will stop human suffering around the globe."

"Don't joke now. I can't help but think we have to do the air strikes."

She knows what I think about air strikes. My mother taught me to read with War Resisters League pamphlets for my primers.

"It's like the Holocaust," she said.

"Don't throw that term around. It has a precise meaning."

"I'm not using it imprecisely," she said. "I didn't say it was the Holocaust. I said it was *like* the Holocaust, the ethnic cleansing. Our standing by, doing nothing." She watched me harder, and Jesse watched her watch me. "We should be sending telegrams, Tim. We should be doing *something*."

I got the distinct impression she meant *me*, not *we*. She'd already done her bit, her stack of letters. I rose from the table and knew without seeing my reflection that my lips were white.

"That's right, Mary Faith. Why don't you write you some telegrams? Emphasis on you."

And just like that, after that brief exchange regarding Bosnia and Herzegovina, I threw my paper napkin down on my artificial food and I stormed out of the house of the only two people I am absolutely certain I will always and unequivocally love. People who sit around the kitchen table on a Saturday afternoon and can't eat for worry.

Let me put this in context:

When I was still an undergraduate—this was years before the big breakdown, back in the days when my hallucinations were exclusively chemical and always intended—I got the heebie-jeebies without benefit of drugs. Just pure heebie-jeebies one day. Woke up scared. Stayed scared. After a while I was scaring my roommate too, who took it upon himself to escort me to a school psychiatrist, one of those doctors Columbia University had designated to take away fear and trembling and dread and longing.

I had one session with the man. One part of a session.

I told him a dream. I had been dreaming the dream every night for six nights, and I was afraid to sleep for fear that the dream would explode on the seventh. I had been up for days.

The dream was this:

A plane crashed in the Due East River, not a block from my house. I was the only one home. No family in my house, no neighbors on the street, not another soul on the Point. I made my way down to the river and there was the wreckage, wedged in the marsh between water and land. People lay trapped, flames licking up around them, limbs severed, faces blown away: no one but me to help them. I ran toward them, but I couldn't bear to look on their misery. I stopped. I made to run away. They called to me. That is where I always woke up: I was planning to flee, and they called to me. Each night the gore was colored a sharper Technicolor. Each night my cowardice ran yellower, down to my very liver. I thought I would never sleep again.

The shrink said: "Maybe your dream is telling you you can't save the world."

I said: "What?"

The shrink said: "Where have all those other people gone? The ones who could help?"

"They won't do it," I said.

The shrink said: "Is that fair?"

"It just is."

"It doesn't have to be," the shrink said. "There are other people who can help pull the victims from the wreckage. They better come out of hiding."

For one shining moment, I thought I had found me a clever psychiatrist, one who would get me to argue my own responsibility. But no. He was taken with the sound of his own voice:

"It's a common adolescent fear that one is called on to do *everything*, that as one enters adulthood one must personally rescue everyone else who is suffering, particularly the other adolescents with whom one is surrounded, but the reality is . . ."

The reality is, he had not grown up with Dolores Rooney. He had not discussed civil rights with his breakfast and political prisoners with his dinner and torture with his supper. He had not been raised, as I was, to take responsibility for all suffering in the world, so long as it was outside the suffering walls of my own sweet home.

The reality was, there was no one else to save them. I was there. I had to do it. I stared at the psychiatrist. I was almost in the dream, right there in his office, right in the big comfy leather chair I sat in. The flames sputtered at the edge of my vision. Somebody called my name, blood gurgling in her throat. I stood from the comfy chair and walked out of the office, and the shrink didn't say a thing. Nobody called me back. Nobody followed me to see I wouldn't hurl myself in front of a car. Nobody ever sent me a bill.

I went back to my dorm, where my roommate shrank from the sight of me. Shrink, shrank, shrunk. I climbed into my bed in the middle of the day and I fell asleep in under thirty seconds. I dreamed the dream for the seventh time. I pulled every single oozing maimed grotesque body from the wreckage, and I woke up happy before I went back to sleep for a day and a night. Then I was cured, and hungry, and my roommate bought me three breakfasts and I did not have a crackup after all. Not then, anyway.

I walked back from Mary Faith's in a high fury, my interior monologue a sort of harried husband routine on the level of *Is there nothing for which she does not hold me responsible?* Crossing from her yard to mine, I was buzzing, electric. But when I approached my own front door, the juice stopped flowing, the switch cut off. I was washed over with an unspeakable weariness. I believe I've mentioned that I'd be willing to diagnose myself as an all-manic personality. I sleep as little as possible, on principle, and never in the middle of the day. There is too much to do, and no one else to do it. But my show of temper must have worn me out. I entered my house and walked directly up the stairs to—

—my sister Dottie's bedroom.

My sister Dottie's bedroom? The creepy beforehand was upon me. I did not remember turning down the hall in that direction, but there I was, in the crypt, the mausoleum, the living memorial my father and I seem to have maintained for my little sister, who died at the age of twenty-one.

I lay down on her bed. You can play that music from *The Twilight Zone* here. DUH-duh-DUH-duh. You can remember the black car in the night. I was sane when I went to Mary Faith's house. Now, again, I wasn't certain. I put my head on Dottie's pillow and breathed in again the sweet strangling currents of dust.

Maybe I was crazy when I woke up. You be the judge.

I can tell you that I felt good, better than I felt after I dragged all those maimed souls from the burning wreckage. I saw through the glass that it was already night. It was Holy Saturday night.

I was the scheduled lector for the Easter Vigil mass. I wore no watch, but I could see from Dottie's bed that the night was already deep outside. I had slept for hours. I rose and checked the alarm clock in my own bedroom. Ten-thirteen. I was due at the church, all the way out near Claire's Point, at ten forty-five, and I still had my shoes to polish. I'd have to fly to make it.

I did my shoes for Easter in the kitchen the way my father taught me, with wax and spit and polish. Dr. Professor Part-Time Academic, o didn't I look the part with my red beard tickling down to my Adam's apple?

My shoes shining, I headed my father's car through the dark out toward the ends of the earth. I would drive past moss-draped shopping centers and packing sheds and fields and country stores: I would drive past civilization as it dwindled. Father Berkeley built the new church way out in the country about the same time he got fired up with liturgical ideas on the order of marching the Stations of the Cross through downtown Due East.

Contempt for the old man I loved shot through my body the same way anger for Mary Faith had traveled it in the afternoon. I eased the car over the first bridge, to Lady's Island, and it came to me as a balloon over my cartoon head that I had spent a lifetime proclaiming religious faith in a century of doubt. Here I was, all alone, ever faithful, on my way to the Easter Vigil. Me and the old biddies of Our Lady of Perpetual Help. I laughed out loud in my father's car and could not even recognize the sound of my own mirth.

See here: I was never one who had to make a leap of faith—I sucked it in, with my mother's milk. When I was a boy I built shrines to Mary and never doubted that she smelled every wildflower I picked her and would shield me from the taunts of children who found flower picking unseemly. I did not have the moments of doubt that are supposed to accompany faith, those doubts that shadowed every step my mother took. Like my father, I believed as I breathed. I believed all through adolescence, all through the first sordid pokings of desire. I believed all through my secular philosophy studies, all through those loose days of the sixties, when we believers hooted at the Church's hilarious sexual pronouncements and thought the hierarchy had been invented for our amusement. I called myself a Christian existentialist and I never stopped believing. I believed as my wife left me. I believed when I joined one of those God-awful (sic) religious communes that sprang up in the Deep South, land not of community but of most awful individuality. I was an anarchist Catholic junkie. O! I was an iconoclast *pro* religion in an age of disbelief. I believed as I went mad, and even as I believed in a malevolent God, a betraying God, a dirty-tricks God who would lead me down into the horror show of madness, I was believing. I still believed when I reentered sanity, and when I wore down Mary Faith and convinced her to marry me and let me be her son's father, I thought I was one of the chosen ones. I thought I was *the* chosen one.

But driving through the dark night over the dark water of the Due East Bay, crossing that bridge from island to island, I knew that I had wakened on my little sister's pillow an unbeliever. I might have spent a lifetime proclaiming religious faith in a century of doubt, but now, as the century ended and everyone and his uncle reclaimed religion, as the *Times* and *Newsweeks* and the yag! *Peoples* down at Eckerds proclaimed "the new spiritualism," as the spectators joined the circus to make their own spectacular leaps of faith, I did the backward somersault into disbelief.

I laughed again, and still did not know the laughter I was hearing. The joke was on me. What everyone else picked up at fifteen or sixteen or seventeen, what any undergrad gets the first time he reads "The Myth of Sisyphus," had taken me forty-five years to understand. Forty-five years and a kick in the head from my girl, a simple little request to make something bad stop.

My first thought was, *I never have to go crazy again.*

And my second thought was, *I will go tell Mary Faith and we will spend twelve hours in bed together.*

I turned the car around at the U-Save-Here sign which marks the first gas station on Lady's Island and I zipped back over the bay, my father's old Mercury a hovercraft. Ooo-eee. I sang "Imagine." I was John Lennon. I saw a lifetime of sanity unfold before me. I saw myself as the true protector of my new family, the good father who does not hide in fear of the Old Tormentor. I saw a life stripped of that self-indulgent agonized search for authentic self: my God, the years I wasted on the neurotic twisted longing of my man Søren. I LEARNED DANISH in my bent God-devotion, I twisted my tongue around words like *afdøe* and departed the world of the sane in favor of the world of the possessed. *Afdøe* means "die away." Yes, ma'am, the joke was on me.

So you can imagine my surprise when I arrived home from the vigil I didn't make to find that Mary Faith had read my mind. She heard my car turn in the driveway and came over the way she had two nights before. You can believe me or not, but she was wearing the same outfit, fake linen and high heels, a hat on her head with cherries bobbing.

"Tim," she said, "I can tell you're feeling better."

First I held her tight, her slender body a graceful bird's, heart fluttering: so slight you could crush her with a stone. I stepped back and looked at the whole of her, one brown lock escaping from the hat, one brown eyebrow raised to question me. I have always felt such guilt about her age. It has always seemed to me that we should seek mates who may have seen what we have seen. But look at her! The slender wrists!

Again I unbuttoned her buttons, same as I had two nights before. You can imagine my delight at the second sight of the garter belt and white stockings. "I can't tell you how much better I'm feeling," I said. And again I slipped her dress down the arc of her shoulders, and folded it neat and tidy on the wing chair. I went to unhook her white bra and fumbled, the way I might have fumbled twenty-five years ago at the first hope of a woman's breast. A small breast, young and perfect, brick-red nipple and enough succor for even a needy man like me. Down, down went my mouth to the nipple when I thought I heard her say:

"So will you take us to church tomorrow?"

I believed I imagined it. I was holding her right breast in my left hand and pulling her down, down to my mother's threadbare rug.

"OK?" she said.

I raised my head from her breast. The cherries still bobbed on her head, the loose lock of hair still spindled. Her lips were smeared with lipstick—Mary Faith doesn't even *wear* lipstick—and now so was her breast. I knew my own lips were smeared as well. The Last Emperor.

"You're kidding," I said, and wiped my mouth with my sleeve.

"No," she said. "I want to do this for you."

Well, *that* was how her face shattered the other night. Wasn't she a sight, one breast pulled free, the garter belt riding up on one side and down on the other.

"Mary Faith," I said, "I have no intention of ever taking you into a church. Ever."

"But. I'd just be going along."

"You think you can just *go along?*" She—innocent, who had been saved all her life from the total immersion in belief so complete it locks out light and air—thought she'd just see what ladies blew a gasket. She had no idea that she was a crumb on the carpet and the great Hoover of organized religion was waiting to suck her up.

"That's right," she said. "So you can have the wedding in church the way you always wanted."

"Oh you," I said, the way you would to a child, and picked up her folded white dress to wipe the stains from around her mouth. She looked down at the wad of it as if *she* were the one hallucinating. She tugged it back, but I'd have none of a fight: I gave it up, her white dress, now soiled, and she began stuffing herself back into her Easter outfit.

"Oh you," I said again. "You have no idea."

But I knew. Hey, I'm offering no excuses. I'm not saying I ran out on her to save her from the horrors religion had visited on me.

O no o no.

I'm not even saying I contemplated the difference in our ages and acted on my uneasiness.

There are no excuses for what I did. My own inauthentic self raises its voice to call my act completely selfish. Unreflective. Guiltless. Ordinary. Unaccompanied by the gas gurgle of acute anxiety that had resided in my gut since I reached the age of reason. No longer troubled by the black sedan of jealousy.

I told you, I'm just an ordinary Joe and faithless in all senses of the word. It's true: that night I said:

"Get on home, now. Get on home and leave me be."

And she looked at me with gray eyes dull with incomprehension.

So I had cast Mary Faith out a second time. I went upstairs to my sister Dottie's dusty bed, where I slept a day and a night without so much as a sneeze. When I woke I left my girl and her son and Due East, and for all I know I left those flaming bodies in the Due East River as well. Just me to save, this once. Just old manic Tim Rooney. At peace after a life of, well, I don't dare say torment and risk your rolling eyeballs.

Let's say after a life spent ill at ease.

DAY FIVE TODAY IS THE FIRST DAY OF THE REST OF YOUR LIFE. HAVE A GOOD ONE!

Monday morning. The rest of the world had a life to lead—Mary Faith off for her final days at Fly Away, Jesse gone to terrorize his teacher —but I had the rest of my life to plot. I rose at 3 A.M. I packed, reshined my shoes, rehung Dottie's door so it wouldn't scrape the floor in closing.

When I was done with Dottie, I finished *The Hound from Hell*. At eight o'clock I watched Mary Faith's car slide out of her driveway, and then I walked over next door to leave the score for Jess and let the brown envelope tilt jaunty in their mailbox.

I waited until nine o'clock (never interrupt Bill Rooney when he's watching the *Today* show) and then I dialed my father's number.

"Dad!" I said, hearty and false.

"Tim," he said. "What mess're you in now? You dump those Dell shares fore they sank too low?"

"I'm sitting pretty, Dad. Today is the first day of the rest of your life."

"There's the right attitude, son."

I must tell you this about my father: when my mother was alive, and he had five children to see through life, he made an art of almost failing in business. He had a little real estate agency on River Street. If there was a trend, he missed it. If there was a chance to make a small investment, he declined it. If there was a profit, he lost it.

We lived on the edge. But after my mother died, and Dottie died, and everyone but his elder son cleared off home territory, he got shrewd. Business picked up. He kept his ear to the ground, and he heard a rumor that a little old illiterate black man, the last living soul on a swampy island called Peter's Gate, did not have the money to bury his wife. Bill Rooney hired a boat and called on the man. He offered him a thousand dollars to bury his wife with, and then, shaking his head at the old man's hesitation, five thousand dollars. *Do it in grand style!* I'll wager he said. *She deserves it!* The man exchanged him the island for the five thousand dollars, and he sold the island a year later for five million bucks to developers who made it the five zillionth golf paradise in the Carolina lowcountry.

My father does not know what became of the little old man after the burial party. Bill Rooney was rich enough not to care. He himself went as far south as he could go, down to Miami—maybe he wasn't getting enough sun or ocean in Due East, maybe it wasn't hot enough for him—and he found himself a Cuban woman named Eliana to minister to him. There she was in the background now.

"Beel, tell him he's a big boy, time he took care of hisself." Eliana wears a blond wig and patent leather high heels to empty the garbage. She never exposes less than six inches of cleavage, but Eliana is neither here nor there. I offer no opinion of her.

"Ellie, I'm talking on the phone!"

I can only offer an opinion of my father who, having soaked an ignorant man, bathed himself in the warm glow of generosity. Before he went off to marry his Eliana he wrote me a large check and introduced me to his new stockbroker. They have stockbrokers in Due East now, now that little old men have abandoned their islands to golf courses. My father's good fortune was my good fortune. I am well off now. I do not have to work, though every semester I take on a philosophy course or two, even if I have to drive fifty miles for the privilege of assigning difficult texts to illiterate good-hearted students who would prefer drinking beer and racing their motorboats on the creek to pondering *Self is a relation which relates to itself—not the relation, but the relation's relating to itself.* You think you could explain it? Sometimes I prefer to drink a beer myself.

"Yes sir," I said to my father, "I wanted you to know I'm shutting up the house today."

"Shutting it up!"

"Yes sir, I'm leaving this morning."

"You and Mary Hope taking you a little early honeymoon?" Mary Faith spent her entire life next door to the Rooney family, but my father calls her Mary Hope, Mary Whatsis, the little girl who got in trouble. He doesn't like her, and she doesn't like him.

"No sir," I said. "I'm off on my own."

"Son, you're not feeling peculiar, are you?" His old man's cranky voice veers off sometimes at a sharp angle, right down Worry Lane.

"I feel GOOD, says James Brown."

"Well, good. You sound all right. So where you going on your own, without your little intended?"

"New York."

"That's not my idea of a vacation."

"No sir, I know it's not." My mother was born on the island of Manhattan and left it to come live with my father on the island of Due East. She never forgave him, and vice versa. And me, I have spent a lifetime bouncing from Due East to New York and back again, and neither one of them ever forgave me for not being able to make up my mind.

"When you coming home?"

"I don't know, sir. Maybe never. Probably never."

"Timothy. Get ahold of yourself there. What are you talking about?"

I was beginning to feel a little Dostoevskian buzz at the top of my head.

"Timothy. Answer me. What in the name of baby Jesus are you going to New York for?"

The buzz was pleasant but I was a tad anxious all the same. Maybe these past episodes of distress were epileptic, not schizophrenic.

"Timothy! For the love of Mike, will you answer me? Have you talked this over with Dr. Black? New York! Why in God's name would anybody in their right mind with a decent income take off for New York?"

We were not necessarily discussing somebody in his right mind. The buzz spread through my skull: could have been a woman soothing my temples. I was visited with a new clarity, sharper even than the Drixoral variety. "Dad," I said, "I'm going to find my wife."

He let out a Bronx cheer. "You haven't even married her yet! Did she take off on you?"

"Not that wife," I said. "The first wife." I was filled with wonder at the sound of my own words. I hadn't let myself think of Bernadette, who left me twenty-odd years ago, after six days of marriage, in lo, these many years. Once—while I toiled away at my one-year appointments, my adjunct stints, my unrenewed contracts—I followed Bernadette's Fulbrights and her NEHs in the *Chronicle of Higher Education.* I gave up following her when they gave her a chair at NYU. But Bernadette, still bearing the name Rooney, was in New York, and now, evidently, I was going after her. Now, I realized, we had some things to settle.

"Not Bernadette."

"It's true, Dad," I said, and I began to sing the Four Tops sotto voce. I knew my father trembled with rage and dismay on his end of the phone wire. I tried to make myself clear to him and to myself: "Yesterday I told Mary Faith I'm not marrying her. Today I'm going off to fetch Bernadette."

"Timothy! Jesus, Mary, and Joseph! Rome decreed that marriage of yours invalid."

True: first thing my mother did, after my wife left me, was get me started on the annulment proceedings. Up until this minute I'd been grateful.

"Timothy! Say something!"

Nothing to say. As many times as I have been glad to be the scabies under that old man's skin, I wasn't about to tell him now that Rome meant nothing to me anymore. It would break his heart to think that I, last practicing Catholic in a family that once included a practicing nun, had left the Church. Even I have my limits when it comes to inflicting pain. I know, I know. You think my walking out on Mary Faith and Jesse meant that I had no limits. Well, judge not lest, etc., etc. Haven't I told you my brain was buzzing? Haven't I told you I was in the throes of fever?

I held the button down until the line was disengaged. Then I lifted it again, so the number would ring busy when my father called back. No time to waste, now that I knew my mission. I was going to New York to find Bernadette. I grabbed my bag, one sorry Samsonite suitcase from my student days, and I hotfooted it out of there before Bill Rooney got the big idea to call the sheriff or the police chief to hold me prisoner. I had told my father I was shutting the house down, but I didn't: I left the front door open for Jesse, in case he needed the piano.

I threw the suitcase in Bill Rooney's trunk and prayed his Mercury's South Carolina plates would not cause it to be stolen my first night in New York. Then I remembered that I do not pray anymore. I cranked the engine but my foot stayed glued to the brake.

This was it. Good-bye, sweet home of my youth and confused middle age. I eased the car through my father's circular driveway, over which hang the branches of one live oak, three pecan trees, and a dogwood. In the spring in Due East those branches are jitterbugging with colors, and the color doing the leading is a green so light-drenched you can almost see right through it to the heart of . . . something profound.

I pulled out into O'Connor Street and in the rearview I watched my father's house recede. In my boyhood it peeled paint and the yard grew in shabby patches. Now my father contracts out the housework and the yardwork, and the place is just as genteel as the rest of the smug old houses on the Point. Their green lawns run down to the river, and the broad houses stretch out like old bankers and lawyers milling at an oyster roast, arms akimbo.

I turned toward my bank on River Street. I was leaving Mary Faith, whom I would love forever, to find Bernadette, who deserted me after six days of marriage. Those six days were not especially smooth, either. But if a life is to be spontaneous, it won't do to question motivation. Too many years lost in the systematic study of meaning and purpose: now I was meant to act!

I wasn't having a breakdown. I was having a new life.

I pulled into the bank parking lot down by the water, next to a waterfront park sprouting low palmettos. Due East is a picture-book town. Even the poverty is picturesque, squatting down as it does in the lowcountry, where sky and land and water meet in one blue point on the horizon. In the bay a catamaran with two red sails floated. The bridge was opening, swinging through the sky like a ride in the amusement park. I dismissed it all with a wave of my hand. All these years I'd been back in Due East, intent on seducing an unmarried mother and convincing her to marry me in a church, I'd been pining for my first wife in New York City. All those years, without knowing it, I'd been losing my religion.

I made my way into the cool dark bank. I'd been using the drive-through for so many years I didn't recognize any of the tellers inside anymore. Didn't recognize the bank either, for that matter. I had to shuffle for some kid in a tie almost as wide as his desk. He peered as he held my signature card up to the light. He scribbled his initials in a backhand and said: "They you go, Mr."—turned the check over— "Rooney. You have a nice day." He had an upcountry accent: nothing the same, anywhere you look.

I cashed a check for fifteen thousand dollars—New York is an expensive town, you try to cash a check drawn on a Due East bank when you're up there—and got back in the car directly. But my wallet sat so fat now that I had visions of the street rats of New York descending on me and picking me clean. If I hadn't had brain fever, I would have had the sense to buy traveler's checks. Sitting in my car down by the Due East waterfront, I divvied up the cash: seventy-five hundred in my left sock, seventy-five hundred in my right. Then I stepped down hard on the money.

And when I was done I looked up to see a dark young man banging on my window. Lately in Due East we have been beset by what the rest of the country knows as real life: crack, gunpoint robberies in Piggly Wiggly parking lots, rapes and pistol whippings and general incivility. Still I wasn't prepared to be set upon myself, not with my fifteen thousand going-to-town dollars.

The young man's face was very broad and very black: I don't mean brown, I mean blue-black, a pure color exaggerated by the sun. When he grinned, he showed off his right eyetooth, outlined in gold. He had a baseball cap set backward on his head and a diamond stud in his ear. When he motioned for me to roll my window down, I did as I was directed.

That would be evidence I was crazy, no? Holding fifteen thousand dollars cash, I rolled the window down?

"Mr. Rooney," he said, and he sang the words in a tenor voice that belonged in a choir, "you gotta be careful. Don't be flashing all that cash."

I waited for him to pull out a knife or a gun. He waited for me to respond, and began to look at me as if he thought I was crazy.

Finally I said: "Thank you. You're right," and he said:

"OK now. You be careful."

I rolled the window back up and, tap on it all he would, I would exchange no more words with him. What could he have to say to me? He set his baseball cap forward on his head and wandered off through the parking lot to go be someone else's guardian angel.

I took this encounter as a good sign. Nevertheless I had to wait fifteen minutes before I could pull my father's car out of the parking lot. The bridge was closed again, backed-up traffic pushing through. Waiting, I got drowsy. When a gap finally opened in the line of cars, the guy behind me had to toot his horn to tell me to pull out. I looked up and saw a broad forehead in the rearview. It was my gold-toothed angel, driving a pickup truck.

I had a hard time concentrating on the traffic signals and hardly registered that I was making my last drive through Due East. The short low row of storefronts on Division Street, the stolid brick Methodist church, the Catholic graveyard, the Due East branch of the university, where they haven't wanted my philosophical services for years. The weariness shadowed me as I made my way up the strip that leads out of town and onto Highway 17 toward Charleston. I only made the turnoff at the last minute, and the brakes on the car behind me shrieked their disapproval.

The rest of the world travels to New York on the interstate, but not I. I had fifteen thousand dollars in my socks and all the time in the world to take the back road up the coast, if only I could stay awake. On the coast road the trees drooped down over the roadway, mossy, and the smells of mud and greens and shellfish swam through the air, conspiring to lull me. Past Gardens Corner, I looked down at the speedometer and saw I was doing forty-five, forty, thirty-five, thirty. The air was musty and rich and sweet and dank. In the lowcountry the land is watery and the water is earthy. The car was veering off for the shoulder.

Drifting off was pleasant enough. The money in my pocket was real. These fields of tomato vines were real. The smells were real. The fatigue was real.

Maybe it wasn't schizophrenia or manic depression or epilepsy that ailed me. Maybe it was narcolepsy. I let the car drift over to a good broad shoulder alongside a field that stretched back out through the country to kingdom come. Tomato vines were just now poking through the earth. I would lay my head against the steering wheel until I was refreshed, and I would be in New York by daybreak tomorrow.

On its way down to sleep, my eye caught sight of a truck in the rearview, a shiny black pickup. It was the same pickup truck that sat behind me on line in the bank parking lot. How ironic it would be if my guardian angel had followed me up a country highway to rob me where witnesses were fewer. I wondered idly if he would shoot me dead. It wasn't an unpleasant speculation.

But the pickup passed on by.

And before its rear wheels had passed my father's front wheels, I had passed on out, again.

REPORT FROM DUE EAST

was in diapers when he went off to New York City. I never knew him, growing up. Then one night my father came home and said: "Little girl next door's gone and drowned herself."

I said: "What?" There was no little girl next door.

"Little Rooney girl," my father said. Oh. He meant Dottie, the baby of the family—but she was no little girl, she was past drinking age already. That much I knew from all the beer she and her father guzzled in the backyard on a Saturday night. She stayed on with her father after the mother died, worked downtown in his office. We were not on waving terms, Dottie and I, not on smiling terms, either, more on nodding if we passed too close and couldn't help it terms. My own mother had always called the Rooneys nuts—*drinking and carrying on that way*—and I suppose my father and I kept the coolness out of habit. It didn't much concern me one way or another, not even when Tim came home to have his crackup and it was all anybody could talk about. He peed right in the front pew of the church. I have to say that is an impulse I admire.

But it didn't much concern me until that night when my father came home and said Dottie Rooney next door had drowned herself and I had to wonder if I couldn't have given her at least a wave now and again, when we were both hanging up beach towels on the back line.

"They're already passing off the story that she was taking a swim and got carried by the undertow," my father said.

"Maybe that's what happened."

"In January? Not hardly. Anyways, I guess we've got to go pay respects. How you suppose they handle this, Catholics? Your momma would know."

"Well, I don't know," I said. "I don't have a clue." I said I didn't think I could carry Jesse screeching into a houseful of mourners, and so my father put on a clean white shirt under his sweater and went over by himself, looking like he was waiting to meet the executioner. I stayed by the window the whole time he was gone. There was piano music dancing out of the house next door, and they'd only just dragged the body out of the ocean.

My father came chugging out not twenty minutes after he'd slouched in. "They're all there," he said. He came back in our front door like he'd just seen a flaming wreck and wanted to make sure I could picture the bodies too. "All four the kids," he said. "And the grandmama's there from New York already, poor old bat. Dudn't know what hit her."

"What about the crazy one?" I said.

"He's there, what's his name—"

"Tim," I said. You see, I already knew his name.

"Tim's standing there at the piano playing ragtime, and the rest of them looking like that is normal under the circumstances! Guess they'd rather not provoke him into losing his marbles again, but if you ask me he's done lost them."

I remember staring out the window again. The music stopped.

"They're fixing to go down to the funeral home, meanwhile they ask me would I like a whiskey sour."

"Did you take one?" I was just razzing him.

"I did *not*."

And I did not hear more of them, or of whether Dottie Rooney drowned herself or just swam out too far in the middle of January, when even the surfers don't go out in their wet suits, until one day a couple of months later when I was chasing Jesse down by the green. He ran straight for Tim Rooney, who was strolling along looking like a goofy mad professor in his chinos and loafers, his hair stubbled up in the light. Tim grabbed Jesse up and my heart stopped beating.

But he delivered my boy back to me. When he got close, his face looked raw underneath the freckles. He looked like he'd been sick.

"Here's your package, ma'am," he said, and then he looked me up and down and over as if to say I was a girl too young to have this little boy, which I was. I wasn't yet twenty, and Jesse was going on four.

"You be good then," he said to Jesse, and looked me over one time more, and this time the look was dull lust, like he couldn't remember why he was supposed to flirt or be chivalrous or gentlemanly or whatever that was he was being. There was nothing behind his eyes, which were icy blue, the color of Aqua Velva in the bottle. Later, when he threw out all the medicine, they came alive again.

And Tim came alive again, alive enough to come visit me two or three times a day sometimes. He borrowed Jesse to go frogging in the pond or just to run the energy out of him.

Once he ran us out to the beach. It's such an everyday thing to do in Due East, run out to the beach, that I swear the significance never crossed my mind until we were walking through the palmettos down to the sand. This was where it happened. It was all I could do to keep up with Jesse. Tim ran along at my side, all the way down to the surf coming in heavy.

The sky was covered with hammerheads and the waves, which generally take their time the way everything in Due East takes its time, were rolling in like thunder themselves. The lifeguards had already packed it in for the day, but you can get a good swim in before the lightning starts cracking, and Jesse knew it.

He went headfirst. The undertow was bad and I'm not much of a swimmer myself. I was counting on Tim, who wasn't behind me the way I thought he was. Time Jesse had been dragged under and tossed around enough for the seaweed to be coming out his nose and the silt mustache to be smearing the top of his lip, we looked around and saw Tim . . . taking a walk. And the first bolt of lightning winking in the sky.

I grabbed Jesse by a fist and nearly dragged him down the shoreline, going after Tim to talk him into leaving. I thought he was off in a daze, no more medicine to hold him together, and we'd have to coax him back into his car. Dottie's car, actually—a little blue subcompact they found in the parking lot a couple of hours before they found the body.

But no. When we got to him, Tim picked Jesse up to carry him and even squeezed my shoulder when we passed through the tall trees again and the lightning crashed down beside us. Huddling in the car, we were all giggly with the weather clapping so close, and it made me bold. I told Tim something I'd never said before, that I was sorry about his sister.

He started up the little car and drove at twenty miles an hour through the rain lashing down, when I expected him to drive like the madman he ordinarily was. He said: "The day she drove out here, she told me she wished I'd go back to the state hospital."

I was straining to hear him over the lash of the rain. I said: "Tim, no."

"Yes, she did. I'd been sitting around the house watching old sit-coms. *Leave It to Beaver. My Three Sons. Dick Van Dyke.* And the Thorazine was so thick I couldn't even bring myself to laugh. That's what got to her, I guess. Not that Dottie was a laugh riot herself."

"I'm sorry," I said. What else could you say? He was right: Dottie was not a cheery-looking person.

"So on her way out the door," Tim said, "I said, *Hey, Dottie it's me. Your lovable big brother. You wouldn't want to send me back there,* but you know, I don't believe I said it with any feeling. She didn't even turn around."

Well. If anybody had asked me before, I would have said there wasn't the least spark of sexual attraction between us. But don't you know when a man hands over his troubles like that you can see the width of his shoulders for the first time? And he had no idea—this is just like a man —no idea whatsoever that I was nearly the same age as his sister, that it wasn't my comfort he wanted but hers.

He's come close to cracking up again, but never this close. I believe, actually, that he's gone over the edge, and all the patience that has seen me through these years has not just stretched thin but torn like old cloth that's not worth keeping. I would have nursed him day and night, I swear I would have, if only he had made his way over to my house. If only he had crossed from one yard to the other.

Instead, he left me, when he knows I've been left before. And he left Jesse. There: the cloth is so ragged it's not even good for a dustrag. He knows I've quit my job. He knows we're all alone here. He knows it took all these years to learn to trust that he wouldn't do what he's just gone and done: desert us.

Maybe now I know how Dottie felt that day. Sometimes, when the only ones around you are that willful, it just looks easier to swim on out to sea.

two

DAY SIX MISS BLISS

I mean to tell you, I woke on the side of Highway 17 on the Tuesday after Easter at 3 A.M. Shank of the night.

You can tally the hours as well as I: I slept through the daylight hours of Easter Sunday, and then again the Monday. I could not have slept as much in infancy as I slept in those two days. And this second time I slept the day away, my head was lodged against the steering wheel. You'd think I would wake with a dent in my forehead and the aching body of the last man in America proud to claim that I have not taken formal exercise since gym class, 1964.

But no: I woke again refreshed, clearheaded, purposeful. Maybe that was the cause of my problems all these years! I just didn't get enough sleep!

Not to contemplate. Only to act. My waking was sudden and complete. I left the car to take a whiz in the deep Carolina night, blue-black as that young man's face in the bank parking lot. The birds would be stirring soon, but now there was only vegetable quiet. The ground was a membrane stretched tight and my piss beat a good swishing rhythm against it. The wet grass brushed my pants legs.

I got back in the car hungry but ready to drive until daylight. I kept myself company, humming *The Hound from Hell* and swinging the car the way the moss swung down from the trees. I was as aware and alert as I had been foggy the day before. I was seeing better through the night than I did the daylight. I skirted two rabbits and a coon caught in the headlights and chased them into these woods where rich men travel to shoot quail and dove. A deer leaped through the trees parallel to me and it was a tossup which of us was more graceful.

Outside Charleston, the land lifted away from the water for a railroad embankment. I passed by that low elegant city long before it woke, long before the light drenched it. All the better, that I should cross its rivers—Ashley, Cooper, Wando—its shipyards, its bridges, without intercourse. I dreamed of women.

I dreamed of Mary Faith. Mary Faith, in the lightening night. In the flesh. O, I loved nothing more than undressing her, and when I loosened her buttons and hooks I could not take my eyes or my hands off her: low mound of belly, hard angle of hip. Small taut breast, nipple puckered as a mudhole. A rush of sensation, all of it physical: saw her, smelled her, felt her, tasted her, heard her, wanted her.

A drive through the night is a wonderful thing. The pine trees had been whacked off by the hurricane, and they too, skinny and vulnerable, reminded me of women. Past the park, along a low stretch, I saw before me a figure in white, thumb out, and I knew a woman had materialized to follow my thoughts. Again, the low whine of anxiety: I rode through the night stiff with desire as I contemplated women, and a woman appeared. Dr. Freud! Dr. Jung! Dr. Ruth! What do you think?

There is no better cure for anxiety than reality, and so I slowed the car to satisfy myself that the hitchhiker was no hallucination. The closer I came, the realer she was: and she may not have been a hallucination, but she was a vision all the same. White-haired, she was dressed in a man's white shirt, underlined with a streak of short tight skirt. In the headlights her legs were dark against white canvas sneakers.

I stopped the car beyond her and waited. Girl stepping out of the middle of the night, dressed like some cross between tomboy and slut: how did she know I was not some lunatic come to pick her up? How did I know, for that matter? She ran for the car in that prissy trot of a girl whose skirt's riding up, and she stuck her head in the passenger door cool as you please.

"Will you take me to New York City?"

I know this sounds made up, fabricated, fantasized: but I swear, that is what she said.

"How'd you know I was going to New York City?" I could hear the shiver and the shimmy in my own voice. Should have been a warning to this girl, or a warning to me, but no, she hopped in and I grinned like an idiot.

"You are? Anyway? I just knew it. I just had a feeling. I let ten cars pass and believe you me there were some real winners wanted to take me for a ride."

I believed her. I pressed my foot to the gas and we were off, to New York City evidently. Together, evidently.

Immediately the nature of my desire changed. This little girl sitting next to me—and I believe we're talking nineteen, twenty years of age—was a, you know, hot tamale. A Sue Lyon of the nineties, a spring wound so tight you didn't dare test it. As soon as we became a syzygy in our bucket seats, the pleasant need driving me up the coast became unpleasant. I felt heat, sweat on my forehead, the usual. Was this why I left Due East? This simple complication of human company, and not brain fever at all? Was I that ordinary a Joe?

"Some hour to be hitchhiking."

"I'm running away," she said.

You can imagine how fast I wanted to pull off the road. I saw myself in a backwoods prison, charged with statutory rape, but I tried to remember carefree youth and keep my voice at even keel.

"Running away?"

The way a shrink would ask. Not all that interested.

"Well, not from home. I mean, OK, I'm leaving home, but I'm not running away from *that*. I'm running away from a wedding. All right, my wedding."

Well! Maybe we were talking a figment of my imagination after all. I allowed myself a sideways reality check.

She was real all right. She smelled of hair goo and night sweats. Even in the dark her hair shone—I thought I'd be able to see some metallic shade of green in it, come first daylight—and she had it trained in a Veronica Lake wave over one eye.

"Don't tell me you were thinking about getting married, your age." I sounded like the ancient doddering fool I am. I sounded like my old man.

"I was doing a damn sight more than thinking about it. We were all set for Saturday. But, I dunno, d'you ever have anything just, like, get to you? Like it just *irr*itated you till you couldn't stand to be in your own skin?"

"Why yes," I said.

But I don't believe she heard me, or took account of my own suffering. "I tell you what was the last straw for me. The presents. Everywhere you look in the damn house. You should see the lines of old ladies coming to see em! You'd think the baby Jesus was sitting up in our house, stead of a bunch of damn candy dishes and grapefruit spoons. I got six sets of grapefruit spoons, that's forty-eight. You want some?"

I looked her way again. She was unbuttoning the bottom of her shirt to get to her pockets, two front slits in a skirt that was melded to her belly and her thighs. Could have been made out of rubber, all I could see. Tucked in the slits, with their little bowls exposed, were a half dozen grapefruit spoons, three in each side. She pulled a couple of them out of the left pocket, opened the passenger window, and flung the grapefruit spoons out into the night. But once she'd tossed the first couple, I wasn't watching her act of bridal rebellion, and I wasn't watching the road either. She was digging in to pull another pair of spoons out from the other side, and the skirt was stretched out across her flat belly and sliding down below her belly button, which was dark and for all I knew furry. I could feel my tongue running along its rim. She dug for yet another spoon and her thighs bucked up when her fingers pressed against the serrated edge. I saw that the car was weaving. Only one spoon left. Do it! Do it! Get it over with!

"What?" she said.

"I didn't say anything." Did I?

"Oh." She closed the window and slouched back in her seat, a solitary grapefruit spoon still resting in her pocket. "I'm sorry. I shouldn't have thrown them out with you driving, you could have got you a big littering fine."

She sounded entirely sincere, and for punctuation pulled her shirt back down. "I just got carried away. I'd like to smash them to bits."

"Hmm. Hope you're not smashing somebody's heart to bits, too." I swear, I didn't know I would sound like Father Berkeley in the confessional.

But she didn't take offense. She snorted. "You kidding? I can't believe he wanted to be sentenced to a lifetime supply of grapefruit spoons either. His old girlfriends'll be calling by tonight, word gets out."

We drove along in silence. I thought a girl capable of throwing grapefruit spoons out the window would be capable of carrying on conversation with a stranger, but conversation was up to me.

"How long you been planning to run away?"

"I didn't plan at all. I woke up past midnight, I looked at the calendar, it said the thirteenth of April, I said, *This is my unlucky day.* I went downstairs, I saw all those grapefruit spoons, I said, *Not me, sister.* I got dressed, I went outside. I thought I was just going for a walk, maybe plant a grapefruit spoon in all the neighbors' yards, but the highway was so close. I saw it and I said, *Hey, I'm going to New York City.*"

She thought about that for a minute and cackled low, first calculated sound I had heard out of her. "Briggs hates New York," she said. "It *irritates* him. He always said, *I'll buy you a round-trip ticket for New York City and all the theater tickets you can fit in your wallet, but I'm not going up there with you.* And I always said, *Fine, I'll go on my own.* And here I go!" She used a hand for drama here, wiping back the Veronica Lake swoop from her eye. I realized it was first light. She swiped the hair back again, and a third time. The last time I could see I'd been right: there was a streak of hard metallic green in her hair. I could also see why it shone so: it was chlorinated hair, swimming pool hair. Now I could make out the hard muscles in her thighs.

"Well," I said, "what are you planning to do up in New York City?"

"I don't know," she said. "Get those spoons out of my system."

"You have someplace to stay?"

"I've got friends all over the place."

I was still thinking statutory rape, maybe thinking it harder since I saw the muscled thigh. I'm sorry, I've always associated physical well-being with an aggressive personality, and it struck me that she'd take advantage of my weakness, my desire. It struck me she might take advantage of my fifteen thousand dollars.

"How do you mean to get by," I said, "if you just walked out into the night?"

From the pocket of the white man's shirt she drew a gold credit card and flashed it in the first watery light. Again my eye drifted from the road.

The name on the card was Angela Bliss. Well, that couldn't be real.

"Pleased to meet you, Angela Bliss. I'm Joe Despair."

"Oh, stop. Believe you me, I'm not all that blissful."

It occurred to me that I should act contrite here. "I'm Tim Rooney," I said, o humble, o bowing and scraping, but she did not bother to answer. We slid past Georgetown, the mills spewing steam, and the air smelled acrid and sweet, metallic and piney at once. We rolled our windows up and pushed on north through the New South: woodsy condos and DON'T BLAME ME, I VOTED FOR BUSH. We passed Brookgreen Gardens, "Where Art Meets Nature." No marshes here.

"I know what let's do," said Miss Angela Bliss. "Let's stop for breakfast at Myrtle Beach!"

She had just walked out into the night. She had just walked out on a marriage and trusted herself to a lunatic. She didn't have a care past breakfast, and as the words fluttered sugary out of her mouth I felt a hunger roar through me, a gaping hole in my belly that ended in shivers at my fingertips.

Maybe it was a *nutritional* problem that had been causing these changes in my thoughts and my behavior. Maybe I was a diabetic! I stepped on the gas.

You may recall that I'd been sleeping on a peculiar schedule, but under the influence of Miss Angela Bliss I stayed awake for blueberry pancakes and all the daylight hours beyond. When the road sign welcomed us to North Carolina, she suggested we swing wide and drive up the Outer Banks that lie beside the mainland. But was this supposed to be a vacation? Wasn't I supposed to be going to fetch my wife?

"Well," I said. A mistake, given Miss Bliss's impetuous personality.

"Oh, let's do," she said. "I mean, are you in any rush?"

I could not protest that I was. With Angela sitting beside me—

strong, action-oriented Angela—I was beginning to forget the purpose of this journey. Now the purpose seemed to be . . . something else.

Miss Bliss directed me to turn before I ever agreed to. (I told you she would take advantage of me. Who do you think paid for those pancakes?)

If you've ever driven north up the Outer Banks you will know you can only get there by boat. You have to drive out to a blip on the coast called Cedar Point, and while you're driving there you begin to remember why people, people like my sister Dottie, head out to the edge of land. The leaves are silver in that Southern light, and the sky does not end. More graveyards by the side of the road than you'd hope to see in a lifetime: people come out here to die, maybe, and they don't join the regular Baptists. The churches are all Free Will Baptist. Free *Will.* All *right.*

They were working on the road here and there. The ride took forever, and every now and again I'd feel Miss Bliss's right foot hit an imaginary accelerator, and I'd obey her at that too. We were doing seventy-five when we should have been doing forty-five, but still when we got to Cedar Point and drove out to the end of the land and the concrete, there was the ferry, swinging its wide hips, pulling out.

We had missed the boat.

Angela pointed to the line of cars bending wide of the docks. "Keyrist. That's the standby line. We wouldn't have got on anyways." It occurred to me that we had hit the road in a frenzied travel week, the week after Easter. It occurred to me that we would be hours on line, but I looked at Angela Bliss's muscled thighs and I did not mind the possibility. We were at the edge of the world. Did I think of Dottie, swimming out to sea? Not for a minute. Did I think of Mary Faith, lonely in her bed? I thought of this blond goddess sticking her head out my car window like a pointer dog sniffing for salt air and the possibility of infinity.

Behind that ferry we'd missed the gulls swooped. Children on board threw Cheese Doodles to the sky, manna to heaven.

Angela Bliss said nothing. I pulled the car obedient into line and went to buy tickets.

When I came back she was lying on the hood of my father's car, a sturdy ornament in a skirt that bandaged the top two inches of her thighs. I saw that, stretched out, she was not so tall as Mary Faith: five-four or five-five maybe. The pleasant obedient size my sisters got to be. But the muscles! The brown arms! She must have felt me watching her. She came down from her pedestal and leaned her hip up against a passenger door. The sun beat down, the wind blew chill. She did not apologize for suggesting this route. She pointed out to sea, meaning to point out the first little island, and said:

"I waitressed there last summer."

I said nothing.

"And then at the end of the summer I dropped out of Vassar. It seemed so—like, pointless."

The ordinariness of it, the banality. Here I was thinking of dropping off the edge of the world, and she was talking about dropping out of Vassar. In the old days I would have thought she was sent to rescue me.

Then she said: "There's wild ponies on Ocracoke." The clear gold light of noontime at Cedar Point gave me a good picture of her, probably as clear a picture as anyone, even old deserted Briggs, had ever snapped of her. She had a lovely high forehead until the cellophane hair, plump cheeks on either side of a polite well-behaved nose, a knobby chin. She had a well-scrubbed look, even after a night in my car, and a fine white fuzz covered every inch of her exposed skin. She did look angelic. She looked like a girl who might have asked me to follow her to the end of the world so's to underline her own wild impulses.

"And we could go hang gliding at Kitty Hawk," she said.

I said: "Hang gliding? Are you out of your mind?" Was I sane, or what? It was bad enough to drive right up to the edge of the earth. I did not want to dangle high over an open sea.

"Let's get out of here," I said, and did not regret the money I'd laid out for ferry tickets. I was thinking of some Family Way Motel up the North Carolina highway for me and this white-fuzzed peach. I was thinking how I had never once in my previous life gone to bed with a woman I did not love. I would say that had left me loving a prodigious number of women, but it wouldn't be the truth. It has left me loving a fair number of women. I've been honorable and decent, though. I married one of them, didn't I? I came close to marrying another. And if I for the first time in my life (not counting acid days when I wasn't too clear on motivation, but who was, then, in that hour of mass insanity?) took into my bed a little girl who was nothing more than—let's say pleasant, because she pleased me—is that so bad?

Why no! It's life-affirming! Haven't we all agreed on that now? No more guilt, etc.?

If I am getting defensive about this, it may be to avoid telling you the things that happened next.

I convinced Angela we didn't have all day to wait on a ferry line, and I backtracked my father's car through the peninsula, the air spun gold behind us, the air ahead of us corrupted with the greasy overlay of fast-food joints. On our way to real life, but what with breakfast and the time on that ferry line, not to mention how far out to sea we'd driven, we were not going to be in New York City by nightfall. Not hardly.

We drove through the thick green fields of North Carolina, and the sky darkened as we traveled. Miles of springtime tobacco struggling up through the earth, and then the rain lashed down in time release, like the cracks of a whip. I began to anticipate the blows, and Angela beside me said:

"Maybe we should pull over?"

Her thighs were curled Buddha-style, and she was trying to look cool, but her full lips were pale. The lightning shimmied. My speedometer was slowing again, down to thirty, down to twenty-five, down to twenty, but I was wide awake this time. Wide awake with the welfare of a scared independent woman in my hands.

"Oh," I said, nonchalant, "it'll let up directly." Nevertheless when a country store presented itself I slid my father's car in beside the gas pumps, and Angela put her strong tanned muscled hand on mine and breathed: "Thanks. I know you're stopping for me."

And I was! Stopping for her! Would have stopped breathing for her at that very moment, but she was content to rest her head back comfy, the rain pounding down so heavy that we could not so much as make our way into Reuben's Groceries: Smokes Beer Pecans Diapers.

Angela yawned. "When we get going again," she said, "we going up the Bridge-Tunnel?"

"I guess we are." I hadn't done this drive in years. She meant the Chesapeake Bay. I'd forgotten it.

"Cool," she said, and closed her eyes. My heart folded in on itself. Cool. The word was as much reality as I could bear. The child riding next to me in my father's car couldn't have had eight or nine years on Jesse, who had so narrowly missed becoming my son.

After she spoke the word *cool*, Angela slept with her puffy Botticelli lips parted, and after a time I pulled out into the lightening rain. She did not wake, and so she did not know, as I did not know, that I headed the car south instead of north. She dozed for hours, entirely unaware that when I thought of Jesse I headed in his direction.

And did not know my mistake until I saw the signs for South of the Border. What happened to my breezy offhand journey? I was a mess! Witless! South of the Border!

I turned myself around and got going in a northerly direction, but now I'd spent the better part of the day missing the boat, driving in circles. Now when I drove past the thick green fields the sun set behind them, white gold, a monstrance. Angela stirred. Black birds chattered on the telephone wires after the storm, black against the blackening night. It would be a good time to make camp for the night, but every time I passed a roadside motel it was too shabby or too slick, or it didn't have a swimming pool for midnight skinny dipping. I hadn't mentioned my motel plans to Miss Bliss, and the burden of looking alone weighed on me. A motel is such a . . . personal matter.

Back through North Carolina, on to Virginia. The doubt that worsens with nightfall descended on me again: did those letters on the shoulder signpost spell the way to the GREAT DISMAL SWAMP? It seemed a message more than a piece of information, and I began to speed up. Miss Bliss woke up beside me and said:

"How'd we get on this little narrow road?"

It was a little narrow road, but it was taking us north again: it said so somewhere back a piece, when I filled the tank with gas.

"I'm working my way back to 17."

"This dudn't look like the way. Where's the map?"

"I don't know the last time I looked at a map," I said. It's true. I haven't traveled far in a good many years. Haven't felt the need. "You might try the glove compartment."

She did. It was empty.

Another sign for the Great Dismal Swamp. "There!" she said. "Dudn't 17 run through the swamp? Turn there!" In the dusk it didn't seem such a bad idea that she take charge. Back in the daylight, the landscape had possessed a definite shape: even at dawn you could distinguish cypress swamp from salt marsh, sandy seashore from dunes. But now the woods we passed were hulking and unnameable. Was that marsh or swamp sucking them down? We crossed a bridge twenty feet long, then another thirty feet long, low bridges that might have spanned ditches. Had we crossed into Virginia? Was this the Tidewater? Were we heading north, or south, or back out to sea?

I overshot the turn but thought to take the next road, hard past the first, and double back.

"You missed the turn," said Miss Angela Bliss.

I thought I might grow to hate her. How was I to know this road would run paved for a quarter mile and then turn to dust and mudholes beneath my wheels?

"I know," I said.

"Well, let's turn around."

"I *will*, soon as there's a place."

We sounded married, didn't we, this girl and I who'd known each other a day? My eyes drooped. That new affliction, narcolepsy, visiting me again. I struggled against it on account of this blond angel I had in my care. Maybe she was a control freak. But what would you think if you were a twenty-year-old runaway bride and some middle-aged man took you down a country road? And wouldn't you think worse if he fell asleep on you?

There was no place to turn around. The narrow road stretched farther than reality. Far behind us the high headlights of a pickup bobbed. Finally a new road appeared at a perpendicular and I turned the car into it.

The new road was narrower than the first. The land was low beside us, but in the dark I could make out neither field nor furrow. We bounced through pits and sinkholes. Wispy branches scraped against my father's car, and it seemed to me I could hear water running in the distance. Ragged pines and scrub oak rose up solitary. I willed myself to think what a fright it must be for Miss Angela Bliss to wake in the night here, in the dark, with a man she didn't know. A man who bought her pan-cakes with a hundred-dollar bill and said he was going to New York City and turned down a country road heading for the Great Dismal Swamp.

But don't you know she said:

"Tim, you been driving all day. You're out of it, babe. Either let me drive or let's just settle in till daybreak."

"Settle in? Here?" What, me worry?

We were nowhere. We weren't even at the end of a road, just in the middle of it, in a dark wood on a motionless night. I swear above the trees I heard the screeching of bats.

"Look up yonder," she said, and when I followed her brown finger in the dark I saw dimly a clearing under a live oak tree. Well. I knew about live oaks. We might be hovering at the edges of a dismal swamp, but we had found us one place of solace for the night. One Family Way Motel, au naturel. I inched the car forward until a big root blocked the path, and I strained to see an expression on Miss Angela Bliss's face. For a moment I wasn't entirely sure she was still there.

"You didn't mean that, did you? Settle in for the night? Out here?"

"Oh well," she said. "We been driving all day. We try to go any further, we could drive around in circles and run out of gas."

I did not tell her I had filled the tank while she slept. I never told Mary Faith I did not go to the Easter Vigil. I said:

"I didn't even buy you supper."

"Well, it's not a *date*," she said. I don't suppose she meant to wound me. "What time is it?"

She wormed her way out of her seat belt and practically into my lap to get herself a look at the dashboard clock. I recoiled: I admit it. She only wanted to see the time, but when she moved her tight swimmers' thighs up off the passenger seat I could see her breasts pitching forward beneath the white shirt and I could smell sweet sweat rolling down between them. I thought to myself, *I have to find my wife.* I thought that I must back the car all the way down this dirt road until I returned to a road that would take me clear and direct to New York City. I could feel the car sliding into reverse already, though I hadn't moved the gearshift. I could hear the engine humming. Or was that the whir of bats' wings, out in the gray night?

I fell asleep. I swear. All at once again, to a whirring sound. But I'd made it through a day, hadn't I?

And even if I didn't know how exactly I came to wake the next morning on a damp low creekbank with Miss Angela Bliss's head resting on my loose middle-aged belly, I did know that her chemical hair was nonetheless gentle to the touch. I know that I was grateful she had dragged me there, and stayed with me the night. I was brotherly, my palm gliding over her polystyrene hair. A spasm of joy gripped me before I realized that I was saying a prayer of gratitude—but I didn't pray anymore.

That was just before dawn—see, Nurse, back on schedule! Waking like a normal man!—just before I was aware that the purple sky indicated a storm, not night. Then the lightning streaked, and the soles of my feet tingled.

I rolled my eyes backward in my head to see if my father's car rested behind us. The lightning flashed again, and I saw that the car was there, driver's door open. I raised my head then and saw the creek we slept beside was narrow and more or less straight. The bank was low enough to let me see the water carousing by.

Then I saw another sight that made me think maybe I was having a vision. On the opposite bank stood a man watching me, and I believed I recognized him. I thought it was that young man with the blue-black face and the choir voice, his belly hanging low over his belt. Was that his shiny black pickup beside him? I understood that he was gesturing to me, and then it came to me that he was hollering as well. Hollering a warning? In the electric air the words shimmered and then shattered. He repeated them, and I couldn't tell you whether I really heard them or made them up or merely interpreted them as I wished them to be:

Creek's rising, came the words. *Get on out of there, now.*

DAY SEVEN **THE BRIDGE-TUNNEL**

I t didn't really matter whether a blue-black man stood across the banks hollering at me. I was not hallucinating the creek, and the creek was rising. Great gnarly branches hurled themselves downstream and crossed each other in passing. The sky spat: once, twice, a third time.

And I called her name—once, twice, a third time: "Angela. Angela! Miss *Bliss.*"

She woke in a state of dismay and confusion, her face a little girl's, lower lip hanging slack, eyes still working back and forth through her dream. Took her awhile to leave the dream and place me. When she did, she said:

"You!"

"Let's go," I said. "Less get out of here. Creek's rising."

Now that she was awake, she took her time stretching, wandered over to where the creek leaked over the banks, saw that I was right, turned around and grinned. The lightning ripped, just as she turned to smile, and made a leering jack-o'-lantern of her face.

"Keyyyyy." She fashioned a little girl's screech and ran to grab me by the arm. That clinging thing women do when they want to appear helpless. The skies opened, and we ran a three-legged race to my father's car.

"Key-rist," Angela said, safe in the passenger seat. "I'm so wet from that little run I could wring my shirt out." And she proceeded to unbutton her white shirt, which might have been damp but which was certainly not dripping. I did not look, but I could see nonetheless: could see hard full brown breasts in the first morning light.

I busied myself with the ignition key and found my fingers fumbling. Here I was, lost somewhere on the Southern coast, maybe hallucinating, facing down a flash flood. Can you blame me? I turned to her and said, fierce as you please:

"Don't do that."

And, fierce as you please, she rebuttoned.

We found our way out in silence. I followed the road which carried us the night before, but soon I could neither see nor hear it. We went jolting. The rain streamed so thick I could not see whether we passed through farmland or the woody edge of a swamp. I did not ram any trees, but I passed close. Angela held one palm out flat against the glove compartment and used the other to twiddle her shirt button.

We plowed. I gunned the motor. We looked at each other and knew we were stuck in the mud the road had become.

"Aw, shit shit shit," said Angela, meaning: *The car's going to die here and the water's going to rise and we'll meet our death together, two strangers.*

I opened the car door, thinking to search for branches to lodge under the tires. The rain lashed in. I closed the door again: a body couldn't see out there, much less go traipsing around looking for likely pieces of wood. Angela was twiddled out and scared. I twisted myself over the driver's seat to rummage through piles of old notebooks and gradebooks from Philosophy 101 and stuffed the stoutest under my shirt. Then I left the safety of the car for the driving rain. I stuffed the notebooks under the rear tires, as if they would make a difference. In the vast space of the rain, they were pathetic, nine-by-twelve cardboard dreams. The lightning flashed, and I grabbed the right rear tire. Those bolts were electric.

Made it back inside the car. *My* shirt was sopping. *I* could have wrung it out.

Angela stared at her fingernails. "So? How's it look?" O cool cool detached. *She* was not going to drown here in the backwater.

I did not answer her but put my foot light on the gas and began rocking the car back and forth, forward and reverse, forward and reverse. By now the notebooks had turned to paste in the rain, wet gray lumps in the dark morning. The tires would find no traction. They would sink in the dark mud and we would sink with them. Unlike Angela, I believed we were doomed. I believed we were going to die on this lonely country road, undiscovered, our bodies destined to become a waterlogged toxic tangle of fumes.

The vision lifted me. I began to rock back and forth with the car, forward and reverse. I began to sing "Take Me to the River" in a bass deep as Samuel Ramey's. No. Deeper. Purer. The engine struggled on. I coaxed the car, swinging like Elvis the Pelvis, like sweet Sam Cooke, like the Everly Brothers, both of them. Angela beside me began to cling to the armrest. No doubt she thought she was with a madman. No doubt she believed there was something sexual in the way I rode this rocking car, and maybe there was. All in an instant the car ground forward: a shifting of gears, a surging of power. Climax. We left the disintegrating shredding sheets of philosophy behind and propelled ourselves through time and space.

See what happens when you take action? See what happens when you take charge?

By the time we hit the highway I was a hero. You could read it in Angela's eyes.

"Tim, I didn't think we were gonna make it out of there, babe. I thought, now don't laugh, I thought it was my punishment for running out on Briggs."

I reached over and pecked her on the cheek. O it was an avuncular act, but my lips stung and the down on her cheek rose as electric as that early morning lightning. And then I rested my eyes back on the road, and the rain stopped, and we headed north again. Two ordinary tourists taking the ordinary route. I was as stylish at the wheel as I had been the night before.

But by the time we stopped for breakfast she had decided to buy herself a map of the eastern seaboard to make sure we didn't get in that fix again. And then she bought herself a red pen and began marking up the map, and then she asked if I wouldn't like her to spell me a little at the wheel.

Well, *I'm* not a control freak. I'm secure enough in my sexual identity to let the woman drive, yes, and to enjoy it. Now I got to be the pointer dog in the passenger seat, feeling chipper, yessir, ready for what the day brought me. Angela Bliss and I were leaving behind our weddings, putting Virginia behind us, pushing on through Maryland, leaving the South. No more rain: the sun shone bright. The landscape grew more moderate—neat packages of smooth open fields opened up beside the road—and the people grew more moderate too, I had no doubt. The land was fenced, marked, parceled. I was content.

Angela was the one driving when we reached the Chesapeake Bay Bridge-Tunnel, and I was a tourist, all agog. *Are we going to drive right out onto the water?* This man-made wonder came on too damn fast for a man in the passenger seat. We rolled through the toll booth and out onto a wide-open bridge, Angela flapping her hands like a loony bird at the big tankers that sat serene as rubber ducks in the great bay. All around us water and sky beckoned. My eyes began to bulge.

When we made the swoop down into the first tunnel, my eyes bulged out past their sockets. What could account for this new symptom? Diabetes? By the time we climbed back up to the bridge, my throat was numb and my heart was beating in syncopation.

We were back out again, back in the air. I got into the rhythm of my heartbeat—duhDUHDUHDUHduh—and I didn't realize Angela was pulling into the parking lot for a rest stop until she had already turned off the engine.

In the middle of the Bridge-Tunnel, o God Bless America, in the middle of the Chesapeake Bay sat a parking lot and a square concrete shop like a fallout shelter where you could buy postcards and geegaws and ice cream floats. Angela turned the ignition off, and I saw we were surrounded by the Easter week vacationers of the East Coast, shivering in their Hawaiian shirts as they traipsed out of their cars and into the souvenir shop.

"Let's go get a hamburger," Angela said. Then she looked out past me and changed her mind. "Ooh!" she said. "Let's get us a look through one of those beenockular things." She was being cute as hell, just adorable, tying up her shirttails as she ran along the edge of the parking lot. She mounted one of the swiveling binoculars and looked out to sea.

Me, I could barely open my own car door. My eyes were pulsing outward, my throat was shrinking inward, my heart was running down the road to its own beat. We were at a gift shop in the middle of the water, out in the magic light, o out on the great sea pass my family crossed by ferry all those years ago when we headed north. The trip north, so my mother could breathe in New York. My father bellyached all the way up the East Coast, all the way across the Chesapeake.

I stared out at the bay. There was my little sister Dottie, strangely enough, standing out on one of those binocular things, mimicking me. But Dottie couldn't be on the Bridge-Tunnel: the Rooney family used to cross the Chesapeake Bay by ferry when we made our pilgrimages from Due East to New York.

The spring sun beat down, and I closed my eyes. Now it was a September sun. Now I was traveling with my family up the East Coast. Here we go. Here we go to deliver the eldest son to his last year in college. Here we go to drop Tim off in New York City, the one city on earth that makes his father crazy. My father made his way to New York too once, to be a musician, but he wasn't good enough or fool enough to stay. He'd rather his children rot in Due East beside him.

The ferryman signals my father to pull the car in behind a logging truck. In front of us, on the flat bed of the truck, lie dozens of unplucked brown tree trunks, contained only by the chains that encircle them. They look as if they might slide back into our windshield any minute. My little sister Dottie, next to me, sucks her breath in horror as we pull close.

Dottie has been sitting next to me the whole trip. Dottie has been following me around the whole summer. She doesn't chatter to me. She doesn't talk to anyone. She is three years old and silent. She has a lazy eye, and my mother cuts her bangs too short and too crooked, and she wears Maggie's and Katie's castoff dresses, too long and too shabby. There is always a little line of grime around her mouth, always a faint smell of pee.

Dottie has been quiet for the last six hundred miles, but now she sucks her breath in and clutches at the door handle. Before we know it, before I can grab her back, she has escaped the backseat and has gone scampering through the line of cars and trucks. My mother leaps from the front seat after her, and my father's foot jerks back and forth on the brake as he eases the car right up to the logging truck. He is apoplectic. Crazy females, leaping from cars.

My mother hollers Dottie's name through the well of the boat—my mother never hollers—and Dottie, abashed, stands safe at the edge of the ferry, wedged between a car and the ferry wall, staring out. Beyond the ferry wall laps the sea. By the time my father has the car settled in and we have all leaped out, it is a big joke, Dottie leaping from the car, and my mother and father share a wink over their smallest child's head, a wink of relief. That is strange, Bill and Dolores winking at each other, but not as strange maybe as grimy Dottie, three years old, thumb guilty in her mouth. Strange and silent, she does not say a word on the entire ferry crossing, this child I will never know, growing up in a family which is no longer mine.

Angela, legs brown in her white canvas shoes, legs swiveling like the binocular she is draped over, was a million miles away. You can't confide in a beautiful woman how the line between memory and hallucination is turning to vapor before your very eyes. Sea spray in a spring sun: you have to hold yourself together. You can't fall apart in front of a beautiful woman.

Angela still pranced atop the beenockular thing, her swimming pool hair radiating the light, and I followed her. I followed her as if she were a star, one of those sad blondes, Marilyn or Jayne or Carroll Baker, and I was one of those melancholy Arthur Millers, one of those decent Joe DiMaggios.

I went to join her. I dropped the quarter in the viewer and I tried to be a good sport, I did, I swiveled the way she did until I could see a good panorama of the bay. The shipping traffic was brisk, the world was at its business. Did I think anymore of silent Dottie, thumb in her mouth? Did I think of Mary Faith, lonely in her bed? I did not. I was out of my mind. I had forgotten them.

I swiveled the binocular around toward the roadway and watched that brisk traffic instead. A dark smudge crossed my vision, and I wheeled the viewer back to follow it. A black smudge. A black pickup truck, shiny, heading north. My entire line of vision went black.

"Get back in the car," I said, gentle and forceful to Angela.

She stuck out her tongue. "I'm getting a hamburger, Tim."

"Get in the car." This time I was only forceful.

"Tim . . ."

"Get in the car!" All around us tourists turned to stare. And Angela, silent and fearful as if a truckload full of tree trunks was about to slide through her windshield, did as I told her. She skedaddled back to the passenger seat of my father's Mercury with only one last look around to see if she was doing the right thing to come with me, or might make a last-minute break. But she came, and she even buckled up for safety.

I threw the car in reverse and knifed it between a man and his wife who had the good sense to look lively and get out of my way.

We were off. I maneuvered the car through the parking lot at twenty miles an hour and then peeled out onto the roadway, the bridge. I pressed the accelerator: fifty, sixty, seventy, eighty. Somewhere up ahead was the black pickup. Angela sat silent beside me, her hand on the door handle.

I said: "Two can play at that game."

She said: "What'd I do?" Her words were outlined in a red thread of alarm.

"There's a guy up there in a black pickup truck's been following me since Due East," I said. "He followed us into the swamp, even."

She would not look at me.

"But now I'm turning the tables on him. Two can play at that game."

She did not answer. And I felt a terrible pity for her, scared like that, thinking that I'd gone off the deep end. She had no idea that I was back in control. I wanted to take my palm and pat her all over. There, there. This is just the way I get, once I get going.

But I couldn't touch her. For one thing, I was doing ninety by then. And for another, she was too far away, curled up small against her door. Now her eyeballs were bulging. Now her throat was numb.

Now her heart was beating in some lonely strange syncopation.

But me, I knew what I was doing. I was going to New York City and track down my wife and the man who'd been hounding me. I wasn't stuck in the past. I was living in the present.

Next morning I woke encased in a sheepskin womb. Wool all around me: I might have been drowning in a shipment of those four-hundred-dollar Aran Islands sweaters you see advertised in *The New Yorker.*

New Yorker! That was it! I was back in town, with no memory of how I arrived. Blackout. No . . . gray edges of memory. Chugging along the New Jersey Turnpike, bound for glory at ninety miles an hour. I lay still. My mouth tasted of wool. It stretched out over my forehead and down to my toes.

Outside the wool and far away were voices. I knew Angela's, firm and low: "I mean to tell you," she was saying. "He was, like, perfectly normal and then he just snapped."

"He was incoherent when he walked in here last night." New voice: female, brusque, candied Southern accent, a voice that goes with beauty-parlor hair and too much eye shadow. "And I don't call it perfectly normal to spend the night in the Great Dismal Swamp."

"Pends on what he was looking for." That was a third voice, this one male, the accent cracker, the tone smarmy.

"He was looking for the road!" Angela again, exasperated. God bless Angela—old friend, sister—pleading my case. Angela, pleading last night. I had a sudden vision of my father's car emerging from the Holland

Tunnel onto Canal Street, the sidewalks jammed with the working poor at rush hour. File clerks in shrinking rayon sweaters. Bins of rubber slippers and pantyhose and Christmas lights in springtime. Angela, jabbering. Me, happy. Ecstatic. Back in town.

The car pushed across Canal to the edge of Chinatown. Hanging carcasses in the butchers' windows, flesh everywhere my eye fell. Old women, color washed out of their lips, toting babies on their backs. And Angela's tanned arm, pointing: *Turn here, turn here!* I screeched around the corner and cut off one of the grandmothers, a little boy in a red cap tied to her back with a length of dull blue cloth. I had a distinct memory of wanting to crawl inside . . . something.

And now here I was inside . . . something. I burrowed my head out from under the woolly cover: nothing but an expensive rug that would have done better on the floor. I lay on a mattress as puckered with lumps as cellulite thighs—must be a futon, torture invention of the yuppie class. The futon rested on a good Shaker bed. When I rolled my eyes back in my head I saw a papier-mâché sculpture-painting kind of thing on the wall, white wads that called to mind those toilet paper lumps on the boys'-room ceiling in junior high. A white paper lamp on the low bedside table. White sheets. Bleached floors. You get the picture. The place was white.

Centered across the foot of the bed was a delicate wood and rice-paper screen. I had the urge to poke my foot through it. Light flooded through the screen, and I knew that my cell began on an interior wall and that the opposite wall, across a vast empty space, would hold a fifty-foot bank of windows. I was in a loft. I was in SoHo. I remembered that hand of Angela's again, that arm stretched out, pointing. *Turn here! Turn here!* When I last lived in New York City, when I was a graduate student ten thousand years ago, SoHo still had *factories*. It was an *out*post. Now it had futons and bleached floors.

"What are you going to *do* with him, Angela?"

"I thought I'd show him around some."

"Show him around! He thinks somebody's *following* him. What I meant was, what hospital do we bring him to? Never mind, I'll call my shrink. Maybe somebody needs to come by with a needle fore we try to carry him anywhere."

I shrank back down inside my wool cover. I understood every word they were saying. I was not hallucinating. I was not paranoid. All right, I could not remember being incoherent last night. All right, I could not even remember *arriving* last night. But somebody was following me. And now, because I wanted to follow him in turn, a perfectly reasonable course of action, they wanted to imprison me! To poke me with their poisonous needles! I would have to call Amnesty International! I would have to remind them how many letters I'd written for them, I would have to say, *Look now, it's time to write some letters for* me.

Or possibly I could escape and not bother Amnesty International at all. Possibly I could slink out of this all-white loft and drive off in my father's Mercury, never to see Angela Bliss again. I could check into one of those uptown hotels which at least have the decency to locate themselves in a swell part of town, far from streets where old women carry children on their backs. And then I could get to work. Then I could search for: (A) the man in the black pickup truck and (B) my wife. I'd almost forgotten B! But now all was clear and full speed ahead. Now I had a good plan. I knew it was.

I was charged with energy. I was almost out on the street already, but I was cunning: I knew I could not leap from my bed, I knew I must hold myself back and slip slide away without their ever hearing me.

I rose one degree at a time, o I was painstaking. I moved through the planes of the universe, and when I rose to the perpendicular plane I examined myself. I had gone to bed, or they had put me to bed, with my clothes on. I lowered my hand one degree at a time to check my pocket, though I could feel from its weight that my father's keys still rested there. Socks on my feet, covering my money. I had only to find my shoes: even in New York City they think you're strange if you walk around without your shoes. You've heard the Bellevue jokes. They're coming to take you away, hah-hah.

I expected the shoes to be doubled up neatly under the futon bed. Down on my knees I went. No shoes. Under the bedside tables? No shoes. I was inching along the floor on my knees. How much time had passed? There! In the Shaker wardrobe that complemented the Shaker bed. Slowly, slowly I opened the wardrobe door. No shoes.

I had exhausted the room. I had exhausted myself, moving in slow motion. I, Mr. Manic, considered lying back down and bringing the wool cover over my head and waiting for the attendants with their straitjackets to come fetch me.

And then, without further contemplation, I saw the solution.

I sauntered, yes, I say *sauntered,* out of my little partitioned sleeping area and made my way down the center of the loft in the direction of the voices. I headed for the spot where my jailers sat over coffee with Angela. They loomed straight ahead, a trio in sunlight. Above their heads twelve-foot strips of gauze clung to the window.

I forced myself to look at their walls: on both sides of me, more white-on-white: monoprints; a white watercolor; white plastic birds, or winged creatures anyway, flying unframed off the walls. In the dead center of the interior wall was a red wall sculpture the width of a fence post. I believe it was an artery slit open. The whole place reminded me of one of those dime-store displays of aluminum Christmas trees with white balls and a blue star on top. The same sensibility.

Not that I would say such a thing to my gracious tasteful hosts, who were at that very moment staring me down. The candy-voiced woman was a shock: she was a stout white woman of thirty or so with blond cornrows and a face as round and white as a turnip's. Her eyes were underlined in purple, as if to underscore the resemblance. She was dressed in black and so was the mountain man beside her, in black turtleneck: you just knew that when he stood up the black pants would be linen and pleated. Mercy. He had a great drooping red mustache and dark hair slicked back and pulled into a little ponytail that curled under like a cartoon pig's tail.

Was I shaking as I drew near?

Was I paranoid?

Ah no. Not at all. The only way I was going to walk out of this apartment free and shod—and you may remember that my shoes, when I began my journey, had been polished twice in two days—was to carry this off. And I did carry it off. With aplomb, if I may say so.

I let an ironic half smile play on my lips and pushed my hand through my (again, if I may say so) boyish fading red hair. When my eyes left the art-covered walls I set them on my stocking feet, and then when I was three feet away from their table I looked up, aw shucks, and I said:

"Listen, I'm sorry that got so out of hand last night."

They looked at me with tight blank eyes.

"I hope you didn't *buy* any of that."

Angela leaned forward over her coffee cup. I gave her an encouraging chagrined grin.

"I just couldn't resist, pulling into New York, you know, trying it out."

The mountain man's eyes narrowed. Angela raised her cup to her lips.

"And, Angela, I never should have done it to *you*. But with the city so close. I just got it into my head . . ." I was draping myself over this, making myself comfy. I shook my head back and forth at my own audacity. "You know, like DeNiro putting on all the weight for *Raging Bull*. I wanted to *get into it* and I knew after half a day with you you'd have . . . an honest reaction. But you guys didn't buy it, did you?"

They looked at each other. Angela's eyes went dull as that old woman's scarf. She didn't mind defending me, but she didn't want to be snookered.

"You did say you taught philosophy?"

Aw shucks again. I *chuckled.* "Well," I said, "that's right. That's what I *have* been. Matter of fact I've been teaching a course called the Philosophy of Drama and, this part's kind of embarrassing, doing little theater. I know, I *know*—little theater in a little town. But maybe you've heard about all the movies they've been shooting in Due East. And I did some walk-ons, you know, big deal, but I, uh, hit it off with a casting director . . ."

Magic words, *casting director.* The blonde licked her lips delicately and let a slow smile work its way north. "You're an *actor?*"

I nodded, bashful.

"And you're coming to New York to try to *make* it?" This was the mountain man, alarmed that some rube would try to park in his loft while dreaming the impossible dream.

"Actually, I've got an appointment with Sidney Lumet next week—"

Sidney Lumet popped into my head because (A) he sounds like a New York kind of director to me, and (B) after Bernadette left me all those years ago, like many American men, I took great consolation from Al Pacino in *Dog Day Afternoon,* the *Attica! Attica!* bit. It occurred to me to try looking like Pacino at the moment, but I'm too tall for the role and not nearly focused enough.

No matter. Sidney Lumet did the trick all on his own. The mountain man sat up straighter and the blonde grinned a tingly grin. Her eyes were darting over the kitchen shelves. What could she make when Sidney Lumet came to dinner?

But Angela's eyes grieved.

"The casting director . . . it's a crazed street person kind of part." I addressed her feet, under the table—a round sheet of glass on plaster pedestals. "It was wrong of me, playing around like that. I didn't for a minute think you bought it. But I guess it was a little creepy. I don't know how to apologize." And I gave a look of Total Remorse.

She stared me down, bright and breezy, and pushed her angel hair out of her face. Then she winked her dark right eye and I knew in a stark moment of revelation that she was sneakier than I was.

"Pretty good act."

"It was so good," said the turnip blonde, "that you better sit you down here with us and get yourself a cup of coffee. Just take a day to act *normal* fore you go talking to Sidney Lumet. Better just let us *all* adjust."

And she rose to fetch me a white mug and pour coffee from a white porcelain jug, and this time my remorse was real and bitter. Because Angela sat now biting her lip, puzzling it through. Distracted, but trained for social grace, she said:

"Tim, this's Velma Ruttledge, her family and mine go way back. And this's her husband Fred."

I could tell Fred's family did not go way back. He patted his chest delicately with his bony hairy fingers spread wide. "Angie tells us you're from South Carolina too. Idn't that something? A roomful of us, looking out on New York City."

I followed his eye out the window, looking south. Opposite us, a row of stolid factory buildings. Beyond, skyscrapers sparkling. Only one of the twin towers fitted in the frame. The buildings and the day were a brown-tinged gray, monochromatic as this loft.

Soon I would be out in the gray day. Soon I would have my shoes. I saw them now, neatly paired on the window ledge. Someone had removed my shoes for me last night. Someone named Angela, I was willing to bet.

"Welcome aboard, bub," Fred said, and I knew that my status had been elevated to invited guest. I had fooled him. I had fooled his wife. It came to me, stirring my coffee round and round, that I used to do the same with Bernadette: even before I married her, I used to drink and drug and go batshit. Later I would persuade her and me both that it was all an act.

Eventually she saw through it. Look at Angela there: she saw through it. And Mary Faith? Did she ever see through it? Was it a noble act on my part, leaving the lover who didn't see through it?

I drew myself up. There was something appealing about formalizing this acting business. Maybe that was my trouble all along. Maybe I didn't have a brain fever bug, maybe I had an acting bug.

Maybe I'd better just work it out of my system.

DAY NINE VIGIL

By the next day my transformation was complete. I was an actor preparing for an audition in which I would play a man on the edge.

Fred and Velma invited me to stay with them on Spring Street, as I knew they would. They said they loved to have guests from down home, why, when the Met did the Ring cycle they didn't know *who* all was staying in their loft.

Velma said they sometimes called themselves Fred and Wilma, as in the Flintstones. Fred claimed to be a sculptor. Were those wads of toilet paper his? Where was his studio then? Why wasn't he in it? He spent the morning grinding coffee beans in an antique hand grinder and castigating Velma for letting the beans go stale.

And what was Velma up to? On her way out for errands, she carried one of those little Louis Vuitton bags, the brown envelope dwarfed by her bulk. What a picture she made: a black-clad beatnik-artiste, an ample mother figure, a conventional hausfrau but for the yellow cornrows tassling along her plump cheeks.

By early afternoon Fred had slipped out too, and I poked around the loft. Angela was still sleeping. They had given her a little cell like mine, adjacent to mine. I hadn't slept all night, listening for her, but she was dead to the world.

Fred and Velma shared a large birdcage at the end of the loft, opposite the kitchen. I peeked inside and saw mirrored squares on the ceiling, over the bed. I slipped inside, just to make sure I wasn't imagining things.

"Oh! You found the mirrors. I can't decide whose idea was that." It was Angela! Awake finally, after all these hours. I had missed her waking, and she had caught me at my voyeurism. But she giggled and the mirror was . . . light-filled. Cheery. Angela had pulled on a pair of the mountain man's jeans. They slipped fetchingly down her hips, and her arms dazzled with that white fuzz that covered her. I found myself watching her reflection rather than her, and in the light-filled mirror she looked like a Christmas angel.

"Wow, it's late." She had caught sight of the time in the ceiling mirror. On the bedside table the clock said one-thirty, but on the ceiling it gave off five o'clock. I twisted my shoulders round to try to make sense of this.

She laughed at me. "Take a walk with me," she said, "after I get me something to eat. Let me show you around."

I had been up all night and now all day too, the glorious spring New York day. Outside, I could see from Fred and Wilma's window, was a spread of gray and brown. In Due East, as I may have mentioned, spring days are rich, bright and dark, the flowers electric, the wind full of promise. Outside this loft the day was damp and heavy and you had to make of yourself what you would without any promise of hope from earth or sky.

I had not ventured out yet. In the morning, while Fred and Velma fussed with yogurts and wheat germs and fruit I did not recognize, shiny and yellow-fleshed, I had paced the length of the loft, working out my character. From the kitchen table they looked on like proud parents. I was a good actor.

And truth be told, I was frightened to leave the loft. I could not remember where anything was in this city. Besides, nothing would be in the same place anymore. Look what kind of people lived in SoHo now. Did Fred and/or Wilma hold artist certification? My God!

"Come on," Angela urged from the ceiling. "You can't stay inside forever."

"No!" I heard the echo of my own protest and caught her eyes flickering above. Since we had arrived she had not ceased puzzling over me. I felt a great tenderness toward her, so protective that there were moments—here was one, right here—when I thought I might weep. I did not want to frighten her again. I could not imagine that I had frightened her in the first place. "I'm into rehearsing right now," I said.

She shrugged and led me across to the kitchen space, outfitted like a wholesale restaurant supply warehouse.

"Suit yourself. I just wanted to show you SoHo."

Oh, Miss Bliss wanted to show me *SoHo*. Miss Bliss, who wasn't even born when I arrived in New York City, age of sixteen, with an acceptance letter to Columbia and the notion that I was young Wittgenstein. I had not so much called a girl on the telephone, much less nibbled on a female ear. I was full of beans, full of promise. Full scholarship! Boy wonder! By the end of my first year, as I believe I have mentioned, I had experienced my first mental . . . crisis. But I was only sixteen. The city was large. The Great Books we read were full of terrifying concepts. Human responsibility! Not to mention eyes gouged out and children sacrificed! No wonder I got the heebie-jeebies so early in life.

But I did not tell Miss Bliss that I *knew* the city already, knew it as the site of my mother's sad upbringing and my grandmother's lonely death. All the Rooney children came to New York eventually, all of us but Dottie. None of us here now but me. The last Rooney in New York.

"Well, I'm going out," Angela said. What could she know of anyone's history? She was all present, pulling plastic containers out of Fred and Velma's industrial-size refrigerator, digging out that yellow-fleshed fruit and sliding it wet through her fingers and down her throat. Finished, she went to get shoes and a jacket, tripping on Fred's trousers and sucking on her pinkies. I followed her down the long hallway and would have followed her into her cell and fallen on her right there on her own white futon if . . . something hadn't stopped me.

Instead I watched her disappear behind her own delicate screen and did not even try to see her shadow as she girded herself for the streets of New York. I paced the hallway again, muttering to myself. Homeless. Out of it. Just out of it, babe.

"You sure? You won't come with me?" She poked her head out past the screen and it was all I could do to resist kissing her full on the mouth.

Then she was gone.

And the long afternoon in the white loft stretched out more terrifying than a changed SoHo could possibly be. I walked the hallway for hours before it came to me that I could venture out myself. I could try my character out on the city streets! I could do Sidney Lumet and Al Pacino proud.

Out on Spring Street it flashed that I had left the car with my suitcase in it in front of the building, against Angela's advice. There was no car there now. I had a moment of profound panic: my father's Mercury was gone. My clothes, my suitcase, the remnants of my life. Then I remembered who I was, a man of the moment, a man meant to act. I couldn't spend my days weeping over stolen cars and a thirty-year-old valise. I offered the car up to the gods of irresponsibility and went on my way.

Halfway up West Broadway I forgot to stay in character. Or you could say I was in new character, rube from Due East, car newly stolen, mouth agape at the Eurotrash in the sidewalk cafés. They all had tanned muscular arms like Angela's and those little brown bags like Velma's. I was sixteen years old again, loose in a city with long-legged women.

I was not, however, the most conspicuous tourist in SoHo. All up the great length of that great avenue were overweight papas in Mickey Mouse shirts. Who could say if they came from Paris, France, or Rome, Georgia? On this spring day they paused, foolish, in front of boutiques.

I crossed Houston Street. A black-stubbled beggar reeking of Ripple pushed me in the chest to indicate I should give him money. I hurried past—manners like that will get you nowhere—before I realized he was playing my role. He seemed coherent, though. Purposeful. What I was supposed to be, playing him.

Up LaGuardia, the bland high-rises of NYU a brown blot on the day. Turned down Bleecker to escape their shadow and found bliss, joy. The Bitter End still standing, still the bitter end. Then I turned up MacDougal and flew higher past the old cafés. I laughed out loud, and the sad suburban girls dressed all wrong turned to stare. Ha! I only meant to share my joy that MacDougal Street in midday was still filled with longhairs from the Midwest and the burbs, that some of them still strapped guitars across their chests, that you could still buy a mud-thick espresso and wail folk tunes for all I knew.

Home! Safe! It might be the nineties in SoHo, but a few blocks into the Village we'd gone all the way back to 1964, the year, I might add, when I first left home for this scene.

I salivated at the thought of Washington Square and picked up my pace. The girls who turned to stare at me, their jeans tight around their crotches, shrank back against a pastry shop when I barreled through. Too rich for you, girls? The money in my shoes slipped to and fro beneath my socks. I'd be covered in blisters by morning. Maybe Angela would minister to me. Maybe she'd bind up my wounds.

I was up to NYU, almost there, heart of the Village, home to my Bernadette's chair. But what was this? NYU students? They all of them, male and female both, appeared to be models. I had been hoping for men in short-sleeve plaid shirts with a passing resemblance to Mario Savio, but instead here came a boy wearing a studded collar, holding on a leash a pit bull with matching neckwear. I turned to watch boy and dog pass by, and by the time I'd straightened myself out had stumbled smack into Washington Square.

Where I was washed with delirium. Springtime in New York—all right, chilly. All right, gray—but that did not stop a one of these greasy longhaired males from stripping right down to their bone-white skin, their hair-flecked nipples, while they kicked a drugged soccer ball around the fountain.

Many changes. The paths in Washington Square converge like the spokes of a wheel and I traveled them back and forth, finding my bearings. Many changes, *plus ça change.* Oh, the first time I uttered those words in New York. I'd been saving them in my pocket with my spare change, waiting to offer them to a girl in braids who knew my suffering. *Plus ça change,* I'd say to her. *Angst. Fear and trembling.* I believe I used all three on Bernadette the first time I stepped out with her. And guess where I took her that first afternoon I talked her into spending time with me?

You got it. Bingo! Double Jeopardy! I took that girl downtown, to Washington Square Park. Now I saw its latest incarnation: wooden playgrounds for those urban parents brave enough to wheel their strollers past these junkies, these reefer-smoking layabouts, these panhandlers.

Back and forth from the fountain, up one path and back down another. Was I pacing? This would never do.

I chose a bench opposite the dog run. What an utterly charming idea, a dog run in a city where everyone is caged. And the run itself hardly bigger than a cage, the dirt flying, the dogs mauling each other while their owner ignored their wounds in favor of flirtation with other owners.

I shifted in my park bench. A boy, maybe three, maybe four, I'm not a father, who's to say, passed by and said:

"Daddy, what's *mercurial* mean?"

The boy was three or four: a mite, I tell you. *Daddy, what's* mercurial *mean?* He pronounced the word perfectly.

Perfect word. I rose to catch more of their conversation, but they had drifted off into preschool talk and out of hearing range. I saw that the tree under which I was sitting had a plaque attached: I sat under the branches of a Siberian elm. Perfect word, again! Bingo again! Final Jeopardy! Here I was in exile, under the branches of a Siberian elm. Wasn't this a sign? Here, in this park, where I first stepped out with Bernadette, I would find her again. I knew I would with all the certainty which once told me there was a God in heaven and a Blessed Mother to protect me. I would set up vigil here under my Siberian elm, opposite my dog run, and Bernadette would cross my path.

Another boy passed, this one seven or eight. A dark-skinned Latin child with a full mouth and round cheeks, his hand tucked in his mother's the way a little boy's would be. *Little* boy. As they walked through the shadow of the Siberian elm he called her Mami and climbed up her arm with his own. Beautiful boy, thick straight black hair slicked down by a Mami who loves him. Gap in his front teeth, eyes dark and slick as oil. He wore a T-shirt that said I'M GONNA SEX YOU UP.

I restrained myself.

I sat myself back down on the bench and looked out on dogs who wear only their own desires and not the ones manufactured for them here in America, land of the sex trade in small children.

Have I mentioned it was my own sexual practices which estranged me from my wife?

Next to me on the bench a wiry man, maybe young, maybe middle-aged, maybe black, maybe white, hard to say: wiry and brown, not from the spring but from the winter too, and a spring before and a winter before, and a few too many bottles of wine. Probably a few too many needlefuls as well. He rocked back and forth and sang a lullaby from Washington Square:

> *"Wind blow oh oh ing*
> *Wind blow oh oh ing."*

You see, they are still singing folk tunes in Washington Square. My vigil had been interrupted, and I knew this was not the moment when Bernadette would appear. She would come to me one day when I sat alone, but a vigil requires patience. A vigil requires time. Enough that today I had found the spot.

And it seemed to me as I sat on my park bench that I caught sight of a dark, stout young man with an earring glinting. But that, of course, could have been anyone.

DAY TEN **PRIESTS**

Woke in a cold sweat. Where am I, all that, the usual.

Looked down and saw right away where I was. In the white womb. In Fred and Velma's, safe for the night, taken in by a pair of rich South Carolinians who'd been taken in by me.

I rose in the dark and prowled through the night. This was where I lived now. This was where I was. In the kitchen the clock said five twenty-two. That would be dawn, not dusk, outside. I sat in the gleaming industrial kitchen. No chance of disturbing anyone. Fred and Velma and sweet Angelina would not be awake for hours.

I sat, and recalled the dream that woke me. No airplanes in marshes this time around. No chance to be a hero. I dreamed the newspaper headlines of the day: small boys and priests. I've told the jokes myself. *What does Michael Jackson get if one more preadolescent boy files suit against him? His own parish.* Personally, I think Michael Jackson was framed. But I still tell the jokes.

Paced the kitchen. I've always been inclined to buy Freud. Blessed relief in Sigmund: a nightmare to sort through, a bland anxiety attack of the sort suffered by males all over the world. Sexual guilt. Sanity. Do you suppose these episodes have been caused by repressed memories of sexual attacks by priests?

No. I don't suppose so either.

Father Berkeley was pastor at Our Lady of Perpetual Help from my adolescence to my flight and he never put a finger on boy or girl that was not placed there in misguided concern. That was not Father Berkeley in the dream.

Slumped at kitchen table. Vague panic. No energy to grind these coffee beans properly, or to walk out into the world and face a coffee shop. Slumped and made vague plans for the day: I would keep vigil in the park. I would hide this from Angela and Fred and Velma. I would tell them I was . . . making the rounds of casting agents.

I was making plans. This, in direct contradiction of my grand plan, to make no plans, to be spontaneous. My eye fell on the gleaming phone in the gleaming kitchen. Where did they find a silver phone? And who'd I want to call? My father? To see if he'd cast his net out to bring me back? O no: he and Eliana were filled with relief that I'd left no forwarding address.

My sisters? Long gone from New York, the surviving two.

My brother? A lawyer. Once my dearest friend. Once advised the family that the wisest course was to commit me.

Mary Faith? No intention of going back to her. Why torment her? Hot on the trail of my wife. Still, getting warmer. Call . . . not Mary Faith, but Jesse. The phone was beckoning me to call *Jesse*. And say . . . what?

I picked up the phone. I dialed the number.

One ring, two rings in the night. I pictured that Holy Thursday night I called my girl and begged her to forgive me. How wise of her to let the phone ring! She'd be all right in the world! What a judge of character!

This time there was a click after the second ring, a whir, and a voice on tape. Jesse's voice:

If you want to say something, hold your horses and wait for the beep.

Hold your horses. One of my lines Jesse mocked, and now he used it on a message machine. Besides which, Mary Faith, machine lover, had drawn the line at answering machines. They required self-revelation, a message, and she was not up to that. See! She made Jesse leave the message. Whatever got into her, after I left, to go out and buy an answering machine? Too many calls for dates? Couldn't keep track of them all?

There was a rackety fumbling sound, the sound of someone picking up over the tape.

I saw in a flash: the machine was for me. They were waiting for me. They believed all along that I would leave a message, and so they left this machine on, their porch light to tell me someone waited up for me.

Well. Talk about your anxiety attacks. They were supposed to forget me. They were supposed to get on with their lives. I wouldn't be trapped this way. I refused. Enough of their false concern, their marriage traps. I was not taking any vows in church. I would not.

I heard myself say: "This message is for Jesse. He will be . . ."

The first eight words were spontaneous. I hardly knew from whom they issued. But no other word came. I did not want to say, *He will be OK.* I didn't believe it. Jesse is a mess. I wouldn't lie to a child.

I didn't mean to say anything portentous, like *He will be tested.* That was the sort of message always being beamed to me, in my childhood. I couldn't do it to him.

Mary Faith was breathing on the other end of the wire. I'd recognize that two-four time anywhere.

"Jesse," I said, and heard in the word the complete sentence. I repeated it: "Jesse will be Jesse."

And hung up the phone.

Anxiety gone, shattered and fragmented, shards of glass on the floor. Replaced now by a weight of sadness that deformed me: my neck could no longer hold such a heavy object as my head, which dropped down to the black and silver table, where it rolled and bounced. Sleep, that old temptress, waggled a finger in my face.

Half a head on the table, I looked up to see Angela standing there in a black T-shirt, the tiniest triangle of panties peeking out. *I'm gonna sex you up.* She was hanging back so's not to disturb my head-banging. I lifted the head, lighter by the second, and beckoned her into the kitchen.

"I'm glad you're up," I said. "I just had a terrible nightmare." I felt like the smallest of children, lip trembling to keep back the tears.

She came round the back of my chair and after a moment she thrust her arms down low around my chest to hug me tight and comfort me from behind. I was comforted. My sadness lifted and was replaced by a roar of energy. I wanted to go dancing, I wanted to dip and twist her and do the shag all night but it was too late, no, too early for clubs. I sat there, letting her comfort me, not moving but roaring, don't you know, and her fingertips on my chest must have felt the vibrations. She leaned her face down over mine, upside down. She found my lips and I rolled my tongue into hers with a subtle lascivious thrust. I wanted so sanely to tie her up that it was all I could do to stand, still kissing her. I ran my tongue outside her lips, licking, licking.

Then I held her in a tango and danced her back down the hall and don't you know, WASP that she surely is, she was a good dancer nonetheless. Melted soft against me and let me lead her down the hallway to my lumpy futon, let me—not throw—but thrust, yes, thrust her down on the bed where she stretched out those muscled thighs and began to pull her black T-shirt over her head. I lowered myself to my knees: roaring, trembling, shagging. I suckled those breasts and closed my eyes and began to peel off her black panties, wanting so sanely to use the T-shirt to tie up her hands and the panties to bind up her feet but knowing all the while she might think me mad if I did such a thing. I slid my mouth down from her breasts to the small triangle now dark with hair instead of panties, a tangle of real, trying to remember to thrust out my lascivious tongue. But it was too late. Back there when I held her nipple in my mouth she had turned to Mary Faith stretched out long on the bed.

Too late: I was limp again, limp dick, no ropes, no belts, can't get it up o.

Had the presence of mind to jump up and say:

"No," to no one, since no one was there. No angels to rescue me in the night. No fantasy you can count on. No hallucinations when you know you're dreaming. No relief at the kitchen table when the dawn comes up over the factory buildings and tells you to open your eyes and smell the coffee.

REPORT FROM DUE EAST

There was a part of me worried to death for him out on the road, that part that maybe even pitied him, and then there was a part of me that would have liked to boil him in oil. When I thought of Jesse, I went for the oil.

Jesse could hear the phone ring at the crack of dawn. Jesse lay stiff in bed, pretending to sleep, when a maniac's voice came on the machine in the kitchen. *Jesse will be Jesse.* To direct such silliness to a little boy you've gone and deserted? It's not like me to fumble with a machine—I can't abide women who priss that way—but that morning I swear I couldn't find the switch to slide the power off.

And couldn't sleep after, naturally. Why was he calling, if he wasn't even asking me to come fetch him? I didn't need to lie awake trying to calculate whether he was in Miami stalking his father or gone back to Kentucky, where he used to stalk Thomas Merton in his religious nut days. If I was going to be lying awake, I needed to be calculating where I'd go to work in ten days, when my already hired replacement would take over at Fly Away. I had nowhere to fly to.

Jesse said he was with a new girlfriend. Didn't have a clue that saying so might pain me, but that was the least of it. Tim's always looked on women with equal parts adoration and terror and if that could ease whatever crazy pain made him screw us over so royally, so be it and more power to you. Only couldn't he have thought to leave a check to tide me over? I gave notice on his account and come to think of it oil's too good for him. I'd like to fry him in memories and let him settle those accounts. His father calls, tanked, at ten o'clock in the morning.

Tim Rooney's father calls rich from Miami to berate me, poor in Due East.

"Mary Hope!" he says. "You heard from him?"

"No," I say, or said, before I let this machine take his calls. "No, I promised I'd call you if I did, and I will."

"He's really done it this time! God Almighty! He's done it this time!"

"Yes, sir," I say. "Yes, sir, he has."

"God Almighty! Sweet baby Jesus! I know he's on drugs!"

"No, sir," I say. "It's just the opposite. He got rid of all the drugs. He hadn't even been drinking lately."

"I don't believe *that!*" says that old slob Bill Rooney, and why should he believe it? He can't get through this time himself without opening his first beer at daybreak and then calling to accuse me of driving off his son, who had his first crackup before I was even born.

Tim told me once his father smashed a Sears guitar over his head, he was so mad. And Tim's mother—the saint, to hear him tell the tale, though I've got my doubts—stood in front of his father and said: "You bring that down on your son's head, you can just bring it down on my head too."

Well, I wasn't offering any similar invitations. It was going on two weeks since he flipped his lid and I'd taken all the blows I could take. Not that I or any woman ever thought there was any justice but can you imagine a man sweet-talking you with a list of physics courses at MIT? I couldn't. Couldn't imagine anymore that I believed I was marrying a man who'd *scrub my kitchen in Cambridge.* Couldn't imagine I went so far as to think he was done with the crackups, couldn't imagine where he was spending his nights and his money, couldn't imagine when somebody was finally going to catch him and lock him up where he belonged. If he belonged anywhere.

As long as it was a million miles from me. As long as I never had to set eyes on him again or watch Jesse, pretending he was just sidling by that machine when he was gaping to see if the light was flashing and the nut who was going to be his father had called again to tell him that he would be himself.

What nonsense. What a fool. No. What fools, the two of us, to think that his kindness would last. I'm the one who believes in empirical data, I should have been the one to believe it was all a chemical imbalance, all beyond his control, but I was not in the mood for science. All his life he'd been bellyaching about the world's suffering and now he'd decided to throw that all over and concentrate on himself.

Little Timmy Rooney.

Selfish, plain and simple, and it's a good thing he left town because otherwise his pompous goofy self would have been in serious danger from me.

Jesse said he was just a wuss and to hell with him. And there were moments when I thought my son had the right attitude, and took some comfort from his words.

three

Saturday night, Sunday morning. Midnight. Due for a rest. After my dreamvision thing with Angela, you see, I willed myself into sweet calm and spent my day at my vigil post in Washington Square. On my park bench, opposite the dog run, waiting for Bernadette. When Bernadette did not appear by midnight I rose and stretched and walked through hordes of teenagers in from the burbs. A hellcat night in the Village.

On down through West Broadway. I willed myself into calm, as I had been doing all day. No need to get uptight in SoHo. You get uptight, you worry about these gray-templed men with little girls in froufrou dresses on their arms, you start to see things. I wasn't seeing nothing, no sirreebob, nothing out of the ordinary.

On Spring Street I walked beneath the flags from stores and galleries drooping down into the street like some medieval signposts and rang Fred and Wilma's bell. Someone buzzed me in without so much as asking who I was. The lobby was all postmodern yuppie, all traces of real work ever having been done in this building obliterated by brown-gray carpeting and triangular sconces on the wall. But they'd kept the old-style elevator, with the grate and the do-it-yourself handle, and it waited for me on the ground floor. Calm was what was called for. I needed to stay rational and not hallucinate if I was ever going to find Bernadette. If she was ever going to find me. You can do a lot through sheer force of will. You can walk through city streets at midnight, you can run an elevator on your own and when it stops a little off the mark you can use the brass handle to ease it down, down, until it lines up just right with the floor.

The elevator opened onto a narrow rectangular hallway. A little moment of panic, more brown-gray carpeting, the floor not entirely level. I could do it. I could navigate this hall and stay with these people. Fred and Wilma's front door was unlocked. Didn't they know they could be murdered in their beds? The loft was lighted, but there was no one there to greet me at the door. I could be walking into an ambush!

Back into calm, back into calm. Ommmmmmm. I'd made it through a day of total reality—and look, who's kidding whom, that was no hallucination at the kitchen table, that was falling back into sleep, into twilight time, when we *all* get confused about what's real and what's vision. Don't we?—and I didn't intend to start freaking now.

And look, there, Velma-Wilma's head peeking out of her room. She'd buzzed me in and now she waved her hand and her blond cornrows vaguely. They were waving in her mirrored ceiling, no doubt. I waved back and made a big show of locking both deadbolts, high and low. A good guest. A thankful guest.

Velma's head disappeared. I had made it through twenty-four hours without anyone carting me off and tomorrow I would make it through another twenty-four. I stumbled into my cell, where Angela was stretched out on the bed, waiting for me.

I could have wept. So close, and yet so far. And o! she looked so real. She had fallen asleep stretched across the width of the futon, her shiny hair pillowed at one end and her legs dangling off the other. She was wearing one of those high-buttoned shirts that's perfectly modest until it stops at the midriff and reveals a glistening roll of flesh. The shirt was white with a pattern of sailor boys saluting in rows. Her pants were sailor pants, laced up across her flat belly and widening at those dangling bare feet of hers, brown as dirt. Her breast nestled on the open pages of a large photo magazine, *Interview* or some such.

So very real. The paper lamps left her in a warm yellow glow, fuzz swirling on her arms and on her midriff and on her upper lip. I stepped closer, right into the dream. Costume, hair, generous cheeks, red fingernails: Angela Bliss, in my vision, was the very picture of American womanhood circa 1942, brassy womanhood unafraid to show a little flesh and a little sass. I felt I could reach out and touch her uncomplicated self. I kneeled at the foot of the bed. If I was doomed to live in a fantasy world, I might as well indulge my fantasy.

I touched the bare midriff and she shot up. She didn't have to do that for me to know my mistake. Real! Real! This time she was real.

"Whoa!" she said. "I thought a metal claw reached out and touched me."

I looked at my offending hand. Metal claw!

But she reached over and pressed her warm fingers, all muscle and sinew, on my cold hand, all metal joint. "Ooh . . . freezing," she murmured, and I suppose she meant the hand and not herself, wakening and trembling. She removed her hand from mine, sat up cross-legged and gave me a smile so direct I couldn't interpret it.

What was she doing on my bed? "What are you doing on my bed?" I said.

She looked around and took her time answering. When she did speak, she held her voice low and made us conspirators.

"I need to ask you a few things," she said.

Trouble brewing. Stay calm. Remember your admiration for the plump lips of Miss Angela Bliss. I chose to act professorial and raised one eyebrow, waiting for my young charge's question.

"Such as what you're really doing here at Fred and Velma's."

This took all my energy and focus. She did not trust me!

"Don't Fred and Velma . . ."

"Oh, *they* believe you. They want to meet Sidney Lucette too."

"Sidney Lumet."

"Whatever. Velma thinks you look like Kramer, except for the hair. She thinks you act like Kramer, anyway."

"Who's Kramer?"

"Never mind. Who are you?"

Well, I had to laugh. Sitting there in her sailor suit, staring so direct through her wide-set eyes, asking the part-time philosophy professor, *Who are you?* There's a scene in *Wall Street* when Charlie Sheen steps out onto the balcony and says, *Who am I?* Really he does.

"Don't laugh. Are you really named Tim? Riley?"

"Tim Rooney. Yes."

"Are you really a philosophy professor?"

"Part time. I was never given tenure by any institution, though Lord knows I tried."

"Are you really from South Carolina or were you . . . heading up from further south? From, like, Florida?"

I shared her dread of Florida but I said, with vehemence: "I'm from *Due East*."

My naming of a lowcountry town calmed her down. "All right now. You scared me out of my wits out on the highway after the Chesapeake Bay and there was something. Something going on. Are you, are you, are, you, really trying to be an actor?"

". . . Yes." I felt this was an ethical answer.

She pouted the Botticelli lips and began to tap on her toenails, curled up in her lap. Rounded shoulders, o I could feel her strong pecs, could imagine them underneath my own hands. No wonder I dreamed I took her in my arms and danced a tango.

"Angela!"

She looked up, startled.

"Let's go dancing!"

Now she looked panicked. "No, Tim, look, I wanted to get this . . . straight."

"Look at you," I said. "All dressed up and no place to go. Don't tell me. You don't have to tell me. You went out shopping today. You waited up for me all dressed up on Saturday night because you thought you'd find out what you wanted to know and then we could go dancing."

A half smile on her generous mouth. I noted an extra chin beneath the knobby one. Angela Bliss was a fleshy young woman, all right, fleshy and muscular. Mary Faith was lean and anemic. I'm just an ordinary man.

"Listen, Angela" (professorial again) "what you want to know is if I'm all right and if I'm going to mess with you anymore. And the answers are (A) Yes, I am all right, I'm sorry I scared you, and (B) having seen how I did scare you, I certainly would never do that anymore. Now . . . don't you want to go dancing?"

The half smile opened up and bloomed. "I didn't think . . . dancing."

"Didn't think dancing! You did, I'll bet, look at those wide legs on those pants, I'll bet you saw them swishing across a floor."

"I did not! When I go dancing, I'll have you know, I wear a dress, and it's black and it's short and it's low cut." She clapped her hand over her mouth and tapped the toenails again. Head down, considering. "I did think maybe we'd take a walk," she allowed.

"Well, let's take us a walk to a dance hall. Why not!"

"Why not? You won't tell me what you're up to. Where were you all day?"

"Washington Square."

"All day?"

"All day."

"Why?"

"Why not?"

Impasse. I was dancing now, I mean literally, a fair version of the tapping my father troubled to teach me when I was twelve. I did a good sliiiiide across Fred and Velma's polished bleached floor and it was a good enough move to make Angela smile her puffy smile yet again. "Washington Square, the crossroads of a nation!" Tap-tap-uh-tap-tap. "The intersection of literary past and pharmacological present!" Tap-tap-tap-tap-tap. "East meets West!"

"Well . . . the thing is, Tim, I'm just . . ."

Scared of me. She didn't have to say it. She thought if she walked out with me tonight I might lure her into an alleyway where I'd hack her body to bits.

"If you'd just . . ."

I stopped tapping. "Just?"

"Just tell me a little more about yourself. If you wouldn't make yourself so mysterious."

I clicked my heels together and sat myself down on the edge of the futon bed, close enough to touch her, far enough to register how frightened she would be if I did.

"Dear Angela," I said, and did not even need to drop my voice down to the sad level it achieved on its own. "I just don't believe in talking about myself. I don't believe in a breakdown of the past, in psychoanalysis. I'm. I'm trying to live in the present. Trying to get on with my life."

She murmured something.

"What?"

"Just one thing."

"What?"

"I mean, just tell me one thing. One little ole thing about yourself that would explain the way you acted out there on the road."

"You don't believe I'm that good an actor?"

"I don't believe you were acting at all."

She wouldn't look me in the eye, but her gaze was steely, staring out beyond me. I told you she was a sharp one. I told you she knew what was what. And I told you, I believe, that I was living a spontaneous life that called on me to act in the moment. Which would account for the uncensored material I spewed out at *that* moment:

"Angela," I said, "when I was nineteen years old I filled a hypodermic needle with gasoline and began to poke it into my arm."

Now. I ask you. What would your reaction be to that piece of news?

But Angela? A champ. She raised her gnarly chin and the fleshy chin beneath it. She looked at me with navy-blue eyes and she said: "Why?" in a voice that betrayed intense curiosity and not a trace of fear.

And, spontaneous and uncensored as I was, I could not for the life of me think of what to say in turn. I had no idea why I had done that. She saw my confusion, shifted in her Buddha pose, and changed the question to:

"I mean, like, how?"

How I could tell her. "Well," I said, "it happened in the middle of a long hot summer when I was sorry I was in Due East. I was reading a book . . ."

"What book?"

Did I tell you she was sharp? "I don't know," I said, though I knew perfectly well what book I'd been reading. I was doing a senior thesis on my man Søren and I was sitting around the hot and steamy Rooney house rereading *The Concept of Anxiety,* wherein were contained my favorite lines: "Anxiety about sin produces sin."

"I don't know what book it was," I lied again, "but a hypodermic needle rolled out the pages. No, wait, it's not what you think. My roommate back at school was a diabetic, and we used to use his needles for darts and bookmarks and to pick out gristle from between our teeth. Anyway."

Angela pitched her magazine aside and stretched back out on the bed, chin in her palm, gazing up at me. Can you blame me for hamming it up a little?

"The needle rolled onto the floor and I picked it up. And remembered from somewhere that if you shot an air bubble into your vein you could die from it. I remembered this very idly. I wasn't thinking about suicide. Suicide had never once crossed my mind at this point in my life, or anyway not since I was a *very* small boy. But for some reason I picked up the needle and I went out into the little shed out back where my father kept an old can of gasoline, and for some reason, maybe the same reason, I poured gasoline into the hypo. My fingers were wet with it, the overflow, and stinking of it, but it was cold against my clammy skin. It felt good. I was thinking of those Vietnamese monks who were setting themselves on fire back then."

Angela looked blank. Another historical reference wasted on the young.

"Well. There it was. I had a hypodermic needle filled with gasoline. Gulf gasoline, probably, that was the kind our family used. It was clear in the needle. I walked back round the house, out front, and I held it up in the sunlight, just watching it the way you'd watch a butterfly in a jar." I stopped there, spontaneously, because now I could remember the hot light filtering down through the mossy trees at midafternoon. I was in the hot light. I am in the hot light. My feet are bare, and the grass beneath them is patchy and filled in with mold and fungus and monstrous gnarled tree roots, real ankle-busters.

My sister Katie is on the front steps, trying to catch some afternoon breeze. She's fifteen or so, that age when some girls get so lovely and others are just spilling out of themselves. Katie's spilling out of herself and her face is just a sorrow, pale and blue as milk right out of the cow, pimples popping mid-cheek. Her hair's the same dark red as mine, as our mother's, only hers is just . . . out of control, just spiraling out from her head in a way that makes you want to weep.

Makes me want to weep, anyway, thinking of the Barnard girls in their berets, their hair long and ironed and sleek. Katie looks up from her magazine—ah, I can catch it, I can *see* it, a *Cosmopolitan* magazine, the magazine she's forbidden to read because our intelligent well-read mother says it demeans women, that's why she's out of the house, not to catch a breeze at all—and she gives me a milky blue sneer.

What have I done to disgust her? Katie's my favorite, I want to protect her from herself. I walk round the house with a needle filled with gasoline and I hold it up in the sunlight. And then I see my little sister, my ally, the first one in the family you could call close to normal, even if she is going through a difficult stage, reading her *Cosmopolitan* magazine, and I. . . .

"What?" Angela said. "What happened next?" She might have been watching the late show.

"I took the tip of the needle and I started poking around my veins. They're hard to see, my veins." I kneeled down and rolled up my sleeve to show her. Angela did not shrink or blanch. She let me lean my elbow on the futon next to her own propped arm. She reached out the other hand and pressed her warm fingers onto my skin, pale as my little sister's, if the truth be told.

"My sister saw me doing this and now, you see, I hadn't even been *thinking* of suicide. If I was thinking of anything it was how the liquid was sloshing in the barrel. The scrape of the needle against my skin. Katie was just disgusted by this. She didn't even look up from her magazine, but she said: *Tim, quit.*

"She didn't believe I meant anything by it either. She figured I was just fooling around and, hey, that's all I *was* doing. But her voice was so disgusted, so hot and bothered, that it made me want to feel the needle deeper under my skin. I wasn't thinking of suicide. I was thinking how cold that gasoline would be, shooting into my veins. I was thinking of those monks in Saigon dousing themselves with gasoline and feeling the coolness of it, and then when they lit the match, that would be"—I snapped my fingers—"that would be a tremendous release, wouldn't it?"

Angela pressed her fingers warmer against my own cold forearm. She could feel how deep under the skin my veins hid. She could see why I wasn't able to get the needle in a vein that day.

"Well, I got the tip of the needle under the skin and then—*whoa, dude*—I freaked. Just froze. Katie'd been spying and she must have seen the needle go in because all of a sudden she's hollering and carrying on.

Tim quit, Tim quit it, but don't you know before she ran into the house to get my mother she took care to roll up her *Cosmopolitan* magazine and stuff it in the mailbox so she wouldn't get caught reading it. And don't you know my mother comes barreling out of the house carrying her own paper in one hand, and Dottie, the little one, comes running after her, grabbing for my mother's hem. And by this time the whole hypo was trying to stand up in my arm but just dangling there, the tip of the needle stuck under my skin but nowhere near the vein. My mother comes charging up to me without a word, bearing down like a banshee with Dottie running behind her hiccoughing and hiding behind the skirt. And my mother grabs my forearm with one hand and then with the other she just slides the hypodermic out, neat as you please, and *then* she says:

" 'Timothy Rooney, don't you ever dare pull anything like that again.' Can you imagine? As if anybody in their right mind would ever again fill up a needle with gasoline and try to poke it in just to see how cold it felt?"

By then I was crying. I mean with Angela, not with my mother. With my mother I was . . . baffled. The paper she's holding, that she's swatting me on the head with—and this is a woman who's never struck one of her children, never, that's our father's job—the paper is *The Catholic Worker.* My brother Andy's come out of the house by now and he's so shook up he can't come a step farther. He stays back on the little square of our front porch bashing a paperback against the front rail. A skinny little book, *The Communist Manifesto.* He must be a freshman at Georgetown that year, if I'm nineteen. My mother sent him to the Jesuits. Later, as I believe I've mentioned, he became a lawyer and advised that I be committed. *Communist Manifesto, Catholic Worker, Concept of Anxiety, Cosmopolitan.* The Rooney Family.

Angela sat up again now, but had the good grace not to resume a Buddha pose. She took my sleeve and rolled it delicately back down my arm. She looked . . . sympathetic. How could she possibly know that in all those years of psychiatric consultation this particular jack had never once before popped out of the box? My mother, meaning no doubt to save me from a real serious beating, never even told my father what transpired that day. We had a good long talk about it when she calmed down and then we . . . let it go.

"You know what my mother would have said?" I felt Angela's fingers leave my arms and venture forth to stroke her own. "She would have said *What about the neighbors.*"

The neighbors! Did Angela have any idea of the significance? The neighbors, when I was nineteen, were the same neighbors as last week, when I hotfooted it out of Due East. The neighbors were . . . Mary Faith. Couldn't I just see her, three years old like Dottie, standing barechested and barefoot at the edge of the road watching the big boy home from college stick a needle in his arm right on the front lawn? She wouldn't hide her face like Dottie. Couldn't I just see her craning her serious long neck, her naked little arms streaming sweet baby sweat in the hot summer day?

No. No more than I could see Father Berkeley laying an evil hand on any of us. I was only conjuring that baby at the edge of the road. "I feel better," I told Angela. "I bet you were a psycho major at Vassar." I meant to say *psych,* didn't I?

She nodded! But it was only a joke! She nodded and said: "You freaked out on the road, didn't you, you thought you saw somebody following us?"

And I began to protest—I *did* see somebody following us—but then I understood the foolhardiness of that gesture.

"I feel better," I said again. "How's about we go dancing, after all?"

She smoothed her fingers down across her flat belly—do women *know* when they're doing that—and shook her head. "I'll make you a promise," she said, and now I didn't like the tone of her voice, mother to son, amateur psycho major to psycho. "We'll go out dancing next Saturday night if you can keep it together till then. Deal?"

I saw those teenagers swarming through the Village in happy herds, those old men squiring their young wives and mistresses through SoHo. Life stampeded down below the windows of this loft, but I was sealed off from humanity.

I didn't like the tone of Angela's voice, but I said to her: "Deal." The truth was, whether I found Bernadette or not, I could not bear to be so weird that no one would ever come dancing with me.

Angela slid out of the room: I believe she was imitating my Astaire sliiide, and the bell-bottom trousers did a lovely shimmy. At the edge of the screen she turned and gave me a little Southern-girl wave, her hand and forearm pivoting back and forth from the elbow.

Ah. I felt chilled and lonely and sad: all these, but I did not feel anxious. It was all real now. I lay down on the futon and practiced breathing until Angela would be safe away in her bed. Through the nose, out the mouth. Now Angela would be unbuttoning the sailor-boy shirt. Now she would be unlacing the sailor-boy pants. Now she would be slipping naked under her own white sheets. The loft shifted and tossed and turned, everyone but me falling into sleep. Outside the city danced and poked and prodded, but here inside, I, Timothy Rooney, practically certifiably sane, breathed and waited.

Silence all around. Now Angela was sleeping.

And if I was good I would get a pass to go dancing with her next Saturday night. I might still be a nut, but I was reconnecting. Nuts to bolts. And nuts to you, Jack.

DAY TWELVE **OFF TO WORK**

I woke at dawn on Monday. New man, new morning.

No sign of activity from Fred or Velma or Angela. They would rise at noon, or one, or two—dilettantes, triflers—but I was up at dawn and casting my lot with the workers of the world, ready to take up my watch in Washington Square.

In the deli they were coming to know me. The guy who poured me my cup could have been Italian or Greek or even Arab: a squat muscled man my age in deliman's whites, his dark hair slicked back over his melon head, his square chin jutting out to hear you the better. He was all business, his wife behind him in a housedress and slippers hopping across the floor to fetch him what he called for. He was moving fast and talking to himself.

"Two bialys, butter," I said. "Poppy seed bagel, cream cheese. Two coffees dark, three sugars apiece." Hear the way I was talking? Joining this world?

"Wha, you again?" He didn't even look up; he was swiveling to speak in sign language to his wife. "You decide to eat this morning, huh?"

"Yeah," I said. "Yeah, I did." Roaring gaping hunger: I thought I might be back for lunch at ten. O! I was sane.

I watched the wan wife, face small and pinched, sparse hair curled tight, lips so thin they could have been drawn on with a sharp pencil point. She looked older: couldn't be his mother, could she? She slapped the bagel with a white-smeared knife and I could feel him urging her on: faster, faster. O! I wished I had a wife. I watched him slap the packages in a brown bag: one two three: and flash me a big fakey Mediterranean grin that rose and set so fast I would have missed it if I had blinked. I left the store shining with intense goodwill.

On to my spot under the Siberian elm. It was still brisk at seven, and I hunkered down in my tweed teaching jacket. For now, I was on duty. The dog pen was full—before-work crowd—more female than male. How cruel and lovely they all looked, the women, half dressed for their important jobs, pearls and silk under their windbreakers, Nikes and Reeboks beneath their well-cut tight suits.

I watched one middle-aged woman in her pink nubby suit and those gray gunboat sneakers. A flurry of dust rose every few minutes from the passing dogs to coat her, and she swatted it with outrage, but—didn't she come here every day? What did she expect? Why do you hang out in the dog run if you don't want to leave dust-coated? She saw me watching her and glared. Oh, I knew her. Dark pageboy with the bangs too short, a thousand lines around the lips but a too firm chin. So she'd had the chin tucked up but was still saving for the mouth job. I knew her. In Due East she wouldn't wear a tight short skirt like that, she'd wear a swinging floral polyester number that's supposed to pass for silk, and when you were waiting for assistance in the lawyer's office, say, and she came out to tell you someone would be right with you, she'd look you over with the vaguest recognition followed by a sudden squirt of *My God! That was the boy genius in high school! And look at him now in his rumpled hair!*

No wonder I robbed the cradle when I went courting Mary Faith. No wonder I was still robbing the cradle when I plotted how to get Angela out dancing and from there to my futon. Women that age, they see a middle-aged man and they're just as likely to see a poet as they are to see a failure. Short on history, long on hope.

And me too. Long on hope now. I smiled at the fierce woman in the dog run and, miracle of miracles, her face loosened from eyes beneath enormous pink horn-rims to her hard mouth and her tight chin. I saw that she thought I was . . . hitting on her! I ducked my head. You can only go so far with this goodwill. You don't want to start . . . misleading people.

Still, head ducked, I felt her staring after me, and my fingertips and my toes began to tingle. Without looking up I tried to reproduce her face to my own satisfaction: under her dark hair a narrow delicate face. The pink horn-rims covered the top half. Pink to match the suit? Or to draw your attention away from eyes so light a green that the faintest sunlight set them to streaming?

I was moving too fast. I was jumping to conclusions.

I sneaked another good look, but she was still watching me: she'd turned so she stood in profile, sneaking her own quick peeks. Watching me because she thought I was hitting on her—or because she recognized me? Recognized me as I recognized her?

Recognized the possibility that this tense middle-aged woman, this woman my own age, this woman in my league, could very well be the woman I'd come here to find, the woman I hadn't seen in twenty years but who could very well nonetheless be none other than the long-gone Bernadette!

My entire body began to tremble in the most pleasurable way. I was moved to call out to her but instead made a bargain with myself: I would walk the perimeter of the park. If she was still there when I returned, it was a sign that she was Bernadette.

I set off at a near trot. This was so simple! You set out to find your wife, you came to a dog run, she appeared. Why hadn't I done this twenty years ago? Already I had crossed Washington Square North.

I had last seen Bernadette twenty-odd years ago, the evening she threw underwear into a small bag to leave for her mother's. It was an *I Love Lucy* scene, comic, not tragic. I knew she'd be back. I wasn't concerned. But she, once she stopped sniffling, once she rode out the waves of hysteria, was cold and driven. I matched her up against the cold and driven woman with the dark hair.

Bernadette, when she left me, had her dark hair twisted back into two braids, as if to emphasize her innocence and my depravity. But she was in fact older than I was—by three years! She'd slept with about three thousand men by the time she got through her first two years at Barnard! I had no sexual experience when I met her. We would walk through Riverside Park, two undergrads at first, then two grad students on fellowship, the chill wind seeping. I thought she meant for me to prove myself.

I proved myself. I was willing to submit to her completely. For years we kept company, and when she finished her dissertation I married her. For the six days we cohabited, I was in heaven. We put off a honeymoon to save the money for my trip to Denmark. She moved into my studio apartment, and I gave her all the file space and all the good light. She was sending out thirty vitaes a day, and the sight of her so driven, so purposeful, so sure of which position was worthy of her, moved me to suggest that I tie her up. This was on the seventh day of our marriage. It was a playful suggestion. Symbolic! I was tripping that day, otherwise I would have read her signals more clearly. I was under a great deal of pressure too, you understand: I had not yet defended *my* dissertation, I was still writing it. I was still struggling with Danish, which is hard to concentrate on when you're tripping. Otherwise I never would have grabbed her wrists that way, *it was just playing, I was just kidding her,* and she never would have shattered into that howling I can only describe as feminist, though I don't think we even *called* a woman feminist in those days, I think we said her consciousness had been raised.

Well. Bernadette's consciousness was raised. She went crying from the apartment into the night, ran home to Mama in Queens after six and a half days of marriage. When she called the next morning, she suggested that our six days together had convinced her of my general mental instability. Still I was not concerned. Everybody was unstable in 1971. I thought she was in a huff. *I only wanted to tie her wrists to the bedpost.* I was a feminist too, in my fashion. I would never hurt her. She was a delicate dark bird with granny glasses and no breasts. I would hold her in the small of my hand. I'm not sure if you understand the significance of this. This was my wife. We were both practicing Catholics. This was the sixties, the seventies, and no one was in the Church anymore, no one but us. We went down to mass at the Catholic Worker, we talked about a pilgrimage to Kentucky to see Thomas Merton. Later, thinking it would bring Bernadette back to me, I joined loony Catholic communes all over the dirty South. I confessed wanting to tie my wife up though I never thought for a minute that it was a sin.

That qualifies as a bad confession. This was 1971, I tell you! People thought it was immoral to be monogamous! Immoral to stay straight!

I did not understand when I confessed the wrong sin that Bernadette's pale anemic lips or her disappearing chin or the boyish chest—and yes, that was my vision, that was my fantasy, I did want to tie her up to see her like a child, helpless, willing to submit to me—that those pathetic features of hers that had me following her around our apartment, slavering, slobbering, would be the features I would remember a year later, or two years later, or three or ten, when it was clear that she (after the senior appointments I could only follow in the *Chronicle of Higher Education*) would never come back to me. When it was clear that those same features that once had made me want to protect her and tie her up had become in my memory sharp-edged reminders of a driven unforgiving relentless castrating bitch.

Who looked very much like the driven unforgiving relentless (castrating?) woman (bitch?) now swinging her broadened middle-aged pink nubby backside in my approaching face. The dark-haired woman was leaving! Her English sheepdog pulled her and her slewfoot sneakers along.

Bernadette was slewfoot! But this could not be Bernadette. Hadn't I told myself: if she was still there when I returned, she was Bernadette? She was not still there. She was gone.

I collapsed under the Siberian elm. I had been so sure.

DAY THIRTEEN **NOT AN EASY QUESTION**

A daily routine is such a . . . grind.

Tuesday morning: dawn long since gone. I had no ambition to go to the park. I would never find Bernadette. It was a crazy notion to begin with.

A quick vision of Mary Faith, her chin tilted up, waiting by the phone. Awash on the futon in the white loft, I passed from sluggish to sick. Mary Faith was out of a job by now, maybe out of money. My God, my God. What had I done? I would have to get to the post office and send her some of these wads of cash that still nestled in my shoes and blistered me daily.

From the kitchen I heard snatches of a gasping hysterical voice— "Sonofa . . . what'll I . . . it's the *suspicions*"—that could only be Velma. How long had I been her guest? And how many words had we exchanged? It was madness to stay with these strangers another minute. I would have to clear out by tonight.

Velma's voice wailed through the loft, and underneath it came my Angela's, soothing and clucking. I resolved to dash uptown and book myself a room this very hour. I'd go to the Algonquin, spend a few weeks in style. I'd abandon Washington Square Park. I'd figure it all out.

I nosed into the hallway, caught a glimpse of the two females down at kitchen end, nosed back into my cell. Took a deep breath, you're a big boy, tried again to slouch past them. Angela called out:

"Tim! Where've you *been?*" in one of those voices designed to cover the fact that someone was sobbing in the kitchen.

"Catch you later." O I sounded false. "Big audition." Big audition. They'd have the attendants from Bellevue waiting for me when I got back for my suitcase. I did one of those tootle-ooh waves and popped out the door.

But when I reached the sidewalk below, I did not grab a cab and head uptown. I was being visited with another glorious impulse. I found myself walking east, instead of north to the park. Now that I'd abandoned all hope of finding Bernadette, I would go to . . .

The impulse wasn't settling yet. I passed through a checkerboard pattern of SoHo storefronts, every other establishment rousing itself for business. Women in thin spring leather jackets jabbered in Romance languages on the sidewalks. Through tinted windows, I ogled breastless mannequins draped in muddy colors. White sculptures, like Fred's. Maybe they *were* Fred's. I felt I was passing through the very soul of money.

At the corner of Lafayette, my impulse turned me north. I still did not know where I was going. I thought someone was following me, but when I swiveled around to check, the sidewalk was bare.

Up Lafayette, past the Public Theater. Was this what I was thinking? That I'd become an actor after all? The spring air was working on me.

Again I thought someone's footsteps trailed me, but when I turned to look this time, I saw only a young mother with pink hair holding hands with her son, who wore a Yankees cap. They were on my heels. When I spun on them, the woman sucked in her breath and cradled the little boy's head in her hands, to protect him from me. I resisted making a madman's face on account of the child. I had no one to protect *me*. I had to look out for myself.

I still didn't know where I was going. I passed a drab little building with the number 339, and the address weighed on me. I circled back. 339 Lafayette. I scanned the directory. Aha. The War Resisters League. Clouds parted, light flooded. This was where I was going this morning.

Inside I climbed the drab wide stairs. I'd had a lifetime of climbing stairs like these. Stairs down to grimy basements, up to stuffy airless cubicles loaded up with the dust of pamphlets nobody wanted, nobody read. War Resisters League. The very notion used to drive my father bananas. He told my mother if she wanted to get mail from a pinko group she could damn well rent a post office box. And my mother damn well did. She handed out those dusty pamphlets on the Vietnam War after the twelve o'clock mass. Sometimes on my visits home from school I'd watch her at her work on the Division Street sidewalk, offering pamphlets no one accepted, Dottie skulking in some corner of the graveyard, mortified, the Marine wives setting their jaws to walk by my mother without so much as a glare. She was invisible, fading away. After a while there was hardly a parishioner at Our Lady of Perpetual Help, including my father, who was willing to talk to her.

Up the stairs I toiled, seized with the sweetest desire to take a load of pamphlets out of my mother's hands. Old Dolores. Old fierce do-gooder Dolores Rooney, with hardly a friend in the world. I—the word that springs to mind is *worshiped,* but I don't want to tie things up too neatly for the Freudians in the audience—I admired my mother. I admired her greatly. When I stuck a needle in my arm, after all, she was the one who said: *Timothy Rooney, don't you ever dare pull anything like that again.* And I never have pulled a stunt quite like that one again.

Maybe this was a memorial trip to the War Resisters League. Up at the top of the stairs, I walked into the pamphlet room—some things don't change much in twenty years—and thumbed a few of the most unlikely. Not a soul in sight. Only shelves of pamphlets and bibliographies and calendars, only reams of paper intended to end war and suffering. *Tim, we should be doing something.*

The space was still. The dust was suffocating. I wandered around the corner to the offices, divvied up from the loft space this once had been. I cleared my throat, but what was I going to say?

Nothing, apparently. No one appeared at the sound of my throat clearing. No one home. Ding-dong. An office full of proselytism, but no one to proselytize. No one typing on ancient Smith-Coronas, no one mapping out the next march on corporate headquarters.

On my mother's account, I grabbed up a load of pamphlets on my way out. I didn't trouble to read what they said. I'd pass them out to people who didn't want them, or maybe I'd just throw them down on the sidewalk myself, to save the recipients the trouble.

I went to leave: but just then a middle-aged woman came tearing out of one of the office cubicles, breathless, and said:

"So sorry. I was on the phone." She gave me the once-over, and maybe she looked worried. "May I help you?"

I was struck dumb. She was a plump tallish woman in a striped jersey and worn jeans, circa 1971. Her feet splayed outward—she was *slewfoot*—and her chin disappeared down into her wide neck, and her hair, graying, was black and plaited into two braids she had pinned to either side of her head.

Bernadette.

And this would make sense, wouldn't it, that my Bernadette would be toiling away at the War Resisters League while she wasn't busy occupying her hundred-thousand-dollar-a-year chair a few blocks over at NYU? That she would, selflessly and without fanfare, burrow herself into one of these little offices and use all her skills as a feminist medievalist to construct new arguments for the cause of world peace.

She blinked at me, and I caught green eyes. Bernadette had green eyes.

"I'm sorry," I said.

"Beg your pardon?"

"Bernadette?"

"There's no Bernadette here," she said. "I'm Sybil."

Sybil! I saw at once that the hair was really dark brown, not black, and that the green eyes were so unnaturally bright that they were surely contact lenses. Also, she seemed to be holding her feet a little straighter now.

"But may I help you?"

"Oh," I said, and here I may even have tossed a hand back to indicate how little I wanted to trouble a woman who was not Bernadette, "oh, I want information on how to stop the war in Bosnia."

She gave me a warm smile—a very warm smile, from a full mouth whose lips, I saw now, were far too generous to have graced Bernadette's mouth—and then she said: "It's not an easy question."

I felt I'd been slapped silly. I saw my mother thrusting those black and white pamphlets, the kind you run off on a mimeograph machine and fold in thirds, into the hands of colonels' wives who pressed the papers back at her and shook their heads, huffing. OF COURSE IT'S NOT AN EASY QUESTION.

Sybil-not-Bernadette, meanwhile, was grabbing up—you guessed it —pamphlets, and thrusting them at me in a way I can only describe as comforting. "We have a mailing list," she said. "Glad you stopped in." She bustled back into her cubicle and returned with a yellow pad on a clipboard, still warm, warmer, I'd say, flirting maybe, the way she brushed my sleeve when she handed over the clipboard, pleased now that she was at this very moment doing something to ease human suffering in the world. I saw that in the last three weeks the yellow pad had been signed by two other guilt-ridden souls.

I took the pencil she offered and found it hard to grasp. A sudden sharp memory of learning to write. Very carefully, very slowly I printed Jesse's address in Due East, and handed her back the pad.

"South Carolina," she said. "We don't get a lot of interest from that state. Visiting?"

While she waited for an answer, the expression on her face changed, changed from full-mouthed generosity to tight-lipped alarm, and she took a step backward, perhaps because I was snarling at the personal nature of the question. Maybe I was shaking my fist, too. I can't say for sure. I can only report that I turned tail—*You think* that's *scary, Sybil*— and descended the gloomy stairs to street level.

Where to my surprise, astonishment, and dismay, the blue-black young man from South Carolina was waiting for me on the sidewalk.

By the time I ran smack into him on the sidewalk the fury was seething through my veins. I pounded my fist into his chest, which you are probably guessing was massive and solid. It was. He grabbed up my wrists—does this ring any bells?—and held me with my arms suspended. I am taller than he is, but I tell you I was looking up into his face. That diamond stud still shone in his ear. Six million New Yorkers passed us, six million New Yorkers saw him take me prisoner, but not a one stopped to gape.

"Quit following me," I said. *Said* is not the right word. I was bellowing, lowing, bullhorning.

"Got to follow you now," he said, and lowered my arms. Still he held my wrists. "See you don't get into any more trouble than you already have."

"I'm not in trouble."

He shook his head back and forth. "You are in *serious* trouble."

By this time I was growling and he lifted my arms again, lifted them until I was dangling clear off the sidewalk. Humiliating. My feet scuffed the air.

"Where's your money?" he said. "Tell me that."

At the sound of the word *money* six million New Yorkers did look at us, began to walk backward on the sidewalk or gape over their shoulders. They believed he was robbing me, shaking me down, but did a one of them stop or intervene? I was ready to blubber. Maybe I was blubbering.

"Where you think I put it?"

He let me down—I must have been blubbering—and loosened his hold. "I think you still got it in your socks," he said, "and the evidence is there in the bulge."

"Why are you following me? You don't even want the money."

"No, I don't, Mr. Rooney. I mean, heh-heh, I wouldn't *mind* that kind of money, but I'm not about to lift it off you."

"What do you want?" I had pounded right into his very flesh, hadn't I? Hadn't I felt that underneath his T-shirt, underneath his silky BRAVES jacket there was muscle and fat? Wasn't I absolutely sure at this moment that he was no hallucination?

"The priest said I might as well follow you," he said then, guileless, and let loose of my wrists. I recommended pounding my fists against his chest, though I will say for the record I would have preferred at that moment to be pounding the skinny old man's chest instead. The priest. Father Berkeley.

"Get away from me," I said, along with the pummeling, and then it occurred to me that I was free to get away from him. I stopped, and looked at him for a minute—o, he was a worry in daylight, your white Southern male's biggest nightmare, a massive smiling diamond-studded gold-toothed young man with his arms folded across his chest and all the time in the world. This time around he wore no hat: his head was covered with coarse blue-black hair knotted into stunted dreadlocks, the Buck-wheat look.

I took off at a trot, and he didn't even trouble to follow me. He thought he knew where I was staying. Little did he know that I was moving out, that I was heading uptown, that I'd be booking a room, that he'd never find me again. I turned on the sidewalk. He was still watching me. His arms were still folded, his dreadlocks shaking back and forth in the spring light.

"Get on back to Due East," I said, and truly believed by the time I resumed my run and crossed Houston that I had lost him for good. The hundred-dollar bills in my shoes slipped up and down against my ankle, under my instep, and cut open the blisters that were just beginning to heal.

Did I check into a hotel uptown?

I did not.

The sight of my young shadow threw the terror into me. He was no guardian angel, he was an avenging angel sent by a pathetic milquetoast representative of the Church. My guardian angel was Angela, and she was back in a white loft on Spring Street. When she opened the door to me I was all atremble.

"Tim!" She held a finger to her mouth. "Back so soon? Hush, though, Velma's sleeping."

I followed her lead and whispered into the hallway. I was ready to catch her up in my arms. "That sounds good," I said. "Sleep. Come sleep with me." I meant it, too: I meant *sleep,* fall into the fog. Drift off, depart, check out.

"You OK? How'd that audition go?"

I panicked. What audition? "Terrible," I said. That would cover all possibilities. "I was a mess. Angela, I mean it. I've got to get me some sleep."

She gave me a look that said she might not go dancing with me, but she'd be willing to sit watch. A hand on my arm, a push down the hall: she urged me back to my room, back to sleep away the day as I had been doing when I began this journey.

And directly I obeyed her and headed for the white rug on my bed. A cover of snow, a blanket of white carnations. Someone was following me.

DAY FOURTEEN **STARVING**

Naturally I woke in early morning, those hours when sleep is sweetest for all other inhabitants of the planet. I woke sharp and refreshed. I woke starving.

In the kitchen I meant to grab me out bacon and eggs and grits, but they do not carry bacon and eggs and grits in SoHo kitchens. From the silver refrigerator, big as a car, I pulled out little white plastic containers. Olives and pesto and grape leaves and hummus. The whole world gone Mediterranean! Even pork-rind Southerners! Well, all right. Why not? I began to eat from an open tin of anchovies.

And turned around, to see by the glow of the swinging steel fixture they call lights around here, that the blond woman who owned this apartment stood before me.

"Hi." I couldn't remember whether her name was Velma or Wilma. "I'm going to clear out of here today I'm sorry I imposed on you this long I'll buy you a new can of anchovies. Naturally. These are *good.*"

I am sorry to report that I was grinning. I couldn't help it. The anchovies were slimy and prickly. They reminded me of women, if you want to know the truth. I wanted to slide them whole down my throat. I remembered that her real name was Velma.

Velma waved away my concern and sat at the kitchen table. She wore a long white nightgown, without so much as a robe to cover herself. Her great breasts caught on the flannel, bunching it like tissue paper flowers. Her feet were bare. Some of the cornrows had got loose, and her roots were growing in. She was a terror to look on, what with those gray porcine lips and that deadly white skin, but I saw that her pale eyes were enormous and beautiful. They were shifting colors in the morning light, from green to blue and back. She put her palm down on the glass top of her table and watched me pop anchovies in my mouth.

"Like one?" I meant that about clearing out. I wasn't raised to impose on people this way! To eat their anchovies and stand around their kitchens. The least I could do was offer her her own food.

Velma didn't trouble to answer. Clearly the woman was clinically depressed. You could tell she hadn't had a poke in a good long while. But a woman with her resources, moving in the world she moved in, didn't have to sit around her gleaming industrial kitchen with her nightgown bunched up like tissue paper flowers. She mentioned her shrink the first night I was here, when she wanted to put me away. Couldn't he help her? Couldn't he put her on Prozac like the rest of the world? I was on it! Until I didn't need it anymore! Couldn't someone listen to her 0 hadn't anybody noticed what sort of shape she was in?

"I thought I'd check into the Algonquin," I said, "it's not a bad address for an actor a little cachet maybe you and Angela and Fred could come up one night have a drink on me hey dinner at least, repay all you've done, and then after we could go dancing I don't know if you're into dancing."

"You don't have to clear out," Velma said, her voice as dead as her skin. "Fred's leaving. As you probly heard yesterday. No wonder you want to stay someplace else."

"Didn't hear a thing," I said, which was true. I was back into sleep mode yesterday but I was by gee by gosh by gum out of it today! I'm sorry to say I was still grinning.

"Well, he is," Velma said. She didn't believe me that I'd missed her troubles. "He is leaving. So you and Angela." It wasn't that she couldn't finish. She just stopped.

Now, other men in this situation—facing a betrayed fat unattractive woman clearly dying to spill out her guts—might want to flee the room.

Other men, what I can tell, might want to jump out the window. But not I. I *love* this stuff. I *love* other people's stories of betrayal and desertion. We're not alone! Hadn't my own wife left me? Come to think of it, hadn't I just betrayed the one woman, the one child I would always and unequivocally love? O. I wanted to drain the oil from the anchovy tin, I wanted it to wash over me. I began eating pesto out of the container. I would have knelt at Velma's feet, to tell you the truth. She was not even looking at me, moving through the plastic containers, consumed with hunger, consumed with this moment at dawn when I was so in love with Mary Faith and so delighted to imagine dinner at the Algonquin and dancing after, maybe at the Rainbow Room, we were all adults. I wanted to go pat Velma's undisciplined cornrows, maybe squeeze her shoulders.

At that moment, however, Fred wandered across the hall from the mirrored boudoir. He was wearing tiger-striped bikinis and nothing else. He was tanned and muscular and covered all over with wiry prickles of dark hair.

"Timbo!" I didn't imagine either the greeting or his costume. I had not spoken to him since the day after I arrived, when we looked together out his large windows at New York City. We had passed in the hallway. We had nodded at each other, waved from opposite ends of the loft. He hadn't been here much, I thought, but then, neither had I.

"Fred," I said. He was not stumbling into his kitchen to see me. "I'm just on my way out the door."

"Don't," said Velma. "Don't go anywhere. Anything Fred wants to say to me, he can say to you."

She was *really* depressed. Five days back, she wanted to call someone to prick me with a needle and lock me away. Now she wanted me as witness.

"I didn't want to say anything to you," Fred said, and tried to belch. "I just wondered what all the racket was."

"All the racket was one human being communicating with another," said Velma. "All the racket was just this complete stranger, Tim Rooney, willing to lend a sympathetic ear."

Well! Let me tell you, I was trapped. Fred stood in the hallway, Velma sat at the table. I was still refrigerator-side. There was no way to slide out of this one. Willing to lend a sympathetic ear, was I? I tried not to implicate myself further by looking at Velma, but really, how could I avoid it? What beautiful eyes!

"Hey," said Fred. He had a glutinous mountain accent—O he'd be from Greer or Spartanburg, where people say *hey* and it sounds closer to *hi*. "Don't let me interrupt your fun. What time is it anyway?"

"Time for you to pack a bag." Velma sat up a little taller.

"Hey," said Fred again. "Calm down."

He disappeared back into the pleasure chamber, and was replaced by Angela, rolling up the hallway. Had we been loud? We had roused the whole household, these folks who never rose before noon.

Angela padded down the long center of the loft in her own bare feet. No nightgown for her: she wore a dark Arrested Development T-shirt. Where had I seen that before? Below the T-shirt her tanned swimmers' thighs pressed forward.

"Oh hon," she was saying to Velma, before she even got close. "Oh hon."

Velma had by that time leaned her dead head down on her dead forearms. She generated no sound, no movement. Angela went to her and patted her head the way I wanted to do, and the sight of it was so—I'd say *loving* if I didn't want to avoid egging on the sentimentalists—so *concerned,* that I moved behind them and patted Angela's blond hair in turn. It rose up, electric.

Angela spun around and pushed me away. "Tim," she said, "you go on back to bed."

From beneath her forearm Velma's voice struggled out. "Let him stay," she said. "He's the only one wants to listen." See how delusional people get, when they're depressed? On the other hand, I *had* wanted to listen. I was hungry for her story, starving for it. "I told him Fred's leaving."

Angela made a face at the air. "That's not true, Vel," she said. "He said he didn't want to leave."

Now Velma raised her head and struggled to raise the rest of her body to some dignified level. The great bunched bosom of her nightie rose and fell. I thought she might breathe fire.

"He is too leaving," she said, but she was not looking at Angela. She did not seem at all interested in Angela's response. It was *me,* Tim

Looney, she was addressing. "He is leaving because I'm not going to support him one more day while he runs around with those—"

Catch. Angela looked downright panicked, and put a hand on my chest, as if she were going to push me back down the hall to my room. Back to bed, Tim, don't want to hear the naughty carryings-on of the world.

"With those boys." Velma finished her sentence and stared at me, very coolly, I noted, with her eyes changing color.

"He *is* running around with boys," I said. "I thought so." Though truth be told, I don't suppose it occurred to me even when I saw the tiger-striped bikinis.

Velma burst into copious tears, fat swollen tears. "Oh, God," she said, tasting them, "oh, God, sometimes somebody walks into your life just when you need help and Tim, I need help now. I am not ashamed to get down on my knees"—I am glad to report that she did not feel the need to dramatize this—"and beg you to just stick around until I can get that man out of my loft and out of my life."

"Hon," said Angela, "that man is your husband."

"*Hon,*" said Velma, "as I recall, you left your own husband standing at the altar."

Well. That exchange wiped the grin off my face and sent Angela back to her room with a black scowl. But here's the strange part. Velma had set me to weeping too. I was filled with a pure and bottomless sympathy for her, her husband running around in tiger-striped bikinis, and for Angela, whose help was not even wanted, and for Mary Faith and Jesse, who wouldn't have any idea why I had to stay in New York and rescue Velma from that fate worse than death, betrayal.

By lunchtime I was ministering to them all. To Fred, in the kitchen:

"Let me make you a sandwich."

"Thanks, Timbo, no, I better get my ass out of here while the getting's good." A wink and a nod from dark hairy Fred on his way out for the day, but all I could see was that ass he mentioned in tiger-striped bikinis. Me, I've always bought the cheap kind of briefs, six-for-whatever at the dime store. As for running around with boys? You pin any man up against the wall, whether he's having a nervous breakdown or not, and he'll be forced to tell you the thought has crossed his mind. Briefly, for most of us. Revolting, for most of us, once we've dismissed it. But there's not a one of us hasn't entertained the notion, however fleetingly. I think we're all bisexual. I think we're all sexual. I think some of us are so sexual it's a wonder we can brush our teeth or read the paper, our minds are so occupied. So who am I to judge Fred? Or Freud?

Maybe . . . maybe my difficulty with marriage was not brain fever or narcolepsy or epilepsy or the acting bug at all. Maybe I was . . . gay?

Fred knew he had me thinking in those terms. He was twitching his butt, in black jeans, as he sashayed down the long white hallway of his wife's loft.

To his wife I brought soup. She was in my bed, where I had led her, what with Fred occupying the mirrored boudoir. I could not say what kind of soup it was, only that it was white, like the loft, and chunky, like Velma. I found it in the silver icebox in another of those plastic containers. The smells that lifted from it were of fungus and cheese, but they were not enough to rouse her. She lay face down on my pillow, and when I put the next ceramic bowl (thick, with a thick black stripe along the edge) on the good little table next to the pillow, she opened her eyes and seemed, for a minute, content to breathe in the ten million calories. Then her eyes closed again, and I saw that her hands rested under her thighs, and that I was meant to go away.

I poked my head in Angela's cell. She was awake! She was stretched out on her futon bed, just as I had once found her stretched out on mine. Again, there was an open magazine. Again, she was not reading it. She was staring out, and when I entered, she continued her stare and implied with it that I was responsible for that blankness.

I sat at the edge of her bed, smelling of fungus and cheese. Again, I wanted her. What madness, that little flash of Fred-consciousness. I may be kooky but, by God, I'm an all-American male.

"She's not mad at you," I said.

"The hell she isn't." O! Angela sounded like a real little hellcat. Where was her sympathy?

"Only him she wants to punish."

"Oh, Tim."

She was softening, wasn't she? I stretched out opposite her, my head at her feet, which were bare as always, the toenails newly painted an orangey red I can only describe as trashy. Her feet were dirty.

"Oh, Tim, I did Briggs wrong, I can't believe I haven't even called. I can't believe it took Fred and then Velma, shit, she has *always* looked out for me, to point it out. Oh shit oh shit, now I've got to call him. I don't want to. There's the bottom line. I just don't . . . want to."

I was about a quarter inch away from taking her trashy orange-red big toe in my mouth and sucking it. I didn't want to make any calls either. I touched the toe. Just an index finger to the tip.

Angela said: "You think I have to, Tim? Anybody ever walk out on you and not call?"

"There was always a call." I moved the finger down the small of her foot.

"On the other hand," Angela said, "he maybe has more pride to claim, like, this way. Huh? As a guy?"

"Don't call," I said.

"You're right. Because in the first place my parents are going ballistic and that postcard probly hadn't calmed them down much. The club was twenty thousand, and I don't know how much you get back for the food when you cancel."

"Twenty thousand," I said. "You're a cool customer, Angela Bliss."

"Oh," she shrugged. "They're loaded. But . . ."

I waited, her toe growing limp above my hand. She wouldn't say more.

"I don't know anything about you, Angela Bliss," I said. "You tell me something, the way I told you."

"All right," she said, and drew her toe back to herself, and sat up to contemplate. "All right," she said again, but I could see she was not honing in on anything. Finally: "I don't have anything, like, so dramatic as pumping gasoline in my veins."

"Thank God."

"All right, then," she said, and probably didn't even know she was down close to whispering. "All right, once we got back from a swim meet late."

I was right! She was a swimmer!

"Daddy drove me. He always did. He coached me some too, used to drive me all over. This one meet I'd just got over pneumonia and I only got one third in the butterfly. But I thought that was pretty good, a white ribbon not but five days after I was in a sickbed. And Daddy thought it was pretty good too."

Now I had to lean closer to hear her whisper. She had taken possession of her foot back and was holding her own dirty toe. Clutching it. "So we pull back into Mount Pleasant late that night and Mama comes to the door potted. I mean stewed. She staggers back to the couch and points at me and she says: *What's it all for, what's all the sacrifice for, if you come back with a white ribbon? You're not trying to win, you're only trying to take him away from me.* Meaning Daddy."

"I'm sorry," I said. "That was cruel of her."

But Angela was trembling now, her toe and the hand holding it and her whispering voice. "It might have been cruel, but it was the truth. She was onto me. I was trying to take him away from her. I thought about it all the time then. I hated her. She never came to a meet. She didn't do *anything* in the house. She's the one who went to Vassar and you'd think she could for God's sake join one of those book clubs or something. But no, it was martinis and bridge, or martinis and golf, and pretty soon it was so many martinis nobody wanted to play bridge or golf with her. I *was* trying to take him away from her. I used to have daydreams— Oh, I couldn't tell you those but—"

She was off. I could see this girl heading into a tirade that was going to last the better part of the day, and I could see that it would include Velma, grapefruit spoons, Briggs as father figure and—unless I got extremely lucky or she was extremely stupid—me. How I fit into this father-daughter picture.

I said:

"—We all have the same troubles, don't we?" And I meant it. Look at me, almost marrying a girl half my age and Angela, crying over a man twice her age. Freud didn't have to figure it out for us. Sophocles figured it out for us. My mother loved me and my father hated me for it. Angela's father loved her and her mother hated her for it. It all seemed so . . . inconsequential. It made me want to go to sleep.

But Angela said: "No. We don't all have the same troubles," and I saw she didn't take kindly to my desire for communion with her. "If you don't mind, Tim." And she swept out her muscular swimmer's arm and pointed toward the screen in the doorway of her cell, as if I were the family dog and she was shooing me off the bed. And at just the moment when I was ready to take her dirty big toe into my mouth and suck on it until kingdom come.

"Tim!" From the other end of the loft came a weak and pathetic cry, Velma calling me to come minister to her. What was her story?

"I'm coming," I called back to Velma. But truth to tell, I was at that very second slipping into a black morass of despair, with the mud rising fast around me. Angela's story pushed me down, down. By the time I stepped into the hallway, with the light streaming from the south, all was black in front of me, behind me, around me: and if I was still walking toward Velma, who needed my help, I was only proceeding by radar.

DAY FIFTEEN BAT OUT OF HELL

Next morning Angela slept, and Velma slept, and Fred—no fool he—stayed away. I made my break for it while I could.

Daylight streamed through the big loft windows, but I stumbled through the dark hallways, only tunnel vision to guide me. I thought I might have tunnel disease too: the bends. I could not walk straight, and when I descended on the elevator I put one hand on the handle and one hand on the wall behind to hold me up. I did not know where I was going. Not to look for Bernadette—I'd given up on that, and besides, I could only see along this shaft of dim light.

Outside on Spring Street it was the dead of winter in April. My bowels turned liquid and my veins ran ice.

He was waiting for me. The blue-black man. There, across the street, keeping a vigil like the one I kept in the park. I could barely make him out, but if I raised my chin I could see the Yankee cap on his head and the longest of his dreadlocks dancing below. I pulled my collar up high and turned away. He'd seen me, though. He was salivating at the sight of me: I could hear his tongue slurping in his head.

Behind me he crossed the street mid-sidewalk and then jogged along, fat basketball shoes slapping the sidewalk. I may have been hunched over like an old man, the walls of the world may have been closing in on me, but the feel of his hunter's breath on my neck made me pick up my pace. My heart was doing double time. He ran through the streets of SoHo behind me.

I walked east, toward Broadway. Soon he would pin me again.

"Mr. Rooney," he said finally, puffing along beside me.

I kept walking. Hard and heavy. My breathing had stopped. I kept walking.

"Mr. Rooney!"

I kept walking. Not to panic. Not to panic. I kept walking.

Until . . . I stopped, and all my fear turned to fury. It seethed through me. I turned to face him, and in turning turned the tables. Now he cowered before me, the bulk of him trembling in the cool spring air.

I hissed at him. "Why did he send you here? Didn't I tell you to leave me be?"

My vision opened up along the edges. Facing me on the sidewalk, he came into focus. I guessed that the light above must be morning light, because it softened his skin and showed me I had been wrong about his color. No one has blue-black skin. He was only brown. The light bounced off his dark face, rebuffed. He was growing a wispy goatee now. He looked puzzled, hurt . . . he looked chagrined.

"Don't you pull that switcheroo on me!" I said. "I'm wise to your tricks."

"What tricks, Mr. Rooney? Come on now. What you talking about?"

"What am *I* talking about? You trail me through the city streets, drive me PRACTICALLY TO THE POINT OF INSANITY, cause me to question what I see with my own eyes, and then ask me what I'm talking about. Oh-ho, that's rich."

I walked again and he chugged along beside me, in terrible shape. I imagined he had high blood pressure, terrible cholesterol, piles, etc., etc.

"Wait up now, Mr. Rooney. It didn't start out this way. I didn't start out following you, you know."

Again I stopped dead and again, as the blood pounded through my head, my field of vision widened. That was a beautiful tenor he had, a John McCormack voice with the wrong accent.

"Explain yourself," I said.

The young man with the beautiful voice pulled again at his goatee.

"Go on. Explain yourself. Explain *him*. Why did he send you after me?"

"Who?" he said. "Father Berkeley?"

"Who else?"

"He didn't send me after you. I was coming up here anyways. He had a feelin you were heading this way and when I say I could look out for you, he says might as well. He had no *idea* I was gonna find you in that parking lot. And neither did I." We were very nearly up to Broadway. "And I sure didn't think I was gonna find you in Washington Square, but I did, and then it seemed almost like I was meant to keep an eye on you. Come on now," he said. "Let's go get us some coffee let me tell you all about it." Coffee shops beckoned, every twelve feet.

"I would burn in hell," I said, "before I would share a cup of coffee with you."

"Thas not fair." Now he stopped on the sidewalk and damned if I wasn't compelled to stop there beside him. "Mr. Rooney, you know thas not fair."

And now when I stared at him the chill passed through me and out, and my body began to heat up. I knew this man, knew him from somewhere. "Who are you?"

"G. B. Brights, Mr. Rooney," he said, with an air of shame. He was pleading that I remember him. He was a very young man, growing younger by the minute, and more strangely familiar.

"G. B. Brights!" I repeated, though I could not remember for the life of me, not to mention the sanity of me, where I had heard that name before.

"I knew you'd remember," he said, and tucked his chin under. "Eventually." But I didn't have a clue. "You said come talk to you I ever wanted to take up more philosophy and . . . here I am."

"Here you are!" I said. I shouted. "In New York City! By God, that's a long way to come talk about philosophy! Sweet baby Jesus, that's a distance to travel!" I could see G. B. Brights, could see him way in the back row of a country classroom. Yessir, I could see G. B. Brights in an evening class at Southdale, only branch of Carolina that has seen fit to hire me in the last five years, a job that took me an hour out of Due East into the dead of the country, where I faced classrooms of the barely literate with *Self is a relation which relates to itself—not the relation, but the relation's relating to itself.* You think you could explain it? G. B. Brights could. I could see his handwriting, large and round as he was large and round, all the subjects and verbs agreeing—a miracle right there! Believe me, you start paying attention to a writer like *that* in Southdale, South Carolina. I could see a pile of bluebooks handed in by G. B. Brights, four or five or six of them for every exam, every other line neatly skipped, every sentence neatly parsed. One of those country kids who got it and liked it and wrote it back clearer than Søren or Martin or Friedrich or any of the boys he was reading in 101 ever wrote it in the first place. Maybe once I wrote on one of those bluebooks *Come talk to me.* Maybe I even said it in person.

"I couldn't place you," I said, "for a minute there."

"Invisible man," he said, and found that hilarious. When he was done chortling and slapping his thigh over his own wit he said: "More like a week you couldn't place me. You were having some kind of crisis. I was worried about you. I was—"

I knew what he was going to say now. He was going to say: *I was hurt when you didn't recognize me in that parking lot. I've been living on those* Come see me *words of yours. I was so hurt I followed you up the length of the East Coast and then trailed you through New York City.*

"G. B.," I said, "you're not into saving anybody, are you?"

He considered this the way he might consider a trick question. "You mean like in religion? Like in baptism?"

I nodded.

"No, sir." He didn't have to ponder that at all, once the terms were defined. "No, sir, I am not interested in religion whatsoever. I liked it when you got into the political business. I was kind of attracted to those existentialists."

"G. B. Brights," I said. "Didn't they call you Geech?"

He nodded. "Call me Geech down to school. My family call me Goober. Preacher use to call me Gabriel sometime."

My heart did a swoop. Hadn't I called him my guardian angel in the bank parking lot?

"Well what in the name of God you doing following me around New York City, G.B.?"

"I told you," he said. "I came to talk about taking up philosophy. But then you start tearing around the country, flashing your cash, what'm I supposed to do? Didn't mean anything by it. Didn't mean anything by following you."

And so I followed *him,* into a coffee shop.

He had tracked me down in Due East. He had looked me up in the phone book and come by my house and found nobody home, nobody but . . . you guessed it, Father Berkeley, parked in the driveway. This was Easter Sunday, that day I slept the sleep of the dead. And all around me their forces were gathering to obliterate me, cross me out, mark me out darker than my very dreams marked me. Upstairs I slept while they conspired below, and I did not hear their smacks on my door. Father Berkeley—traitor, traitor—told him I had not shown up for the Easter Vigil. They drove out to the beach together, to make sure I hadn't followed Dottie.

It was pure chance he saw me in the bank parking lot the next morning. He had given up on talking to me; he was heading out for the rest of his journey. He was on his way to Brooklyn, coming to live with an aunt and get himself enrolled in Brooklyn College, if they would have him. That was why he came to see me, to ask me if he should be a philosopher.

G.B.

Now.

Don't be a fool.

He must have been all of twenty. He put away an omelet, a plate of toast, home fries, an order of bacon. Then he asked for grits. No grits in New York, G.B. He let me pay for the meal, but he said:

"Watch it now, pulling that money out your sock. There's people watching you all over."

As if I didn't know *that.*

Back out in the sunlight the world was reconfigured again. Whew. That was a close call, bad way to start the day. Real bad. We passed a liquor store and I remembered how long it had been since I took a drink. Too long. Way too long. Maybe my vision had started to fade because I was an alcoholic! Maybe it was better just to treat that need than to ignore it. Maybe these last two weeks could be explained by a simple lack of Jamesons.

"Come on out with me to Brooklyn," G.B. said. "Come meet my aunt. She knows I been running into the city try to catch you. Come say hello. She'll be home bout three o'clock, she's a teacher. We can talk meanwhile. Come on out."

Now that he was fed, he was a regular little chatterbox. That voice, o, sweet and light as honeysuckle. Irresistible. And wasn't he treating me as a normal person again? *Running into the city to try to* catch *you.*

"G.B.," I said, "I have never in my life explored the bowels of Brooklyn, and I don't intend to start now."

"What's the matter? Too many black folk for you?"

Whoa-ho. Just twist the knife in there, buddy. We were up to the corner of Houston Street. Why did he call me Mr. Rooney? Out at Southdale they called me Professor and Professor Rooney and Tim and Professor Tim and hey, you. What did I need him for?

"Come on now," he said. "Do you good get away from this part of town."

The subway stairs loomed below. I had just escaped one tunnel.

"Come on now," he said and, without waiting for an answer, led me down.

I had not been on a New York City subway train in lo, these many years. The stench of warm piss rose up immediately to tell me what a mistake I'd made, following G. B. Brights just because he told me to. I began to picture that bottle of Jamesons. The lack of it explained everything. I was once a heavy drinker. Some people might have even called me an . . . alcoholic. Well, all right. Call me what you will. I tapered off round about the time Jesse Rapple started complaining about my language and my whiskey breath. Maybe I wasn't an alcoholic, I let it go so easily. But look what it had cost me. I was paying now.

The trains were new. They called to mind sleek silver flasks, the kind they might sell in a jeweler's. The kind that might fit a half pint of Makers Mark. The kind would calm you down.

The trains were also quieter. Not that they sneaked up on you but surely no subway train ever came in so fast and silent back when I lived in New York. G. B. Brights let one go by and then another, but when a D train pulled into the station, he muscled on board as if he'd been living in the bright lights, and not some backwater, all his life.

Inside, the car was all done up in orange plastic. I felt ill. I needed a drink. Whatever possessed me, to come with him, this man who had been stalking me? Now he led me to a seat. The car was half empty, heading out to Brooklyn on a weekday. Its passengers looked large and dark. They looked like . . . G.B. Floaters swam before my eyes. I blinked and blinked again.

"You OK?"

"Yes, I am. I am perfectly OK."

"Just checking. Listen, man, I was just kidding about too many black folk. It's innegrated out there. You sure you OK?"

I found I couldn't swallow. An anaphylactic reaction! My throat was closing up. I must be allergic to something on this train. I must be allergic to . . .

"Cause anyway you was always fair in the classroom. People thought you was a little crazy maybe, but fair, you know. People thought you *were* a little crazy." I was having an allergic reaction that would possibly lead me to my death and G. B. Brights was correcting his own grammar. So that subject-verb stuff didn't come all that easily to him. Plus he was calling me crazy. I found I could swallow again.

"Grand Street," he said, before we pulled into the next station. Like a conductor, for the tourist. I sat on the orange plastic seat experimenting to see if my spittle would ease down my throat.

It would, and it did, and I could breathe. Dust must have made its way into my windpipe, but I had beat it back. I settled into the seat because, truth to tell, I have always loved the New York City subway system. They may have taken out all the old gray benches, all the old cane two-seaters, but they can't take that away from me! We picked up speed and G.B. said: "Next stop Brooklyn."

We went for a good fast dark run through the bottom of Manhattan and then we emerged, praise be, astride a great blue bridge, the Manhattan, looking out over Brooklyn ahead and the city behind and out in the harbor, jumping Jehosophat, the Statue of Liberty.

"Look," I said.

G.B. shook his head. "You thought you been hanging around the cool part of town. See here, this here's where all the cool stuff is. Out to Brooklyn." He put his hand on my thigh, and I jumped half a foot in the air. This was too much. Way too much. My windpipe closed.

He removed his hand.

I calmed again in the watery light. He hadn't meant anything by that hand. By God, it was a beautiful day. The Brooklyn Bridge beside us was so stalwart, so brown. There was Walt Whitman down in the harbor, on one of those sloops.

Why hadn't I done this before? Why hadn't I ever crossed over before?

The tracks swooped down, coming off the bridge, and we came into the tunnel again. Now I felt we'd crossed the Rubicon. Besides the floaters and the throat closing that old thirst came up fast and insistent.

"Any place we could get a drink?" I said.

G.B. leaned his big wide head back and laughed. His gold-rimmed tooth showed. "Not till we get out the train."

I settled back again, chastened. I shouldn't have given up looking for my wife. I made a resolution to look for her again tomorrow. This afternoon, if possible. If I ever got out of Brooklyn. At least I had found the man who was following me. I was functional. I was functional and *effective*.

At the first stop in Brooklyn three Latin boys got on one end of the train car, jostling each other and carrying on, whooping and shrieking. One of them—tall skinny boy with his hair slicked down neat—carried a big shopping bag that was doing its own jostling. A couple of women fled from them and one managed to jump out of the train before the doors closed. Either the bag was gyrating, or I was losing it. The bag was alive.

"Uh-oh," said G.B. beside me. See, I wasn't losing it.

Meanwhile the end of the car the boys were on had cleared out and there was a crowd mid-car, where we were sitting. I can report that I was certainly the only Irish-American headed into Brooklyn at the moment. All around me were the rest of Brooklyn, in various shades of brown, in turbans and baseball caps and secretary dresses. The boy with the bag was laying his package down on a seat.

"No, fuck, don't let it out!" The other two boys began to back away, but the bag lay quiet.

"Oh my God," said a fat woman beside me.

"What they got in there?" said G.B.

"Gotta be a squirrel or something."

"Must be a rat."

"Somebody pull the cord!"

"Don't pull the cord, you wanna be locked in here with some crazy rat?"

The first boy stepped gingerly, gingerly over his shopping bag and tipped it sideways. Still no action.

"No, man!"

He poked at the bottom of the bag. Still no action.

He picked the bottom of the bag off the seat and rustled it and from the mouth of the brown shopping bag flew . . .

A bird, I thought. A pigeon: no, a blackbird. I was cool, it was interesting in an anthropological way, here I was in Brooklyn, no, here I was under Brooklyn, for the first time in my life, and three teenage boys had let loose a bird in a half-filled subway car.

But it wasn't a bird. It was a bat.

I figured that out with everybody else, with its first swoop down the length of the car. Women stood clumped together with their little fists clenched against their breasts and ran en masse from one end of the car to the other. The bat followed them, or fled them, the line of passengers and the lines of the bat making the same sweeping motion. G.B. and I sat in the midst of this, G.B. shaking his head back and forth, a half-smile playing on his mouth. If they would just sit still, the bat would find a perch, crawl back in the bag: something.

A wiry brown little man, couldn't have been bigger than five feet, took off his shirt and began to swing at the bat whenever it passed close. He had hard dark pecs that reminded me of Angela and abundant hair curling over his net undershirt: a manly man. The bat's sweeps took a shorter turn, more confused. Meanwhile the crowd, still running from safe haven to safe haven, shouted to the man: "Don't kill it! Don't kill it!" They fled the bat and begged for its life simultaneously. And I, sitting in the midst of this, having forgotten my throat and my thirst, remembered how lucky it was that it was a bat and not a bird that flew through our subway car. A bird in the house means a death in the family.

The little man managed to strike the bat, finally, with his shirt. The bat flew off faster and then circled back, lower. The train seemed to be slowing: soon we would be pulling into the next station. A fat woman clawed at a door, trying to pry it open even as we moved. The bat's route was unpredictable, goofy. It wasn't until it changed its trajectory and swayed past me—I mean directly past me, I mean grazed the top of my red head—that I found myself jumping from my seat, G.B. beside me doing the same, some strange batlike shrieks emitting from our mouths just as they had been emitting from all the female mouths on the train.

And then we were huddled against a door—maybe we were clawing at it, like the fat lady—while the train lumbered on. Still it had not pulled near the light of a station. The bat too seemed to slow, and the wiry man had given up swinging at it with his shirt. Now he was flailing with his bare hands. Now he was connecting with a batwing and now, good God, he seemed to be pummeling the body. I could not look, but I could hear. He swatted the bat the way my father once swatted me when I displeased him. All around me women were shrieking for the life of the bat who scared the living daylights out of them.

I was strangely elated: not that the bat was dying—wasn't I covering my own head as it received its blows?—but that I was able to remember my father's blows about my head. I saw the swoop and pinch of his belly as he stood above me. I swallowed, and I was in Due East. My father is standing above me. His belly puckers out above his belt: a black belt, cracked with age lines.

"Timothy," he says, "your bow is on the kitchen counter again." He holds each word back at the corners. I don't look up past the puckers.

"I was fixing to get it," I say.

"That bow," says my father, "was seventy-five dollars. Seventy-five dollars and a trip to Charleston."

"I'm fixing to get it." I am at the moment sitting on the old green velvet couch, playing a guitar I bought myself from Sears for forty-nine dollars and forty-nine cents.

"Maybe you're giving up the violin," my father says. "Maybe a boy can't loosen his bow and put it in the case can't appreciate a seventy-five-dollar bow the whole family sacrifices for. Your mother dudn't have proper shoes."

His belly heaves on above me. I am not giving up the violin, I am only tuning my guitar for the talent show because the Daydreamers have finally agreed that I can do two verses of Bo Diddley's "Who Do You Love," fast, so no one can hear the words. In exchange I have promised not to make faces while they sing "Lemon tree, very pretty."

"Maybe you've also given up answering your father in a civil fashion," he says.

Still I do not answer. My father taught me piano himself—he plays Gershwin like an angel, he is the only man in Due East who goes on pilgrimages to hunt Stephane Grapelli records—but he stands before me now as Neanderthal man. I feel my mouth snaking and humping itself, spelling out the very letters of the word *sneer,* trailing off with the tail of a cursive *r* as written by a fourteen-year-old boy.

And I feel simultaneously the guitar slipping out of my hands and see that my father has taken it up and wields it over my head. My sneer turns into a wide contemptuous grin—he can't mean to do *that*—and my father, knowing he can't hit me over the head with a guitar, swings it down hard on the coffee table. The soundbox cracks. I groan. The show's tomorrow night. This eggs my father on, it's just a cheap Sears guitar after all, the honey wood splitting, the white plastic tuners flashing through the dim Rooney living room. He swings the guitar again and at this I finally rise, maybe in fact I rise *into* the swinging guitar and that first blow to my head is not intended at all, but having been accomplished, having been met by the sneering grin still stretched across my face, he does it again, soft, slow. And again. And again.

And I stand with my knees pressed up against the velvet couch while he swings a cheap Sears guitar down on my head and I say: "It's a joke, it's a joke," and this makes him—not crazy, *I'm* the one who's crazy—but reverted back past Neanderthal man to Australopithecus. He is ready to swing it slow once again, he is enjoying this, the balance of it above his head, the stunned sneering head below him.

But my mother comes flying down the stairs and through the living room. My father stops in wonder and I stare at her too. Look at her go, French twist falling out of its black hairpins, the black flats on her feet flopping up and down. She flings herself between us, between husband and son, like a bat out of hell, and a high-pitched something, not words, emits from her as she struggles with my father to wrest the guitar from his hands.

I swallowed, my throat open wide, ready to split open the head of my father and this wiry man and anybody else who looked at me cross-eyed. I looked at G.B. for confirmation that something momentous had just happened. Outside the train door I saw light, finally. We were pulling into the station. I made out the name in tiles on the wall—Atlantic Avenue—and then I passed out, into a deep and dangerous unconsciousness. G.B. would have to carry me like a baby from the train.

The bat was dead.

REPORT FROM DUE EAST

The old man had me so upset I couldn't think straight, couldn't sit down for a minute without jumping up, couldn't answer Jesse without snapping at him.

Father Berkeley had called before, of course. He called first thing Tim went missing and told me he'd never shown up for Easter.

"Tim's lost his faith," I said. I didn't mean to. I blurted it out, and it was a betrayal, plain and simple.

But Father Berkeley said: "He's lost his mind, you mean."

I didn't argue with him then, on the phone. I hadn't seen him in years, had been dreading it since I made the decision that I would marry Tim in church. But I'd always told Tim, and it is the truth, that I do admire anyway the fierceness of his religion. Like the Jews. If he were a Presbyterian or a Methodist, I don't believe I would have troubled myself.

The priest didn't call before he showed up. He was waiting for me when I pulled in from one of my last days at work, sick with worry about how I'd be buying groceries a month from now. There'd been no money and no word.

Jesse had let the old man into the house and, here's a curiosity, had fetched him a glass of tea and was sitting there with him in the dim little

TV room where my father used to hole up all night with the game shows. Jesse had given Father Berkeley my father's chair, the lounger. He himself was crouched down on the footstool. They weren't talking. They weren't watching TV. They might have been stuffed birds, sitting in that room day after day in the same position until I walked in. Then they stood up together. I have never seen Jesse behave in such a way before or since.

"Miss Rapple," the old man said, pronouncing *Miss* with that little kick in the rear to make sure you know he knows your marital status. I had nothing but contempt for him, but I couldn't have imagined he could ever get so old. Even in the dim room I could see how light and protuberant his eyes were. I towered over him. Jesse towered over him. He is retired, but he says a mass every Sunday and of course it would have been him, old friend of the family, marrying Tim and me. Tim said he's gone wild with religion in his old age, flamboyant where he was once shy and restrained. But Tim said, too, that there were years when Father Berkeley didn't believe a thing, and just stayed on in the Church out of duty.

So I had nothing but contempt for him. Duty. And then there was the injustice of an old man standing trembling before me, his head jerking back and forth mid-sentence, but sure of himself too, self-righteous and smug. My own father died before he ever saw the age of fifty. There were gravy stains on Father Berkeley's jacket. His hair had gone yellow and soft over his pink freckled head.

"Miss Rapple," he said again.

"Yes, sir." Already he had me on the defensive. Already I had stumbled. "Yes, Father."

"I've come about Timothy," he said.

"Jesse," I said, "why don't you get out and get you some fresh air?" As if he normally did such a thing in the afternoon.

Jesse shook his head. "I want to hear." He sounded himself, a little sullen maybe, but so serious you couldn't deny him. I wouldn't deny him, anyway. The priest would. "Go on out now, Jesse," he said, without so much as a glance in my son's direction, and Jesse rose and did as he was told. Wonders will never cease.

When Jess was safely gone, Father Berkeley sat himself back down, lord of the manor, and said: "We have to go after him." Just like that. Without further introduction of the subject.

"Oh," I said, still stinging from the way he turned my son out of his own house. "Does this mean you know where he is?"

"I think I do."

I waited, and the old man shook his head back and forth, or let it shake. He was waiting for me to guess. I'd be damned.

"Where's he gone, then?"

"New York," the priest said.

"He might have gone to Miami," I said, "where his father is."

The priest shook his head no, so it was trembling and shaking at once.

"He might have gone to Kentucky," I said, "or those people outside Atlanta, or he's always been crazy about New Orleans. He might just be holing up in Savannah."

"He's gone to New York," said Father Berkeley.

"Father," I said, and then I sat down on the footstool myself and had to hold my tongue so I wouldn't go weepy in front of him. I wanted to say that the passage of these two weeks had made me grateful, finally, that we hadn't yet made it up to the wedding. Now I could not remember loving Tim Rooney. I might be filled with dread of the future, but I'd get by, one way or another, and the prospect of that filled me with peace —whereas the prospect of ever seeing Tim again filled me with a hatred so black it should not rest on anyone's soul.

"I'll pay for gas," the old man said, "and meals. You needn't trouble yourself over money."

That took me by surprise, and when I looked up I saw that it took him by surprise as well. He was dabbing at the corner of his mouth with his priest-handkerchief. It was as yellow as his hair.

"Father," I said, "my son is in school. I can't take off like that."

"I'll tutor him," said the priest. "Have him bring his books. Do you drive?"

Have him bring his books. And you, young lady, you can deal with the Due East school system which will have Jesse's hide and hold him back a year, besides. "I can drive, Father Berkeley," I said, "but I'm not going with you."

"Whyever not?"

"I told you. My son's in school. I'm not having him fail sixth grade on account of a trip to New York when Tim may not even be in New York. And." I bit my tongue.

"And?"

"And," I said, "I hope Tim gets the help he needs, but this is where I get off the train."

He pulled his toes up and stared at his wingtips, black and dull, unshined. No one was taking care of him. Maybe they put him in a back room of the rectory and let him struggle through every day on his own.

He said: "Surely you didn't intend to marry him with that attitude."

He came into my house and took me to task like a tenth-grade girl caught smoking in the bathroom.

"Father," I said, "I didn't know, when I said I'd marry him, that he was going to walk out on me."

He spluttered. That's the only way I can describe it. *"Walk out on you?"* he said. Just like that.

"Excuse me," I said, "but what else would you call it? He walked out on me and on my son, who loves him like a father. I didn't know when I said I'd marry him that he was going to have me quit my job before he left me. I didn't know he would tell me to leave his house when . . ."

The old man dabbed his mouth.

"He called and left Jesse a terrible message."

He leaned forward. "Where'd he call from?"

"I don't know."

"When? What did he say?"

I was purple with frustration now. I could not have explained why I still sat and talked with him. "He said, *Jesse . . . will . . . be . . . Jesse.*" And then I sat biting my lips from the inside, to hold myself back from saying more.

Father Berkeley slapped his knee. He was still leaning forward. "Of course," he said. "Of course."

Oh sure, of course. I didn't give him the satisfaction of a single word.

Finally the old man said: "Has he called since then? Written? Did he leave you a note?" I did not say a word.

"Listen, Mary Faith"—he took to calling me by that name just as easily as he took to sitting in my father's chair and lecturing me—"you cannot call it *walking out on you* when he's having a breakdown. It's not the first. Surely you knew."

"I knew."

"And you knew his sister drowned herself in a state of despair."

"I did."

"And you knew his mother, before the stroke, renounced her religion and her husband and moved into a separate bedroom and lived apart. That his father was driven to distraction and almost had to be . . . restrained."

I stared at him.

"And knowing these things, you would still hold him to the behavior you'd expect of an ordinary man?"

I couldn't believe my ears. Suddenly it was wrong of me to ask Tim not to leave us. Suddenly it was wrong of me to resent his asking me *to leave him be.*

"We don't even know he's had a breakdown."

"Do you have another diagnosis?"

Yes, I wanted to say, *yes, I have another diagnosis. I'd call it the big walkout, plain and simple. I'd call it a man freaked out about becoming a husband and father, a man turning to his old tricks.*

"I tell you, Mary Faith, this trouble has been going on since Timothy Rooney was fifteen years old and playing in a rock and roll band. It was going on when his mother sent him to New York City, and it was going on when he was traipsing around the country joining religious communes. When he finally had to be hospitalized, Mary Faith, he was in desperate trouble."

Still I did not say a word. I could not say a word.

"We have to go fetch him. Unless," Father Berkeley said, "unless you did not know the extent of his troubles. Unless you've changed your mind about marrying him."

"I wasn't given the chance to change my mind."

"You're thinking in the wrong terms, Mary Faith. He hasn't left *you.* He's left his senses."

And I didn't intend to leave mine. I had passed through the pitying stage, passed through the worrying stage. I'd passed out of the stage when

I thought that Tim's troubles were sweeping over him. I believed Father Berkeley was right. I believed he was in New York City. I believed he was acting crazy, and I believed he'd get over it. I believed Jesse was right. Tim was with another woman.

"Listen," the priest said, "you have the chance to make a choice now. You can choose not to take on the nursing of a man who will have these . . . incidents all his life. Because he will, you know."

And that was the point at which I could not help but go weepy after all. Not over Tim having *incidents* all his life, but over my father, wasting away in a hospital bed in this very room, more childlike every day, dying with *Jeopardy!* on the soundtrack and the shame of a catheter in his bladder. And I was weeping over the men I used to sneak out and meet when he was alive, all of them gone back to their wives or off to their wildest dreams, as far from Due East as they could run. I was weeping over Jesse's father, who overdosed of pills when he wasn't but sixteen himself, and left me to face bringing up a son on my own. Wasn't that enough? I was weeping over priests sitting there on your father's old lounger and asking you to believe that this really is a woman's lot: to nurse men and to wait on them, to send them off to their crazy adventures and then, when they've made it too dangerous for themselves, to go fetch them and forgive them and be steady and faithful. Well, I've got news for you, Father Berkeley. I was wiping my mother's cancer face when I was nine years old. I've taken care of plenty. I've done my part.

The old man heaved himself out of the deep old chair and came and put his hand on my head while I cried. It made me sob the harder, the weight of it there. I couldn't bear his soft fingers. He smelled of mothballs and nicotine.

I willed him to say something, something that I could slap away with the back of my hand. I wanted him to say something smug and ready-made, *But God will give you strength* or *Let us call on Him for courage.*

"I'm not going with you, Father," I said.

He stopped patting my head. He stood over me for a minute and then creaked on over to the doorway. "I know the way out," he said—oh, like the parting line in a movie and the other kick in the rear, that I didn't have the good graces my son had, to show him to the door.

I didn't care. I sat sobbing on my footstool until I'd cried myself dry.

When I got up, I'd cured myself of any doubts the old man had planted. There was Jesse's supper to make.

But in the days after I felt I could jump out of my skin and go screaming the heebie-jeebies into the night myself. I felt closer and closer to what Tim must have felt, that hard cold ball of self in the center of my body. And the closer I was to what he had become, the more I despised him, him and me both.

So that by the time a pamphlet arrived for my eleven-year-old son, with a reading list on The Balkan Conflict, and a return address from the War Resisters League, I had no trouble determining that I could never forgive him. It wasn't until later that the address registered. New York City.

four

DAY SIXTEEN **TOO GOOD**

This time I was not in the white womb. This time I was in a sensible bedroom about the size of a coffin. I lay on a single bed. There were blue flouncy curtains on the window, and the smell of a woman, a woman's powders and lotions and sachets, and there was the sound of a woman outside my door too.

"G.B.," she said, and I knew where I was. That would be the Brooklyn aunt. G.B. had rescued me, when he promised he wasn't into saving souls.

"We cannot leave him in that bed out cold. Listen here now," she said, "I got to get off to work. But if he hadn't come around time I get back at three o'clock we're calling 911 and we're carting him out of here. Matter of fact we should be calling 911 this minute and if I didn't have to make roll call I'd make sure you did it. Just like Etta, I swear."

"It's not just like Aunt Etta," G.B. said. This time there was no long hallway to echo or muffle their talk. They were right outside my door, and I got a sense of the scope of this apartment. It would be two, three rooms, two or three rooms all scrubbed this clean and smelling this . . . female. There was green light coming in the windows, the tops of branches. I was high in some square apartment building, and once again I was in someone's hands. Once again they thought I was mad. I took a look out the window: three stories up, at least. Otherwise, I definitely would have shimmied out. Or . . . maybe not.

"It is too just like my sister and don't you talk back to me, and don't you go bringing in white boys having nervous breakdowns off the street you want to stay with me while you go to college. I'll send you packing you do. I swear I wish it was just drugs. I wish I could believe that."

"Well, it's not drugs, Took. I told you. He passed out when he saw that bat. And he's not a white boy, older'n you. He's my professor."

"Professor. And stayed sleeping in that bed for sixteen hours? Some South Carolina excuse for a professor. You mark my words, Goober, he's gonna wake up the way Etta did. He's not gonna know where he is and he's not gonna know who he is. Didn't you say he was acting crazy the first place? And where'd you put that truck? And don't you know I got to leave in the next fifteen seconds I'm gonna punch in on time. Give me those keys. Just give me those keys."

"He's not gonna wake up crazy, Took. It's not like Etta. Truck's on East Fifteenth bout halfway down." The sound of the keys flying through the air, caught neatly.

"No. No. *Tell* me you didn't put it in that garage like I told you."

"Can't afford it, Took, not and go to college in September."

"Not gonna be a truck out there is my bet. You put the Club on?"

"Course I put the Club on."

And then the door slammed and she was gone. Whoa. What a near escape. She sounded like a woman who wouldn't cut you any slack. I decided to get out of G.B.'s before I came into further contact with her, direct or indirect. I was fully clothed in yesterday's clothes, and this time my shoes were on my feet. All I had to do was make a polite getaway, thank you and good-bye to G.B. Fully sane. I knew exactly where I was. I knew exactly who I was.

Something—maybe that feeling of full sanity—caused me to linger at the window, looking down. I pictured the bat and the rabid look of the man who beat him to death. It was real: hadn't I just heard G.B. telling his aunt? I had followed this chubby overage kid into a coffee shop and he had changed from my nightmare shadow to my protégé. A surge of hope passed through my body like an electric current. No need to check into the hospital for the shock treatment this time. He looked up to me as a father figure, for advice and concern, and by God I had pulled myself together in time to be one for him. I hadn't felt so warm toward another human being since . . .

A twinge of panic. Never mind. Setbacks occur. Shit happens. I had managed to slip into a deep unconsciousness, had managed to miss the night when I intended to begin drinking again. Another small setback: the memory of drink. No, no. Orange juice would get me over this hump. Coffee. No need to buy that bottle of Jamesons until nightfall. Surely a little drink between a mentor and his . . .

The doorknob twisted as I stood at the window, and G.B. entered on tiptoe, meaning to check, I suppose, if I was still breathing. He stopped dead at the sight of me risen.

"Mr. Rooney. How you *feeling?*"

Warmth and hope increased. The window's east light warmed my back and G.B.'s face both, turned it cherry, the same rich sheen. How had I ever pictured it blue-black? The glass diamond in his ear looked downright rakish. What a charming fellow.

"I feel GOOD, says James Brown."

"Thas great," G.B. said. "Cause my aunt, she was worried about you—"

"I heard her."

He shook his head. "She's not that bad, really. I wanted y'all to meet. You think you ought to go get your blood pressure checked or something? I heard low blood pressure could do that, or you know you might have sugar diabetes, something like that. You was, you were, passed out a *long* time."

I laughed a deep paternal laugh. "I guess I needed the sleep," I said. No need to worry the protégé. "And I'll meet your aunt one of these days. I'll write her a note!"

"Thas a good idea," G.B. said. "C'mon, she left the coffee on. You wanna walk over to Brooklyn College with me? Tell me what you think? You know anybody there? You feeling good enough for that?"

I told you he was a chatterbox when he got going. There was nothing I wanted less than to walk over to Brooklyn College. What I wanted was —I had no idea. Maybe I would walk over to Brooklyn College with him. Maybe I would be his mentor. Maybe we'd have a beer.

The apartment was just as I expected: a living room with white flouncy curtains, a sofa where one of them had slept flat and a wing chair where one of them had slept sitting. G.B. had sat up all night waiting over me. We passed through a narrow hallway into a narrow kitchen covered head to ceiling with church notices and children's drawings.

"Who finger-paints?"

"Everybody," G.B. said. "All the nephews and nieces. Aunt Took everybody's favorite cause she hadn't got any of her own. Always sending us presents and such. Books. This was her idea, me coming up here. Tell you the truth, I think she was lonely. My father and them, they were twelve in that family. She was used to having somebody around, under-foot. She even sent me half the money for a car to get up here, only . . ."

"Only I bet she wasn't so pleased you got yourself a pickup truck to drive around Brooklyn."

He shook his head and laughed. "No, she wasn't. See, she was think-ing I could make enough being a livery driver to pay my way. But there was this sheriff's auction and I saw this truck somebody been using to haul dope. Wasn't but six months old. I don't know what I was thinking, but I'll tell you this. I got a good buy."

And a distinctive vehicle, I said to myself, picturing that truck whizzing along the Bridge-Tunnel.

The next voice I heard was Aunt Took's:

"I don't know what you were thinking either."

I don't know how she got back in the door without either of us hearing her, but there she was, any fifth-grade boy's nightmare. Aunt Took. She stood there in the entrance to her own apartment like the FBI, holding the keys to the truck in one hand and slapping them hard as you please into her other, open hand. You could see her in her classroom slapping a ruler back and forth on her open palm. I squirmed in my desk, giddy with fear, but it was not an unpleasant sensation. She had a face as dark as G.B.'s, only hers was triangular, not round. Her forehead was broad and high and sat under hair straightened and dyed red and twisted into a knot at the back of her neck, a knot so tight it hurt to look at her. She had thick black brows, lashes made up thicker yet, and a mouth so full and painted so red the lower lip looked bee-stung. She was wearing one of those sensible schoolteacher pants suits, khaki-colored, and she had a khaki-colored raincoat hanging over the arm with the keys. She might have been twenty-five or thirty-five or forty-five. Once you got past the makeup she was all epaulets and military bearing, so trim and tidy she was just irresistible. And of course there was that smell about her.

"No, I don't know what you were thinking, G.B. There's no car on East Fifteenth and now I am late for work and out fifteen hundred dollars. Not to mention in for the headache of my life. All of which could have been avoided if you had just put the truck in the garage like I asked you to the first place."

G.B. had reached me down a coffee mug and had been in the process of setting it down on the counter. It was supposed to say *Jesus* ♥s You, but the paint had scraped away until it looked like *Jesus Yo.* With his aunt arrived back from the world of the living, the mug hovered, suspended between cupboard and surface. Should I have rescued it? Should I have offered this harridan a peace mug?

No. She was only getting rolling. "We'll be spending the next three weeks of our life down in that damn good-for-nothing precinct filling out eighty-six thousand forms and I'm gonna have to take a sick day which I can ill afford, all right, don't laugh at me. That was not intentional. I see *you're* up."

She turned on me with those eyelashes fanning the fire. I didn't think she was really waiting for a response.

"Let me get to that phone, y'all, out of the way now, you think Mr. Benedict's gonna like me calling in twenty-two minutes before the start of the schoolday. I don't *think* so."

"Give me the keys, Took."

G.B. meant to hold out his palm for the keys, but he was still holding out the Jesus mug. I scrambled to get out of Queen Took's way, dancing from counter to dinette and back, but there was no clear aisle in the space of that little kitchen. She'd just have to manhandle me to get where she wanted to go.

"What you mean, give you the keys? All I got left of my investment, I'm not handing them over now."

"The Club's on that car, I know it's still out there. Just give me the keys, I'll drive it up to the door."

What a look of disdain and pity. She put the keys in the Jesus mug. I told you she was irresistible.

"All right, Goobie, you just run on out there in the street and make a fool of yourself like I did up and down East Fifteenth. See you run across any of the folks helped me look. Ask them do they think we're *all* blind."

She manhandled me just as I'd hoped she would—put her arm around my shoulder and swiveled me so she could get by, stiff military breasts brushing me. I was weak-kneed. G.B. grabbed up the keys from inside the mug and made his escape out the front door.

Then she made her phone call. The principal on the other end of the line was scared of her too, I'm sure he was. "Thank you, Mr. Benedict," she said. "I'm gonna tear em apart with my bare hands I find em."

She hung up and gave me the once-over. Finally she put the Jesus mug in my hands and said: "Might as well get you that cup of coffee. This is gonna be a *long* day," and manhandled me again, o joy, before she beat her own retreat out into the living room.

Well, what could I do? I was in for the short haul, anyway.

I poured myself a cup of her coffee, and even that smelled perfumed and tidy, womanly, and I made my way out into the living room and stood respectfully by while she sat in the wing chair with her ankles crossed and her face down into her open palm. Finally she looked up and said:

"You all right?"

"I'm just waiting for G.B. to get back. I'm supposed to walk him by—"

"No. I mean are you all *right?* G.B. says you fainted. You better not have brought any drugs into this house."

I summoned all my dignity. "I don't do drugs," I said and then, in an inspired afterthought, added: "And I don't drink." At the moment it was technically true.

She gave me that adorable look of pity and disdain she'd given G.B. and I knew just what she was thinking. Whiteboynerd. "What happened to you, then? Are you *ill?*" O, I loved the way she pursed her lips and her shoulder simultaneously to get that out.

"Yes, I am," I said. "I am ill." And I was. I was sick with longing for her and for Mary Faith and for Bernadette and for my Angela and for Velma. There wasn't going to be enough of me to go around.

"You better get to the doctor, then." She said it absolutely flat, and I said:

"What happened to Etta?"

"I beg your pardon?"

"What happened to your sister Etta that made you worry that was what was wrong with me?"

"Listen, Mr.—"

"Rooney. Tim Rooney."

"Mr. Rooney-Looney, don't you come walking into my house when I just lost my sole means of transportation which happens through no fault of my own bad judgment to be a 1993 Chevy *truck* and ask me what happened to my sister when it is none of your damn business."

"Excuse me."

"And don't you *Excuse me.*" Here she did one of those high mincing voices that a man is supposed to use when denigrating a woman. "You ask the question, you better listen for the answer. What happened to Etta was she passed out in the classroom one day right in the middle of the spelling words and woke up crazy as a jaybird. Schizophrenic. Hearing voices and seeing lights."

Well. I wanted to ask what spelling word this sister was calling when she passed out, but—it was not the moment. Took still sat in her wing chair, but she was bearing down on me nonetheless.

"What happened," she said, "was it took her eighteen months to get well enough to get out the state hospital. My folks had eleven others to worry over. She wasn't back on the farm more'n six months fore she went crazy again. And almost took some of the rest of us with her."

We sat in silence for a while. This was as respectful as I get.

"She was the eldest, Etta. She was the first one graduated college. There was a lot riding on that girl. She was doing fine up to that point. Doing just fine. When she went into the hospital the second time she stayed for good. Second time she hung herself, hanged herself, right there on the locked ward. Just like any crazy nigger. Broke their hearts."

"Excuse me. I beg your pardon." It was like being at a wake. Hard to know just the right thing to say.

"Well, that is what you get when you ask. That is what you get when you ask, you get somebody's sad story, and don't walk into somebody's home asking that kind of personal question you don't want to hear that kind of personal answer."

I did not tell her that I had been a patient in that very same hospital as her sister and that those wards were enough to make anybody hang himself. Or herself. I did not tell her that nowadays they can get you in and out in days: miracle drugs. You don't have to hang around and hang yourself. These days there's no such thing as despair.

She said: "They told my parents it was a *virus*."

"What?"

"Yessir. That's the craziest thing of all. Those doctors thought they were talking to ignorant country colored people. They told my mama not to worry, wasn't anything they did. They said they were right on the verge of discovering what caused that kind of craziness, and they were sure it was going to be a virus."

"Brain fever!" I said.

She shot me a look. "Brain fever, ha. We all knew what made Etta crazy. Trying to be too good. Trying to take care eleven brothers and sisters and go off to college when nobody in the family ever got past the tenth grade before. Trying to be too good. And my parents didn't cut her any slack. No, they didn't. She came back from the hospital and they were still lacing into her. *Quit your moping around. Get out there and do some weeding.* Didn't cut any of us any slack, either, after she killed herself. I'd say they got meaner."

"So you were worried that I was going to wake up crazy too."

"I don't know what I thought," Took said. "I knew I didn't like Goober bringing home a passed-out body to lay on my bed."

Ineffable sadness pressed down on me. "Thank you, though," I said, "for the bed."

She grunted.

"And you a teacher. You trained to be a teacher after she died."

Took looked past me, fierce. The sadness lay heavier than ever. I'm the eldest son! And did anyone feel like following me? Ah no. Quite the opposite. I cause people to swim out to sea.

"You don't look so good," said Took. "Maybe don't drink that coffee."

I knew my mouth was quivering.

"C'mon now," she said. "You feeling faint again? Don't *do* that to me, I got a stolen truck to deal with, can we just get out of the house before you pass out again? You feel good enough to get into a car service?"

But I was saved from the indignity of a car service by G.B., who came into the front door holding the keys aloft and triumphant.

"I knew it!" he said. "It was on East Sixteenth. How come you didn't check Sixteenth?"

Took rose and shook out all her fury. "I didn't check on East Sixteenth because you said East Fifteenth. What you mean putting me through all this?"

G.B. said: "Well, now you can get on off to work anyhow."

"What? When I just got off the phone saying my car is stolen? How you think that looks, showing up in the very truck fifteen minutes later? He'll think I overslept!"

"Tell him the cops got it back."

"First off that's a lie and second off it was the truth he wouldn't believe me anyway. You know anybody in Brooklyn ever got a car back from the police?"

"I don't know anybody in Brooklyn period," G.B. said.

"Well, you're not likely to meet anybody either, the way you're going." And she snatched up the keys to the truck and made ready to leave despite herself.

"Just get him out the house," she said to G.B., right in front of me. This time I was the invisible man. "Just get him on back where he belongs fore he passes out again. Call a car service. Here. Here's twenty dollars."

My heart lifted a little at the thought that I might be worth twenty dollars to get rid of. Took stared at me again and must have satisfied herself that I would make it home. She swept out, raincoat on her arm.

But it was too late.

Maybe it wasn't schizophrenia or manic depression or diabetes or narcolepsy or an acting bug or homosexuality at all that made me this way. Maybe I was just trying to be too good.

DAY SEVENTEEN **UNDER THE BUSHES**

"**W**hy'd we do this?"

That was G.B. speaking. I looked over at Goober in the morning, uncombed and unwashed, and he looked exactly the same as Goober when he's all shined and polished. Those cornrow dreadlock things are very handy for sleeping out of doors. I took a second look and saw he had twigs and acorns and berries adhering to his hair and to his shirt. We had rolled too close together, on a grassy patch under a low hedge. Behind us rose a spiked fence and I saw that we must have climbed the fence and dropped to this little patch below. Only, I don't do that sort of thing.

"Why'd we do this?" I sent his question back to him: that's an old philosophy teacher's trick.

"Cause I didn't wanna face Took and you didn't wanna face Manhattan?"

I was terribly confused. My face was pressed against cold dirt but I sensed the sun shining out bright beyond us. I sensed, too, that if we rose we would be seen, and I had not yet determined where we were or whether it was safe to be seen in this state. I would have thought we'd gone to sleep in a park, but square imposing brick buildings rose all around us. My sinuses were completely blocked: I wished I had some of that wonderful Drixoral: maybe it wasn't schizophrenia, etc., maybe it was an allergic reaction that was causing this brain fever.

Because any doctor would have diagnosed brain fever if he could have seen me, forehead flushed, clothes rumpled and reeking, this incredible blockage across my face. And the cold panic to go with the cold ground. And the weight of sadness Took rested on my chest, like clods of dirt. I might have been in my grave.

"Why you call her Took?" I said. See, another symptom. Flitting from thought to thought, unable to focus, to concentrate, not even the image of that disciplined and sweet-smelling woman enough to bring me back.

"Short for Entuckia."

"Entuckia? What kind of name's that? Kentucky in pig Latin. No, that would be Entuckikay. Entuckia. You're pulling my leg."

"Don't have to be so nasty about it. Don't be so loud, huh? I'm not pulling your leg. Matter of fact you're the one doing something to somebody's leg, and it's my leg. You're pinning it down."

I raised my head enough off my elbow to see that my leg was thrown across G.B.'s large thigh. I couldn't feel a thing. There was no sensation in the leg whatsoever. I jerked it up and off just as fast as I could manage to drag the dead weight. Maybe I couldn't focus, but I sure as hell didn't want to give the wrong impression.

"Brain tumor," I said.

"What?"

"Brain tumor. My leg is sound asleep. The rest of me is full of aches. How else would you explain it? It's not a virus at all, I've got no sensation in my extremities and I can hardly breathe. Listen." And I demonstrated how hard it was to get air through my nose.

G.B. rolled into a fetal ball and chortled away until I thought he might be the one to stop breathing.

"Yeah, well. Right. Just yuck it up about my neurological condition."

"Oh, man. You carry on this way every time you got a hangover?"

Hangover! That explained it. That explained it, including the bottle now making its presence known under my rib, a fifth of Jamesons. An empty fifth. Where had I acquired that? I seemed to be drinking again. That would account for the blackout. Last thing I remembered was Took's backside in her belted safari suit leaving her apartment. On another morning. In Brooklyn.

"Brooklyn." I didn't know I was going to say it.

"Yeah," G.B. said, "and keep your voice down. They's folks going to and fro, they got Saturday classes. I don't want some guard arresting me for being homeless or something, then I can't ever get to school."

"Brooklyn College."

"Shit, man. Are you with me?"

"With you . . . where?"

"Shit. You remember anything?"

Had to be brain fever. What I remembered was so incongruous, my father's bed, my leg across my father's middle. My mother lifts me up, pressing me against her big breasts, her nightgown sheer and pink. My father: "Let him stay," in his sleep. My mother ignores him, carries me back to my own bed, where I am once again filled with cold panic.

"You remember tag team poetry? Those white boys from Brooklyn College? You remember the bar? The Junction?"

I remembered riding my father's shoulders at the beach. A school of porpoises swims along the horizon, black knives in the water. Dottie in the waves. Dottie can't breathe. She is a baby choking with croup, and I run her outside the house so she can breathe in the cool night air.

"You with me, man? You OK, Mr. Rooney?"

I was crying again. I knew it from the heat of my tears down my cheeks. "I'm allergic to everything!" I said. "Damn it, this has gone too far. I sleep outside one night, one lousy night, and I can't breathe and my eyes are stinging like nobody's business."

"Ought to get you shots. Listen man, we got to get you to the doctor. Maybe after we dry out. Look. We go over to Took's, she'll be at exercise class, what you say we take a shower, then get you on the train back to your folks. They'll be worried about you too, your friends. Gone two nights."

How did he know I had friends? You could hardly call them friends. "My father used to beat me," I said.

"I don't think it's allergies," G.B. said.

"Don't you tell me what my symptoms indicate."

"Listen, Mr. Rooney, keep your voice down. It wouldn't do, somebody finding us here, look like, you know. . . ."

"And I cannot be in his presence, I mean not so much his voice on the phone, without my nerve endings singing the Hallelujah Chorus. But he is not cold-blooded. You can't accuse him of that. He's a warm guy, you might say he's warm when he's not hot. Hotheaded."

"Listen, Mr. Rooney, you're starting to scare me some. Look, my father beat me too. You know any man didn't take a whupping from his father? But you don't have to go off the deep *end* about it."

O G.B. He made me laugh: I mean literally.

"Mr. Rooney? You pulling my leg this time?"

I reached down and pulled his leg, heavy as a piece of timber.

"Oh man, you had me going for a minute there. I'm not kidding about the doctor, though, you just don't look right."

"Am I not making any sense?"

"No. That's just the thing. Most of the time you make perfect sense. I mean, hey man, I was proud to be sitting on the bar stool next to you last night. I thought to myself, *I'm on the right track. I did the right thing, coming after this man.* Tag team poetry. What's that one you did?

"Quit that fear and trembling, Søren.
Don't you know right now it's more'n
I can bear."

The porpoises were diving back. I had controlled my drinking all these months, and then I found another young man who asked me to be his father.

"I'm just not up to it," I said. "I'm sorry, I have a manuscript to finish, and three articles to get out. It's just I have so much on my plate already. Really I do."

"Yeah." He sat up and started brushing his shirt, one eye out for passersby.

"I didn't mean to hurt your feelings."

"Yeah."

"Now. G.B. Listen to you. Sulking like that. Listen to yourself. We'll stay in touch."

"Mr. Rooney, you are losing it. Come on back to Took's and take a shower. Get you some warm food."

"Did you say it was Saturday?"

"Listen, we can take you to Took's doctor. She's got some kind of health plan."

"Saturday. I'm going out dancing tonight. With Angela."

G.B. was hardly listening to me. He was checking out the grounds, eyes darting this way and back, looking as if he'd die to be caught here, under the bushes, with me. It was first light, early dawn, and Brooklyn College was deserted. What was he talking about, people going to and fro? I didn't see a soul. I could slip on the subway and back into Manhattan without anybody being the wiser. I could creep through the streets of SoHo, and Velma would buzz me in. I would shower and present myself to Angela sane and ready to dance.

God! A hangover is a terrible thing! For a minute there I thought I was losing it too.

"You can't get on the subway by yourself," G.B. said.

"You can't appoint yourself my guardian angel."

And I rose up quick before he could see my allergies acting up again and my doubts coming back thicker than the cloud of pollen that rained down from the trees. I thought he would come after me, but he was no angel. I stumbled in a circle through Brooklyn College, looking for the street, but they had locked us in. Brooklyn College looked like any leafy campus, and I lost my bearings. I climbed a walkway over the street and, reaching the middle of it, panicked. I leaped to the pavement below and thought at first that I might have cracked both ankles.

But no. The Jamesons still padded me. I might have cracked the sores on my feet open, but I could still walk. I could still walk to the source of more alcohol. That would brace me up. On my left I passed William James Hall, and I knew that I was on the right path.

DAY EIGHTEEN OFF THE WAGON AND CURED

I bought a can of malt liquor, the only alcoholic beverage available, from the only store that was open in Brooklyn at the crack of dawn on a Saturday morning. With the malt liquor in me, I found the subway station and rode the train without passing out. I didn't exactly remember the way home—I had to go up to the Bronx and then back down—but I was almost there. And the first can tasted so good, I bought another one in Manhattan. By then it was eight A.M. With two malt liquors in me, I was stabilized.

By the time I got to Spring Street I was thirsty again, so I bought champagne and orange juice and a dozen red roses, and when Velma rang me in I kissed her on both cheeks, pressed the roses into her plump hands, and said:

"I made it to the final cut."

"Tim?" She was wearing her bunched-up nightie again, and I could see a film across her eyes that matched the film across her breasts.

"It's down to just the two of us," I said. "For the role. Sorry I couldn't call. Sidney had me working with a dancing coach. Then he made me sleep outside to see what it was like. Where's Angela? How about some griddlecakes and mimosas?"

She yawned, but she was smiling. Smiling and maybe blushing a little. Happy to see me. "Good God, Tim, it's the middle of the night. We thought you'd been mugged on the street. We thought your body was lying unclaimed in the city morgue. I called the city morgue, matter of fact." She yawned again, smiled again, walked down the hall back to her mirrored boudoir. Waddled, really, but I didn't care. I was home, back where people called the morgue to check up on me.

I had to drink mimosas by myself until the two of them got out of bed sometime in the midday. I drank all that Saturday, and by midnight it was clear what had been wrong with me in Due East and on the highway and in New York those first days. I had been suffering from a delayed case of delirium tremens. My body needed the alcohol to achieve its normal metabolism, to stabilize. Once I started drinking again, I was as stable as Vatican City. I was coherent. I was not seeing or hearing anything. I knew what was real. I was ready to forgive my father, but I was so on top of things that I knew not to call him. He could track me down. I wouldn't put it past him.

"OK, Angela," I said. "Listen to that. The clock strikes twelve. It's time to go dancing."

And the dancing bears on a little china clock did their pirouettes somewhere deep in the Spring Street loft. We were sitting in the kitchen, the three of us. I had mixed us up gimlets before dinner and then ran out and got a couple of good bottles of Graves for the meal. Not that I could remember the meal. I could remember the Graves, though. At this rate, I'd run through my fifteen thousand in no time. I told you this was an expensive town. Now we were working on Rémy Martin. The only thing I could carp on about the Rémy was that it made Velma close those beautiful eyes of hers, right at the table, right over the crème aux marrons she'd whipped up for my homecoming. One fist clutched her gooey fork and the other curled around the stem of her glass.

Angela pouted. She was flirting. She pouted again, and I said:

"Come on. One week. Time to go dancing. Didn't you say . . . ?"

Angela tilted her head with a smile to indicate her pleasure at my progress and, at the same time, her distress that we had to baby-sit for Velma. But of course I meant for Velma to come. Of course my intention was that the three of us do the town. And after . . . we'd see.

"Vel-ma," I whispered. It's a wonderful thing, when your personality reintegrates, how utterly yourself you become, how right it feels to whisper an unattractive woman's name and convince her, in the space of those two syllables, that she is the most irresistible creature on earth.

She blinked her eyes open at me. And was that a flicker of annoyance in Angela's eyes, sitting beside her?

"Come on, Velma," I said. "We're going dancing."

She closed her heavy lids. They were painted black. "Oh no," she said, but with my newly reintegrated personality I knew she meant for me to beg her. And I did.

"Come on, darlin," I said—see how I slipped that *darlin* in?—"come on with us. We're going to . . . where're we going, Angela?" I had in mind the Rainbow Room, tuxes and froufrou dresses. Surely the absent Fred had a tux hanging in his mirrored closet.

Angela said: "Do we want elegant, like nightclub, or funky?"

"Elegant," I said.

"Funky," Velma said, with closed lids, and Angela made a face. Velma managed to hold her eyes open and dip them my way. "Fred and his friends used to hang out at Intergalactica's for a hoot." Her fleshy lips, the lipstick worn off by the meal, pursed. "Course now they're hanging out at Ramrods and Stick the Whip Up Your Butt."

Angela rose to massage Velma's shoulders and offer her sympathy, but Velma would have none of it. She was awake, suddenly. She sat up straight and shrugged Angela off, her silky blouse billowing over her voluminous breasts, and she said:

"And why the hell not? Why shouldn't I go over to Intergalactica's and throw bottles on the floor if I want?"

Bottles on the floor wasn't exactly what I'd had in mind, but Velma's fury was convincing, and I was feeling so *right*, so back to myself, so back to normal, so sure that on Monday I really would get to the bank and wire Mary Faith some money, and call NYU to track down Bernadette and give her my regards after all these years, and maybe take Took and G.B. out to a good meal if they could steer me to one in Brooklyn, that I said:

"Intergalactica's it is!" And then looked down at my khaki pants which Velma had so kindly washed and pressed for me and knew before I even saw the place that I was dressed all wrong.

We took a cab over to the Bowery. The streets got darker the closer they got to the sound of that name, but even the mean streets, even the bums, even the guys wanting to wash your windshield couldn't get me down.

"Just think," I said in the back of the cab. "Last night I was sleeping in Brooklyn. Under a bush." It was gratifying to tell the truth that way.

"Oh my God," Velma said. "They had you do it in *Brooklyn?* Is that where they're shooting? Tim, I love you dearly, but if you get the part, this is one set I don't think I have any interest in visiting. I've never been to Brooklyn. I don't know anybody's ever been to Brooklyn."

"I've been in Brooklyn," Angela said. "I had a friend at Vassar lived in Brooklyn Heights. It was *nice.*"

"I live in Brooklyn," the cabdriver said.

We were all quiet, the implications of that settling in on us. Velma broke the silence. "Well, where do you *shop?*" she said.

The cabdriver winked at her in the rearview. "They have stores in Brooklyn," he said. He was small and brown and wiry, Indian or Pakistani, maybe. I wondered if he could be the man who killed the bat on the subway. He had the same aggressive posture, even sitting down.

He pulled up to the curb and I paid him from my shoe, scared to look him in the eye. When I reached a hundred-dollar bill from my sock, Velma said:

"That is so *cute.*" All my blisters had hardened into carbuncles.

Angela rolled her eyes. "Don't egg him on, Vel. He's gonna get hit over the head he carries his money like that. They can tell us coming twenty blocks away." Us meaning Southerners, me in my prof pants, Velma in her silk blouse and, I hate to say this, black tights—I believe they're called leggings. You can only imagine how all wrong they were on her. But they made me love her more, that she should . . . perse*vere* that way. Angela was the only one of us who might have passed, chic in a short little white dress that covered those broad shoulders and muscular arms of hers, her hair a shiny cellophane cap. O I was a lucky man. I had Michelle and Mama Cass both.

I took them both on an arm to cross the Bowery and they squealed, really they did. That's kind of a Southern thing too—except that Mary Faith would never squeal. I missed her. Utterly. In the middle of the street, in the middle of the Bowery, with two squealing women on my arms. Mary Faith didn't dance. She didn't spend money on champagne and Rémy and cabs. She didn't like music especially, unless it was Jesse playing it. I knew I was sane, I knew I was reintegrated, when I remembered her solemn self so clearly. I felt she stood before me. I felt I could reach out and stroke her cheeks under those sad gray eyes.

"C'mon, Tim." That was Angela, tugging.

There was a gaggle of children—what else could you call them?—all lined up on the sidewalk around this place, this Intergalactica's. I had a little moment of disorientation at the sight of them. They all appeared to come from another era, from the era of *my* youth, with their torn jeans and their black peace symbols on white T-shirts, with their wispy goatees and mustaches, their bobbing braless breasts. How'd they all get here? Intergalactica's. Teleportation.

"C'mon."

I thought at first that it was one of those places with a line out front where they look you over, but no: it came to me that all these children lined up outside Intergalactica's really were children, too young to get in. I thought they might bar the door to me too. Too old to get in.

They didn't bar the door, but then I was with Angela. She breezed in first, down a single step, and Velma and I squeezed in behind, into the dark and cavernous space. We entered a huge concrete room at street level, the kind where you might expect a barn dance. This was no barn dance. This was stepping from the first circle to the second. Strange violent murals painted on the cinder block, boys in leather holding knives and hand grenades. Black lights, drug-crazed faces. A mental ward was nothing compared to this. I didn't know why Velma thought we could go dancing here: there was no music, no conversation either, only smoke and a nasty baited silence.

Angela pushed forward into the crowd and then stood with her hands on her hips, cracking her gum. Where'd she get gum? She had one hip thrust forward, in one of those sexual-aggressive stances women sometimes don't even seem to know they're pulling. Velma's hand was in mine. I must have grabbed it, to pull her through this press of sullen bodies.

Angela troubled to take one hand off her hip to point out the bar, meaning that I should go fetch us all something, and I saw that she was still pouting. Pouting at me. For holding Velma's hand. It made me squeeze Velma a little tighter before I left them. I couldn't help it. I was feeling sane.

It took me three or four minutes to push my way through. Pipes hanging down, industrial lighting. Tough guys in sleeveless T-shirts, cigarettes hanging out their mouths. Dudes in loose black shirts buttoned up their Adam's apples.

One sip of my cognac and I felt better. I had one sip of everybody's, just to even things out. And to ease this anxiety coming on. Probably I had not been watching my alcohol intake to insure its smooth and even absorption by my body. It's just like a drip in the hospital: it has to be scientifically measured.

On my way back to my waiting women I saw the reason for the silence in this hall: the band, or their flunkies at the moment, were setting up onstage. I could relate. The Daydreamers—remember?—when I was fourteen. I played guitar and portable piano and the first electric violin anybody in Due East, South Carolina, had ever dreamed of. This was at Due East High School. We played the cafeteria, which was also a big cavernous space done up in cinder-block construction, though you couldn't call it as threatening as this place. Actually, we played one dance. And the talent show, the one for which I had no guitar, since it had been broken over my head. Anyway, the Daydreamers never made it big in Due East. I liked Chuck Berry, the Shirelles. The rest of the Daydreamers liked the Chad Mitchell Trio and the Limelighters. It was hard to get a coherent sound out of us. The other guys were juniors too, but I had skipped a couple of grades and trailed them by a couple of years. I hardly had hair under my arms. The rest of the Daydreamers wore loafers. They found me amusing sometimes. Every once in a while. They only let me try the electric violin once, at practice, even though I'd gone all the way to Savannah for the pickup. They didn't let me sing, either, though I have a tenor almost as honeyed as G. B. Brights's, and I can produce a bellowing bass at will. They made me go out and buy a pair of loafers, which just about broke my heart. I always suspected that Father Berkeley called somebody's mother and that was how I got to be in the band. I had a little wisp of hair over my lip, and when the rest of the Daydreamers were feeling warm and expansive they would tug on it.

Male bonding. I may be sounding a little whiny here, high school misfit, all that. I got over it. I'm sure I did.

Now I was bonding with females. Angela gave me another cool pout, but Velma snuggled close when I was back with the cognacs.

"Who's playing?" I asked.

Angela shrugged. Velma said: "The Walking Wounded, I think. Leastaways, that's what somebody in the little girls' room said."

Velma looked more incongruous than ever in the purple light, her cornrows straggling. G.B.'s stayed so neat. White people shouldn't do cornrows. I'd have to talk to her about that, about saying *little girls' room*. No I wouldn't. I knew better. You don't call women on things like that. I found I couldn't stop staring at her, though, the deep shiny rose of her blouse turned the color of blood in this dark space. Her nose was enormously broad, and though she'd repainted her mouth it was chipping away again. Angela watched me watching her with unmasked contempt.

But Velma was pleased as punch. "Tim! Quit looking at me! Is my blouse unbuttoned?"

"Not yet." Did I really say that? "No it's not. You . . ." I was about to say, *You remind me of me, back when I had that wisp of hair over my lip,* but that would never do. For one thing, Velma had a wisp of hair over her lip, a dark one, and she would think I was being literal.

"What? I what?"

"You look like a woman who needs to dance. Is this a dancing band?"

By now Angela was seething, scowling, curdling. She proceeded to turn her back on the two of us. But just in the nick of time, to save me from my dear angel's scorn, the band itself, the Walking Wounded if that's who they were, meandered onstage one at a time. I liked the look of them, myself. They all looked wasted away, and under his T-shirt the bass player had tracks on his arms. The tracks of my tears. If only I'd had the courage to really get into drugs, instead of fiddling every now and again with acid. Acid, pffff. These guys had the right idea. Tracks. Needle full of gasoline. Uh-oh. I swallowed the rest of that cognac just as fast as I could, but I could still taste the fumes. This was one of those moments when it was going, quickly. No closed throat, no blackouts: I was skipping the preliminaries. Just the sensation that right outside my field of vision there were flames licking, shadows that couldn't be explained. Just sounds merging so it wasn't entirely clear what direction they were coming from, and who was talking about me. They were all talking about me.

I wouldn't let it happen. Wouldn't.

"Ladies?" I held out my empty glass to the gals to indicate I was on my way for another. I was absolutely on top of this.

Angela said: "I never saw somebody put away so much in the space of a day. Are you all right?"

To prove I was, to prove it to myself, to prove the D-D-D-D-D was the sound of the guitar tuning up and not my own musical imagination, I pulled my arms high in the air and walked a straight line. I refused to hear any sounds that were not there. I was all right.

And a strange thing happened as I walked the straight and narrow. I felt my knees buckle slightly, elegantly. I clapped my hands and my glass over my head: a smarmy Mediterranean gesture. Not the sort of thing I do. Have ever done. It turned the walk into a Greek dance, a Zorba-Anthony Quinn thing. Well, all right. I was an actor, wasn't I? A real man, whatever the Daydreamers thought?

A miracle happened. The dense crowds parted for my performance. It was not what they were used to seeing at Intergalactica's. The band was still tuning up. They were extremely loud. I was still dancing. Knees bobbing, hands clapping. The money in my sock scraped up against my feet, violently. It provoked me. Sexually, I mean. The band was now tuning up to my dancing, following my lead. I'm not a dancer, usually. Bernadette and I didn't even dance at our wedding. Tell you the truth, I like to watch a woman move. I don't like to strut my own stuff.

But now I was strutting it. The lead guitar was doing a slow twang, a bluesy kind of prolonged Albert King bit that he shifted into feedback-Hendrix. You'd think it would be hard to dance to Hendrix, but it wasn't hard at all. You keep those hands over your head, you keep your balance. You're seeing nothing on the periphery of your vision. You're feeling your calves stretching and your shoulders dipping and your butt twitching the way Fred knew how to do it. And here came the women after me, throwing themselves in their skinny little dresses at my aging body.

Here was one in particular, right on the edge of the throng, in one of those black satiny slip-y things and a skirt so short I could have slipped my hand right up, if I'd wanted to. The thing was, I wanted to. Even as I danced with my hands over my head, I wanted one of those hands, both of those hands, right up that skirt. I burned with fury. If she didn't want a hand up the skirt, why'd she wear it? Why'd she dance with me that way, tits grinding on—excuse me, I guess I'm supposed to say *breasts*, I guess I'm not supposed to suggest any compliance on her part until she fills out the form that says *Yes, I want you to stick your hand up my skirt* and has it notarized. She must've been about twelve. Ten. She had green hair and maroon lips. She came up to my belt buckle.

My anger burned so high it might have been coming from above. Actually, it was coming from above. That was the warm glow of a spotlight shining down on me and this . . . child. But the panic was gone. I was not going to have a breakdown in Intergalactica's. I was not going to have a breakdown at all.

And with that foreknowledge, clear as a prophet's, my body stopped dancing: that is, it continued to move, but it stopped its spontaneous gyrations. I could feel my elbows again, and my creaking knees. I was fourteen again, only I was a doddering middle-aged man. I was one of the Daydreamers, and the real band was onstage. The spotlight shone down, but I couldn't feel the heat. All four limbs moved separately. I—musician, composer—couldn't find the beat. Had I been *clapping my hands* over my head?

I came to my physical senses not a moment too soon, because now there really was a vision at the edge of my sight: just outside the pool of spotlight stood Velma and Angela, united now, shoulder to shoulder, gesticulating. *Quit it, Tim. Stop acting so goofy, Tim.* Like my little sister Katie, embarrassed that I should be her big brother. If my limbs had been functioning in unison, I would have defied them.

But my limbs were not functioning in unison. They had broken down. The music had broken down: I could hear it one note at a time, and then I could hear the note spray out, mist from the droplet. I was not having a breakdown, but everything was disintegrating around me. I turned away from the fright-child in the green hair and back to the women who waited for me.

"Tim," Angela said. "I think we've bout had enough for one night."

O! Glorious sanity! She was speaking to me, and though there was background noise, I heard nothing else.

"You mean you think I've had enough for one night," I said. I was

OK. Really I was. I was talking and everything. Out on the street I had missed Mary Faith. Now I wanted her: all of her, talk solemnity long white narrow frame guilt duty, all of her. I was out of the spotlight, but now it shone down. That was why I left Due East. Wasn't it? So she wouldn't see this happen? So Jesse wouldn't? Some animals go away to die. Some people go away to crack up.

But I wasn't cracking up. This time I had kept it at bay.

"Tim," Velma said, and I heard her call me in the very same voice I had used to call her at the dinner table. She even turned my name into two syllables. "Ti-im."

"What?"

We were shouting by now. Shouting over background noise, but all the sounds were real. The Walking Wounded was screaming something a capella that sounded like *Why don't you pull the trigger, baby? Why don't you just pull?* Pretty good lyrics.

"Come on home and let me put you to bed." Velma said *bay-ud.*

Angela glared. O, if you could bottle that jealous rage. Bottle it and then spread it out over the two of them, a glistening oil. O, if we could all console each other for all the ways we had been betrayed and stand here all night knowing we weren't hearing things.

Let me tell you about Catholic guilt and sanity.

The alcohol and the near miss of total crackup made me as clear-eyed as I get. I needed some relief, somewhere. So when my two angels brought me back to the loft that night, supporting me by either elbow as if I were a wounded soldier, and Velma said, "I'm gonna have to put you to bed, hon," I let a bleak smile lounge on my mouth. Anything you say. I thought Angela would be right behind us. Meanwhile I slurred my words to get all the nursing I could squeeze from Velma: "Velma, my shishter. . . ."

"Your sister what, Tim?" She led me into my little cell and laid me out on my bed—all right, her bed—and she ran her chubby palm over my forehead. Nurse. Mother. Etc. My own mother was never big on the physical stuff. This was ecstasy. This was enough. Angela was in the cell right next door: we both knew it.

I opened my eyes. Velma was leaning over me with that dark wisp of hair over her gray lip. "Let me get that shirt, off, hon," she said, and I moved my shoulders just enough to ease her struggle. Mostly, though, I was dead weight, a victim of her ministering.

I kept my eyes closed while she unbuckled my belt and slid my pants down my legs. But when she got to "Let me pull that underwear down for you," in a stage whisper through the lips I knew were gray and mustached, I pretended to pass out. Pretended: what rich irony, after all these lapses of consciousness. Because as she tugged away at those dingy Jockey shorts that have seen me from Due East to New York, as she pulled them down, down, down, past my knees, past my ankles, I knew I couldn't get it up for her. Not for those rolls of . . . flesh. My poor uglies, the only consolation she needed, were left shrunken and exposed. I could have given her that moment of mercy, that small act that would have cost me so little but would have steeled her against Fred's rejection. But I had lost my will, and I wasn't even ashamed. I didn't want her. I lay there with my eyes closed, pretending to be unconscious, attempting to make my very toenails droop, all the while praying that she would just hurry up and get the message and tiptoe on out of there. Making room for Angela, who waited next door.

She took her time, though. She seemed to need total rejection.

She kneeled at the side of my bed—all right, her bed—and bent over to kiss me, up the length of my bony shin, my bony thigh. I felt a terrible pity for her, but my cock felt none, and stayed as soft and gray as those lips of hers pressed against it. And I breathed deeply, the way children and skunks do when they're playing at sleep, until she gave up and draped the sheet over me. Like a corpse.

A guilty corpse. *Come back,* I almost said. *I could try harder.* But I didn't. She drifted off without a word and I waited in my bed, perfectly awake, perfectly conscious, for Angela to appear.

I knew she would. I knew her all along, I had a handle on her from the moment I spied her on the side of the road. Five minutes after Velma left me Angela tiptoed in past the white screen in one of her ubiquitous misleading white T-shirts and whispered my name. I could hear the jealousy floating through her breath and I knew she'd listened to Velma's ministering. Had waited for Velma to leave me, naked under the sheet.

I called her to me in my bed: "Come over here," I said.

She didn't wait a modest second but was at my side of my bed in a flash. "Tim, are you all right?"

Was I all right? I was awake, I was alive, I was not going to have a breakdown. This limp dick of mine had sprung to life. This time I was real and she was real and this was it. This is what we live for. This is what my wildly successful generation has been handed, on a platter, like John the Baptist's head. Endless free uncomplicated lust and instant gratification. Even in the dark I could see Angela's muscled thighs under the T-shirt, and o I wanted those thighs to squeeze around me, I wanted to taste her and drink her in the way I had the alcohol; it wasn't drink I needed, any fool could see.

Now she leaned over my bed—all right, Velma's bed—and hovered in that sexual aggressive pose, one hand on her hip. I reached up my hand just as I had wanted to do in Intergalactica's and felt that underneath that T-shirt her belly was flat and then down, down: wet soft sinking. Mud. Swamp.

I reached up and pulled her down onto the bed. She rolled atop me, the sheet that Velma had draped over me between us. She straddled me in that practiced aggressive way I knew from the moment she thumbed me down on the side of the road and she took her index finger and put it in my mouth and it smelled of her, I was her slave, I took it in and ran my tongue around it and heard myself moan, helpless as any man with a woman on top.

She kissed my eyelids and my ears, she shifted her muscular body atop mine, she pressed her lips against mine and tasted her own finger. Then she drew her hand out of my mouth and down, to stroke me through the sheet, the sheet with which I wanted to tie her up, the sheet which Velma had drawn up over me, the sheet which made me a corpse and I saw nothing and for a moment felt nothing but only heard a sound knelling, behind me and above me and through me: and I lost it and couldn't get it up again. Not even for Angela, angel, object of my lust, not when I was newly reintegrated, but she floated in separate terrifying pieces all around me.

The guilt theory for Catholic males: Your mind is too puny an object to understand that you don't want to do what you're about to do. So grace enters another organ and renders it useless. Your body takes over and stops you from yourself.

Only I wasn't a Catholic anymore. I had to develop a different theory of impotence, a crazy man's theory. Mental illness slows you down, sexually speaking. My sexual fantasies, when I'm on the edge, are terrifying. Like suicide, rape is not in my repertoire of breakdown acts. But just before, I often feel I could hurt someone. Someone could hurt me. Priests and small boys. Large women with terrifying teeth. Decrepit flesh. Death.

Often it's just that word, tolling through my head: death, death, death. Dong, dong, dong. And that is right and just: if something's going to undo me, it should be a sound. When I have no control over the notes I am hearing, when someone else is singing the tunes, then I know finally and absolutely that I have lost my mind.

We all slept through the day and woke at evening to an ordinary sad soundless displaced moment. Disorientation, hangover, lingering female scents on my bed sheets: normalcy. Back from the realm of the almost mad to the realm of the profoundly unhappy. I had come very close this time to going crazy.

I lay in the darkening room, evening already closing in on the city outside. I listened to Angela and Velma moving about the loft. The sadness that Took had pressed on me in Brooklyn weighed heavy. I knew, as I had known all those times past, that I was coming out of it.

I had taken a new route this time. This time, I had not subjected everyone to my crackup. No more Dottie swimming out to sea. This time, I had fled my family. I had saved Mary Faith and Jesse from myself. From what I am capable of.

Lying in a rich woman's bed, I knew I could never go back, not to the Church, not to my lover, not to the boy who was going to be my son. Even as I regained control of my actions—even as I lay in bed trembling with indignity and shame at the image of who I'd been these last weeks (a doofus! a faithless ordinary man!)—I knew the breakdown had, in fact, been my mind's limp dick, my mind's refusal to stay in a Church when I no longer believed, to be a father when I could only harm the son.

Outside my cell, I heard the two women laughing together.

The first time I went utterly and completely over the edge, that Christmas I peed in Our Lady of Perpetual Help, the whole family dragged in when they heard about the desecration, but it was my little sister Katie who kept watch. She wasn't so little anymore, she was a good-looking redheaded actress living in New York. My father and Dottie were in hysterics. Father Berkeley advised them to consult a Jesuit psychiatrist. My brother Andy advised them to get a court order. My sister Maggie, the ex-nun, advised me to straighten up and fly right.

Katie stood watch. She wouldn't let them commit me. She waited for a sane moment and drove me to the hospital and struck a pose while I signed the papers. I worried that she stayed with me in that sad house that Christmas, keeping watch, because once, when I was about to put a needle in my arm, she took the time to stuff the *Cosmopolitan* out of sight before she ran to get my mother. Catholic guilt.

The air was gray and heavy, even inside the loft. It was hard to breathe, now that I'd moved out of lunacy and into depression. Lunacy was preferable. Much more pleasurable. But I had sweated it out, avoided their pills, stumbled back into sanity.

And now I only had to crawl into a new life for myself.

It was after midnight when I was able to rise and make my way to the kitchen. I only wanted water, to ease the swelling in my head. Only a hangover, I knew now. Not brain fever. Only the damage I'd inflicted on myself.

Angela and Velma sat at the table, fluffy in short skirts, their hair gooed in Velma's case (to get those cornrows to behave) and slicked in Angela's (to make her more severe). She looked pretty severe to me anyway, smiling in that cold and distant chlorinated way. I knew from the way they smiled at each other with their eyes, these women, that they'd had a heart-to-heart and exchanged their own limp-dick theories. Sane, I had a new vision of who I was to them: a pet, a child, a needy man they could mother. They would both try to sleep with me again. I knew they would.

"Well, well," Angela said. "Welcome to the world of the living."

"Tim." Velma could see the slump of my shoulders at the sink. I could barely move through the room, much less turn the expensive fixture they called a faucet. Where was the cold? The silver stick went round and round. "Tim. Get you some mineral water from the fridge. Don't drink that icky tap stuff."

See? Before the night was out, they'd try to sleep with me again. My sadness was going a little . . . jittery.

"We're just going out," Angela said. "Want to get dressed and come?"

I stood drinking the tap water and thought I could talk again. I didn't want to go out. "What time . . ."

That was as far as I could get. But when you have women ministering to you, women who have already deluded themselves that you are a trustworthy man, you don't need to go any further.

"It's going on twelve-thirty. We promised to meet somebody over at the Lion's Head." The Lion's Head! That's where everybody from the South ends up to look for literary lights in the big city. O, it made my head ache and my knees go weak. I took Bernadette to the Lion's Head when we were innocent grad students looking for innocent kicks. In its heyday of extravagant loudmouth drunks. We pretended once that we saw Brendan Behan there, on his last legs, but it was just a fat drunk from the neighborhood.

Angela nodded to Velma: some signal they had going between them. "We're just going to hop in a cab."

I shook my head, as far as I could shake it. Not very hard. I was hardly there at all.

"Oh come on Tim." That was Angela. You could hear the disdain in her voice. I hadn't performed up to expectations. I hadn't performed at all. "You're in New York City. You can't stay here all alone all the time. You'll go out of your mind!"

She had a point.

It was a two-minute cab ride to the Lion's Head. We rode up Sixth Avenue and, in my sanity, I saw all the places where I had courted Bernadette: Carmine Street (zeppoles at the feast), the Waverly (French movies), St. Joseph's (hip liturgy). The rage I had felt for her when I was so close to the edge had disappeared. We'd just been kids. The kind of kids who flock to Manhattan, all of us misfits in high school, all of us too smart or too weird or too miserable. I had no anger left for her. I would have left me, myself.

The cab wound across Waverly and looped over to Christopher. How wise Angela was in her disdain. How good to get me out of the house. We pulled up to the Lion's Head and I could have wept with nostalgia. I paid the driver from my sock and nearly sprang out behind Velma and Angela. O home of my youth. The round red awning, the four steps down. I could see already the dark dingy bar, the television blaring. There'd be two or three depressed souls there facing the framed jackets. In the back room there'd be a drip in the ceiling.

Velma was already descending, but Angela waited on the sidewalk for me. I fairly bounced to get in, but she put out a warning hand. Velma, at the door, waved a sheepish good-bye and disappeared inside.

"Wha—" I might be sane, but I was still something of a cartoon character.

"She's meeting Fred."

"You said—"

"Well, I wanted to get you out of the house. She's meeting Fred. He wants to patch things up. Come on, let's walk around. I promised we wouldn't go too far in case . . ."

"In case he brings a boyfriend?"

Angela made a funny face I couldn't read and we began to walk Christopher Street in our desultory South Carolina fashion. The graceful stone and brick buildings, great and small, still rose up the same; but the shopfronts were different from the ones I remembered: in those days the windows said LOVE BEADS. Now they said TANNING, HAIR, LEATHER. Boys boys boys. I'm just an ordinary man with all the ordinary prejudices. We passed the Stonewall's glass facade, a picture window to look in on. I cheered them on at the Stonewall, I'm just . . . conflicted. I pictured Velma inside the Lion's Head with Fred, ready to write him out another check if only he'd stop by the loft at night. And meanwhile he'd be cruising these streets, following these good-looking guys in their tight jeans, half of them doomed to disease and death, the other half to a perfect physicality: bulging biceps, tight asses, expensive haircuts, good shoes. O I'm just an ordinary threatened man. I realized how much I liked Velma, how delicate her kisses had been the night before. Some women have so much grace on the inside that there's none left to decorate the facade.

We crossed the square and turned onto Waverly. At Gay Street Angela turned us again, but silently, looking up that curving alleyway at the brick dollhouses like the tourist she was. She was up to something. When we'd reached the end of the block she headed us back toward the Lion's Head. Martyrs to the mouth of the beast.

"Don't want us to go too far."

"All right," I said, "but when we get back do we get to go in and have a drink at least?" I was ready to admit my alcoholism! But I could only take on one fight at a time. And keeping my sanity around Angela was getting tricky. She was . . . up to something. I was sure she was.

"No," she said, "we can't go in and have a drink and ruin everything." She was worse than sulky. She was edgy. My heart sank. She wasn't even flirting.

We walked back along Christopher, until she said:

"Tim, who else do you know in New York?"

That stopped me on the sidewalk. I was being asked to pack my bags. "I've got an ex-wife here somewhere," I said. "That's it, I guess." *That's it.* No mentors, no old pals from grad school I could call on. Even in philosophy, they're wary once you get a religious bug. And I had Bernadette to pine for all those early years, and then I never made it past a three-year appointment. I didn't do the conferences. I hadn't kept in touch. I wondered if Angela was trying to draw me a therapeutic picture: man in isolation.

"Don't worry," I said. "I've been meaning to move out to a hotel anyway."

"You don't have to move out. Velma's crazy bout you. I mean do you know anybody I could stay with?"

"I thought you had friends all over the place!"

In the streetlight her face looked almost as green as her chlorinated hair. She was ill, I thought.

"I do, but they're all living with somebody or they got studios that aren't big enough or they're out in Long Island City or Hoboken, wherever they are, and I don't mean to find out. Oh, I know I'm just gonna end up going back. Back to Briggs. They'll make us have a little wedding. Just the families. To punish me for running out on the caterers. Oh shit."

I put my arm around her shoulders—just a sympathetic reflexive gesture, I assure you—and felt her shrink beneath my touch the way I'd shrunk beneath hers the night before. Tit for tat and shrink shrank shrunk. Still. I had a creepy feeling.

"Don't you think Velma might need you," I said, "even if she does take Fred back? Especially if she takes Fred back?"

She didn't answer. She sucked on the same finger she'd stuck in my mouth the night before. I didn't like her. It descended on me, all of a sudden. I didn't like her. Didn't dislike her all that much, just didn't . . . trust her.

"Did Fred make that up about—boys?"

She looked at me with distaste.

"Well, duh," she said. That's another of Jesse's favorite expressions. My chest began to cave in.

"Fred's not gay?"

"Did you think he was?"

The fact is, he had a certain charm in those black jeans. "But why would you make a thing like that up? Unless. Unless Velma suspected him of something."

She gave me a bored look. "He said the first thing came into his mind. I told him it was very revealing."

"It is, too."

The bored look turned vaguely resentful. "Well, tonight, he's going to say he never really acted on it, it's just something that bothered him, you know, like an identity crisis. He thought he'd look around but he didn't ever really sleep with any guys. And that'll be true. I hope."

I must have looked about eleven years old, staring up at her.

"Well, look, Tim. He's got to go back to her. He'd never survive here without Velma. It's not like he doesn't like her."

"I like her too! I like her more than I can say. She's so . . . ingenu-ous. She's just spilling out of herself." A sorrow, like my sister Kate, age fifteen. "It was you," I said.

Angela gave me a look of withering pity.

"You slept with him while you were a guest in their house."

"Oh, sorry, Mr. Manners," she said. "You tried to sleep with the two of us on the very same night while you were a guest in their house. You guys would fuck mud. You've got a nerve to be accusing me."

"I guess I do." Did she say *mud?*

"Don't you dare—"

"I wouldn't dream of it."

"Cause she has been like a big sister to me since we were itty bitty."

I hate it when women do that doll talk. I hate it especially when they're more muscular than I am.

"Tim?"

I didn't answer. We were back to the Lion's Head and from the sidewalk Angela peered in the window overlooking the back room. I peered behind her. I swear I saw a drip plopping down from the ceiling.

"They're still at it," she said. "Looks intense. Let's walk around one more time. Then . . ."

She was acting as if I hadn't just learned something gargantuan and catastrophic. "I need a drink."

"Look, we'll get you a drink. Just promise me . . ."

"I already promised." I heard my voice go flat and affectless. I disliked Angela more and more. I didn't want to share the same sidewalk with her. She was as bad as I was, faithless and duplicitous. And treacherous: look how she'd betrayed Velma. The way I'd betrayed. . . . everyone. It wouldn't do to have the two of us under one roof. If we belonged anywhere together, it was down in the ninth circle.

Of course I knew someone else in New York: I knew G.B. And Took. I thought I'd better get myself out to Brooklyn before anyone else crawled back in my bed. Before Angela and I did any more harm.

I took her by the elbow, an old-fashioned gesture. I didn't want to touch her, but it was the only way I could think to hurry her. I had to go find G.B. She yanked her arm away and I felt myself float with wonder. A couple of weeks ago I thought this white-haired strongwoman could save me from myself. Now I only wanted to hurry out of her life.

I reached for the elbow again. Again she jerked away. A little shudder of self-recognition: grabbing someone's elbow is a lot like tying her up. Once at the state hospital a halfway intelligent female psychiatric intern said to me: *Why do you suppose you have this fascination with belts?* and I said: *Because that's what my father used to threaten me with.* We were both so pleased by this obvious and elementary revelation that we hugged each other. Then she was horrified that she'd touched me in that context, sorry that she'd hugged me at all. She looked around to see what supervising psychiatrist might have seen, what nurse would tell on her. The moment was ruined. And what good had it done anyway? I still want to tie women up. At the very moment of revelation, I couldn't think of anything I wanted more than to tie up the intern. And here I was, still grabbing after women on a New York City sidewalk, in this case a woman I didn't even like.

Another woman coming across Waverly toward us was watching our pantomime. She had the brisk air of someone out for a quart of milk at one o'clock in the Manhattan morning, the *I-know-I-shouldn't-be-doing-this-but-I'm-keeping-my-wits-about-me* look. I shoved my hands in my pockets and looked her straight in the eye to prove my innocence.

She was a good-looking middle-aged woman with her graying hair cut short and poofed high. She was wearing a long elegant pantsuit, also in gray: just the sort of suit David Bowie and I would favor. She had no pocketbook, only the grocery bag in the crook of her arm and her keys dangling below. She seemed amused by my struggles with Angela, and as we passed she looked straight at me with remarkable wide-set green eyes and she said:

"Tim?"

To which I had no reply at all. I only reached out a third time to connect with Angela's elbow, and this time she could not refuse me. I pushed her along Waverly Place, the woman behind us, and Angela said:

"Who was that?" with a certain grudging admiration. That woman could have been her mother, but who wouldn't want such a mother, sure of herself and amused by the world? I wouldn't mind such a mother myself.

"That was my wife," I said, and knew this time, at its most far-fetched, that what I spoke was the truth. I had finally found Bernadette.

I turned to look over my shoulder, and Angela turned with me. We watched Bernadette turn into Gay Street with her bag of groceries. She lived in one of those little houses we'd just been staring up at. And she didn't look back.

I didn't sleep that night. I knew it wasn't healthy to stay up, not when I'd come so close to losing it, not when I was feeling so threatened by Angela, not when I should have been calling G.B. and making my arrangements to move to Brooklyn with him and Took. I knew it wasn't wise to wait up the night in the Spring Street loft, but I was as incapable of sleep as I'd been when I was eighteen and took my Bernadette to Washington Square Park.

Bernadette lived! And she was a good-looking, sure-of-herself woman of the world.

I paced through the night so that the next morning I could head back to Gay Street. Couldn't help myself. Had to see her. I kept running that line through my head: *Tim?* She remembered me! Her tone was so . . . beneficent. But then I had shunned her. Maybe she wouldn't forgive me. The suspense was killing me.

In the early morning I hiked up to Washington Square, kind of a memorial visit to convince myself that I was officially seeking Bernadette again. I stopped under the Siberian elm and watched the dogs in the dog run, doing their doggy things, their sniffing and their licking, one tail lowered to another. That's all I wanted to do: get a whiff of Bernadette, a reminder of who I'd been when I married young. I'd lower my tail for her. She could dominate me all she liked.

On to the top of the park, over on Waverly Place. I was a little lightheaded, a little trembly. I shouldn't have stayed up all night, not with such a recent near miss at madness. When I was in my teens, when I was in my twenties, there were all kinds of near misses. But I was out of practice.

The Village was crowded as a gym with robust types in shorts taking their runs and their power walks, thrusting out their dumbbells. I wished I'd stopped at my Thompson Street coffee shop, where the deli man's rabbity wife could have wrapped me up a bialy to go. Not that I was hungry. I was only trembling.

I stood at the corner of Gay and Waverly for a long while, looking on the small, respectable but charming townhouses. But Gay Street curves at the big apartment building, and though you can see through to the other end, someone fast might elude you. It came to me that Bernadette might leave the block at the other end. Panic.

"Excuse me." I grabbed a young man in a business suit: shined shoes, glasses, briefcase. I shouldn't have clawed at his elbow that way. He drew back. He thought I was a street person: too bad Sidney Lumet wasn't casting that movie after all. I let loose of his arm. "What time is it?"

"Seven-fifteen," he said, scared not to answer. He didn't even bother to check his watch, and he took off on the run.

"Do you know Bernadette Rooney?" I was running along beside him the way G.B. had run after me.

He looked at me over his shoulder in fear and loathing. He looked at me as if I were mad, truth to tell, and then he made for the subway.

Back to Gay Street. She could have slipped out in the meanwhile. I decided the most efficient watch was a walk up and down her street. But I was happy! That I had seen her! Happy and trembling.

In the old days I would have prayed that she show up but now that I was a nonbeliever I discovered that miracles happen anyway. I spotted her. Up at the corner of Gay and Waverly.

Jogging home herself. Just like anyone. Just like all these people in the Village, dressed in one of those shiny sleeveless little shirts and shorts. Her legs were good. This threw me off: she was older than I was, after all. She looked just fine in shorts, better than Angela with those muscled daunting thighs. I felt weak and thin, myself, one of those guys who get sand kicked in their faces. I knew I should have exercised sometime in the last twenty years. I knew I forgot something.

"Bernadette!"

I must have called out in a louder voice than I realized. Two more businessmen all the way out on Waverly stopped their business on the street. Up above, someone raised a window. I did it again, just to hear what I sounded like, and what I sounded like was Marlon Brando calling for Stella.

"Ber-na-dette!"

She stopped at the corner, arms akimbo, feet splayed. Old slewfoot Bernadette with good long milk-white legs. She was smiling at me. Absolutely. I could tell from a distance.

And then she advanced on me and I panicked momentarily, thinking it would make more sense to back up than to face her, this woman who had walked out on me after six days of marriage, this woman who had last seen me with a belt in my hand and that hallucinating puzzlement on my face.

There she was, though, with her good haircut, skin glistening after her morning run, arms delicately muscular. She worked out in a gym, too, it was clear she did, though in the old days a long walk used to send us for our naps. She was a delicate bird when she left me. But these were the new days. This was how you got a chair at a major university. You lived in the world. The world got fit, and you made adjustments.

"Bernadette," I said.

"Tim." She was still smiling, still beneficent. "I *thought* that was you last night. With that . . . child. That wasn't your—daughter, was it?" She was laughing at me.

I was miserable. She'd caught me with Angela. I hadn't meant anything by it. Hadn't my own body known what I didn't want to do with her? "That was—an acquaintance," I said.

"Are you living here? In New York?"

"I am."

"How long?"

"Long as I can take it."

"No, I mean how long have you been here? Have we been in the same neighborhood for twenty years and not known it? Where are you teaching? Want breakfast? Let's go up to the Waverly and grab a bite."

I was definitely lowering my tail for her and she, woman of the world, chairholder, knew what was what. She—I swear this is the truth—she took me by the elbow and began to steer me to the coffee shop on the corner. I understood that she was steering me away from her home. When she was a girl, she used to grab me by the hand and drag me along Broadway. I was raised by a strong mother. I was always delighted to follow Bernadette. And Bernadette was delighted as long as she was in charge.

"So—are you married?"

This as she charged into the narrow doorway of the coffee shop and insinuated herself past the waiters, pointing out a corner booth, still not cleared. New York powerwoman! You would never do such a thing in Due East. I was still trembling. Up above the booth, in a row of framed pictures of two-bit comics and actors and on-the-make New Yorkers, there was a picture of William Kuntsler, celebrity and signifier of my generation's confused past.

I shook my head stupidly and, because I was trembling, said: "No, I just ducked out on my wedding in Due East, matter of fact. Is that William Kuntsler?"

She had not stopped smiling in all this time, even as she peered up to look at the photograph. The other head shots were black and white, but there he was, defender of the political outlaw, in garish living color, all confused himself. It was a wonder. We were squeezing into our booth. Bernadette looked . . . affectionate. Glad to see me. "Oh, Bill," she said. "He's up the street. . . . So that's what you were doing with that little blond girl. Ducking out on a wedding."

"Yes," I said. "That one's been company. But I don't—like her any-more."

"Oh Tim," said Bernadette. "You big goofball."

She called me *goofball.*

"You know who you remind me of?"

"No," I said.

"You remind me of Kramer."

"Everybody tells me that." I was ecstatic at the moment. She'd just called me *goofball.* "Well, not everybody. Another woman I'm . . . fond of . . . called me that. So that makes two women I'm fond of who think I'm like Kramer, whoever he is. I'll have to ask Jesse."

"Who's Jesse?"

I could not believe I'd made such an error. I waved my hand over the dirty dish in front of me to wipe out Jesse, and felt in the gesture that now I had truly and irrevocably betrayed him.

"Well, it looks like the whole world's still in love with you. Beautiful young women, anyway. Oh Tim. There were so many times I thought to call."

I looked at her strangely. Did she think the whole world had ever been in love with me? Did she ever think to call? These were the sorts of things a Southern woman says without even drawing in a breath, and you and she both know it means nothing. But Bernadette was never coy. Bernadette came from *Queens,* and if anybody's straight-talking, it's a girl from Sunnyside.

She saw the strange look. "I know," she said. "Silly. I was so jealous."

"You were never jealous." A small dark man was removing plates beneath us, but I was only aware of his shadow. Bernadette was blushing, charming pink splotches busting out all over cheeks.

"Well, sure I was," she said. "You know. You'd drop a tab and get all expansive and put your arms around every girl you saw . . ." More splotches. But she was all wrong. That was my father, that was big Bill Rooney, out front at Our Lady of Perpetual Help every Sunday morning squeezing every high-heeled lady in a girdle, while my mother handed out her pamphlets and pretended she saw nothing. I never did such a thing!

Bernadette waved the air the way I had done. "I haven't seen you in twenty years and I bring up that." I did have a vague memory of being— friendly. But I hadn't messed around. She knew that. I was an old-fashioned kind of guy, the kind of guy who, if he can't be married, might as well join a monastery. Not that one would ever take him in.

"You were the one with all the lovers," I said.

"Goodness gracious, Tim. Two lovers in college!"

Was that how many it was? She was so experienced, I always thought. "Say something else," I told her. "It's good to hear you talk." It was. *Goofball. Goodness gracious.* It was so good to be around a smart old-fashioned woman my age I almost burst into tears. Bernadette was a little gawky when we were married. Her hair was always braided in a way that was two steps out of style. And there were the glasses, so you never saw those green eyes, flecked with gold. The glasses must have covered those two tiny moles below her left cheekbone, black precise dots. I didn't remember ever seeing them.

"I don't know what to say, after all this time. You still look like a kid, Tim Rooney." Her voice was that wisecracking voice of my mother and my grandmother and any girl brought up in a working-class neighborhood. You could hear that they'd once snapped gum, back when they wore parochial school uniforms.

"I am still a kid," I said. "I've been so childish these past few weeks I can hardly believe it. My thought processes have slowed down. Sometimes I sound—retarded. What about you? Your thought processes slow down? You get married again?"

"Three times. Let's hope this last one takes." I saw the ring then, a thin elegant band, thin and elegant as she. I had no right to feel such deep sorrow. She was still wearing my name, anyway.

"So you're not in the Church, then."

Her smile faded for the first time. "Can't be a woman in the Church, Tim, not and live any kind of life." I could practically hear her gum snapping. "If my work weren't so damned Church-suffused, I might miss it sometimes."

"I don't miss it." Maybe I said that a little fiercely, which would account for why she leaned back so far against the booth.

"You? You left the Church? I don't believe it! You said, after . . . what about the monastery?"

"I didn't get around to inquiring back then. And when I finally did, they wouldn't take me. Psychological troubles. You were right all along."

"I'm sorry."

"Thank you, Bernadette." Really, you would have mistaken us for a peaceful old married couple, the loyal wife offering the husband solace.

"How's your family? How's that adorable little sister of yours?"

It took me a minute. First I thought Katie, because eventually Katie did get to be adorable; but then I knew she meant Dottie, who was the flower girl at our wedding. I never attached the word *adorable* to Dottie: she was so pathologically shy, that child, and so stern. Her bangs too short, and her dresses too long; and the lazy eye, the glasses. My mother wasn't a fussing kind of mother. But if I thought back to our wedding, I could see Dottie with her thin brown hair all gussied up in pin curls and a fluffy pink short skirt and those little white socks that really do make little girls, all little girls, adorable.

"She drowned herself," I said.

Bernadette put her hand over her mouth and made a terrible sound, that shrill death screech we all made when the bat died on the subway.

"I'm sorry," I said. "I should have made something up. Everybody else did. They all said a riptide carried her out."

"When, Tim?"

"Oh, right after I had my nervous breakdown."

The hand again, this time without the sound.

"I'm sorry, I'm shameless. Why am I telling you these things?"

"Because we were married, a million years ago? When we were kids?"

The tears drooled down my cheeks, the way they had with G.B., but I wasn't under a bush, and I wasn't on the edge, and I didn't pretend I had allergies. I was only shameless. "I said terrible things when I was crazy, Bernadette. Worse things than when I was tripping, and you were witness to how bad that got."

"Yes I was. I will never understand—"

"I know. Why somebody that close to the edge of the roof would want to wiggle the loose shingle he's standing on."

"What did you say?"

"When I was crazy? Oh. I said, evidently, that I wished I'd just gone ahead and slept with my mother. Though I don't remember saying that. That's what Dottie said I said. She was twenty-one when she drove out to the beach. She'd never even had a date. She'd never had a boy call her on the phone. She said I said—oh, I couldn't tell you that. Terrible things." A terrible pounding in my head. Obscenities, in rhythm.

Bernadette tried a solemn smile. I smiled back and wiped my face with the back of my hand. We smiled at each other for a while. I was all right. I wasn't trembling anymore. The litany of vile terms was only an echo. The dark little man hovered, couldn't seem to interrupt us, went away again. I began to think that maybe I should pay Bernadette for this psychiatric session, best one I'd had in years.

"She was very controlling," Bernadette said.

"Dottie?"

"Lord no, that little girl? Your mother. Was very controlling. The way she had you all lined up against your father."

"He used to beat me," I said. "I didn't need my mother to line me up against him."

"If he used to beat you," she said in that Sunnyside voice, "she should have left him and got you out of harm's way."

"Well, it wasn't that bad." Listen to me! Defending my mother by defending my father! "You remember. He had tantrums."

"I know. But you joked about it. Guitars banging and plates whizzing by your head. I never thought you were in any danger, Tim, any more than I ever thought I was in any danger when you wanted to . . ."

"Never mind."

"Well. It sounded like he just liked to make a lot of noise. If there was any danger, I always thought—"

"What?"

"I always thought it came from her."

"My mother?" That was a stunning notion. It was my mother who proofread my papers and helped me write my application to Columbia when I was fifteen years old. It was my mother who pulled the needle out of my arm and never told my father. Never told my father.

"I'm sorry, it's none of my business. It must have broken her heart when your little sister—"

I found I couldn't answer her. My mother was dead when Dottie drowned herself. It was my mother's death, in fact, that precipitated my breakdown. My breakdown that precipitated Dottie's suicide. Regular dominoes, we Rooneys.

Before my mother died, she moved into my old bedroom, Andy's and my room. She moved out on my father but never left the house. And my father called me up, nights: *Tim, tell her. Tell her she dudn't even have to move back in the bedroom, if she'd just go to communion. She's so cold, your mother. It's not right, what she's doing, she dudn't even speak to me, Dottie gets me my supper, I can go for days without seeing her and she—* I didn't call my mother to tell her to go back to communion. I called her with another offer: I asked her if she wanted to come stay on my couch in Georgia. If she wanted to leave Due East for good. She said she didn't know what to say. She said she would write me a long letter. The letter never came. One day shortly after I offered her refuge she just blew her lid. Kaflooey! Killer stroke. She wasn't even sixty yet.

"Tim." Bernadette leaned her elbows on the table between us. The waiter, who'd come back finally to get our orders, gave up again at the sight of her intensity and single-mindedness. "Tim, you mustn't blame yourself for Dottie's . . ."

"Suicide." I never knew why people didn't just say it.

"Way back then, way back when she was that adorable little flower girl, I could see she was lonely."

She was lonely. Dottie was the only Rooney who never finished college, the only Rooney who didn't get as far away from my father's house as her little feet would carry her. Though I guess one day she did hop in the car and drive as far as she could go. Right on out to sea.

"You're kind, Bernadette. You always were." I meant it. She was controlling too—no wonder she and my mother didn't get on—but often she was kind. I had stopped trembling, and I was only happy to be in her presence and I wanted to tell her:

"The marriage I ran out on, Bernadette. She's so much younger. It didn't seem right."

"Don't say that!"

"Why not?"

"My latest marriage isn't exactly age-appropriate either. I seem to like those young men who haven't yet finished their dissertations."

I began to cry again.

"Her son . . ." I was sniffing. It was not in the least humiliating. Bernadette was smiling the most benign smile from her thin lips, a medieval Madonna's smile. Her life's work. I didn't need to ask her if she had any children. She was a woman meant to mother grown men.

"I couldn't see messing him up."

"But Tim, you'd be a wonderful father." I felt stabbed in the gut. She hadn't wanted me to be the father of her children, had she? "Because, you know, you've been through a lot with your own."

"Why did you leave me?"

"You were a mess."

"Why are you being so lovey-dovey now?"

"Because you're still a mess." She wasn't smiling anymore, she was clipping the words and rising up on her haunches, ready to leave before she'd ever had her breakfast. She was getting concerned, right through the sweet talk.

"Where's the waiter?" I said. "We don't even see who he is, some shadow behind us. Some dark little shadow! Well, I'll tell you, Bernadette. I don't want to be a father, thanks anyway. I don't want to be a father to my wife and I don't want to be a father to my son."

Now her thin mouth unhinged itself again. "And what exactly do you want to be, Tim Rooney?"

I set my own mouth firm.

"Did you come here to get my permission to marry again? Did you want me to talk you into it when you chickened out?"

Firmer still.

"Come on, Tim. What do you want?"

I craned my neck up to see the picture of William Kuntsler on the coffee shop's hall of fame wall and remembered the long days of our mass insanity, our shared hallucinations, our concurrent demands for peace and the right to blow up the Bank of America, the days of social justice and hokey folk masses, the nights of sweet delicate Bernadette snuggling up to me and thinking I could protect her. What I wanted to be was back in 1968, when we all went crazy together.

"I want to be an outlaw," I said.

REPORT FROM ON THE ROAD

We stopped the first night in Myrtle Beach, which is ordinarily only two and a half hours out of Due East, so you can tell exactly what time we were making. Father Berkeley insisted on going up the seacoast instead of the superhighway, and he stopped at likely restaurants to show Tim's picture and ask if anybody had seen him. Maybe he'd been watching reruns of "Father Dowling" on the television. Naturally no one had seen Tim, and if they had why should they remember him from two weeks back? Though I had to admit the priest had found a picture that captured Tim and why he might stay in a waitress's mind. It was a snapshot of him and Dottie at some rectory dinner meant to distract them from their mother's death. Tim is wearing his old gray corduroy jacket and a rumpled white shirt underneath. He has his arm around Dottie's shoulder but it's not really touching flesh, it's just floating there. His hair has gone wild, combed maybe, but not contained, and his eyes are just—blazing. There's no other word for it, even in black and white. It must have been a few days before he cracked up. If you wanted to illustrate the word *maniacal,* you could use that picture. He looks like an overgrown boy, his lips all white and puffy and the freckles scattered on his face like blisters. Dottie's a foot shorter than he is, under his arm, gritting her teeth. She doesn't even try to smile. When I took a look—the priest insisted—for one pure minute I remembered why I'd been so crazy for Tim and why I didn't think I could ever forgive him. Then Jesse looked at it and just hooted, long and hard. "Look at Tim's *hair.*"

Father Berkeley drove his black Volvo up Route 17 with one hand on the wheel and the other thrust out to cradle the passenger seat. Jesse drove in front with him, thrilled to bits. I thought I might be losing my boy and my mind all on the same journey. The speedometer slipped from sixty to forty and then climbed back up again, like the old man's energy. I was afraid I might have to reach from behind and grab the steering wheel any minute.

And then that first night, at the Pink Seashell Motel, I thought I'd choke when he pulled out a gold card to put the two rooms on the one credit card. Where does a priest get such a thing? And there's the black Volvo, like a comfy undertaker's car.

After the embarrassment of his paying for our room, he turned to me right in front of the desk clerk and said: "I guess you and Jesse will be running over to the amusement park."

I didn't have a penny to spare for amusement parks and he should have thought of that before he picked this town to stop in and dangled these pleasures in Jesse's face. "I think we'll just turn in early so we can get an early start, Father," I said.

"Oh come on, Mom," Jesse said, and my mouth fell open, not because he wanted to go to the amusement park like any boy but because he doesn't call me Mom, he calls me Momma. But he wanted to be some kind of junior man of the world around the priest, who was at that very moment drooling a thin trickle of spittle down the side of his mouth.

"Jesse." That is all I have to say, with one eyebrow raised, and he knows then that the subject is money and that there is nothing I can do. These last few years, with Tim indulging him, have thrown us off our balance.

"Allow me to treat you," the father said, and out of his wallet he pulled a couple of twenties. I didn't know whether to spit in his eye or weep, it was so humiliating, the desk clerk witnessing this and now a family signing in behind us, a regular mother and father and sister and brother, gaping. Jesse and I looked like the homeless, taken in by the priest as an act of charity. He was as insensitive as any man.

"Come on, Mom," Jesse said, not wheedling, which he has never done in his life, but more imploring me. I was flabbergasted.

"Jesse, really, I think I'll pass out in the heat. I've got to go lie down." Which was what you could call a transparent lie, at the end of April. The thermostat hadn't gone above eighty all day long.

"Perhaps I could mosey over there and put Jesse on the roller coaster."

He must have seen the bitterness in my face, he must have, even as I said yes, he and Jesse could *mosey over there.* He must have heard my voice going as folksy as his and burning all the while. Because I knew as we stood there in the lobby of the Pink Seashell Motel that I would spend the night rigid in a plastic chair while the old man took my son on the roller coaster and the gravity-defier and the Scrambler, and tried to steal him away from me.

I did spend the night rigid in a chair, but the priest brought Jesse back after an hour and even that made me mad, his thoughtfulness. Mainly I just wanted to burst from having agreed to make this crazy journey. When I washed my face that night I looked myself dead in the eye and promised again that this trip was only to fetch Tim back to where he could get help. That was the end of my obligation to him. And once that burden was lifted, I was going to order a stack of graduate school bulletins and wait tables if I had to, to support me and Jesse until we could get out of town and never ever rely on a man again.

But the next morning I thought how strange it was that I had thought of waiting tables, since I have never done any such thing and probably would not be good at it. I can barely bring myself to smile at a stranger. It must have been the sheer volume of waitresses we had talked to, going up the coast highway, or maybe the kindness of them, taking the time to peer at that snapshot of Tim, willing themselves to remember him when they hadn't seen him or anyone remotely like him in all their born days.

Leaving Myrtle Beach, Jesse asked for pancakes and we stopped at one of those chain restaurants and sat ourselves down in a booth. Naturally Father Berkeley pulled out the picture just as soon as the waitress brought us our ice water. Why do they subject middle-aged women to those frills she was wearing, on her apron and round her collar? Her name tag said DARSHA, which is a name I have never heard, but I tried not to hold it against her. Look at my own name. She was one of those black women whose skin is so light it would make more sense to call her white, but we don't. We don't call her white.

"Miss Darsha," the priest began, and I blushed all over at the sound of his quaking voice. I was afraid he'd shame us, as if he hadn't done that already just by enlisting us in this chase. "We've lost a dear friend," he said, "and we think he may be in trouble. I wonder if you'd mind looking at this picture? He might have passed through Myrtle Beach two weeks ago."

"What kinda trouble?" Darsha said, before she'd take up the picture. She wasn't being unfriendly, just curious. She was hoping it was interesting trouble.

"Mental instability," Father Berkeley said without missing a beat. "He's not dangerous in the least, only troubled."

"Oh." Darsha picked up the snapshot and you could tell from the way her eyes narrowed that she saw something there right away. But she wouldn't commit to it. She called over another waitress—"Leitha, come here a second"—and pressed the snapshot into the other woman's face.

"You see this man two three weeks ago? Member that girl with that white hair? Member those big bills? Pulled em out his sock."

"I member them hunner dollar bills falling all over the floor." Leitha nodded with pleasure. "Wish I got me one fore that girl scoop em up. She was *fast,* unh-huh, I got to hand it to her." Then she looked over her shoulder and back at us to see if she'd just slipped up and revealed something she shouldn't have.

She had, but the priest acted like he didn't know it. He thought he was a detective again and asked whether this couple said where they were going next. This couple. He and Jesse leaned forward, into the question, Jesse forgetting even that he'd come to order pancakes and neither one of them in the least perturbed that Tim was traveling north with a girl with fast hands and white hair.

And the two waitresses went on chattering, kind as all the other waitresses had been. I sat stiff as I'd been the night before when my son went off with the priest. I'd known it anyway. I'd known Tim went off with a woman, and I can't say how I knew he was thinking of it. I'm not sure he knew he was thinking of it. He'd never been unfaithful to me, but there was something about his lovemaking that told me it wasn't possible for him to take the pleasure if he couldn't find him some pain to go along with it. If he'd found another woman so soon after he left Due East he must have wanted to feel guilty all over, wrapped in guilt, covered in it. Tied up in guilt the way he liked to tie my ankles and then pretend the next morning he didn't know what came over him and scramble to thread the belt back through his trousers before Jesse came wandering into the bedroom.

"Look like one of them surfer girls to me," Darsha said. "I bet they right here in Myrtle Beach. Either that or up to Wrightsville."

I saw Father Berkeley's head jerk in disagreement. He thought he knew which way they were going, and he thought Jesse and I were still with him on this trip. But I knew different. I knew I was going back to Due East.

I wasn't going after Tim if there was a surfer girl with white hair looking after him. A woman like that would be better for him, anyway. She wouldn't get all tangled up in his guilt. But me, I had my boy to look after. I had my ankles to untie.

five

got Took's number from Brooklyn Information: Entuckia Brights. Good luck she had the same last name as G.B. A good luck omen. I waited until eight o'clock to call, when she'd be gone to school. Otherwise I might start wooing her and that was not my mission. Not my mission at all.

It took G.B. twenty or thirty rings to get out of bed and answer the call. First thing I'd have to work on with that young man was some discipline.

"G.B.," I said, "you got to join me here. Today. Say, eleven A.M. Let's synchronize our watches."

"Who's this?" he said. "That you, Mr. Rooney?"

"It is I, G.B. Brights. Hold your voice down. Speak in complete sentences. I want you down here at eleven A.M. sharp."

"Where's here?" He sounded stern, stern and fatherly if the truth be told. He thought he could switch roles on me. We definitely needed to work on discipline.

"Downtown," I said. "East Village, something. Somewhere I'm not familiar with. I'll get you cross streets. This is East Fifth and . . . wait, I'll have to go to the corner."

"Man, don't go to the corner. You got to get yourself to the doctor."

"G.B., you don't understand! The trouble with doctors is, it's all this personal stuff. Embarrassing stuff, sex and diapers. I don't intend to go crazy and spill all those beans, nosireebob. I'm marshaling my resources, I'm going to get a little political action going. I can't do it alone. You see that. I'll need you, and then we'll bring Tuck into the . . . not cell. Unit, perhaps. Fighting unit."

"Mr. Rooney, you are having a nervous breakdown. You had it under control awhile there, but now you are definitely having a nervous breakdown."

"You're not listening to me," I said.

"Took told me not to come after you anymore. Listen, I'm sorry, Mr. Rooney, but I got to protect myself too. Took says—"

"You're not listening to me! I'm talking politics. I'm talking being an outlaw for a decent cause! I'm talking action. I'm *taking* action! You're not listening to me!"

Which was true, because he'd hung up somewhere past the word *outlaw*.

Some father figure.

I stood for a while cradling the receiver, because he has such a beautiful voice and it seemed to still be singing through the wires: *protect myself, protect myself,* gentle iambs that turned to song. Remember "Respect Yourself"? D a h - d a h - d a h - d a h-d a h-d a h. I was peaceful there, hearing the echoes, there on East Fifth, was it? East Seventh? East Zero?

But then some little she-devil wearing her slip out in traffic came up and snarled at me to get off the phone.

I went on my martial way. I could do it alone. You always do it alone, anyway.

"Velma?"

"Tim? Is that you? Honey, you have got to stop disappearing on us. Where are you?"

I was on a street. There was a phone in my hand. I could not get any more specific than that. G.B. wasn't going to join me. I hadn't been sleeping. Every few hours the cops did a sweep.

"Velma, I need assistance here. I need a squire. Or a lady. You could be either one. Either one that appeals to you."

"Tim?"

"Velma, come be with me."

"Tim, honey, where are you? You're not in Brooklyn, are you? I'll come get you anywhere if you're not in Brooklyn."

I could not say for sure that I was not now in Brooklyn. There were some . . . gaps in my memory. I might have been on a train. I looked around me but I was having trouble focusing my eyes. The buildings were low. The phone was in front of a bodega. It could be Brooklyn. But there were a lot of young white people around. A lot of those skinny girls in their underwear.

"I'm across from a park."

"Tim, you don't sound good."

"I smell Chinese food. I smell like Chinese food."

"Tim, you sound terrible. You didn't get the part, did you? They're not making you act something out? You wouldn't do that to me, would you? You're not just playing a role, are you, fooling with me on the phone?"

What role? I was an outlaw, wasn't I, wasn't I turning myself into a countercultural knight, disappearing off the face of the earth and giving away my money?

My money! Gone! My feet felt so light and dry without their damp cushion. There was nothing there beneath my socks. In fact, there were no socks. I remembered giving some of those hundred dollar bills away in the park. I remembered their clamoring for more, grubby faces out of Breughel, Gregorian chants in the background. But I didn't recall giving it all away. Could they have picked me clean while I napped?

No matter. Better, in fact. Purer this way. I would fight for every scrap of food, and Velma would help. Velma was loaded.

Yag. Guilt attack. I looked down. My feet seemed to be bleeding in my loafers. My feet were dry no more. Where were my socks? Maybe I'd traded them for this can of malt liquor in my hand.

I couldn't remember why I was holding the phone, though there was a sensational sound coming over the receiver, a sound like a blob of Jell-o on a plate sliding and squeaking. It sounded for all the world like my name tolled again and again:

Tim? Tim? Tim? Tim?

Benny Goodman was playing the Mozart Klarinettenquintet with the Budapest String Quartet, which accounted for my calm and the graceful-ness of the pedestrians who strolled past me. Of course, I was pretty graceful myself, sitting on the steps and swaying my shoulders. A-major is the most hopeful of keys. First Mozart takes leave of the body, then the mind. Jesse used to move his feet one over the other, listening to Mozart, until he spun into dizziness. I used to feel that way after communion, myself, out of body, inflated, floating off on the de-light balloon. I was doing something like that spin now, with my upper body, stretching shoulders and arms until I had been pulled up on my feet to swoop and swirl with the clarinet. First time my father played Goodman for me, I started saving for a clarinet.

The sane interludes are always the worst. The anxiety comes then, so you like to burrow down deeper into the dark, if possible. It's not always possible. Now I was moving into the larghetto, and there was nothing to do but cry. I never mastered the clarinet. I was overextended: piano, violin, guitar, all the projected musical hopes of a failed businessman. Aquinas, Avila, Weil, all the projected intellectual hopes of a miserable do-gooder housewife.

This was a sane interlude. I was sitting on stone steps. I might have had a few snatches of sleep in the last few days. I'm not sure. Someone woke me as soon as I drifted off. A common torture technique. But they couldn't get to me. I was not tired. I had no money, and I was not one of the regulars back in Tompkins Square. No one would share a lousy malt liquor with me even if I'd provided the money for every one of those flea-bitten losers to souse themselves. Always the outsider. Think they're so cool. I was sobered up. So hungry I didn't want food. So smelly I couldn't smell anymore. Couldn't remember how I got here, wherever here was. Stone steps.

I moved into the menuetto and twisted myself around to see whose stone steps I listened from. Holy God, we praise Thy name! The music stopped. The passersby stopped too, to peer at the madman tripping backward down the stone steps. I sat on a church's steps, a church set close to the street, and it was a dimly familiar church. St. Joseph's, Sixth Avenue, Greenwich Village. You know who St. Joseph is, don't you? Patron saint of fathers. O, the jokes we play.

I, atheist, outlaw, had made my way back to the Village, to Bernadette's stomping grounds, and had sat myself down on the steps of the very church where we once, as I may have mentioned, sought out hip liturgy. O I was hungry. O I was tired of tracing back the source of all sounds that vied for my attention.

A procession of small girls in white puffy dresses, little white anklets on their feet, crossed my line of vision. I could summon neither Mozart nor Goodman to help me out here. I never cared for visual hallucinations! Auditory was my game! But look at them, dark stern little girls, their bangs cut too short, their palms pressed prayerfully together. And at the back of the line an especially melancholy child, a loner, a homely stout shy-unto-humiliated-to-be-seen-in-this-line-of-marchers little girl whose flounce drooped down as melancholy as she.

Wait a minute! Did I say melancholy *flounce?* That couldn't be a hallucination. That last little girl in line bore a white satin pillow on which was perched a crown of flowers, a diadem, and it descended on me in all its reality.

I sat on these stone steps on May Day! Workers of the world unite! and all you little girls descended from Mediterranean and Caribbean countries, hold on to your traditions! Today we crown Mary Queen of the May!

And I didn't even believe in her anymore. I was sobbing. This crying stuff was getting out of hand.

Slowdown slowdown slow down. Ommmmmmmmm. It was just that Mary . . . Just that women . . . Just that Dolores Maggie Katie Dottie. Bernadette. Angela. Velma. Took. I was leaving somebody out. O the sweet comfort of all of them, remembered and forgotten. I may have mentioned that as a small boy I built shrines for Mary, hauled stones across town for grottoes in the backyard. Doesn't take an analyst to know the flowers were really for that other mother, Dolores, beaming on me from her kitchen window. Bill was furious: *You'll make him into a pansy!* And who knows maybe she did because I believe I have also mentioned that there's hardly a minute of the day when my thoughts are not directed toward sex and, believe me, this compulsion could be eased by anybody passing my way. Any body.

"I'm sorry, you can't block the doorway." I was sitting again, on the top step. I knew that because the church door swung open and punctured my back. Anyone else would have jumped up, but not I; I groaned and leaned my head down into my knees on May Day, Mary's Day, International Timothy Rooney Appreciation of Women Day. And a female voice behind me, firm not prissy, said again:

"I'm sorry, you'll have to move out of the doorway."

I twisted around to see who disturbed my first moment of peace in hours, in days, in weeks. It was a nun: no doubt about it. She was in disguise, but she was a nun, all right. Short no-nonsense hair, a drab polo shirt and a dark skirt not long enough to be long but not short enough to reveal anything interesting. Polo shirts on nuns! Do you wonder why I would flee such a church?

"Here for the meal? Around the corner." She looked on me without the least bit of concern, because I'm redheaded and freckled, graying and faded and potbellied though I become. My sister Maggie was a nun, for a while. Any nun worth her salt knows I could do her no harm. I sank my head back down into my hairy bony knees. There were no untoward sounds anywhere.

I sank my head down, but this time she kneed me. Kneed me, I tell you, in the back. In the kidneys. To prod me along, to poke me on my way. I descended one step.

"And over to the side. That's it. All the way over."

I slid along, the slap of her voice easing me down the length of the step. I told you I'm happy when the woman takes charge. As of course she never does when you need her to, unless it's that passive-aggressive stuff. Unless it's not telling your father you stuck a needle in your arm.

My head was still down in my knees but I listened for the sound of the nun leaving me. No door closing, no spongy sucking sneaker descending the step. The street sounds began to confuse me: the traffic boom-box crying baby soothing mother sounds. I could have been anywhere. I was dizzy. I could have been anywhere. I chose a church with stone steps, but I was losing the surface of anyplace. The sounds were rising. The B-52s were on my airwaves, singing "Love Shack." That boom box could have accounted for "Love Shack," but that's not your general B-52 mode of transmission. "Love Shack." It could have been emanating from me. O dark soft sinking, o terror.

I raised my head, hoping against all hope that the nun would beam down on me but she was gone, lost, teletransported, maybe had never been there. And the little girls in flounces? Not a trace.

I rose, with difficulty. It was hard to walk out onto the sidewalk, my eyes unfocused that way. And yet, and yet even with unfocused eyes I could look down on myself in that very same pair of chinos I wore to start this journey, now pee-stained and drooled over, and see that I was becoming what I wished to become, maybe had wished to become all along, not so much pilgrim as pilgrim-outlaw, not so much outlaw as outlaw-knight. A noble fanatic like Stonewall Jackson (see what we Southern boys are raised on). Stonewall Jackson, only on the right side this time.

I stood a little taller and Mozart and Benny G returned to me, the fourth movement, allegro. By God, I could take them all on. I could rise above these streets and fool them all.

"Mr. Rooney!"

Though it might be hard to pull off, to make my way down this sidewalk, if the voices continued.

"Mr. Rooney!"

So insistently. From that direction yonder, the direction of the Waverly Coffee Shop where I had made my intentions clear to Bernadette. The precision of the music kept me high-stepping along Sixth Avenue. I didn't have to listen to any voices.

"Mr. Rooney!" Now the sound brushed by my very ear and hot

breath fanned my sweating neck, some Orwellian all-sense delusion descending and blocking out the music, my music, the music that soothed me and enabled me to believe that I, Stonewall Pilgrim Outlaw Knight, could . . . be of use.

But so all-over was this delusion that it began to shake me to my roots, to my feet that is, which I believe I have mentioned were by then scabbed and bloodied.

"Mr. Rooney, I been looking all over town for you, man. I been crawling through East Fifth Street since you called from there, man, you were living in the park with them crazies, those crazies, they told me bout the money, I been down to SoHo went through every loft in that building you were staying in to find your friends, Mr. Rooney, say something, say something let me know you're alive because looking at you I can't say for sure that you are. Alive."

"G.B."

"Praise Jesus. No, don't get upset now, I know you don't like that talk. Calm down now. Just an expression."

I might have been flailing at him. I might have been hollering: "Supposed to be a woman."

"What's supposed to be a woman?"

"A woman come to my aid."

"Dint you ask me come git you?"

"I asked you to come join me."

"Well, what am I doing?" he said.

I looked him over: the large dark fullness of him, that hopeful hair of his in those stunted dreadlocks, the tooth outlined in gold, the diamond stud gleaming in the spring air of May Day.

"G.B.," I said. "It's May Day."

"Workers of the world unite," he said. He knew the pass code! My man knew the pass code! I didn't have to do it on my own after all.

"Take me to Took," I whispered. The relief of his signing on was telling on me. I was weak in the knees and the heart and the groin. I thought I might pass out on the sidewalk if someone did not offer me a sip of something on a sponge.

"Ah, Mr. Rooney, that might not be such a good idea. We better think up another plan."

My knees buckled, but he held me up.

"Take me to her." He could hoist me up, this G. B. Brights, and together we would proceed. Took would keep us in line. Took would keep us on the straight and narrow.

Now, truly, I would ride the streets aloft. I raised my hand for a carriage to take us over the mountain.

REPORT FROM THE CHESAPEAKE BAY BRIDGE-TUNNEL

We were stopped at one of the rest stops they have on the Chesapeake Bay Bridge-Tunnel, but we might have been in Istanbul or Kismet, it seemed so strange to Jesse and me. We'd never been farther north than Chapel Hill, where Tim drove us once after I told him how I'd pined for Carolina when I was fifteen and pregnant and knew I wouldn't be going off to college any time soon. So Chapel Hill is as exotic as we had seen up to that point, and even if the women professors there all look like Virginia Woolf, with their pinned-back hair and their wide-legged trousers, it is still the South, still defined by the day the dogwoods bloom and the size of the president's house.

The Bridge-Tunnel was definitely not the South. It was not even land anymore, just a concrete route through the sea. It gave me the willies and made me giddy all at once, to be standing in a parking lot on the water, and Jesse stood there trembling under the heat of the sun and the shimmer of the air.

"He's been here," the priest said. He was just leaving the car, straightening his twisted back and knowing, probably, that the time it takes him to get in his walking position has filed down the sharp edges of my feelings toward him. But this *He's been here* business, which he was pulling out of his hat more and more the farther we went on our journey, was just too weird. It was like traveling with a diviner, if you'll pardon the expression, waiting for the wand to sense water so we could slake our thirst. I'd never let Jesse so much as play with a Ouija board and, little as I knew about the Catholic faith, I doubted *He's been here* was part of any sanctioned doctrine.

I let it pass, though. The old man was failing, the tremble constant now in his hands and his jaw. Every day when we stopped for the evening meal he sent Jesse off to wash his hands and then said, like a ritual chant, "Oh, I wish I had a drink tonight." He was a terrible drinker once. Everybody in Due East knew it. It seemed to me he had a milder look in those days when you saw him from a distance. Kinder. I liked the way he admitted the longing now. The strange thing was, I felt the strain of looking so much by evening that I'd been wishing I had a drink myself.

But we didn't get ourselves a drink, not so much as a beer with our supper. Our stops tended toward the seedier side-of-the-road home cooking spots, where Father Berkeley was convinced Tim would stop. I was not so sure. There is a Howard Johnson's side to Tim, particularly when he's feeling *the nerves coming on,* which is the expression his family uses for his trouble. If I had been playing this detective game I believe I would have picked the cleanest tidiest chain restaurants and motels up Route 17.

I was not in the driver's seat, though. It had taken us five days to get from Myrtle Beach to the tunnel, a half-day's journey, and no one since the waitress in Myrtle Beach remembered seeing Tim. Three days before we had started up the Outer Banks but Father Berkeley decided in Ocracoke that Tim hadn't come that way after all. So we doubled back through North Carolina—the poor old man set the car going in the wrong direction at one point, in the rain, and was so shamed by his mistake that I pretended to be sleeping when he turned us around. Then we pushed on north through the Virginia tidewater.

Now that Father Berkeley had straightened himself, he and Jesse walked over to play with one of the silver binoculars, setting their sights out on the shipping lanes. The day before I had seen Jesse slip his hand in the old man's for a minute, neither's face betraying the gesture. That child—and don't forget, he is almost heading into the teenage years—has not held a man's hand, not even Tim's, since my father died. It softened me, too, that Jesse trusted the old man, but the priest had known that would happen all along. He has just waited for me to come around, knowing in that diviner's way of his that we are two of a stubborn type. He makes no apologies. No sweet talk out of him. I thought at first that he did not like women, but now I am not so sure. Maybe he just doesn't like me.

When they were done, we headed into the snack bar and got ourselves Cokes and salted peanuts (Father Berkeley) and Twinkies (Jesse). That was a ritual too: the first day I fussed about the sugar and Father Berkeley rolled his eyes heavenward. It came to me what a terrible trip this was for that child, even if we found Tim. Especially if we found Tim. It came to me, as the old man meant it to, that a package of Twinkies might give him some comfort.

And then we sat. "You forgot to show the picture at the cash register," Jesse said, and the old man said, "So I did."

He fumbled for his wallet and pulled it out slowly, Jesse breathing down his neck all the while, tapping his foot. Maybe I was wrong to let that child get his hopes up. He believed the old man utterly, believed that Tim had been to this place, believed that we would find him. I was beginning to believe myself.

Father Berkeley found the edges of the snapshot finally and then, for the first time, passed the picture over to Jesse.

"Me?"

"You go ask," the priest said, and Jesse blushed to the roots of his hair. He went off sheepish, scared to make conversation with a stranger but scareder still to question anything the old man said.

When he was gone I said: "Do you think—"

"No, I don't."

"You don't let me finish my questions, Father."

He didn't answer. He could blaze out a speech when he wanted to make his own point, but otherwise he wasn't interested in conversation. Most of these meals had been consumed in utter silence.

The silent treatment got to me, and I liked to poke at him a little. "Do you think, I was going to say, it's such a good idea to involve Jesse that way?"

"Showing the pictures?"

"Yes. I mean, I've told him plain and clear that Tim and I aren't getting married anymore, that Tim's not going to be his father. Should he be—"

"Showing pictures? Perhaps not. Perhaps he shouldn't be traveling with us at all."

"Father. I've never left that boy in his or my life. And even if I'd had someone he could stay with, I wouldn't do it, not even for Tim. Especially not for Tim, not after . . ."

The old man's jaw trembled and then stopped, abruptly. Out of the corner of my eye I saw Jesse up at the cash register, hanging back. "Look here now," Father Berkeley said, "Tim Rooney's father asked for my help the first time around. I had no help to offer him. One of Tim's sisters had to come home to show us what had to be done, to sit patient until he would go to the hospital with her. I was of no use."

Again I remembered the days of Father Berkeley's drinking: he used to shuffle through the streets downtown, a little muddled, his light eyes a little unfocused.

"This time around," he said, "his sister doesn't know where he is. I mean to go after him. And you have agreed to come along. It's of no consequence what you choose to tell your son about your romantic life. A romantic life is not what's at stake here. Perhaps you should consider not telling Jesse anything about your plans with Tim. He is a child. He doesn't need that burden."

He took my breath away, and I hated him again. *I* wasn't calling it a romantic life. I was talking about a man who'd had me quit my job, for God's sake. But I didn't have the presence of mind to stand my ground with him. I only set my own jaw as firm as his was now holding. Oh yes. I should tell Jesse nothing but he could send Jesse off to the cash register with a picture of the man he thought was going to be his father.

Jesse came back downcast and threw the snapshot on the table, where it landed on a wet spot. Father Berkeley made a point of picking it up by the edges and wiping it down with a paper napkin and smoothing it and putting it away in his wallet. It took forever. The old man's hands were trembling again, and now so was his jaw.

"They hadn't seen him," Father Berkeley said.

Jesse didn't trouble to answer. He looked out over my head, as if he were straining to see out to sea.

I found my voice. "We should be getting on. You want some more of that Coke, darlin?"

Jesse kept on looking right over my head. I felt as if he were looking through me. He rose and made his way out the crowded snack bar. He had his shoulders slumped down in imitation of the way the old man walks, and I shot a look at the priest.

"Forgive me," Father Berkeley said, and sank his neck down. "You were right. That child shouldn't be showing this picture to anyone. He doesn't need that burden, either."

I stared out past him.

"We needn't show it at all, here on in," the old man said. "We'd best get on our way to New York. I know Tim's there, but I don't know how much longer."

six

DAY TWENTY-SIX CUT ME SOME SLACK

I had a new symptom and a new position to go with it. I was rocking myself in a fetal ball on Entuckia Brights's couch in Brooklyn and I was helpless to stop myself doing it. Until I fell down close to sleep, woke with a start if ever I did drift off, and commenced the whole operation again.

They had been letting me do this for hours now. I had been singing at first, trying out some atonal chanting, but Took came at me with her fist balled and I was able to quit that quick enough. Now I was watching myself rock in silence, but my vision was fuzzy.

I was not hearing anything anymore, nothing but the real sounds of real people in a real apartment fighting to the death over my fate. Well, maybe not to the death. Maybe it's that kind of hysterical exaggeration that got me rolled in this ball and rocking in the first place. My grandmother Rose's legacy. The rocking had been going on for the better part of a night and a day, ever since G.B. got me home to Brooklyn and got a little chicken soup spooned into me. From that point on I had shifted into clarity and terror and the need to confess.

But there was nobody to hear my confession, nobody but good G.B., who would be dirtied if he were to hear the half of what I've done. Took would make a better confessor, I thought, having entertained so many hateful thoughts herself, but Took didn't want to hear anything from me. She had lifted the receiver a dozen times to call the ambulance, and a dozen times G.B. had stopped her.

If she wouldn't hear my confession, I would have liked her to slap me silly.

I rocked in the cradle of my wickedness. I had left Mary Faith high and dry and bereft, dear tough struggling high-minded sad Mary Faith.

I had lusted after Angela and had grown to despise her. Her body parts still floated into my consciousness.

I had led Velma on, just like any other man who'd ever crossed her path.

I had projected all my ambivalence onto Fred and probably egged him on in his pursuit of Angela.

I had harassed Bernadette, who, I could see now from my cradled position, had never done me any wrong.

I had feared and despised my father all my life and of course

I had deserted my son.

There were no hallucinations, I tell you, only the terror that came with these visions of myself: black and white, grainy, a little lewd. And the funny thing is, I was so inflated with love for all of them, for Fred himself, I tell you, for Dottie too, so stern and unforgiving, and for my father who let me crawl in his bed at night and for my brother who once wished me safe in a hospital and for Angela who listened to my sad stories, that I was surrounded by a warm zone of air that cushioned and protected me and made my thoughts perfectly clear, anyone could have followed them, until Took or G.B. tried to talk to me and I forgot the safety zone and came unhinged and could not speak but only chant.

I rocked on a good woman's couch.

"This is it, G.B., what you think, I can't take another minute. Look at that."

I willed myself to stop rocking, for her peace. The spirit was willing, but the flesh was still weak. I wanted her to shake me by the shoulders.

"Where's an ambulance gonna take him?"

They had had this little exchange a dozen times already. Took would answer they were going to take me to Kings County, and the sound of the two words together pierced the cushion around me. The two words together sounded bad even to Took, because as soon as she spoke them she put the receiver down. She couldn't do that to anyone, not even to me.

Then one or the other of them paced while I rocked. G.B. paced with his arms flung out and his chest heaving. Took paced with her fists closed and crossed across her chest. O I wanted to ease her suffering. I was so glad to be under her roof on her clean couch smelling of Scotchguard and lemon bubble bath I didn't want to ever venture out again. That pilgrim-knight stuff was a madman's game and I wanted no more of it. I had spread fifteen thousand dollars on the park benches of New York. These people were from home. These people would understand. They'd fix me ribs and patch me up.

"All right then, I'm calling H.I.P."

They had had this exchange, too. G.B. would say: "What you think H.I.P. is gone tell you?" and Took would say: "They're gone tell me to call the ambulance take him to Kings County" and there—they would be back to Go.

I managed to slow the rocking tempo and I heard them both breathing easier. I had an insane desire to whistle and cheer them up. It had been so long since I'd written a song. Maybe that was what had sent me out onto the streets as a bum, not brain fever at all but the creative urge! Or maybe I wanted to whistle because that soup G.B. heated from the can was tainted! These things happen. People drop dead. All the times you wish you could drop dead, and all the dread you feel when it's visited upon you. Mercy.

"I'm calling Reverend Smalls," Took said.

Here was Took shaking me into vision. I couldn't say if she was waking me after a long night or after a short pause, I could only say that I had turned the dial too far the wrong way. There was a click, and then the flutter of a broken spring.

"OK, buster," Took said, and of course I wept for joy. The way all these women talked! Mary Faith said I was acting *kooky*. Bernadette called me *a big goofball.* And now Took called me *buster.* I had come home to the right place.

"You're out of here." She was whispering, so I had to bend down to hear her soft words. Her tone was not unkind. "G.B. won't let me call the ambulance, Reverend Smalls says I don't have a choice. The men are always willing to tell you what to do, but are they here doing it? You're not staying in my house ten minutes more. No sir, not and have two nervous breakdowns on our hands. I don't *think* so."

Because of that click, because of that broken spring, it didn't register at the moment that I was no longer rocking. I'd had a few spoonfuls of soup and a few fistfuls of sleep in the last days. I may have been crazy, but I was hungry and tired too, and Took was grabbing me by what was left of my front pocket. I could feel from the way she heaved me how much weight I had lost, and it occurred to me that I had lost inches from my height as well. From my head, maybe, sizzled away with the brain fever. The way she was looking at me. With such terrible pity.

It was night. I opened my eyes, and saw that we struggled in the dark. In the distance I heard G.B. snoring. That was real snoring. Took had waited until G.B.'s guard was down, and now she was going to toss me into the night. Isn't this what I wanted? The slap? The chance to confess on my way out the door? Why then did I struggle? In the dark I saw she wore pajamas as military as her teaching suit, plaid men's pajamas. She'd let her hair loose from its tight knot but it only sat, beaten down into a thin rope, at the nape of her neck. She tugged at my shirt, one hand behind my shoulder, and she looked at me with her full mouth trembling out the purest hatred any woman has ever breathed in my direction. That Etta must have broken her heart.

The sleep had refreshed me in a curious way. Even if Took came along to torture me like this, to turn me out into the night, I had found my bearings.

"Come on, you big lug." *Big lug.* O I loved it. I even shifted for her, to make her burden lighter. I felt myself standing for her, and I felt the small of her palm against my back, pushing me toward the door.

I went willingly, this was the penance I deserved, these sores on my feet scraping against my shoes, I must be cast out the way I cast out my dear Mary Faith. I walked along, docile, and Took's hand pushed me only metaphorically.

But when we reached the door of her apartment the terror flooded again. I only wanted a little chicken soup and some tough talk. *Cut me some slack,* I wanted to say, but I could not find my voice.

I heard the door click behind me.

I stayed in her corridor, on my knees, praying for Took to take me back in, all that long night and on into the morning. She came out the door dressed for work in a brown safari suit, hair knotted and tucked, smelling that yellow smell. I stayed on my knees, hands bridged together.

When she saw me still in her hallway she hollered back inside the door: "G.B., he's still out here. You let him back in you can go back to South Carolina together. Any of the neighbors ask, you tell em you never saw him before in your life." The way she was bellowing, it wasn't likely the neighbors would have anything to ask.

She leaned down low and hissed at me. "Scat," she said. There. All right. Someone had recognized me.

And then she sauntered on off down the hallway to press the elevator button. She smoothed her safari jacket over her hips while she waited for the car to come, and never once looked in my direction.

I stayed on my knees praying that G.B. would smuggle me back in, keep me under the bed or somewhere equally appropriate for the lowlife Took recognized me to be. Young Gregor. I believe I may have been there for hours. People left their apartments and took note of me, but they must have heard Took's admonition. No one asked any questions. I might have been a newspaper folded in the hallway for all the concern I caused.

I slept kneeling and rocking. I woke with my head lodged against the doorway and the doorway giving, pulled from inside. G.B.!

He peeked out, saw I was still there, closed the door again. He was leaving me to my fate. I tried to rise in response to that—if G.B. had given up on me, I gave up too—but as I struggled up the wall, my very limbs disconnected from their sockets, the door opened again and G.B. slipped out, his arms cradling jars and dishes and cartons. G.B. with food. I slid back down the wall.

"Come on, Mr. Rooney, let's get you some breakfast now. Then we'll see bout getting you to the doctor."

I heard the word *doctor* but it had no impact. G.B. had a sack of rolls in his hands. He sat on his haunches and began slathering the bread with butter and jam, then picking off little pieces to poke at my mouth. Birds. He thought we were birds. Death omens.

At first my mouth held stiff against him, but my tongue slithered out and caught the buzz of sugar in the jam. What a drug, sugar. Sublime. From there we made progress.

"Here you go, Mr. Rooney."

I began to cry. "Stop calling me that," I said, "it's so distressing. I don't call you Mr. Brights. It's so—"

"Mr. Rooney," he said, "that's the way I was raised. You were my teacher. That's what I call you."

We made more progress after that. I fell asleep once or twice during the proceedings but he stayed steady throughout, now sitting on the floor, his feet stretched out patient, waiting until he could bring me round to consciousness. He poked the carton of milk toward my mouth, and it slid down my throat like honey.

Yes. I realized absolutely the totality of my regression, realized that I was being fed like a baby and that when this operation was through we would have to go clean me up, because I was about to soil myself in the hallway. I could imagine the stench I let off already from the way G.B. held his face to one side while he got the food in me.

I thought of Walt Whitman in the war hospitals. He would think G. B. Brights a fine strong lad.

I was lucid, though I was allowing myself to continue in the infantile state: no. I was lucid *because* I was allowing myself to continue in an infantile state. I was coming around. If they would only let me stay. If only I could be nursed for a little while.

Finally I was fed to G.B.'s satisfaction and he rose and collected the packages he had brought to me. "OK, Mr. Rooney, you stay right there. I'm gonna go get myself a shave and then I'm coming back to get you to a doctor."

Still the word *doctor* did not register. What registered was that I had soiled myself, just as I predicted. Fed, I no longer kneeled but sat, in a pile of soft shit. I did not have the words to speak such a reality. Once, to shock me, Mary Faith said, *Inter urinas et faeces nascimur.* She'd won the state Latin award in sophomore year of high school. She didn't shock me. O a moment of utter bliss and sublime inner peace, to think that she could not see me here, this low.

G.B. made a face. "You are far gone," he said. "What you have to do that for? How'm I gonna get you on the train?"

He looked up and down the hallway for traitors who might report him if he led me back into Took's apartment to clean me up, but we were alone. "She's gonna have my hide she knows I let you back in," he said.

But he helped me rise up and steadied me through the doorway and on down through the little hallway that led to Took's antiseptic cheerful bathroom. There were yellow curtains over the frosted glass.

"Sit down on the toilet," he said.

I began to cry.

"Oh, come on now." He raised the lid of the toilet and then unbuck-led my pants for me. They slid down onto my bleeding feet.

"Go on now," he said. "Pull your drawers down."

I couldn't do it, not in front of him. I could do nothing but watch myself, a baby again, old Dolores brisk and no-nonsense before me, talking away so that no time, not bath time, not wiping-the-shit time, would be wasted, but all would be used to further my education and hence bring glory to God. Dolores chanted, *Trouble deaf heaven with my bootless cries.* I couldn't pull my drawers down.

He did it, and I remembered Velma doing the same and her gentle gray lips on my gray pecker which sat now like a baby's, half perky, full of interest in this scene.

"Oh sweet suffering Jesus," G.B. said. "You step out that mess now," and that I could do, with him there steadying my arm. I was progressing, I knew I was, because I couldn't bear to look down on him picking up my shit from off the floor. I screwed my eyes shut and heard him say:

"Shit!" and then the plop of it into the toilet.

I opened my eyes.

"All right now," he said, "you think I'm cleaning that off your butt you're too far gone to live. I'm leaving you in here to wipe yourself, you holler if you feel faint. Hear?"

I heard angel choirs.

"I'm going to fetch you one a my shirts. You like the Yankees or the Braves?"

"Yankees," I said.

"There," he said. "There you go. You gonna be all right, Mr. Rooney."

"You're all right too, Mr. Brights," I said and felt again that resurgence of hope and light and possibility. It was enough to make me weak in the heart and the groin and the knees, which it did, and I fell, down onto the toilet. I felt cold air beneath me and knew I was about to be sucked into oblivion. He reached out and steadied my arm again.

"Come on now," he said. "You get yourself together. I'm gonna draw you a bath, that's what we do with you, oh sweet Jesus, look at your feet, oh my God, and we getting out of here."

Then he left and I tried, I swiped away.

He was back with a clean shirt and a pair of Took's pants, pleated and military green, wouldn't you know it, because of course I would swim in G.B.'s trousers but Took's would only be too short. I could follow it all, the logic of it and the beauty of it too.

The bathroom filled up with sweet clouds of mist. Maybe I would be cleansed and born anew.

I had to strip to get down into the tub and believe me, I felt no shame, not with G. B. Brights steadying my arm. But when I put a foot in the hot water tears of humiliation filled the backs of my eyes. Someone held a branding iron to the soles of my feet. G.B. pressed me down from the shoulders and I sank into the hot water, thinking for one minute that the pressing of his thumbs meant that he would prefer to drown me, that he was drowning me, that it was right and just that I should be drowned, down into the waves like Dottie, down under, down deep.

But he was not drowning me, he was setting me down proper and I sat, yes, like a baby, yes, my feet extended, my uglies floating there on the rising water and the filth washing off of me.

He didn't shave me. I was a sight in Took's pants, but they were clean by God, a little baggy in the backside but more functional than I was. I had a navy-blue Yankees shirt on my back. I had socks on my feet. My hair was still damp from where he'd wet it for me and then gone at it with a cold metal comb. I clung to him going down on the elevator and in the lobby. An old granny fetching in her groceries stared at us in terror and disgust.

After we were outside G.B. said: "I bet she thought you and me was lovers. Were lovers. I bet you that's so, Mr. Rooney, and I'll tell you what else. You so weak, I bet she thought you got AIDS."

He was screeping with joy at the old lady's mistake and maybe with the pleasure of being out in the warm May day, the sunshine flooding down on us, but the light churned to terror for me. AIDS! That could explain everything. This was not brain fever. This was not insanity, only the dementia that meant I was in final stages. I couldn't for the life of me remember where I had contracted AIDS. The last needle I poked in my arm was at the old Rooney homestead when I played with gasoline in the sunlight. And Fred may have had me singing the identity crisis blues but I swear I have never so much as let a man touch my thigh. So I had a case of inexplicable AIDS. I would be the subject of a congressional inquiry. They would carry me in on a litter, like the leper to Jesus's feet. They would try to explain me, and then I would be dead.

I may have moaned, clinging there to G.B.'s arm as we made our way down the sidewalk, because he said, "Those feet hurting you, Mr. Rooney?"

I may have moaned again.

"Where are we going?" I said, and the clarity of my speech and my thought took me by surprise.

"I'm taking you on the train to Manhattan," G.B. said.

"Where we going in Manhattan?" How well I spoke! How strong I was growing, walking along. The bread had revived me, my blood growing thicker, the terror thickening with it. But the air struggled through my lungs. Maybe it wasn't AIDS that was killing me, maybe it was TB. O to die of Kafka's disease. I was unworthy. So hard to breathe in the harsh Brooklyn light. This was like the Long March, through sidewalks strewn with paper wrappers. The stragglers, the out-of-work, the mothers with children crowded the sidewalk, most of them black, some of them brown. And then the ones like me, white and consumptive, limping along.

"You just leave that to me," G.B. said.

Well. I'd heard that line before.

"We're going to Bellevue," I said.

"See, Mr. Rooney? You still understanding everything that's going on here. That's right. That's where we going. I talked to that friend of yours last night, Velma, and she said that's the place to go, she's gonna call somebody she knows make sure you get you a good bed and they get you a good doctor. She said don't even worry about the insurance just get you in there and she'll see to anything you don't have covered. Then we can call your family they can come see about helping you along."

"That's good," I said. They could call Katie and she could come and sit, patient by the bed, next to G.B. They'd get along fine. She'd bring *Cosmopolitan* and they'd get into small talk, this and that, home. Home.

I could feel G.B.'s arm tightening with pleasure and anticipation under my hand which clung to it still, clung to it tighter.

"All right, Mr. Rooney," he said. "All right, you are really going to be OK. I know it now. Oh man, I am relieved. I am relieved you'll all right bout taking care of this. And oh man, Took is gonna be so relieved she's gonna show up by your bed with a chicken in a pot, you take my word for it."

"She can come," I said. "Katie, Took. Let em all come. We can use a crowd in there, G.B., because believe you me it gets lonely on those wards. It gets lonely and then of course you're sharing a room with someone with whom you have absolutely nothing in common. Nothing except psychosis. We'll need the company."

His arm tightened again.

"Won't we?" I said. I heard my voice go high and hid my head in shame. The terror had completely flooded my vision again. G.B. was answering something, he was chattering away, but the terror had filled up the entire cavity that was my head so sound was no longer being processed. He was patting my hand, the hand that clung to his crooked arm, he was saying something sweet, I'm sure he was, because he is a sweet boy, a fine strong lad, Walt and I are so fond of him even if he was saying that he wouldn't be there to nurse me the idea was that I go alone into Bellevue where of course they shoot you with *real* life-threatening drugs and leave you in the company of real loonies besides. You hear the saddest things. There is no one sadder than a patient on a psycho ward. That's why we all turn our heads. That's why G.B. wouldn't come stay with me.

On the subway I pulled myself together and withdrew my hand from G.B.'s arm out of respect for his dignity. I sat straight. The food had strengthened me. I took in everything. We were on the number two train.

"You know what Took told me the cops call this train?" G.B. said.

I was attuned to everything.

"They call it the Beast. But I never had trouble yet."

I wasn't about to get into small talk on my way to Bellevue, especially not tricked into small talk about cops. I didn't have much time. I didn't know the Brooklyn trains. There would be cops on the platform, there are always cops at big stops, even in the daytime. But an outlaw like me, newly strengthened with milk and honey, would be able to outrun a cop and a fine young lad like G.B.

I wasn't going on any psycho ward. No, sir. No, thank you very much. I had misjudged them all, Took and Angela and Velma. And G.B.

"Next stop Atlantic Avenue," the conductor said, with marbles in his mouth, but I was attuned to everything. Chomsky at the wheel, I could take in his garble and reconstruct it so it came out as clear as my own plans, which were to make a run for it at the first express stop, a sly run before G.B. knew I was gone.

"Change there for the zheezheezheezhee." It was all Chinese. I couldn't be expected to translate from the Chinese! Danish was difficult enough. But I could run. With socks on my feet I could run from my captors and go out into the world to be the outlaw pilgrim I was meant to be.

The train lurched into Atlantic Avenue, but I did not lurch with it. Ah no. I closed my eyes in case G.B. should think to look over me, my hand unhooked from his, my body slouched physically but mentally coiled, ready to run, my six-shooters at my side. All around me passengers stood to change trains, but I did not stand, I sat patient next to G.B. until they were all boarded, I sat patient until I heard with my newly strengthened supersensitive hearing that the doors were just fixing to close.

Then I leaped. Maybe I had to push a few people out of my way. I hope not. Maybe I had to dive headfirst onto the platform. It's all a blur, that kind of break for it. I hope I did not frighten any children in their strollers. I leaped, and behind me G.B. rose. He was fast, but I was faster, and the doors closed on him. I could hear his fists pounding on them even as I ran through the station, even as the train took off with G.B. aboard and me cut loose. Free.

I missed him already.

I took off down a flight of stairs, through a dank dark corridor crowded with raucous children released from school for the day, and up another flight of stairs. A train was pulling in and I boarded it, my heart pounding out a rhythm that did not belong in any Western musical tradition. The heart would burst, that was all. G.B.'s train was off in another direction. What would he do, a young man from South Carolina, having lost the patient he was about to deliver to a mental hospital?

He would tell a cop, that's what, inform a policeman.

I tried to sit straight in my seat, I swear I tried, so that no policeman would make note of me, but my knees trembled violently and gave the game away. People sat next to me, got a load of my trembling knees in Took's knife-pleated trousers, and took off running. Still the train had not left the station. At any moment a cop might board and find me. Where to run? I stood, meaning to bolt the train and take off, perhaps through the tunnels, but at that moment doors clanged shut. I tasted metal and heard chimes.

By the next station I was rigid and could not move, not even when the chubby policeman came and stood at my door. He was dark-haired and thick-browed, Italian probably, no more than a boy. I felt a pitying affection for him even as I trembled in his presence. In my day they all called the cops pigs, but I never did: my mother was a child of the Irish working class that delivered these public servants into our midst, some of them even blinded by their faith in good works. This cop's walkie-talkie crackled, a toy in his belt. Or not a toy: it opened its gaping mouth. At any moment he would be hearing news of a runaway mental patient and I would be swallowed up.

It was unbearable, I tell you, my imminent capture. I thought my heart would explode in my chest and coils of brain unfurl in my head. The fever left me drooling in sweat and whimpering in my seat. The cop heard my low cries and turned his chin in my direction, tilted his head to hear my ravings, and moved . . . down the length of the car, away from me. Even the police would not look on me.

On and on the train sped through Manhattan. At every stop the cop stepped to the door and leaned his head forward onto the platform. Then he stuck his head back in the car. He did not bother to look my way, but I knew whom he was pinning with his silly charade at the door. He was waiting for reinforcements. I was trapped beneath the earth.

Then, at the next stop, an extraordinary thing happened: the policeman left the train entirely. A ruse? A trick, to lure me out? The policeman left, the doors closed, the train left the station. As we sped away I read the sign on the station's posts: 47–50. What a strange notation. A strange sign, a biblical verse, a hex, a curse. 47–50? 47–50?

Another stop. No cop to stop me but paralysis down the length of my spine. It was a trick, but if I were quick enough I could outwit them the way I'd outwitted G.B. Through the chimes I heard the conductor announce Columbus Circle, and though it meant nothing to me at the moment, I willed my body into action and leaped again onto the platform. But there! I'd been tricked! Another policeman stood guard—no, wait, the same policeman, it had to be, same chunky body, same limpid bored dark eyes in pouches. A terrible thrill ran through my body. They were hiring policeman clones now.

I had no choice but to run past him and follow the streaming light until it led me up the stairs and out the station. I looked over my shoulder and saw no one in pursuit. That would be another trick. Hordes of them, armies of clone policemen, waited around some corner. In the light I saw that I had emerged by a low stone wall, in another country: I was surrounded by pacific green leafing down around me.

Central Park.

"G.B.!" I cried. How could he have let me leave? Now I had to cross Central Park alone to escape my tormentors.

I leaped the fence and struggled through bushes, scaled rocks, crossed the teeming roadway. It was hard to breathe again but I ran through the green walks of Central Park in spring. I heard a fluttering behind and turned to see not policemen but bats.

Bats! A swarm of them, bearing down close behind, their plump bodies spangled in the airy day, their wings jeweled with rubies and jade, the rubies and jade swirling into mandalas. Bats in the daylight? I laughed for the first time in long days. Bats in the belfry. I was crazy, that was what. My laughter turned to . . . well, fill in the blanks. A madman, I looped through the great expanse of the Sheep Meadow and crossed it to the other side, but I had shed neither the bats nor the insanity. I could go no farther.

I curled under a park bench, doubling myself to fit beneath the legs, speaking in tongues as strange as the flapping of those bats' wings until even my tongue could go no further and fell into the only relief available, that retreat from consciousness that had served me so well these last weeks.

I woke up better.

It was morning now, midmorning maybe, and there were no bats in the park. I lay in a woman's pair of pants, under a bench, drenched with sweat or the morning dew or maybe both, on the outer edges of the Sheep Meadow. I was alone in Central Park, retracing the outline of sanity, and starving. I crossed the meadow, the roadway, the same green graceful walk I traveled the day before. I found myself again on Columbus Circle, surrounded by little men with little carts. Food, food, everywhere, and not a crumb for me.

I approached a withered man behind a hot dog cart, his white shirt-sleeves rolled up halfway to his shoulder and his mustache drooping beneath his long nose.

"Mister," I said, "I'm starving." It was all that drove me.

But even before he could hear my words he was shaking his head. "No," he whispered when I drew close. "Go way."

When I turned from him in my hunger, I had a vision of Mary Faith, cloaked in blue and white. It wasn't a hallucination—I tell you, I wasn't allowing any more of those—it was a vision, Mary Faith large as the sky, tall and thin and graceful, a diadem of flowers on her head. I could see her clothed and unclothed, the blue gown revealing and obscuring her simultaneously. The vision was wavering, like a movie shown on sheets, and I pursued it to the edge of the sidewalk before I stepped out into Broadway traffic unawares. I believe I have mentioned this is a pattern with me.

The cabs screeched around me. I escaped with my life and heard what the vision told me: I was an outlaw. If I needed food, I should take it.

That was a relief. The hunger was clawing at me. I shuffled up Broadway and made my way into one of those big instidelis that have sprung up all over New York, one of those glass-fronted crowded anonymous places with a basket of rolls in front of the high glass cases. No little German man here to slice you your pastrami, no little rabbity wife on Thompson Street, only young men wiping the sweat from their brows.

At my approach, the crowds parted—I seemed to be having that effect on people—so I swooped down into the basket and pulled me out not one but two bagels. One was onion, which I've never cared for, but I didn't want to push my luck. I swirled, my old Fred Astaire training keeping me light on my feet, and I left the store with my food in my fists and a counterman yelling out, "Hey! Hey!"

The customers all turned to stare, but they did nothing more. We are not our brothers' keepers.

There was nothing to it. I strolled up Broadway, eating my bagels as delicately as I could, which was not very, given the state of my hunger. When I was finished, I was thirsty, and I repeated the process in another anonymous instistore. I strolled to the refrigerator case, got me a large bottle of purple juice, and strolled back out.

This time one of the young men chased me. I got a glimpse of him before I hightailed it—he was as tall as I, and sallow, and hopeless in his deli whites—but I tell you, I've never been so exhilarated in my life. To take what you want, and then be held accountable. A simple human interaction, but by God it kept my legs pumping long after the boy dropped off his chase, all the way up Broadway past the whited sepulchers of Lincoln Center and into the 72nd Street subway before I knew where I was heading.

I was a thief and an escapee and now that I was in motion I knew no way to stop. There was a cop by the token booth and the sound of an incoming train below. I vaulted the turnstile. No gyms for me all these years, but by God I still had a spring in my bloodied step and, the cop in hot pursuit, I could slide too, down the stairs and right into an uptown local which cradled me in its arms, shut its doors before the policeman reached the platform, and trundled me on my well-fed way.

An outlaw. This time I sat smug in my subway seat, as if I knew where I was going, and took the trouble to dust last night's Central Park dirt from Took's pants. The cleaning improved them so, I rolled the bottoms up. The pleats were still sharp, the starch still stiff. The day before folks had fled the crazy man but now they smiled indulgently at the sight of me making my morning toilet. We all admire an outlaw.

The doors opened and shut, opened and shut. When they opened at 116th Street, Columbia University, I got out, thinking that I had to get back to the dorm. No, that was wrong. I had to get back to 113th Street, where Bernadette was filling up my filing cabinet. I shook my head.

And exited the station outside Columbia's gates. I walked north, afraid to enter. Across the street leafy cool female Barnard beckoned, but I was shy of it. A redheaded girl in a filmy skirt and jackboots preceded me up the block.

I turned the corner at 120th Street, afraid to enter, afraid to leave. I was circling Columbia, that was what I was doing, outsider as always. Beside me it towered like a walled fortress. How many years had I let pass before I returned to this place where I squandered my youth? How many years before I could return to the scene of terrifying freshman seminars and vicious competitive graduate school and a six-day marriage from which I had yet to recover? Was it because I remembered how vast the buildings were, how cold? And the sidewalks were so clean! Surely they had never been swept like this when I was a boy limping through *The Sickness unto Death*.

Across from Teachers College a man in rags stretched across the sidewalk, his boils edging toward green. Me, I kept on my way, circling Columbia warily, trying to remember my obligations here. Paper due? Footnotes to check? Wedding to dress for? Protest march? Occupation of a building? On Amsterdam, I drifted in through the gates onto campus and set myself down on the cold library steps looking down and out toward Butler. The names shimmered out over the great white building: Homer. Herodotus. Sophocles.

Then a wondrous thing happened. That red-haired girl in the filmy skirt and the jackboots passed me by again. She was a little gawky, her thick black shoes tripping up her gossamer skirt, but she would be lovely one day, one day when she had her Ph.D. and a chair at a major university. Her arms stretched out bone white, wounded with freckles. As if she felt my eyes on her arm, she raised it to brush away her hair, dense with curls and escaping the rag she'd tied around it in back.

I knew why I'd come.

Bernadette walked by these steps in 1967, with her black braids pinned to the sides of her head like some old peasant woman and her stockings and her loafers, a girl who hadn't heard that the times they were a-you-know-what. It was my first vision of her, and I sprang up, knowing like a prophet that she was a shy girl from a Catholic school and that we were kindred spirits.

Before I could retreat into my terror of women I ran alongside her, panting. "I'm Tim Rooney," I said, "from South Carolina, no I'm not kidding. Want to go down to Washington Square? I know a place where we could get espresso." And then, seeing the look of terror on her own face: "I'm a philosophy major."

She stopped and gave me a look that made it clear she thought I was out of my mind. Then she tilted her head, her black braids curling into her shoulder, and said: "Philosophy? Well, OK. When do you want to go?"

"Now," I said.

I closed my eyes right there on the steps.

The sanity was descending on me too rapidly. I sprang up again—had to keep moving, had to keep the visions at bay—and set off down Broadway for unlucky 113th Street, where I once lived in happy bachelor bliss.

Those years after I left my dorm room, I lived in an undistinguished apartment building on a street filled with undistinguished tenements and chipping brownstones and drab low-rises. Nothing romantic about my block, but when Bernadette was feeling rebellious, when she was feeling the sixties pulsing in her good-girl veins, she left the girl grad students on 114th and came to me instead, and we sinned in guilty pleasure. Pleasure! Bernadette's low moans dissolved into giggles and then, when she was feeling sentimental, tears. Crying because she was sentenced to a lifetime with me?

When we married, for six days we shared the same small quarters in back, our books piled so high we could hide from each other behind them, our window gated to keep out maniacs on the fire escape. Through the gates we looked out on a view of brown bricks.

Now I stood on 113th Street, unsure for a minute which of these undistinguished buildings was *my* undistinguished building, and I wept uncontrollably. Bernadette had imported lace curtains from Sunnyside, Queens, to frame the brown brick view I'd been looking on for years. To obscure the gates. After she left me she came back when I was out and took the lace curtains down.

This weeping was getting out of hand. As I stood amid the used Kleenexes and cracked beer bottles of 113th Street I was not standing on the terrifying streets of the Upper West Side. I was standing in the terrifying confines of my studio apartment. Six days married. I held a belt in my hand. I wanted to tie Bernadette up with the belt and if she would only let me, it would be a sign of trust and faith, sure as those low moans of hers, a sign that I could live out the rest of my life without asking more. Only that. Only in the sixties. Only when you could move beyond the rigidity of reason. Only while other people were wife-swapping. I only wanted to tie her up.

I only want to tie you up.

"Tim, did you drop acid again?"

I smile stupidly. Behind her, atop the books, a platoon of khaki-green plastic soldiers spray us with gunfire. AK-47s. The soldiers come and they go. Cannonball Adderley's playing, the quintet, Nat's cornet pop-pop-popping with the soldiers' gunfire, but I'm pretty sure the stereo's not on.

"Tim, that's the stupidest, you *know* what that does, you *promised,* you're up half the night when you don't take anything at all trying to figure things out. Tim, you promised. You said when we got married."

Only half a tab. Half a tab doesn't do anything to anybody, didn't used to do anything to me, used to make the tips of my toes more accessible, the print on the spine of a book clearer, but lately . . .

"Are you hallucinating?"

I smile yet more stupidly. I'm not letting on to those soldiers. Bernadette would not find it amusing.

"Are you freaking out?"

She's seen me freak out. The soldiers whirl on her, drill through her back. Her kidneys dribble out. Mercy. Glutinous pattycakes, miscarried organs. O put the kidneys back. Reverse that. I pull my belt out my pants so I don't have to look at the soldiers and I hold it up, stupidly, stupid belt, stupid smile, stupid gift. "I only want to tie you up. I'm OK."

"Look, I told you, I don't like it when you do that, I mean I do like it, that's what I don't like. It makes me feel creepy after, so let's not and say we did. OK? I don't want to wake up wondering why I did something I didn't like doing the first place. In women's group . . . oh, never mind, you're not listening. You're tripping your brains out."

Damn straight, not listening. When she got on a roll Bernadette could talk you to death. I stand there smiling stupidly and it occurs to me that I could talk too, talk and hush her up. I know as soon as I open my mouth it's the wrong move, but at least I'm not watching the soldiers anymore.

"It's not wrong if it's between us, Bernadette, it's symbolic of course of your putting your trust in me but don't you see it simultaneously confirms my trust in you that you would allow me to bind you, to confirm our mutual binding when I have already"

I know I sound like I'm wearing my tweed jacket and drawing deep on a Salem underneath the classroom NO SMOKING sign. I know I sound foolish but it keeps me from seeing the plastic soldiers and worse, worse, a wavering Madonna up there on the wall where if this were a good Catholic household we'd have a crucifix at least. There is no Madonna there, I'm pretty sure there is no Madonna there. I cannot look that way. Bernadette has started up again.

"Please," she says. "Puh-lease. Don't give me that, Tim, you're out of your mind tripping and why'd you do it anyway, after two weeks ago freaking out like that? Huh? What do you want to do, tempt fate and see if you can make it happen all over again? That one I thought, *OK, it's the wedding,* OK, but what about two weeks before that and two months before that and oh, there's too many to count."

Her hair is loose. She's beginning to look like a woman of her time, of her day. She wears a thin white T-shirt, my T-shirt in fact, and no bra underneath, just those barely there breasts, those breasts that might have been a boy's, those rose-tinged globules meant for suckle. I cannot stop, no, wrong. I can stop. I cannot stop toy soldiers from dancing atop my books, that's physiological, but I can stop this if I care to, only I don't, I want to reach out for her breasts, especially now that the new look has crossed her face, the look of despair, granny glasses sliding down her nose, eyes above them gone blank and glassy with the tallying of all my episodes and the realization that if she lets me touch her now, if she lets me tie her up she will be all tied up with craziness for the rest of her life.

Some of us embrace it.

I grab for her wrists, but hey I'm only playing, this is only a joke, if I assert myself in a manly way she'll be tickled to go along, along, all the way along to the low moans that yield to giggles that yield to cries under the sad Madonna that may or may not at this very moment be looking down on us in our vale of tears and women's groups.

"Get your drug addict hands off me," she says.

I look down at my hands, red hairy knuckles and flat smooth palms, my fingertips callused from the guitar. "You don't get addicted to acid." I hear myself smooth, sophisticated, man of the world. "You just get you some vision."

And then I make the fatal mistake, the mistake that sends her fleeing: and even as I grab again, even as I put behind my trembling biceps all the rage and pity I feel for her contempt, I know that I am calling the shots here, that I am controlling this scene, that I, grabbing for my wife's wrist and pretending that I want to tie her up with the same leather that struck me somewhere in another life, am sending her on her way and good riddance. Good riddance. Does any man want a woman to see him perceiving the world in some cubist Dada Man Ray Fellini Magical Mystery Tour vision? Toy soldiers and a sad Madonna? I ask you. Do you want a *witness* to that?

"Oh!" she cries, like the fifties, like Lucy McGillicudhy Ricardo. "Oh!"

And I pull her close and she struggles but I, knowing she is on the way out, am free to feel this pure angerlust, this disdain for her contempt, this rising pulsing need to punish punish if only she will

kick me in the balls.

She kicked me in the balls. And packed a bag and plaited her hair into braids, to emphasize her innocence, and ran into the night, into the subway, gone back to Sunnyside, home to Queens, from whose safety she could make her new assault on the world without me, me, loony Rooney, sliding now down the studio wall to crouch on my heels opposite my books and hold myself still against the rising panic hearing the dissociated chant *I love you, I love you* and recognizing even in the repetition of the sound, growled now by Cannonball Adderley on a stereo that wasn't playing, the utter falsity: I love no one, shooed away a little sister on account of her slow dull need. Scram, you bore me, you needle me, you wear in the grimy ring around your mouth all the sad sorry voracious hunger of this family. I'm gone, I'm out of here, out of this family, out of this marriage, out of town, and it is right and just that I should stand on 113th Street with a Kleenex sticking to the sole of my shoe and the green glump spreading through that other soul. Bernadette. I could reach out and touch her. I could reach out and drive her away.

I was on 113th Street. I was not hallucinating.

I fled the grim buildings staring down on me. I fled the street where I lived with my first girl, my prosaic wife, the one who drank wine with me in the park and listened to post-beat poetry with me at the West End.

When she left I knew that I would never live with another human being again.

Well, ha. The joke was on me. I landed in Christian communes, trying to split logs when I'm not so good at cutting my own overgrown toenails. I landed in Due East and lived with big impossible Bill Rooney after his own wife departed his presence. I ended up living with a little sister I drove right out to sea.

I poked my eyes with my fist and propelled myself back to Broadway. At the corner I forced myself to swim upstream against the tide and breathed in through my nose, seeking calm. I passed a restaurant that had never been around when I lived in these parts. I was beginning to get jumpy again. Just beginning to sizzle a little around the inner ear.

The restaurant was called Grandma's. Well, I can read a sign.

Grandma's.

I remembered who I was and, passing a news booth, stole a *New York Times.* A great halloo let out and a gauntlet of folks stretched out their arms to slow if not detain me. Or maybe they just wanted to touch me, Outlaw and Pilgrim.

But I was hot, o the split blisters under my sock urged me on. I loped up Broadway and down into the subway. By then they'd all given up the chase, and I felt the surge of well-being that comes with being an accomplished petty thief.

I was on my way to Grandma's.

DAY TWENTY-NINE LACE CURTAINS

Maybe I slept on the trains. The next morning I found myself walking Dyckman Street in the hazy light of day. I was in Inwood, tip of upper Manhattan, where for many years I went to visit my grandmother out of a sense of duty and fear and fascination.

I could not remember waking. I still held yesterday's stolen newspaper in my hand, as if I had clutched it all through the night. The words shimmered up: *Bosnia, Steinbrenner, talks collapse.*

I was worried about my appearance. This was not the sort of neighborhood where you wear a woman's pants rolled up, not when the starch is getting flaky and the pleats are falling out. Inwood wasn't Irish anymore, not on Dyckman. The shops sat under Spanish names, the children's faces rested under thick dark hair. The stores sold beepers, the cars blared out Tito Puente. On my way to my grandmother Rose's I used to stop for fortification at an Irish bar, a Mooney's or a McQuade's or a Maloney's. Now, with all the landmarks changed, I couldn't remember the street. Now I couldn't find an Irish bar. But maybe I had spent the night in one? That would account for a blackout.

I turned up Seaman. More fortresses: this part of Manhattan is built up and braced against the Hudson's winds by the tall stout apartment buildings that stretch out block after block. I trudged the hill and found me some Irish faces, faces of my ancestry, my link to humanity. Everyone I passed was stooped over with a plastic shopping bag, the old men in worn dark ties, the women in jaunty little berets. I felt disrespectful, unworthy of being connected to their hopeful dignified presence, and swatted at my clothes. Dirt crawled off: had I spent the night in another park, then?

Already I was up to Rose McGillicudhy's, where my mother Dolores spent her childhood. A great chill passed over me, a long shadow, and my vision darkened. Had I entered this dark courtyard recently? Last night? All we Rooneys were scared to the bone of Rose McGillicudhy's apartment, because surely that was where our mother grew so sad and so earnest.

The building's paths diverged into two wings from the courtyard. My grandmother's apartment would be over there, to the right, down a dim corridor suffused with the smells of working-class food, sodden vegetables, stewing fat.

I pushed against the heavy glass and ironwork door. Unlocked! Only in Inwood. For a long while I stood in the doorway, waiting for someone to stop me. No one appeared. I bowed my head, crossed myself, and entered. Whoa there. Where'd I think I was—church? I cast a guilty look over my shoulder, but I was alone. I toiled up the dark gray stairway to the third floor, where Dolores and Rose lived alone after my grandfather ran off with a floozy. *Peroxide-blond floozy,* my mother used to say.

I made my way down my grandmother's long hallway and stood in front of her door. It looked exactly as it did when I was sixteen. It was painted exactly the same shade of dried blood.

Before I met Bernadette, and even after for a while, I came up every Friday to see my grandmother in her three little rooms, just beyond this door. I could see right through the door: Rose sits me down on her patched velvet sofa, its springs riding beneath me. My own springs are a little riotous, loose maybe from the whiskey in Mooney's, maybe from the joint I breathed in on the hike from the train.

"Oh, Timmy," my grandmother says. "It is a joy to have you here." Her voice smells of sachet. She is a big lanky woman with bad teeth but she makes her movements small and distracts my eye from her teeth with a surreal lavender lipstick. Sometimes I have the strangest feeling that she's flirting with me.

We sit for hours in the dark, the television and the radio both transmitting a low hum. She forgets to feed me, but she encourages my manly smoking and rises to wipe the ashtray clean with each cigarette. No whiskey in the house, though. She is a cheery teetotaler. She has me dig in her narrow closet, her only closet, for holy cards in cardboard boxes. *She was so pious about the drinking,* my mother said. *She drove my father away. And those holy cards!* There are thirty or forty boxes, the cards in waxed paper slips, smelling of incense, smelling of funerals.

"Here," she says when I've found the right one. "Brendan the navigator. He'll steer you through that college of yours."

She regards the halls of Columbia as heathen, and by God she's right. But I've smoked a little hash and it doesn't seem untoward for me to ask her why she didn't let my mother go.

"Go where?" Her voice chirps high and fluttery, an incongruous sound from her big bass body.

"To Columbia." My mother wanted to go to Barnard: we all knew that: and my grandmother wouldn't let her: and many years later my mother peered over my shoulder while I filled out my application to Columbia.

"Your mother did go to college," my grandmother says. "I'll never forget that Sister Perpetua. The arrogance."

I raised my eyebrows in encouragement. This is her favorite story, how my mother deserted her.

"And Lorey had already agreed," my grandmother says, her voice now low and conspiratorial, "that she'd go down to Wall Street. A smart girl like that. She'd be executive secretary in no time and we'd both be comfortable."

"But she had the scholarship," I say.

"She had two! But of course there was no question of college at all, much less a college that wasn't Catholic. I was shocked to hear she'd applied, behind my back like that. When Sister Perpetua showed up on my doorstep—"

we look together at the very doorstep

"—and told me they needed her at Mount St. Martyr's, what was I to say? Was I to break her heart, so that we'd live decently? She shamed me, that nun did, shamed me into signing the papers then and there and never a more bitter mistake did I make, because if Lorey hadn't gone to Mount St. Martyr's, and hadn't been running around with those smart and sassy girls, she'd have never been running down to Greenwich Village . . ."

where she met big good-looking black-haired Bill Rooney, jazz musician, in the only year of his life he ever took a chance, and ran off with him and down to South Carolina, and left Rose McGillicudhy alone. There is no choice for my grandmother but to trail off. "Italian!" my grandmother says. "Italian, with the nuns. I was shocked to hear they taught it." She rummages back in the box and draws out a snapshot lodged between St. Pius I and St. Innocent I: her own big handsome ruddy black-haired husband, gone forever, married to two other women though he never divorced her.

"Lorey adored her father," she says.

"That's not what I heard." It's the hash talking.

"What do you mean, Timmy? She adored him, and well she should have, no matter what he did. I believe it was some virus that overtook his brain, and prevented him knowing right from wrong." My mother hated him for leaving, and that was why she never left my father, so she would not repeat his sin, and that is why I'm smirking now. That and the hash.

My grandmother rises, flustered, and stands under the doorway where the television's drone meets the radio's hum. The sound waves bounce off her great heaving bosom. It must be radio waves that transform her like this.

"Don't you look like that, Timmy Rooney. Lorey adored her father."

I sit dignified and serene, agreeing with all her delusions, but the hash must be distorting my features. The next thing I know the cardboard box is beating down on my head, holy cards flying through the air all about me, fluttering down: I catch glimpses of St. Ignatius Loyola, St. Barnabas, the manly saints, the adventurers, the builders of the Church, free-falling in my grandmother's sad apartment to the shabby rug while my grandmother beats my head with their cardboard coffin box and shrieks:

"Laugh at me, go on. Laugh at me, college boy. Smirk at me! The way Lorey smirked! Italian, when we ate lima beans six nights a week! Laugh at me! Running off that way, all of you, oh, so smart, with your foreign languages." Now she begins to cry as she beats me and I see for the first time that she is beating me the same way my father beat me, about the head, and they aren't even related! Except of course through my mother, and—my mother despises them both! I cover my head with my hands—cardboard doesn't hurt—and I laugh pretty uncontrollably because of the hash, and my grandmother cries harder and says:

"She was such a happy thing! We were so happy together!"

And at that I rock, all curled up, saving myself, thinking that she is right off her gourd. She never leaves her apartment. A neighbor boy fetches her groceries. She cannot bring herself to join the other old ladies, in their jaunty berets, at bingo. She sits for long hours, drifting away, remembering her faithless daughter.

And the next morning she calls me to tell me she is sorry, it must be some virus, she has a terrible headache and

The sound of salsa crept along the floorboards of my grandmother's building. The music was real. I was sure it was real, but I could not determine if it came from under my grandmother's door. I could feel garlic scraping my fingertips. These halls were supposed to smell of soft cabbage, not arroz con pollo. Everything changing! My very past.

My grandmother sat rotting in her apartment for days before anyone found her. Now I saw an eye at the peephole of the door I stood before, a watery unfocused eye. I'm sure I did. I forced myself to walk back down the corridor, down the three long flights of stairs. It was all I could do not to break into a run. I used to pat my grandmother's hand, sitting there with her. It's a wonder my mother didn't lose her mind.

But that was my job, losing my mind. My mother couldn't go to a secular school, so I went. My mother couldn't love my father, so I did, when I could. My mother couldn't go crazy, so . . . They designate one of us in every family. I was the sacrificial son. My grandmother put the lace curtains up, and Bernadette took them down.

The hazy light streamed merciless once I left the darkness of my grandmother's building. I longed to sit in a bar on Dyckman Street and hear brave false tales of gunrunning from the neighborhood boyos. But I drifted instead toward the light and the river, the sky hanging down close over my head. Storm coming. Storm brewing. I was hungry again, and not hungry. I was moving beyond it.

I climbed my way up the hill and into the park. I had been in this green lately, very lately. The spring foliage was so dense that I could barely see New Jersey, but still I was drawn to the river, the great Hudson that flowed by my grandmother and Bernadette. I never stood up high above the Hudson without wanting to throw myself in. Was this where I spent the night? I sat myself on the great swoop of green that slopes down from Indian Road.

I still held the newspaper in my hand. I opened it, fearful, and seeing the front page remembered that Mary Faith and Jesse wanted me to stop the ethnic cleansing in Bosnia. But I was so tired. And the sky was so threatening. And I'd had nothing to eat, nothing to drink.

I sat with my grandmother's ghost in this park where my mother must have come, as a girl, to plan her escape. And my mother came and sat beside me, right on the grass.

Tim, she said, *I didn't hate her.*

I didn't say a word. My grandmother was soft and oblivious on the other side of me. My mother'd never said a word against her.

I tried not to hate her, my mother says.

I tried not to hate my father.

She forgave him, my mother said. *I never could, and I died bitter, and then Dottie died bitter at me. Maybe it's better to drift off the way she did. I don't want you to die bitter, Tim.*

I don't want to die at all, I said. "I don't want to die at all, sister."

And a dark lanky boy dribbling a basketball stared over his shoulder at me on my patch of grassy ground, and I saw in his expressionless gawking eyes the look that the neighbor boy must have given my grandmother when he fetched her in the groceries.

woke atop a park bench instead of beneath one. I knew where I was: my mother's park. I stood and looked down on the Hudson, the gray sky stretching over it like an ether haze. There was no storm. It was only a darkening of my vision.

I was weak, and the newspapers I had spread over me for a night's cover were scattering in the damp and breezy morning. I stooped and grabbed up the front page, and again the words swam before me: *murder* and *rape* and *Bosnia*. No one to stop it but me.

My mother did not want me to die bitter. All right, and hadn't Dolores Rooney always had a sense, too, that if you don't do what's right in the world you're liable to lose your mind? Dolores and her pamphlets, Dolores and her discussion groups, Dolores lining up her five children at the kitchen table to lick the stamps for the latest letter-writing campaign.

I had to stop the war in Bosnia. No one to pull the burning bodies from the flames but me.

The plan unfolded broad and complete as the sky above me. I was to go to Union Square, that old rabble-rousing center. I was to gather disciples around me. I would preach, and they would come. I would lead them up Fifth Avenue and down Pennsylvania Avenue. We would build a boat if needs be, and sail across the seas. I would go myself, Walt Whitman among the wounded, and I would not die of bitterness.

I trembled. I tripped over the cascading papers flying down to my mother's Hudson River, flying down beneath the great leafing trees. I knew at last my mission.

REPORT FROM THE NEW JERSEY TURNPIKE

Father Berkeley lost his nerve after the accident. We were all right, and it wasn't really his fault—it was the truck that sideswiped us, not the other way around, even if he was only traveling forty miles an hour and maybe weaving a little.

But we were holed up in the motel room for five days, waiting for car parts, and that is a long time to be on edge. He shared all our meals, but in the middle of eating he would disappear to make mysterious phone calls. He seemed to know people in New York, and I imagine he was troubling them with the search. He always came back to the table grim.

Now more than ever it seemed to me that this was a fool's errand. The last night, Father Berkeley said: "It's been twenty-six days." They were delivering the car to the motel in the morning, and we would be in New York by afternoon. "No. I shouldn't count from Easter." He got out a pocket calendar and began to count the squares. "Didn't you say he started acting strange on Holy Thursday?"

I couldn't remember saying any such thing, and I never would have referred to Holy Thursday. That day has no significance for me. It all started a long while ago, that was all I could remember. I had moved past my anger and now felt I was in mourning. Tim was a dead man to me.

"Twenty-nine days from Holy Thursday," the old man said, "and tomorrow it will be thirty." He had gone past divining, straight into numerology. I begged him not to count the days in front of Jesse.

"I won't," he said, stung. "I wouldn't, of course." We sat drinking our coffee after dinner, the two of us longing for something stronger. Jesse had gone to play the basement video games.

The old man leaned over the table the way he does sometimes, trying to startle me. "The last time Tim had a breakdown," he said, "he put together a file box with index cards. Terrible thing. Just terrible."

"Cards?"

"They represented the ways man betrays God and vice versa. You could flip them over, depending on which betrayal you were interested in. It was bizarre and"—here he laughed a bitter, brittle laugh—"I've heard some bizarre tales in the confessional. It takes a lot to shock a priest. Now we're getting on to forty days."

"And you think forty means something to him?"

"Forty years in the wilderness. Forty days in the desert." I believe Father Berkeley enjoyed my bewilderment. "Forty days when you might say Christ Himself imagined insanity."

"No," I said. I felt a dull panic. I knew exactly what the priest suspected: that after forty days, Tim would follow his mother and Dottie. If the old man was right, Tim meant to destroy himself. I searched back to that first night when he turned on me. "I believe it was a Thursday," I said. "It was, I'm sure, because the next day I went to work and then . . . It was. Thursday."

The old man leaned back finally into his chair. "Then tomorrow will be thirty days," he said. "And we'll have ten days to get to him."

Seeing the self-satisfaction on his face, I could have kicked myself for falling into his superstitious trap. Forty days! Christ imagining insanity! It was hard to believe I sat with this old man in the twentieth century. I felt at that moment that I lived in the Middle Ages, where signs and portents held people locked in place, just as Father Berkeley held me to my unwilling part in this trip.

The mechanic didn't bring the car by the motel until after lunch. By then we were all out of sorts from the strain of still more waiting. Father

Berkeley asked me to drive, and I said: "I've been offering all this way up the East Coast."

"Is that a yes or a no?" he said.

I took the wheel and Jesse sat beside me. Father Berkeley was in the back seat, trembling every now and again, drifting off for most of the trip. His head lolled and the picture in the rearview reminded me of nothing so much as a baby. I was scared driving the turnpike, I don't mind saying, but I held my own with the tractor-trailers and made good time through New Jersey.

Jesse scribbled in a notebook, as he'd done most of the trip. It gave me the willies to see it, an old-fashioned composition notebook Tim gave him. It was something Tim's mother used to have her children do, fill notebooks with little jottings and drawings. She bought them a new one as soon as the old one was filled, and that was the practice Tim had started with Jesse. Whenever I'd peeked—I knew I shouldn't, but I was sure Tim's saintly mother took a look too—Jesse's book was filled with doodles, and now and again a horrific monster drawing guaranteed to make any mother close the pages right quick.

Midway through the trip Jesse slammed the notebook shut and said: "There," which, believe me, is as open an invitation to conversation as I am likely to get from my son.

"What you working on?" I said.

"Finished the opera," he said.

"What opera?"

"The Hound from Hell."

I'd forgotten all about *The Hound from Hell.* It caused so much friction between Tim and Jesse that I'd tried to forget it even when they were working on it. Now my anger burned bright again.

"What happens?" I said. "In the opera." I was dreading the answer.

"Well," Jesse said. "It's a long story."

"That's all right."

"Well. The dog, you know, Clover, Clover's got this father he's never seen. So he takes off on a trip to find him? And naturally his owner goes crazy that Clover's missing, the owner's a kid, and so *he* sets off after Clover and the father. The father's The Hound from Hell."

If Tim had been in the car, I would have torn him limb from limb.

"Three acts," Jesse said. "I did twenty-seven songs. Like, arias and stuff."

"Twenty-seven songs!" Jesse was holding up his composition book and thumbing through the pages. He wasn't kidding. Page after page of his crabbed handwriting flipped before me. I'd need a magnifying glass to read it—as if I could bear the reading. *Bastard,* I thought. Leaving him with that. *Bastard.*

"I inkimllikeit," Jesse said, his voice as small as his writing on the page.

"What, darlin?"

"I said, *I think Tim'll like it.* Maybe now he'll come home."

"Jesse! You don't think Tim left because you guys fought over the opera?"

Jesse stared out the window.

"Oh, Jesse. It's nothing to do with that. It's nothing to do with you. Tim's—"

I couldn't get the word *sick* out. I didn't believe it. And I wanted to rewind and swallow back *It's nothing to do with you.* I believed from the start that it had everything to do with Jesse.

Jesse sat up straighter, over the silence, and said: "When he sets the music to it, it'll be like Massenet, the way Art Tatum plays him."

"What?"

That was Father Berkeley sitting up bolt upright in the backseat, unwilling to let me and my son have a minute's privacy to struggle through this.

"Like Massenet, the way Art Tatum plays him." And right there in his seat belt Jesse hummed a jazzy little tune that took off into outer space. "The trick with the words is, you make the rhyme corny enough to get your audience to smile, but not so corny they groan." It was so weird hearing Tim's voice coming out of my son's mouth that I thought I might drive the car right off the turnpike.

"When did he start you on this project?" Father Berkeley said, and I tried to shoot him a look to warn him off this numbers business. He wouldn't meet my eye in the rearview. I would have set him out on top of a guardrail if he said anything crazy to Jesse then.

"I dunno," Jesse said, "sometime," and Father Berkeley didn't press it. We were back to silent driving, and I was steady at the wheel.

Jesse fell fast asleep, he and the priest breathing deep and slow together, and I pushed the car faster than I might have if they'd been awake to catch me at my speeding. But night was threatening to fall, and I was frightened of New York at night. Remember, I'd never driven north of Chapel Hill before. They'd see me coming on the streets of New York. Father Berkeley had arranged one place for himself to stay, another for the two of us.

Thirty miles out of New York the two of them stirred, and when they woke they caught the excitement of being so close to the city.

"What's it like where we're staying?" Jesse said.

"I'm sure it will be comfortable," the priest said. He seemed stiff, but he was just waking up.

"Is it on Park Avenue?" Jesse said. Where'd he hear of Park Avenue?

"It's not on Park Avenue. It's downtown. In an old part of the city called Greenwich Village."

"I know," Jesse said. "Beatniks."

"You'll stay in an old house. Small, I believe."

Jesse started squirming in his seat and, I admit it, I was excited myself.

"Where are *you* staying?" Jesse said.

"I'm staying in the other direction. Uptown. I'm staying with an old friend, in a community of Jesuit priests."

"What's a Jesuit priest?"

"It's a priest who's learned, but worldly at the same time."

Jesse sucked on that for a while, and then he said, "Like you. You're a Jesuit priest?"

Father Berkeley laughed, and I realized I'd never heard him indulge in that warm a pleasure. It set me smiling myself. "No," said Father. "I'm an old fumbling priest."

"So who are we staying with? Beatniks?"

Father sat back, stiff and formal again, and we had to strain to hear him. "I don't really know her myself," he said. "She's connected to the Rooneys by marriage, or she was at one time."

My blood ran cold.

Jesse said: "What's her name?"

"Bernadette Rooney," the priest said, and I went into shock. I thought I might slip into a coma then and there. The priest was putting Jesse and me into Tim's wife's house.

"She wadn't married to Tim's father was she? Cause now he's married to Eliana."

"No," the priest said.

Go on, I thought. *Go on. Tell him. Tell me you did this.*

And he did. "She was married to Tim," the old man said, "but the Church declared that marriage invalid."

I thought Jesse's eyes would pop out of his head. "Tim wadn't married before."

"When he was a young man," Father Berkeley said. "The Church said that marriage . . . didn't count."

Jesse began laughing one of those high-pitched laughs that means he's scared. It was a wonder that, between my rage and fear, we stayed on the road at all. Somehow I kept driving but, straight ahead as the road stretched in front of me, I couldn't help but think I was going down, down. Jesse's laugh tapered off, and when he said:

"Look! Look!" and we saw the city rising up out of the low earth and sparkling before us, I thought of a fortress or a castle, and knew that my part was to be in the dungeon.

Already I felt I was in chains.

seven

was *much* better. Those bagels I'd eaten three days before were made,
like my vision of Mary Faith, of miracles. I no longer needed food. I
hobbled along, my blisters oozing, the socks G.B. put on my feet glued to
my sores. But I knew where I was going. I knew what I had to do.

I circled Union Square more than once looking for that cruddy disreputable scene of demonstrations and harangues, that urban oasis for
politicos, sane or insane. But this square I wandered now could not be the
same square where I once heard Yippies flamadozzling. This square could
not be the same square where my mother listened rapt to Wobblies. This
square had become a marketplace. Commerce, in Union Square!

Union Square was ringed with carts and farm trucks, and all along
the periphery stood innocent vegetable vendors. An Amish woman selling butter and cheese. Some out-of-work actor selling someone else's
spinach. Either this farmer's market was real—either I had come to the
village square on a Saturday—or Bernadette was trying to confuse me by
reconfiguring the city in medieval design. Filled with the good will of my
mission, I decided it was real.

I hobbled along, looking for likely recruits. Nothing and nobody
looked likely among this prosperous crowd. They might have been in
cornball medieval costume after all: they were dressed in tights, the men

and the women both. Arses, arses, everywhere, and not an arse for me. Ah, but I was far beyond that need. Beyond food, beyond sex, beyond money, which these folks wore in belt pouches round their tights. Belt pouches and jackboots! Jackboots and rollerblades! Bicycles with more power than the car I drove to this city!

The car I drove to this city. I had abandoned that long before I gave away my money. Even then, even in those lost days of mental crisis, I must have known to prepare for my mission. Now I needed nothing but the news, which I clutched in my hand. In the park I read the dispatches from Bosnia again and again, until I could make the words come together in a straight line on the page. Straight line, straight path. I had been forced to steal another paper this morning. The news from Bosnia was worse. The news from Bosnia was horrific. Mary Faith and Jesse had asked me to see to this. They had asked me to do something. For a month I had tarried, and the news left the page in a long straight line of grief and sorrow.

I scouted a speaking site and climbed into the flat center of the square, unprepared for flower beds in *this* hothouse. I considered speaking dead center, in front of the flagpole and the Declaration of Independence, but the spirit of humility pushed me back to Abe Lincoln's statue, with the backs of the food stalls facing me. Young fathers sat poised for action on park benches: they were watching their toddlers spilling out from the playgrounds while the young mothers made the rounds of the stalls. I'd seen them there, pawing through asparagus. Plenty of junkies interspersed among the well-to-do young families—*plus ça change*—but the fathers stood their guard. Young fathers. Energetic strong handsome confident fathers. Unlike the failing businessman father of five who sired me. Unlike the failing-courage father on the lam I turned out to be.

Never mind. My mission now was not fatherhood but lifesaving.

I limped around my site, claiming my speaking territory, and sized up the crowd. A tough audience, fathers and junkies with shopping carts, a few derelict skateboarders. Everyone on wheels, everyone mobile, most of them fenced in the grass by the flagpole, staring out at me. I would have to hold them with the oratory of mission. This was why I lived in communes of like believers for so many years! It wasn't so much work when we all believed the same.

"Fellow New Yorkers," I began. A sexist beginning. When you

work a crowd in bicycle tights, you should watch the words. You should always watch the words.

I began again. "Brothers and sisters. BROTHERS AND SISTERS." No one looked my way. I had not counted on how distracting it was to speak with no one listening, how the words struggled up from my lungs. Of course! These people were used to beggars, to street people! They thought I wanted their money.

"I DON'T WANT YOUR MONEY. I DON'T WANT ANY OF YOUR MONEY. I'M A RICH MAN, MYSELF."

That got a few sideways glances. *Rich* might be stretching it, but I was rich in love, wasn't I? Hadn't G. B. Brights stooped to clean my mess?

"I COME HERE TODAY"—I went for the lowered voice—"I come here today to ask for your goodwill and your courage. I come to implore you to consider joining my peace-loving army in solidarity with the people of Bosnia. I come here today to ask if you will help lift the siege of Sarajevo." My low voice had attracted a few glances. A toddler of indeterminate sex in one of those bibbed overalls came up to make cute with me, hands on knees, winking eyes. I had to stop speaking. A beautiful child, with a mess of dark curls and blackberry eyes, the kind of child Jesse might have been before I came around. But the father, in a flash, scooped the baby up and looked on me with the contempt he reserved for child molesters. Hot wet shame drenched my face.

"Lift the siege of Sarajevo, I say! Can you sit here in good conscience, in this sunny square, while Karadzic's henchmen savage the countryside? That man has the devil on his side; no, that man has the devil in his pocket. Ethnic cleansing? Crimes against humanity, I tell you. The Muslim girls they rape are twelve, thirteen. Look at their faces. Look on their faces, dazed with disbelief and sorrow." And I unfolded my paper for a visual aid, though I was not sure whether the picture was on newsprint or in my mind's eye. The words were leaving my mouth cracked and splintered. Otherwise why did they reach no ears? None but that baby's, who winked at me still, safe in a retreating father's arms. None but my own. The flames lifted higher in the marsh.

"Brothers and sisters, we can do it! We can undo it!" Do? Undo? Panic. My voice broke high. In all my days of teaching my voice never split this way. My judgment, maybe, but my voice, never. I was a performer, I tell you, a Daydreamer. Only this week I had rolled down the rocky cliff of insanity and crawled back up. I folded my paper and pushed on.

"We can undo the damage, the pain, and the humiliation of being betrayed by all who watch, who watch from the village squares and the Union Squares, and wring their hands and say they can do nothing."

A tomato connected with my solar plexus, and I doubled in pain and surprise. It was hard: May isn't the season for tomatoes. My breath was taken away, but I was buoyed all the same. Someone was listening. Somewhere on the outskirts of this inattentive crowd someone heard my words. I scanned the faces and found there were faces to scan. A little crowd was forming inside the fence and staring out at me. The little beginnings of a peace army. The ranks of young fathers seemed to have swelled.

"Isn't it a shame? we say." I wiped tomato from my shirt, the hot pulp giving me courage. "Isn't it outrageous? But so far away, and so many problems everywhere. We can't take it all on. We can't be our brother's keeper. But brothers, brothers and sisters, we are, you know. We are our sister's keepers."

I was beginning to irritate the junkies. I interrupted their trade. A low rumbling came from their midst. The others, though, the young prosperous Manhattanites buying their vegetables fresh from the farm, listened now with half an ear, their faces turned in profile. How I must look to them: gaunt, from these days without food; weathered, from the nights in the park; filthy; disreputable. Mad. But I knew, too, that my light eyes burned, tempered steel and needle-sharp. I knew I pierced their skin. I knew they wondered, for just a little moment, if there was a prophet speaking in Union Square, under the statue of Abe Lincoln in his cloak.

"Rise up out of our apathy, rise up out of our fear. We are on a mission. You say there will be more Bosnias, all over the globe. WELL, OF COURSE THERE WILL BE." The babies hid their faces in their father's broad shoulders.

"There will be more, and we will meet them. But we will never act if we look out into the void. Look down the road, friends! One step at a time! Look and see the young girl dragged from her house. Go after her, brothers and sisters. Run to her aid." They stared at me now, thirty or forty of them, sad guilt in their eyes and a hunger for guidance. O the burden was heavy. The words were slipping away.

"One step. One step. First things first. And what comes first? Make peace with yourself! Hallelujah! You got it, friends. Bingo. Double Jeopardy. Peace with yourself." I was losing them again, losing the young fathers, the baby with the blackberry eyes. I was losing them, my army, the words. I stretched out in the day, my long gaunt prophet's body, to seize them back, and my voice came roaring out, hot wind across the desert.

"Make peace with yourself, and make peace with your families, I tell you. Make peace with your mothers and your fathers, your grandmothers who smell of sachets and clichés, make peace with your sisters and your brother who wants to lock you away, make peace with your daughters, your son who thinks you can save the world. Make peace at home, brothers and sisters, and then you'll be able to step one step at a time, down the road without tripping, my wife and my son asked me to do this, to send me to you, they've asked me to save them, one step at a time, DOWN THE ROAD WITHOUT TRIPPING"—I was losing the words, I was losing the beat, I was losing the crowd—"AND IF THE ROAD LEADS TO THE WATER, YOU'LL MAKE A BOAT, WON'T YOU, AND YOU'LL CROSS THAT SEA ONE NAUTICAL MILE AT A TIME, YOUR SAILS FULL TILT full tilt full tlit full flit full clit."

I was alone under Lincoln's statue in Union Square. My knees buckled, but when I reached the concrete I still had the strength to grab one leg over the other and to sit, in the lotus position.

I did not detach. I howled, I am ashamed to say. Union Square, where no one is afraid of the scuzz, the thugs, the bullies, and the pimps, was afraid of me, and, o, I was afraid too. I was a human broken record, a man gone haywire, my brain gone as kaflooey's as my mother's, whose very being exploded from the strain of all it could not forgive.

I had no more words, sitting there alone, only sounds. Ommmmmmmm. I tried to chant, but no sound emerged. Moooooooo blew down between my ears and then Mommmmm and then I was truly panicked. This was worse than bats in the belfry: this was hearing what I'd said.

I'd said: *My wife and my son.*
I'd said: *They've asked me to save them.*

When I reached the arch in Washington Square I thought I could go no farther and fell to my knees.

I crawled, one knee at a time, to the dog run where I'd begun my search for Bernadette. Bad as Imelda Marcos crawling up the altar when they acquitted her! I found my Siberian elm and curled up patient on the walkway to die.

I was not waiting for Bernadette. I wished her well.

I was not waiting for my mother, though I saw her face that night, under a head of fiery hair, when she was still my young mother. Her skin was so very pale, her eyes pinched with the tiny lines of worry just forming there. She was peering out at my backyard grotto.

I was not waiting for more visions of Mary Faith, but grateful for the one I'd been sent.

I had only gone numb, walking and crawling these last paces, and knew I approached the state opposite nirvana, the state of despair.

So when G. B. Brights stood above me, and asked me if I could speak, I could not respond in any way.

I woke encased in white wool: the white womb. The gated city, the temple walls. I was a small boy and an old man.

A large figure hulked in front of the rice-paper screen, and a smaller one flitted at my bedside. The Buddha and Tinkerbell.

"He's awake!" Tinkerbell. "Just in the nick of time, too, I'm not kidding. How are you feeeeeeling there, Mr. Rooney? Pretty big fuss, huh! Pretty big fuss you put your friends through!"

"Don't worry," said Buddha. "Don't worry, Mr. Rooney, she's a nurse, thas right, but you're not in the hospital, you don't have to go the hospital you don't want to. Velma said she put you up long as it takes you to get on your feet, she's putting me up too till I can talk my way back into Took's good graces, which might be never, heh-heh. You know *her,* Mr. Rooney! Hey! Maybe you'd like some real food, what you think? He could take some real food, Sophia? Some rolls?"

The womb was dark, the screen was white. A bottle of clear liquid hung above my head and traveled down to my arm. I was under the white wool, but high on a hospital bed.

"You rushing it, Mr. Brights. Toast and tea, a little sip. Give him time! Don't rush him! He only just opened his eyes. Wasn't easy cleaning

265

you up, no sir! You put up such a big fuss I didunt think we ever get you to bed, but the last day you've been sleeping like a baby. I told Mrs. Ruttledge, that blood pressure gets any lower, we bring you to the E.R. you like it or not! Whether Mr. Brights here likes it or not! I want to keep my license, don't I?"

She flitted back and forth.

"I told you he was starving."

"You were right, Mr. Brights. Starving and exhausted. Maybe today you let me shave you later, no? We see."

"Hey! Maybe he'd let *me* shave him."

G.B. had removed the diamond stud. His gold tooth glittered. The nurse had straight black hair cut in bangs. Her eyes were black. She was no bigger than a bird. She looked so young.

"............................"

"What? What you say, honey? What you want?"

"A you a lim?"

G.B. leaned down low over me. "Say it for me, Mr. Rooney. I'll catch it. Say it again, Mr. Rooney?"

"Are. You. A. Muslim?"

"He says are you Muslim?"

Tinkerbell let out a merry cheerless laugh. "No, honey, I spent the night praying to the Virgin Mary you'd make it through without having to strap you down in the ambulance. My name is Mrs. Sanchez. Can you say that?"

"I'll protect you. I won't let them rape you."

She turned to G.B. Her back was to me. I couldn't see her eyes. The womb was dark, the white wool was warm. Still I was cold. I tugged on this vein that hung from my arm.

"No, no, honey! Don't pull that out. No sir. We be in big trouble then. I don't want to put that thing back in your arm."

"Don't worry, Mr. Rooney, it's just the what, dextrose, is it, Sophia?"

"Just a little a sugar water, honey. We just get you strong, long as you promise not to fight us so baaaad. Just so we can shave you, get you looking like a human being."

My feet were bandaged under the white wool, underneath the cold sheet.

"Am I . . ."

"What, Mr. Rooney?" G.B. leaned down low again, and I knew the answer from his warm breath even before I asked the question.

"Am I dead?"

All the next day I drifted in and out of sleep. Dottie raised her fist to me, then stretched her white hand out in the gray waves. I grabbed it and pulled her from the flames. She was only a small child in anklets, caught in the crossfire. Karadzic's army advanced on us, but I held them off.

Late in the day, G.B. came to feed me soup.

"Why do you stay?" My whisper rasped.

"Took won't let me come back just now. I told you that."

"No," I said. "I mean. Why'd you follow me all over this city? Why you keep looking for me?"

"You just keep making the same circle, Spring Street up to Washington Square. I knew you'd come back there eventually." He'd found me in front of St. Joseph's Church, and that was way outside the circle. He'd followed me to the War Resisters League.

"G.B.," I said, "will you help me stop the siege of Sarajevo?"

"Sure, Mr. Rooney. You figure out how to stop it, I be right there with you."

You hear that? I had to reach out and touch his hand, pretend I was helping him guide the spoon to my mouth. The chicken broth tingled down through my extremities, hands and feet and nose and cock all remembering animation.

"The thing we got to watch for, Mr. Rooney," G.B. said, "is that you don't travel the same circle with the crazies. You been up and down, up and down, sane and insane. We got to get you stabilized here. We got to get you steady a couple of days. Don't want what happened to my aunt happen to you." I remembered. Etta. Hanged herself.

His words soothed me and I closed my eyes, ready to rest up under his care. I heard him laying the spoon in the bowl and moving to the hallway to confer with Velma and the nurse. Ah, Velma! My benefactor! She'd come in this morning, to lay her plump moist hand on my forehead.

I felt myself drifting again, then lifting up from the hospital bed, as if on a cushion of air. Maybe I was sleeping, but I was not dreaming. I was deep in the throes of memory. *We should set a deadline,* Velma seemed to be saying. *Maybe a week.* And the little nurse might have answered, *I tell you right now he's gonna be the same in a week if he's not taking his meds. You haf to put your foot down. Put him in a good psychiatric hospital! He'll thank you for it.*

But I couldn't thank anyone for anything. I was elsewhere. I was in Due East, in the backyard on O'Connor Street, the shabby backyard with the rusty swings and the overgrown browning grass and the weedy flower beds. I was seven years old. I am seven years old. I am tending to my shrine of the Virgin Mary. It is First Communion year, and I have attained the age of reason. Now I am capable of sin.

Mary's statue is plastic, not even blue but tan. I am saving for a better one to buy from Father Sweeney in the rectory. The one I have is only six inches tall, but I will buy a bigger one each year until she is lifesize and stone. The one I have now I got for free. Across the bottom of Mary's pedestal is a peeling label that reads: *Catechism Honors.* Maggie and I win all the catechism honors. There is no competition in this hick town.

I've piled rocks and bricks for Mary's grotto. I stick in oyster shells in the gaps. My father says it makes the backyard look like a junkyard, but really he doesn't like it because it makes me look like a pansy. Every day I pick a flower for her, but our flower beds are plumb out. We don't have pansies. I have decapitated all the daisies and the azaleas are long since gone. I am not allowed to touch the camellias, but they are too big for the glasses my mother gives me anyway. Every now and again my father breaks the glass. I've seen him do it. Then he comes in and says it looks like a junkyard out there, you can't balance a glass on a pile of rocks and bricks and what do I think, he's made of money?

Today I steal a rose from the Percys' yard down the street. It's OK, when I get to First Confession my sin will be wiped away. But it's so hot that the petals from the rose are falling out of my hand before I even get it into the glass. My mother's given me a metal glass so Dad can't break it when he is being a ratfink. It is so hot I feel dizzy. The sun shimmers above the pecan trees. It is so hot, Andy and Katie have to stay inside.

The rose looks terrible, falling apart like that, so I try to stick some of the petals in the top of the glass at least. The water in the glass is boiling, and it hurts to hold the metal. The petals look stupid in the metal glass. Except it is gold metal, the same color as a chalice.

"There you go," I say, and put down the glass on the rock. It balances fine. "I'm sorry it's not so hot. I mean, it *is* so hot."

Mary smiles at me.

I look again, because the statue does not have a smile. It is tan, and Mary is sad, and that's always looked right to me because mothers are always sad. Now Mary is smiling and her eyes, which were just tan ridges before, are blue.

"It is hard, Timmy Rooney, to be so all alone," Mary says, in a cheerful way, in the kind of encouraging false way your teachers say it when they want to tell you they are sorry you turned out to be a boy genius, which is about the worst thing that could happen to any child in Due East, South Carolina, especially when his father is teaching him three instruments and his mother is reading the family *The Lives of the Saints* for bedtime stories.

"So hard, Timmy," Mary says again, and this time her voice is not cheerful, it sounds exactly like my mother's voice, firm and brisk and sympathetic and sad.

I stare at her for a long while, but her eyes have gone back to plastic ridges and her mouth is a smooth straight line again. I want to pick her up, but maybe I will hurt her. It is so hot maybe she needs some water. It is so hot I don't know what to do.

Finally I run up the back steps into the kitchen, hollering bloody murder. It is a sound like the one characters make in the funny pages, an ARRRRRGGGGGGG sound from deep in my throat. It feels good to make it. My throat's on fire.

"What?" my mother says. "What?"

My mother is standing at the lunch dishes, her blouse wet from the sink because she never thinks to wear an apron the way other mothers and Mrs. Cleaver do. Her hair is red like mine, only she wears it piled high in a French twist with red bobby pins and every morning when she gets up she clips on fake pearl earrings she lets Maggie wear any time she wants. Katie runs to her skirt when she hears me screaming and tugs on it, as if my mother hasn't noticed me. But my mother's running toward me, the dishrag in her hand dripping on the floor and on Katie's head, and on me. Andy sits at the table with his notebook. He doesn't know whether to get interested.

"Oh my God," my mother says, "you're burning up. Let's get the thermometer."

"She moved!" I say.

"Who moved?"

"Mary, Mary moved, her eyes were blue, she said something to me."

"Mary the statue?"

"Yes!" I shout. "Mary the Mother of God!"

"What, Timmy? What did she say?"

"I can't tell you, it was just for me and her."

"Just for her and me. You must always put yourself last."

"Her and me. But she stopped saying anything and now maybe she's dead."

My mother is kneeling in front of me and flipping the dishrag back over her head into the sink. She misses, and it falls on my sister. Katie begins to wail.

"Shush, Katie. Andy, come take your sister by the hand. Your brother's very sick."

"Let's go see the statue," Andy says. "Let's go see it talking. Let's see what it says to me."

"It won't say anything to you. It's only for me and her, HER and ME."

"Take your sister, Andrew, before she catches it too."

My mother is still kneeling. She stares straight at me and her eyes are ringed with those tiny lines. Mary had those lines! Worry lines. My mother is worried. She thinks I'm weird. She thinks I'm maladjusted. "Mary is all right, Timmy," my mother says. "Just think who's watching out for her! And now we'll see to you."

Katie's wailings follow us up the stairs and Maggie comes out of her room to see what the racket's all about. She has *Little Women* in one hand and a Nancy Drew in the other. She likes to read two books at once in case one gets boring.

"It's all right, Maggie," my mother says. "Timmy's sick. Get me the thermometer."

And she puts me to bed and Dr. Black comes and shoots me in the behind and my mother gives me an alcohol rub and I cry out, *I want to go home. I want to go home.*

"You are home, Timmy," my mother says, but I know that I am not. I am not home at all. Home is where Mary is. I am going to be a priest.

And when I wake in the night and go to pee hot yellow lava, I hear them at the foot of the stairs.

"What do you expect, Dolores? You fill his head with cockamamie notions, you get a cockamamie boy. I'm telling you, it is not normal for a seven-year-old boy to be worshiping a statue and if you don't believe it after this I'm paying Father Sweeney a call and he'll tell you. He'll tell you a seven-year-old boy worships God with a fishing pole in his hand." But I don't have a fishing pole, Dad. You don't even have a fishing pole. We've never been fishing.

"Oh, Bill. It's just the fever."

"It's too much mother and not enough father is what it is. Well, the father puts his foot down on this one. That grotto goes, tomorrow."

"Hold off, Bill. Let him take it down himself, if you insist on that. Don't let him come out of a fever to find it gone."

There is a low grumbling from my father, but my mother is cool and serene.

"He is a very spiritual child," she says, and her tone says she is agreeing with him, but her words say just the opposite. "Fever or no. We can't any of us stop that."

I know that what I have is a brain fever. I know that I have a longing for God and that only Mary can help me home and I do not know if this is part of the sickness or if the sickness is the devil tempting me away from what I want.

From the hallway I might have heard Velma say, "I must be out of my own mind, bringing a mental patient in for a houseguest."

I grew stronger, and the little nurse shaved me. I was terrified she was going to slit my throat with that razor, but I lay still. The drip was out my arm, anyway. The radio said the Either Orchestra was on a nationwide tour.

The next day Velma told Mrs. Sanchez she and G.B. could handle me, and the nurse was gone. G.B. moved my hospital bed from the white womb to the kitchen, where I could hear the talk. Velma had a theory about insanity.

"I had an uncle in Charleston, Tim, crazy as a June bug. And you know what we did with him? We made him sit in the kitchen and just listen to all the women in the family talking. He got well right quick. Not that I think you're crazy. Well. Yes, you were. You went a little crazy. Anyway, you do me good, to have you here."

O, she did me good too, fat kind gray Velma with the money to take care of me. When she got middle-aged she'd be a do-gooder like my mother, only she'd have the money to actually do some good. She said she'd banished Fred forever, but Angela was still in the loft. Her sleek strong thighs glistened under her white T-shirt and she brushed her stiff white hair out of her eyes.

"Hello, Tim," she said, soft. "I'm glad they found you." She had that look she'd worn the first night in the city, when she looked right through me.

"I know who you are," I said, and Angela's eyes narrowed all the way to slits. She leaned low over my hospital bed, so strong, so healthy. She might throttle me. She might beat me around the head. Bad enough she stared at me so.

"Who am I, Tim?"

"My grandfather's blond floozy."

"You're a floozy too, Tim Rooney."

"Hey now!" Velma said, from across the room. "We're trying to get him better."

"Sallright, Vel. He called me a floozy and I told him he's one too."

"Course I am. I knew that. Now we're back where we started."

"No we're not," said Angela. "We're not where we started at all."

I watched her strong retreating back make its way down the hallway, and I knew I wouldn't see her again. That one knew what was up from the start.

"Thanks, Angela," I called after her, and she might have heard me. That might have been a wave coming from down the hall.

I was weak still, and G.B. fed me when he was not on the phone begging Took to take him back in. Velma hovered, always.

"Velma!"

"OK, Tim, it's OK."

"I have to wire money to Mary Faith!"

"Who's Mary Faith?"

"She's my sweetie, my sugar dumpling, the girl I'm going to marry."

"Tim, you mean to tell me you took off for New York City and left behind a fiancée?"

"A wife, even, you might say, the way we've been carrying on these years. I left her and my son besides and I'm not proud I did it."

"Tim, a son!" The look in her eyes was pure alarm. They flashed blue-green-blue-green-blue.

"Jesse. He's eleven, there's a picture, actually several pictures, in my billfold if you get it out my pants." Though before the word *billfold* was out of my mouth I knew it was gone forever. "I'm going to adopt him soon as we take the vows. But he's my *spiritual* son now." Something about the word rang false. I was forgetting something that had happened. There were large . . . gaps.

"Tim, uh, do they know where you've been?"

"O, Velma, help me, won't you? I'm too weak to go to Western Union, take that money from my socks, take all fifteen thousand and send it to her. Tell her I flipped my lid but I'm coming home. I have a little more work to do here to stop the war in Bosnia, but then I'll be on my way."

"OK, baby, slow down. Just lie down there. First thing, the doctor has to get back here and say it's OK for you to be up and around. Also, we've got to talk about taking that medicine."

"O, Velma, doctors, doctors. A ringing in my ears. I know, the doctor, I'll see to it, but first the money and then the war . . ."

"Baby, you're spinning. Listen, I've got to get out and get some food in this house with this gang. Angela can listen for you."

"Not Angela!"

"What's got into you? I thought you two were the best of pals." She said it with a little sneer, maybe.

"Not Angela."

"All right. Tell you the truth, she's wearing my patience a little thin. G.B.'s here. I'll tell him to write *paranoid* down on that symptoms list."

I wasn't paranoid! I wasn't! I saw . . . the danger. "O Velma, see to Western Union. I've got to get the money to her."

G.B. came back into the kitchen looking weary, and wearier still when he saw Velma frowning over me. She turned to him.

"G.B., you're the one with the patience. I'm going to leave you to tell him what he did with all the money. And Tim, I don't want to be tight about it, I'm not *like* that, but private nurses and doctors who make house calls in New York City are not cheap. I'm investing a small fortune in you, darlin, and I don't think I can start investing in a girlfriend too."

"Good God, she's not a girlfriend. I tell you, she's the love of my life."

She looked on me with blue eyes going green.

"Please, Velma, just take the fifteen thousand out my sock. And I'll pay you back the rest, I'll be out of here in no time, I'm stronger already, aren't I?" I could get down the hallway to the bathroom.

"Tim, there is no more money. You gave it all away."

"I did?" This sounded vaguely familiar. But Mary Faith and Jesse had no money in Due East. And there was the war to stop, which would take serious funds. I leaned up on my elbows and began to rise from the bed.

"Just where you think you're going?"

"I've got to go find the money, or else earn it."

"Tim."

"I've got to find the money and stop the war and go get married. Father Berkeley—"

"Yeah," said G.B. "Father Berkeley. But there's no answer."

"You called Father Berkeley?"

"Hadn't been an answer in weeks. I hope the old man didn't up and die."

"Die!"

"Tim," said Velma. "Lie down. You don't lie down this instant I'm calling them to take you away in a straitjacket to Bellevue and I'm not kidding."

She wasn't, either. O, I love a strong woman. I lay back down, to appease her, but my blood was boiling and the songs were dancing in my head. Get money to my family! See if Father Berkeley's still alive! Stop the war! Appease Velma!

"G.B., don't give him any more sugar now while I'm out, hear?"

"I don't think it's sugar, Velma."

"No," she said. "I don't suppose it is."

REPORT FROM GAY STREET

Bernadette Rooney's house made me feel like I'd been buried in a small town all my life, which I had. First off, you could see that not everybody in New York had a whole house to themselves, not on a quiet little curving alley like this, all the city noise not but a block away. Then she had shelves of books from the floor to the ceiling and framed prints and rugs with streaks of turquoise in them. Jesse and I were on the top floor, where the ceiling was low and everything was pine and unpretentious, and I could have cried myself to sleep from pure envy. Or from the heat. It was hotter on that top floor in New York than it was in our cool house that caught the breeze in hot Due East. I stayed up there in the heat as much as I could. I could not believe I was in Bernadette Rooney's house.

And I could not believe Bernadette Rooney. First off, she was old enough to be my mother, which of course made Tim old enough to be my father, in case I hadn't thought of that before. I did not need the wrinkles around her eyes to remind me every time I looked at her. It didn't surprise me that she was good-looking, or that she dressed herself so well. Tim used to see a woman in Due East before we started going out, an artist from New York City who looked like she knew what was what. Tim has always tried to play up the crazy card, but the truth is, he has always wanted a good-looking woman on his arm, and from what I could piece together, he'd generally managed to find him one. You can see from the pictures that his mother was very beautiful, though all I remember is a thin, tired woman in an ill-fitting housedress hanging wash on the back line. She had a head of faded hair pinned flat.

Bernadette, on the other hand, had probably never owned a house-dress. She didn't stay around the house much. She was polite enough, but cool—like me, if the truth be told. I saw the shock in her eyes when we rang the front doorbell and she saw how old *I* was.

About the same age as her husband, though I wasn't sure if *husband* was just a word they used so we poor conservative Southerners would not be offended. He wore a ring in each ear and a nose ring as well.

"What do you do when you've got a cold?" Jesse said to him.

"Ah, it's a mess."

"Mom, I want one." See, I was Mom for good now, not Momma, and my son had gone to New York City and decided he wanted a nose ring. I had to keep my eye on him every minute.

Bernadette's husband's name was Fran, for Francis. I can guarantee that no boy in Due East has ever gone by the name of Fran. He had a hawk nose, thick black hair, and black eyes. You might have said he had a brooding look, like Al Pacino, but he was always heading off to the gym, which I just couldn't see Al Pacino doing. I caught myself the first night wondering what he saw in an older woman, even one who looked as good as Bernadette, and then I thought, *You hypocrite.* He sees the same thing you see in Tim, with his skinny legs and his bone-white skin and his belly going to pot. The same thing, which you have never been able to figure out and better not to try, under the circumstances. I thought Bernadette's Fran was just a bodybuilder, a gigolo even, but the second night we were there he climbed the stairs and said: "Well, it's off to the salt mines. Got to finish that dissertation someday."

"What do you study?" I said, to be polite. He looked like somebody in business administration.

"Philosophy."

I sucked my breath in. "Tim teaches philosophy!" Jesse said.

"What's the dissertation?" I was getting queasy.

"It's pretty technical," he said. "I'm working with Heidegger." I stopped listening right there. Tim never had the time of day for Heidegger.

Father Berkeley called in the mornings with the same news, no news. There was a kid from Due East up to visit a relative who was supposed to be looking for Tim, but the kid had moved out of wherever he was supposed to be. He'd been a student of Tim's. Where did Father Berkeley find these people? Where did he find me?

"I can't stay but a few more days," I told him.

"There aren't but a few more days," he said. "We're up to the thirty-fifth day. Five more to go."

"I can count."

"I'm sure you can."

Father Berkeley and I sounded like the old married couple. He had called every hospital in the city, and filed a missing persons report with the police. He was walking the streets around Columbia University every day, looking for Tim, and Jesse and I were doing Greenwich Village. We were supposed to have a better chance, because Bernadette had seen him down this way, but to tell you the truth I didn't even scan the faces anymore. I was just going through the motions on account of Jesse.

I took to walking the city right away, and never once thought about being scared. We'd start out in the morning heading toward West Street and maybe even cross over the highway to look at the Hudson River. I have never lived anywhere but Due East, so I could not make out why I felt like I was home. On the way back, if we were walking Bank Street I'd quiver, almost, at the sight of the row houses so close to the street and the flowerboxes filled with pink and purple. I'd lie and say to Jesse, *Let's pop in this little bookstore, this looks like someplace Tim might like,* when I was the one lusting after every volume they put on the shelves. I might die from the magazines alone. This might have been our life, in a city like this, if he'd meant what he said about scrubbing the floors while I studied. I eyed the biggest flattest buildings for a roof where I could make my geodesic dome and look out on the city spread below.

By lunchtime we'd head over to Washington Square. Jesse was too old for the playgrounds, but he liked to make the rounds of the dog runs and the chess games and the boys without shirts kicking a soccer ball around the fountain. The two of us could wander for the better part of the afternoon, round in circles and back again. But here, too, I had to watch him every second. I could just picture him buying a vial of crack. *Cool,* he said about everything he saw. *Cool.* And *Mom, you can't be following me every step around the park. Look at the other kids.* He was right. The ones his age walked right through on their own. My heart was in my throat.

One afternoon we saw Bernadette hurrying across Washington Square. Jesse and I were sitting on a park bench, nursing our tired feet, and here she came like a Mack truck, in her white linen suit, with a black leather backpack, swishing along like Queen for a Day. She looked like she belonged in this city and we looked like—well, come to think of it, Jesse was coming to look like he belonged, too. He wore the same clothes he'd worn out of Due East, and he combed his hair the same way, but there was something about the way he held his shoulders now, walking the narrow streets of the Village. Sometimes I thought he'd run people down. I'd so forgotten that we were looking for Tim that I spent my time daydreaming about how I might get a job in a travel agency and a little room in one of these little houses. I'd enroll in night classes. Every time I allowed myself such a notion, the plane of the universe we sat on shifted, and everything was on a slant, and I was dizzy and a little nauseous.

It was somebody like Bernadette, somebody who knew where to get a haircut and buy clothes, who belonged around here. She was barreling right past us, not even aware we existed in the same world she did.

Jesse broke the spell. "BERNadette!" Even something about the way he hollered. He'd picked it up here, in Washington Square, in the few days we'd been coming.

She looked right over and came our way, that cool polite smile on her face. "This is a good idea," she said. "If he's wandering, he'll come this way eventually."

I might have been the schoolgirl, tongue-tied, and Jesse the adult. "He plays chess," Jesse said. "Also he likes dogs."

"He doesn't like dogs," I said. "I thought that's why the opera's named *The Hound from Hell.*" Look what I'd done to Jesse, staring out with his jaw set the way he does. "Oh, Jesse, you're right. I guess he likes Clover all right."

"He told me a little about you," Bernadette said to Jesse, "when I saw him." Oh. Lovely. She looked ready to sit, and actually moved her hands in a little shoveling motion. She was telling me to slide over. I was flabbergasted. I slid over.

That first night we got to New York, after I got Jesse settled in the room, I'd come back downstairs to hear her tell Father Berkeley about seeing Tim. I'd listened to as much as I could bear.

Now Jesse said, "What'd he say?" His jaw was still set. You could hardly hear him speaking.

"He said . . . let me think and get it right for you. He was going to ask you who Kramer is."

"TIM DUDN'T KNOW WHO KRAMER IS?"

"No, I told him he looked like Kramer, and he said he didn't know who that was, but he'd ask you and you'd know."

"Heh," said Jesse. "What else?"

Bernadette put her hands on her linen knees and I made note of her fingertips, filed in elegant rounded edges but unpainted. Just what you'd think. My own are chewed to the quick, and sometimes beyond.

"He said he was worried about what kind of father he would be."

She hadn't mentioned that one the other night, with Father Berkeley there.

"He should be," Jesse said. "He can yell fit to bust."

"His dad was supposed to have a bad temper too," Bernadette said. "But I always kind of liked Bill. He was a funny guy. Great piano player. Crazy about Tim."

She looked to me for confirmation, but I had none to give her. Bill Rooney was loud and overbearing and full of himself. He'd wounded Tim over and over again.

Maybe she was reading my thoughts. "Tim's never hit you, has he?" Bernadette asked Jesse, and there I drew the line.

"I'm sorry," I said. "He doesn't have to answer that from you. Do you think I'd let my child stay around a man who hits him?" I didn't even trouble to look at her when I said it. I had set my own jaw in imitation of Jesse's, and looked out at a million people in the park, at nothing.

"I'm so sorry," she said. "You're absolutely right. I'm way out of line."

Jesse said, "Well, I'd put his eyes out, he ever hit me."

She said, "He wanted to talk about you first thing."

Again I felt I was sinking, wearing chains. Tim sat in New York talking to his ex-wife about my son.

"Jesse," I said. "Go run check those chess games again. See if he's been by." There. I could let him loose a little.

When he ran off, I turned to Bernadette and didn't even try to smile. "How crazy did he sound to you? When you saw him?"

"He sounded OK at first. He sounded good. And then he sounded a little inappropriate"—right there I hated her, right there with that word, *inappropriate* when a man you're supposed to have loved is losing his mind—"and then he . . . he got scary. Hostile. He said he felt bad about running out on his wedding, that he thought he'd make a terrible father. Then he got mad, and madder, and finally he just ran out of the coffee shop. He knocked the waiter down. I haven't seen him since. . . . I'm sorry I wasn't thinking more clearly, I'm sorry I didn't get a number first thing. I guess I wasn't counting on his being crazy. I guess I wasn't counting on Father Berkeley showing up to look for him."

"Nobody counts on Father Berkeley," I said. We sat in silence and I decided to say it right quick, before I could change my mind. "Did he say anything about another woman?"

"I'm sorry. There was . . . I saw her. The night before we talked, when we just stumbled into each other. She was very young, I mean younger than you." She said this as if it were a physical impossibility to be younger than I was. "Very—oh, I know I shouldn't make snap judgments, especially about other women, we don't need that, but she was very young and very sophisticated at once. I would have said she was spoiled."

I was having a hard time breathing, not to mention sitting still.

"Did she have, uhm, white hair?" I figured when Jesse came back I'd swing by Bernadette's house and pack our things and call Father Berkeley to come meet me. Let him buy me a train ticket home. Let him explain it to Jesse.

"Yes, blond. White, I guess. I asked him about her the next day," Bernadette said. "It was very strange. He said he . . . didn't like her.

282

Actually, they looked like they were fighting the night before, but you wouldn't have called it a lovers' quarrel. That's why I was staring at him, instead of looking the other way. I wanted to make sure the girl, the woman, oh hell, let's call a spade a spade, she was a little girl is what she was, I wanted to make sure she was OK. He was grabbing her by the elbow. But when I got close I could see she was perfectly fine. She could hold her own, that one."

"May he burn in hell," I said.

Bernadette started to laugh, which didn't seem like a real friendly thing to do under the circumstances. I thought of how Jesse and I would get through the packing and how I'd have to tell him after all—couldn't leave that to Father Berkeley—and I said to Bernadette, just not caring anymore, just furious that Father Berkeley had put me in a situation like this:

"What are you laughing at?"

"I'm sorry, I was thinking of all the times I thought that very line about Tim Rooney. And he never went off with anybody else, he just . . . likes women. All through college it tormented me, and then graduate school. We were together a long time, I don't know if he told you. We were together until we got married."

"Well, you left him finally. I'm leaving too. I'm not fetching Tim home from some peroxide blonde's house." Peroxide blonde! When was the last time I had heard such a phrase? And then I remembered: that was what Tim called the woman his grandfather ran off with: *my grandpa's floozy. My grandpa's peroxide blonde.*

Bernadette knew better than to touch me, but she leaned into me a little, there on the bench, as if to give me warmth, or touch. "I don't blame you," she said. "He's guilty, you know, that you're so young. But crazy for you, if you'll pardon the expression. I'll tell you the truth, and I know I have no right, given the age of the men I've chosen to marry. But in the abstract, I just don't approve, not even of me, but especially not of men, you know, these middle-aged men and the girls who could be their daughters."

What was I supposed to say to that?

"But I could tell, from the way he spoke about you, that you're not someone to stroke his ego. It's just the breaks sometimes. Sometimes you just fall in love with somebody inappropriate." There was that word again. "And then what can you do?"

"I'll tell you what I can do," I said. "I can pack my bag and get out of this town where Tim Rooney's shacking up with somebody else."

Now I wanted to suck my words back, about getting out of this town, not because I ever wanted to see Tim Rooney again, but because Jesse and I had finally found us a place that lifted our spirits. And now I'd gone and proclaimed my intention to leave it.

eight

They worried me day and night over starting the Haldol. I was sitting up most of the day now, in a kitchen chair, growing stronger and weaker at once. I ate everything they put in front of me, and asked for anchovies on top of it all, but I could not focus my eyes or my thoughts. Velma called the shrink every morning and reported my progress. She reported that I was *lucid*. The shrink had seen me the afternoon they brought me here. I had not seen him. I let them jabber away, G.B. and Velma, and when they told me the doctor was coming back the next day and now we really had to get serious about the medication, I nodded my head. Ever so polite. Sure thing. Doctor. Medicine. Whatever.

Because I knew I was drowning. No matter how much soup G.B. spooned into my throat, no matter how many rolls he popped in my mouth, my brain was going under water and my soul would soon follow. When they left the *Times* on the kitchen table, I could not read the words. No words but *Bosnia*. The sports pages read *Bosnia Bosnia Bosnia*. The weather forecast said *Bosnia Bosnia Bosnia*. My wife and my son asked me to save suffering souls, and I went off to find myself.

My docility soothed G.B. and Velma. They thought I was getting better. Velma sometimes sat with me, her lower lip pouting. She thought I was so much better that now I could help her.

And I could see her suffering, she was right about that. "You miss Fred?"

"And I can't ever take him back," she said. "I'll get AIDS for sure. I don't care what they say about condoms. You can't put a condom round your heart, can you?"

"I don't think he's gay," I said.

Velma just shook her head.

"I didn't mind supporting him," she said. "That's what nobody understands. I didn't mind his taking advantage. He's a genius. Somebody has to support him. Somebody has to think of the little things so he can think the big thoughts."

"I don't think he's gay," I said again.

And Velma shook her head again. What did I know? I was crazy.

And I was crazy, too. When they pleaded that I take the Haldol, just get started, just so the doctor could see was the dosage working, the whispering came back. At first it was a constant irritating unmelodic fluttering bad Ingmar Bergman mutter. I was so blue I paid it almost no mind. Who wants to sit around in one of those grim Swedish movies all afternoon?

Then Florence Henderson took over the role of the whisperer. Remember when she did that ad frying chicken and singing *Wessonality? When chicken tastes this good, as crispy as it should?* It almost drove me out of my mind at the time. Now, when I *was* out of my mind, the voice returned. Last time out, Bobby What's-his-name on *Dallas.* This time out, Florence Henderson. I had no connection with these people. That they should enter my hallucinations seemed entirely unjust and capricious; worse, they seemed to confirm those theories that our dreams are not meaningful at all, but arbitrary. That we are not talking about meaning or form here, but a synapse problem.

The further down I sank, the chirpier Florence became. *Take the medicine. It will soothe your spirits. It will feed your soul.* But if I took the medicine I would not be able to do anything about Bosnia. I did not trouble with Florence Henderson's voice. I did not even answer her back. No. When you are drowning the water is rising a little, every day, and so you know that the voice will be washed away soon, swept away forever. The voice is not worth troubling over now.

"G.B.," I said. "Brooklyn College'd be OK. City College'd be OK. They'd both be fine. But I have a feeling if we sat right here and you drafted an essay you could get yourself into Harvard or Yale, you wanted. You could write your own ticket, G.B. Only. We'd have to get to that essay today. If you want me to look it over." I thought of it as my last will and testament.

"Why?" G.B. said. "Where you going in such a hurry? Anyway, Mr. Rooney, I can't even imagine Harvard, you know what I'm saying? I just want Took to take me back in, thas all I need for now. One step at a time." Where'd I heard that line? "And what you so worried about today for? Cause the doctor's coming tomorrow?"

I didn't have my own voice to answer him. If I opened my mouth, Florence Henderson would sing out my answer. My flurry of interest in Harvard for G. B. Brights was the sudden flash of light you see when you're going down, the sun in the sky. It's comfort, I'll say that. I imagined that Dottie saw that flash of light when she was going under. There is nothing like the light in Due East, South Carolina. Nothing so vast and empty as those skies.

At night G.B. rolled the hospital bed back into the white womb and I knew that that bed of white carnations would be falling on me soon. I had a blank longing for Mary Faith, for Jesse: I would think those words, *I have a longing for them,* but I'd feel no corresponding warming of my spirit. And Florence would sing in the background, mocking me. *You long for them, as crispy as it should.* The waters were cold in January. I was drowning.

I almost expected G.B. to kiss me good night sometimes, the way a father would, but that was because of my mental confusion. I was crazy. Drowning. I lay there in the night and the voice talked dirty if I got close down to sleep. *Cunt,* it would say. I just let the voice go on. Its toes were already wet. It'd drown with me. *Dash this temple down,* it would say, and I did not even need to answer.

That last night I was there in Velma's, though, a new voice started in: Angela's. It took me awhile to place it, because she'd been laying low, knowing that I kept her secret. In the night she plotted a conspiracy. The old voice whispered, *Fuck her, fuck her,* but Angela's voice rose strong above. She must have been throwing the voice from my head into the hallway and all the way down to the kitchen. Because I should not have been able to hear a voice that far away. The voice, then, emanated from me. *Fuck her, fuck her.* She had been slinking around this loft, knowing that I knew her secret. Betrayer!

"I don't think it's good for you, having Tim around," the voice said. It must have been my own voice. "You were right in the first place. That first night you said, *Let me call my shrink,* and I should have let you. We should have put him away then. I don't know what I was thinking. That he was *cute* or something? He's not cute. He's out of his mind."

And I was, too. Out of my mind. Drowning. And so heavy, so cold and heavy that I lay like a stone in the hospital bed waiting for the carnations to fall on me. So heavy I can't imagine that I climbed out of that bed. Or that I left the loft in my bare feet, in the silk pajamas they'd laid me out in. Fred's silk pajamas.

But I did. I must have. I must have left the Spring Street loft and made my way down to the corner of West Broadway. Because next morning, at first light, that is where I found myself, curled up on a cellar door in a puddle.

The waters had not yet even come up to my chin.

Fred's pajamas were too short, but they were the right color: black. They looked like clothes, too, like the clothes the Eurotrash in SoHo wore, and the only problem with my passing for human was my bare feet. It was a long walk up West Broadway, in my condition, and the path was strewn with policemen. Or so I thought: I envisioned them everywhere with their dark pouched bored eyes, ready to lock me and my bare feet up, to throw me in the dungeon. But I didn't pass a single cop in the long hour it took me to find my way.

It was that hour of sun dawning. I had trouble remembering the direction I was to take, more trouble remembering the purpose. Florence was completely distracting now. If I walked the middle of the sidewalk, she chirped out, *Walk in traffic, this tastes good.* My progress was slow, but I was strong, strong and heavy. I was drowning but still plowing my arms through the water. The fluids in my lungs rose higher. I was heading toward water, but at this rate I would not need the water to drown.

The city woke and came to life as I scraped along the sidewalk, suits and skirts swishing to work. The crowds reminded me that I hadn't yet reached the water, so I quit plowing my arms and lowered them to my side. Even the insane can be reasonable members of society.

I drifted west, and knew then that I was heading toward the Hudson River. That would be right. That would be the place to go. My mother sat by the Hudson when she was a girl. Bernadette and I sipped wine by the Hudson. That was my destination.

But I was leaving a bloody trail on the sidewalk. All my old wounds had opened. Now I drifted north, and found myself in the middle of NYU again. The students—the girls, anyway, it's always the girls who make eye contact—gave me strange probing looks. One, short and plump and Asian, with straight bangs like Mrs. Sanchez's, put her hand to her mouth the way Bernadette put her hand to her mouth. It was the sight of the blood on the tracks. All the women who saw me seemed to be considering whether they should inquire after my health.

My health was bad. I tell you, I was drowning.

And so, when I found that I had drifted all the way into Washington Square, practically my starting place, I thought that perhaps I was not to go all the way to the Hudson. Perhaps I was only to go to the fountain. I pushed on, but there was no river in the fountain. There was no water in the fountain at all.

I had to sit in order to breathe. And as I sat there in Washington Square, quiet, Florence's voice left me in peace. For a long while I saw nothing, but soon enough I saw that I was fulfilling my mission. A great calm descended, and I was able to sit, on the steps leading down to the fountain, for hours. I folded my legs in and held my arms out. My heart beat slowly and the fluids in my lungs promised to hold off their surge until I could finish my work.

Hours. I did not chant—I could not risk the sound of even a single syllable—but held onto the dark and the quiet even as the sun rose high in the sky above me, even as the rabble-rousers descended to play their soccer and deal their drugs and murmur sweet talk in each other's ears. I could not hear the sweet talk. Could not hear the boom boxes. Could not hear the speaker system when a stand-up comic took the center of the fountain, could not hear the jokes even when he said, *What does Michael Jackson get if one more preadolescent boy files suit against him?*

I could not hear the joke. I tell you, Michael Jackson was framed. I was floating, safe and aloft, until the moment arrived.

The moment arrived sometime after the comedian packed up and the sun ascended. It came on a chill breeze, when the sun was covered with a sheet of dusky clouds. I woke from the calm and found that my lungs were clear. I was able to stretch and stand. I made my way to the center of the fountain: I could have raised myself up to speak, I could have done my preaching loud as a bullhorn if I'd wanted. I was strong and fired up, but I knew to sit there quiet and only to talk.

I only needed to teach: all I'd ever wanted to do.

So I sat on the center pedestal, and I started out with the hard stuff. *"Self is a relation which relates to itself, not the relation, but the relation's relating to itself,"* I said. I spoke in a low sonorous voice, my own voice.

No one paid me any mind, but I had learned a great deal in that practice session up in Union Square.

"You grow weary of self," I said to the crowd that had not yet formed. I knew now to be patient. "You grow weary of analyzing self. You decide to leave off reflection, you decide to act instead. And what do you find? You find that your jerking at the chains of self is only stoking your jailer's fire. He loves to see you struggle there, pulling against the chains.

"Stop pulling," I said. "Sit awhile." I heard my voice grow stronger, and saw that the crowd grew with it. "Sit awhile. Sit quiet and the jailer will fall asleep." They sat all around me, my students, and some of them really were students, in overalls and backpacks and thick black shin-kickers. They sat, secretaries on their lunch hour and junkies and Danish tourists and high school kids playing hooky. A few of them watched me now. The others pretended to be staring off, but they listened: I knew they did.

"When that jailer falls asleep," I said, "reach over and pull the keys from his pocket. Unchain yourself." A few more souls descended the steps of the fountain and joined our symposium. "When you all leave the dungeon," I told them, "you will hear the cries from the next dungeon down the road. Well. You have to go on down there. You'll have things to do on the way, you'll have a life to lead along the road, but still you must walk in the direction of the cries."

I found that if I stared out straight ahead the folks in the immediate vicinity watched me intently, trying to get a handle, trying to run an ID, a blood test, a DNA match on this strange dude. I stared out to my left: my old friend Garibaldi's statue, looking on benignly. I took it as a sign to continue.

My students were maybe a little too stoned in the midday sun to be much good for listening yet, but full of the questioning spirit.

"What is it you need to do?" I asked them.

No answer. No questions. Very well. I would speak for them.

"You need to let the relation between self and its relating to itself take care of itself. You need to accept that Florence Henderson lives in you! Bobby What's-his-name on *Dallas* lives in you! Selfish seductive blond swimmers live in you!" I had to pause, this notion was so confusing. It happens all the time when you teach, of course: you say something so startling you must simply take a break and absorb it.

I closed my eyes again. I felt certain that the water level in my lungs was descending rapidly. I was a swimmer. I was a *swimmer*. I was not going to drown. This was the moment, then.

I stood on this central pedestal and did my bullhorn bellow. "BOSNIA!" I said, in that Samuel Ramey bass. "BOSNIA! BOSNIA!" And the third time I said the name of that suffering country, I leaped down from the pedestal and wandered the rim of the fountain. I'd been approaching my philosophy lesson all wrong.

"BOSNIA!" came the scattered cries back through Washington Square. A stubby fellow in the soccer game stopped his foot mid-kick to look my way.

"BOSNIA!"

Again the echo, scattering in from different corners of the park. O brother, you are not alone in Washington Square, no sir, not in a city populated by the weirdos from every small town in America, whoa baby, not in the city populated by the wandering souls of Europe. Nah-uh, in Washington Square, where East meets West and literary past meets pharmacological present, where the trendsetters meet the nerds, where the nerds *are* the trendsetters, in their sideburns and their slipping pants and their thick-soled shoes, where everybody is actively seeking something, anything, you can always connect.

"BOSNIA!"

The echo bounced back. See there. Mary Faith wasn't the only one couldn't eat for worry. I walked the rim of the fountain in my black silk pajamas, my hair newly cut by Mrs. Sanchez, my body supple with all the days' rest and reflection it had received. I could not feel the wounds on my feet. I said:

"Remember Al Pacino in *Dog Day Afternoon?*"

You *know* there were film students down in that crowd, boys in goatees and girls in shrinking T-shirts. Somebody said, "All *right.*" Somebody applauded. This was a game show symposium. "I'm not paid for this," I said. "This may look like a paying gig, but believe me, I'm doing this because my chains have been unlocked. I'm doing this because my son, my eleven-year-old boy, has asked me to do this, because the love of my life, my corn muffin, has asked me to take some action. This is the only action I know how to take!" The words spun out in black and white, mimeographed pamphlets of the free airspace in Washington Square. I, unemployable teacher, was teaching, so far beyond self that Florence Henderson had left the chicken frying in the kitchen and gone on with her career in musical theater. I let out a rebel yell and then a cowboy WHEE-HAW to underline it. I said:

"Remember Al Pacino when he paces up and down in front of the bank? Remember? *Attica, Attica, Attica, Attica?*" And I was not only saying it, I was doing a perfect Al Pacino imitation, tall as I was, red-haired as I was, skinny and doofy and goofy as I was, I had become dark brooding Al Pacino, and he had become Sonny the bank robber and we were all chanting *Attica, Attica, Attica, Attica.* Joy in our anarchy, joy in our purpose. Outlaws! Pilgrims!

Now the passersby stopped to see what was the fuss. Now the whole center of Washington Square held as we took up the chant: *Attica Attica Attica Attica,* and when I slid it over to *Bosnia Bosnia Bosnia Bosnia* they slid over with me, without missing a beat.

"BOSNIA! BOSNIA! BOSNIA! BOSNIA!" I was on dry land. I wasn't drowning. This was totally inadequate, this was only words, only touchy-feely words after all that connected us one to another, we student filmmakers and wealthy tourists and knockabouts and junkies. Still, I was on dry land, not drowning but teaching, moving toward something, moving toward . . . Jesse?

Jesse?

Jesse, who was pushing himself through the crowd that ringed the fountain and making his way down the steps toward me.

Jesse?

Even in the midst of my chanting I stopped and stared. It was a boy who looked exactly like Jesse: black curls, narrow face, dark eyes, a nose ring, narrow and gold. Nose ring! And even more psychedelic than his nose ring his thin lips: smiling, joyful, beatific.

Couldn't be our Jesse. Not this little cherub. Jesse doesn't smile.

Not even if that appeared to be his mother pushing her way behind him, a she-lion reaching for his T-shirt as if she actually thought she could tug him back.

Jesse was calling out, "BOSNIA! BOSNIA!" and as he raised his fist the crowds parted for him. I called it back to him. He was calling to me and he was coming toward me and I waited on dry land. It didn't seem to matter whether he was real or not. It didn't seem to matter that he couldn't be real, not with a nose ring.

His mother was real, though, descending behind him. She had her hair pinned up flat, her long neck arching. She wore a flowing dress, blue and white, and you can be sure it didn't come from the Due East discount stores. No straw hats with cherries on Mary Faith this time, no high heels, no outfit. Mary Faith. In New York. Come after me.

She was not calling out, "BOSNIA!" Her lips were white and tight with fury, as if I'd just given her trouble next door and she'd crossed our lawns to have it out.

This was top of the pops. This was Junior Walker and the All Stars. This was the mother of all visions.

All around us the chanting continued, we outlaws and pilgrims tearing loose through the center of Washington Square, remembering for one minute the souls outside ourselves. Outside our selves relating to ourselves, I might add.

Jesse reached me and I scooped him up and believed that this was real flesh. He is a tall child, but slender, like his mother. I was able to lift him up and hold him out to the crowd, and we both raised a fist and cried out, "BOSNIA!" I would have gone on, I would have continued, I would have chanted FREE TIBET! and MOZAMBIQUE! and TIANANMEN SQUARE! So many souls to save.

But Mary Faith had finally broken through the chanting crowd and was making her way down to the steps. When she reached us where we stood in the center of the arena, she put her hand on my arm that held Jesse and then she stood on her toes to touch my cheek.

"Tim Rooney, from a distance you look like you're on fire," she said. "You're burning up with fever." And for all that she is young enough to be my daughter she sounded for that moment just like my mother, and I knew then that we were all of us in this scene just as real as real life gets.

REPORT FROM THE SICKROOM

We put him to bed in the little guest room on the top floor where Jesse and I had been staying. He let me take his temperature, which was a hundred and three degrees. Bernadette and Fran were all in favor of the emergency room, but I put my foot down. I remembered the stories about his family trying to commit him and called Father Berkeley. He said he'd come take charge. It was all I wanted. I was so weary, and Jesse's eyes were bugging out of his head.

Tim meanwhile had fallen into a deep sleep. Even his own coughing could not wake him, and by midnight I decided that the thick hacking couldn't be less than pneumonia. Father Berkeley still hadn't come. On the phone he said he'd be there soon as he could locate a doctor to come with him, but there was no knock on the door. I kept a vigil down where Jesse and I would spend the night in the parlor. Bernadette and Fran were already all snuggly in bed. What did they have to wait up for?

Sometime after midnight Tim cried out, and I was the only one who stirred at the sound. I climbed my way up to the low bedroom where he stayed in the hot night. Even on the stairway the sound of his labored breathing threw a black fear into me. Bernadette and Fran should have put him in their bed, where the ceiling was high enough to let a breeze blow through. I stood in his doorway watching him struggle on the narrow bed, the sheet wrapped around his naked legs like a shroud. I thought he was dying. I had no faith that he would make it.

When I came close I heard that he whispered in his sleep, a string of obscenities I would not repeat. I stood there over him, my hand on his hot forehead, until he slipped into a deeper, silent sleep. I was remembering the night my father died, in front of the television, the catheter still chaining him. He died while I was cooking eggs, food for Jesse, food he could not eat, and when I came in to check on him and saw his blue lips and understood that his body was cold, I let out a long single cry that whistled through the hole in my heart and I fell to my knees. My father had been helpless for a year already, but I thought if he could only stay breathing in that bed, in front of the game shows, that I could go on.

That night Tim heard the strange cry I let out and came running over from next door and let me bury my head in his chest. He understood to stay silent. He understood that I could not bear a single word. He shored me up that night and now, standing over him, I thought that if he left this world too I could not bear it. I didn't care whether he was sane or insane. I didn't care if they stuck tubes in him and he never came to his senses. If he could only stay breathing on this earth, I could go on. I stood right over him and whispered, "I won't leave you," and then heard the words after they left my mouth. What had I done?

I imagined that he'd heard, though, and the thought comforted me through the rest of that long night, when I curled up on the rag rug between the twin beds and lay stiff. Hour after hour, I thought, *If the priest doesn't come the way he said he would I'm calling that ambulance myself.* Bernadette and Fran and even Jesse slept, oblivious, below. And hour after hour passed without a knock on the door, until sometime near dawn when I was so beside myself with worry, with calculating whether Tim's breathing was better or worse, I slipped into my own sleep.

I woke to find a strange bald man in the doorway and Bernadette smiling behind him. I started up, and reached from the floor to touch Tim's forehead. Cool. Cold, even. Dead, I thought, and then heard again the thick breathing and knew that he was alive and that the fever had broken.

"Mary Faith," Bernadette said, "the doctor's come," as if I was retarded, and I ran crying from the room in such relief and fear that I'm sure the poor psychiatrist thought I was the patient he'd been sent to see.

I knew nowhere to run but to Jesse, all the way down in the parlor, but when I got there I saw that I was too late. Father Berkeley was already there beside him, the two of them talking head to head so that they did not hear me come into the room with my hiccups. I had to cough to tell them I was there.

"Mary Faith," Father Berkeley said, "I'm just telling Jesse the plan."

The old man was certainly driven. We didn't even have a diagnosis yet, but he already had a plan.

"The doctor says if he's well enough to travel we can bring him home in the car. He doesn't like it, but he understands I insist on getting him home. He believes we can sedate him adequately. Do you think you can handle that? In the back seat? Or should we wait for his brother?"

"I think he has pneumonia," I said. "All night he sounded like he was drowning."

The priest put a finger to his lips. "Well, that's different. If he has pneumonia, we'll put him in the hospital here. For the pneumonia. But as for the psychiatric ward, you and I are not even related to Timothy. His father would have to commit him. And I don't think that would be . . ."

"Wise," I said. We looked at each other. "If we could call his sister . . ."

"Kate," Father Berkeley said. "I did. She'll come if we need her. She's been waiting all month for word."

It was Kate who sat by Tim the last time and talked him into signing himself in. "She could talk him in again," I said, and believed it, and hated myself for how fast I wanted to slap him in a ward where someone else could wait up all night.

"I knew when I heard him in the park," said Jesse, "I knew we were home free. How long you think the adoption papers'll take now, Mom?"

Last week he said he wouldn't let Tim adopt him if he was the last living male on the planet. The chains tightened around my ankles. What had I promised in the night? I had not kept a single resolution on this trip, not one of those promises to myself that I would slip out of this nightmare and go set myself free. And now I had promised to stay in the dark with Tim.

Later the doctor came downstairs to say that it was not pneumonia at all, he was sure of that, even if his game was more brain than lungs. A touch of bronchitis, maybe, from being exposed. A bad cold, plus being crazy. The doctor said we were looking at a couple of weeks' hospitalization, maybe a month, it depended on how fast Tim responded to the medication and how well his body healed up from the exposure. He said we should sit tight for a day or two to see whether it was really possible to travel with Tim. *You may just change your mind about that scheme,* he said, *and it may surprise you what good care he could get here in the city.* But I could see the set of Father Berkeley's mind, and it was concrete. He was bringing Tim home, and I was along for the ride.

It didn't seem possible that a bad cold could have set Tim on such fire that he was able to make that speech in the park. There must have been two hundred people carrying on at the sound of his voice. It is a lovely deep voice, deep enough to talk all those folks into chanting along with him like they were at one of those happenings in the sixties. One of those be-ins. Maybe the speech had set the fever burning, not the other way around.

After the doctor left, after Bernadette and Fran left—as if nothing unusual was going on in their house, as if it was perfectly reasonable that the priest and I should sit watch with a mental patient all the day—I sat Jesse in front of the mindless television and went to Bernadette's kitchen to stand and shake. I could not climb the steps and relieve Father Berkeley just yet.

I had been weak and wavering all this trip, but it wasn't until now, his body in the same house, that I was able to remember how solid and steady and sane he'd been, all the while my father was dying, and all the while Jesse was causing trouble, and all the while I shrank from him. I shook, and poured myself a glass of water. I couldn't bear not having him to lean on. I couldn't bear his knowing, always, that I had seen him this way.

And as soon as I finished the water and stopped my trembling, I saw that I didn't have the patience to be anywhere near him. I kept picturing the peroxide-blond floozy and wondering what kind of father a faithless crazy man would make for my son. I was back to wanting to boil him in oil. I opened all Bernadette's cabinets and fingered her thick white bowls with their blue stripes and her green glasses and her half dozen casseroles, with their dark glazes, and her Russian and Greek and Moroccan cookbooks, and I included her and her life in all my bitterness. Then I shut the cabinet doors. I'd have to hold steady enough in the days to come.

When Bernadette finally saw fit to come home from work, not a minute before her regular hour, which is already well into the evening, she saw how agitated I was and asked me if I'd sit in the kitchen with her while she ate the food I'd fixed.

"Did he eat?" she said. She herself was mopping up corn bread like she hadn't eaten in days.

"Fran?" I said. "He ate with us, and then he went out to the library."

"No," she said. "Did Tim eat?"

I couldn't help it. I still felt jealousy stabbing me between the ribs.

"He didn't eat," I said. And then I added, and I can't say why I would confide such a thing, "He didn't know me. All day." *But all night I lay next to him,* I wanted to say, *and promised him I wouldn't leave,* and now here I am with that package to hold in my hands.

"I'm sorry," she said. "These are good."

She meant the black-eyed peas. I guess I laid it on heavy with what my mother used to call country food. I would have thrown a slab of fatback in too, just to remind them we came from elsewhere, but they don't seem to believe in animal protein of any kind in New York City. I couldn't locate fatback.

We sat in silence, not even the cover of company to let us look one another over. Finally Bernadette was done with her food, and she said, "Did he ever tell you about the vision when he was a kid?"

I shook my head. "Tim doesn't talk to me about religion," I said. "I don't have the patience."

"Good for you."

But I couldn't stand it, that she should know but that I would never. I was going to have to nurse him back, wasn't I? "What vision?"

"He was just a little boy, I don't know, six, seven. He had a little statue in the backyard he used to bring flowers to. One day when he had a fever he thought the statue talked to him. It was Mary, you know—"

I thought of Jesse at six or seven, those years when a boy might think the clouds are talking to him, or the winds in the trees.

I must have looked the way I felt, which was out of patience again. What I wanted was to get an engineering degree and earn my own way. What I wanted was Tim sane and Jesse in the company of someone who admired his nose ring. What I wanted was to build a geodesic dome for the three of us and set it on top of a factory building down by the Hudson River.

Talking statues was just a little more than I could bear to take in, at the moment.

"Good night, Bernadette. We'll be out of here soon."

"Get out of here," I said to the old man. It was like being in a permanent confessional, a smelly priest in the next bed, for Christ's sake. When I was teenager and he took over Our Lady of Perpetual Help from Father Sweeney, he tried to seduce the family. He came by the house with books for my mother and 45s for me. He brought me back the Clancy Brothers and Tommy Makem from Ireland and the Beatles from England when all I wanted in 1963 was Gershwin, because my father loved Gershwin. But Father Berkeley was in love with my mother, and ingratiated himself in any way he could.

"Get out," I said. "I don't believe in that stuff anymore. I've given it all up." He wouldn't take it personally. He'd seen me worse. Between bouts, you might say he was my best friend in Due East. Once my mother died, of course, and we cleared that air between us.

"You've given up plenty," he said. "It's none of my business at the moment."

Well. This was a new tack from our clergy. I wasn't sure where they'd imprisoned me this time, but there was no air, and there was an informer in the room.

"What is your business?" I said, thinking he'd slip up and reveal himself.

"Make sure you don't go running off the way you've been doing for a month and more," he said. "Make sure you don't go breaking that little boy's heart one more time."

"O, lay off the guilt." I was feeling feisty, and the terror was setting in fast. They wouldn't have Jesse here, would they? They wouldn't have pulled that one. They must have talked me into swallowing some of those bitter pills, after all, because I was beginning to remember some smelly details, piss on my pants and a nasty incident in a hallway. If I'd taken the medication, I didn't have all that much longer to act like a total asshole.

"Fine," said Father Berkeley. "As long as you knock off the speeches."

"You weren't there." I remembered the speech, or at least a moment of glory. I remembered Garibaldi winking.

"I'm here," he said. "Here and now. And I can't tolerate that pop mumbo jumbo you're spewing out another minute. *Florence Henderson is in me?* Who is Florence Henderson? What fluffy nonsense are you trying to pass off as psychosis? There's no one in you but you, my dear boy, and that at the moment is the problem."

My dear boy. He was laughing at me. And he'd forced the medicine on me and there were things I had to do.

"Florence Henderson was imposed on me," I said. "It's my own affair if I make use of her now."

"Oh?" said the priest. "And was Maynard G. Krebs imposed on you? And Spin and Marty? And Penny King?"

Maynard G. Krebs! Spin and Marty! Penny King! They must have strapped me down in front of decades of television! I could only imagine what I'd been saying the last day and a half. Only: what was that about Jesse?

"I'm getting better," I said, and closed my eyes. "Aren't I?"

"Not much," said the priest. "But I may be prejudiced, since I am sharing the room. Mary Faith thinks you're better."

"Mary Faith! Where have you hidden her?"

"I haven't hidden her anywhere. She'll be back."

"I don't know why you're all carrying on this way. I'm perfectly able to carry on by myself."

"Tim."

"And if you don't think I can, why don't you just have my brother commit me? Why don't you just get Andy to do your dirty work?"

"He's on his way to Due East," the priest said. "He's probably there now, in the house. Katie's there. Maggie. Your father. No one's going to commit you."

"Well, why the hell not?" I said. "I've been acting like a lunatic for a long while here."

"That much is true," said the priest. "That much we can agree on."

"Is Jesse here?" I said.

"Yes. You saw him not but an hour ago."

"Mary Faith?"

"Yes. She's a little short-tempered now."

"Did you call G.B.?"

"He came by. Remember?"

"Will you hear my confession?"

"Not while you're out of your mind," said Father Berkeley. "But I will hear it soon, if you find you still believe in that stuff."

It was hard to leave New York City, and not just because I knew the heartache that faced us, between hospitals and the shame Tim was showing already, coming to his senses. I couldn't even say whether there'd be any money left. It seemed he'd been giving it away, on the streets of New York.

But there he was, in the backseat with me. He wouldn't let us put the seat belt on him but lay instead with his head in my lap, his eyes closed.

"Forty days," Father Berkeley said. "We just made it."

"What you think I'd do?" Tim said, his eyes still closed. "What you think I'd do, kill myself after forty days?"

"Timothy Rooney," the old man said, "I've given up figuring your next move."

"Well, that wasn't it," said Tim. He sounded perfectly sane, as he did now for an hour or two at a stretch. And the weight of his head in my lap wasn't a burden at all, but a comfort, even if the next time he lay it down his eyes might well be glazed over from the medication. He and Jesse might be at each other's throats, we might be stuck in Due East for the rest of our days, with Tim running off with blond hitchhiking floozies every few years. But still, the feel of his head there, the look of his red hair fading to yellow, his chin rooted through with deep ruts and stubble, was a comfort for the moment.

"Did you get the stamps?" he said. His eyes were still closed. Father Berkeley was lurching through Manhattan traffic and I closed my own eyes, too. I couldn't bear to look.

"What stamps?"

"The stamps to send the letters about Bosnia," Jesse said, from the front. "The letters to Bill and Hillary and the dude at the UN and I forget-all."

Tim had already drifted off. "When did y'all write letters for Bosnia?" I said.

"Well, duh. We hadn't written them yet," Jesse said. "Tim's been crazy, remember?"

"Jesse, don't speak to your mother that way."

"Father, watch out!" We dodged a cab and Father raised his fist, triumphant. We slid down into the Holland Tunnel. It would be a miracle if we all made it home.

In the back of the black car, I felt almost like someone on the way to a funeral. It wouldn't just be nursing Tim, helping him fight off the demons. It would be fighting off my own bitterness too. It was just hard to imagine that I'd ever forgive Tim. That was all.

But I was sane, and I could see the road ahead. Here we were, pulling out of the tunnel already, on the grim New Jersey side. We were heading south. We were heading home. And the weight of Tim Rooney's head was a comfort on my lap, a comfort for the moment. Even if he was a mess.

It felt good to have someone else drive the car. But I can tell you one thing. I'm never asking him to take me to church again.

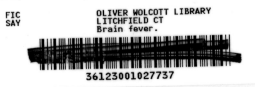